Extraordinary acclaim for Lauren Beukes's
The Shining Girls

"A triumph. . . . The smart and spunky Kirby Mizrachi is as exciting to follow as any in recent genre fiction. . . . Each chapter in which Harper appears holds a reader's attention, especially the sharply described murder scenes—some of which read as much like starkly rendered battlefield deaths out of Homer as forensic reconstructions of terrible crimes. This book means business."

—Alan Cheuse, NPR

"The next *Gone Girl*." —*InStyle*

"Science fiction and psychological thriller collide spectacularly. . . . A heart-thumping tale." —Tina Jordan, *Entertainment Weekly*

"Clever story, smart prose." —Stephen King

"Unreservedly recommended." —Joe Hill

"A haunting, suspenseful meditation on fate and free will. . . . In less assured hands, the two narrative strains might clash, but Beukes finds a way to make the hardboiled-crime and science-fiction tropes complement each other. Much of the novel's power comes from the way Beukes faithfully portrays the women who fatefully encounter Harper Curtis. . . . The author forces the reader to acknowledge their heartbreaking humanity. Expertly chilling, *The Shining Girls* marks Beukes as a distinctive talent with a bright future ahead of her."

—Michael Berry, *San Francisco Chronicle*

"A masterful twist on the classic suspense novel." —*Shape*

"Excellently written. *The Shining Girls* makes brilliant use of a nonlinear narrative to create and build tension."

—Liz Bourke, Tor.com

"Why's *The Shining Girls* so special? First, the concept. Harper is a 1930s drifter-turned-murderer who finds himself able to jump through time, making him all but impossible to catch...a refreshingly ornery heroine in Kirby, the only girl to have survived the killer's knife. And, crucially, it's the girls' stories that are being told—not Harper's.... By placing the victims center stage, Beukes celebrates each girl's life and transforms a genre that often seems sickly sensationalist. Forget *Gone Girl;* now it's all about *The Shining Girls.*" —Sarah Hughes, *The Guardian* (UK)

"One of the scariest and best-written thrillers of the year, not to mention the most memorable portrait of a serial killer since *The Devil in the White City.*" —Kevin Nance, *Chicago Sun-Times*

"Tautly written and sharply plotted. Deftly told from many points of view and in many time zones, *The Shining Girls* is a tremendous work of suspense fiction. What's more, it's a fabulous piece of both time-travel and serial-killer fiction, using the intersection of those two themes to explore questions of free will, predestination, and causality in a mind-melting, heart-pounding mashup that delivers on its promise." —Cory Doctorow, *BoingBoing*

"Gripping. A strong contender for the role of this summer's universal beach read with many gasp-worthy moments."

—Janet Maslin, *New York Times*

"*The Shining Girls* is enthralling and dazzlingly inventive. Lauren Beukes risks everything with a startlingly original structure that's perfectly executed. A huge accomplishment."

—Deon Meyer, author of *Blood Safari*

"[Beukes] is so profusely talented—capable of wit, darkness, and emotion on a single page—that a blockbuster seems inevitable. . . . *The Shining Girls* marks her arrival as a major writer of popular fiction." —Charles Finch, *USA Today*

"I just started *The Shining Girls* last night, accidentally, and it has already ruined my life. Stayed up for hours—crime thriller with a sci-fi angle, and such good writing. Am hooked, and jealous."

—Ann Lamott, *People*

"One of the most thrilling and accomplished novels of the season, a genre-blending tale of good vs. evil with plenty of pace and, in its portraits of some of the murderer's victims, a surprising heft."

—Jim Higgins, *Milwaukee Journal Sentinel*

"I loved *The Shining Girls*. It really is a new kind of thriller, sitting somewhere between *The Time Traveler's Wife* and *The Silence of the Lambs*. A dark, relentless, time-twisting, page-turning murder story guaranteed to give you heart palpitations. It shines."

—Matt Haig, author of *The Radleys*

The Shining Girls

ALSO BY LAUREN BEUKES

Moxyland
Zoo City

The Shining Girls

Lauren Beukes

MULHOLLAND BOOKS
Little, Brown and Company
New York Boston London

Copyright © 2013 by Lauren Beukes
Reading group guide copyright © 2014 by Lauren Beukes and Little, Brown and Company

Mulholland Books/Little, Brown and Company
Hachette Book Group
237 Park Avenue, New York, NY 10017
mulhollandbooks.com

Originally published in hardcover by Mulholland Books, June 2013
First Mulholland Books paperback edition, January 2014

Mulholland Books is an imprint of Little, Brown and Company, a division of Hachette Book Group, Inc. The Mulholland Books name and logo are trademarks of Hachette Book Group, Inc.

The publisher is not responsible for websites (or their content) that are not owned by the publisher.

The Hachette Speakers Bureau provides a wide range of authors for speaking events. To find out more, go to hachettespeakersbureau.com or call (866) 376-6591.

Library of Congress Cataloging-in-Publication Data
Beukes, Lauren.
The shining girls: a novel / Lauren Beukes. — First North American edition.
    pages cm
ISBN 978-0-316-21685-2 (hc) / 978-0-316-24521-0 (large print) / 978-0-316-21686-9 (pb)
I. Title.
PR9369.4.B485.S55 2013
823'.92 — dc23   2013003018

10 9 8 7 6 5 4 3 2 1

RRD-C

Printed in the United States of America

For Matthew

The Shining Girls

HARPER

17 July 1974

═══════════

He clenches the orange plastic pony in the pocket of his sports coat. It is sweaty in his hand. Mid-summer here, too hot for what he's wearing. But he has learned to put on a uniform for this purpose; jeans in particular. He takes long strides—a man who walks because he's got somewhere to be, despite his gimpy foot. Harper Curtis is not a moocher. And time waits for no one. Except when it does.

The girl is sitting cross-legged on the ground, her bare knees white and bony as birds' skulls and grass-stained. She looks up at the sound of his boots scrunching on the gravel, but only long enough for him to see that her eyes are brown under that tangle of grubby curls, before she dismisses him and goes back to her business.

Harper is disappointed. He had imagined, as he approached, that they might be blue; the color of the lake, deep out, where the shoreline disappears and it feels like you're in the middle of the ocean. Brown is the color of shrimping, when the mud is all churned up in the shallows and you can't see shit for shit.

"What are you doing?" he says, putting brightness in his voice. He crouches down beside her in the threadbare grass. Really, he's never seen a child with such crazy hair. Like she got spun round in her own personal dust devil, one that tossed up the assortment of random junk splayed around her. A cluster of rusty tin cans, a broken bicycle wheel tipped on its side, spokes jabbing outwards. Her attention is focused on a chipped teacup, turned upside down, so that the silvered flowers on the lip disappear into the grass. The handle has broken off, leaving two blunt stumps. "You having a tea party, sweetheart?" he tries again.

"It's not a tea party," she mutters into the petal-shaped collar of her checked shirt. Kids with freckles shouldn't be so earnest, he thinks. It doesn't suit them.

"Well, that's fine," he says, "I prefer coffee anyways. May I have a cup, please, ma'am? Black with three sugars, okay?" He reaches for the chipped porcelain, and the girl yelps and bats his hand away. A deep, angry buzzing comes from underneath the inverted cup.

"Jesus. What you got in there?"

"It's *not* a tea party! It's a circus!"

"That so?" He turns on his smile, the goofy one that says he doesn't take himself too seriously, and neither should you. But the back of his hand stings where she smacked him.

She glares at him suspiciously. Not for who he might be, what he might do to her. But because she is irritated that he doesn't understand. He looks around, more carefully, and recognizes it now: her ramshackle circus. The big top ring marked out with a finger traced in the dirt, a tightrope made from a flattened drinking-straw rigged between two soda cans, the Ferris wheel of the dented bicycle wheel, half propped up against a bush, with a rock to hold it in place and paper people torn out of magazines jammed between the spokes.

It doesn't escape him that the rock holding it up is the perfect fit for his fist. Or how easily one of those needle spokes would slide right through the girl's eye like Jell-O. He squeezes hard on the plastic pony in his pocket. The furious buzzing coming from underneath the cup is a vibration he can feel all the way down his vertebrae, tugging at his groin.

The cup jolts and the girl clamps her hands over it.

"Whoa!" she laughs, breaking the spell.

"Whoa, indeed! You got a lion in there?" He nudges her with his shoulder, and a smile breaks through her scowl, but only a little one. "You an animal tamer? You gonna make it jump through flaming hoops?"

She grins, the polka dots of her freckles drawing up into Dutch apple cheeks, revealing bright white teeth. "Nah, Rachel says I'm not allowed to play with matches. Not after last time." She has one skewed canine, slightly overlapping her incisors. And the smile more than makes up for the brackwater brown eyes, because now he can see the spark behind them. It gives him that falling-away feeling in his chest. And he's sorry he ever doubted the House. She's the one. One of the ones. His shining girls.

"I'm Harper," he says, breathless, holding out his hand to shake. She has to switch her grip on the cup to do it.

"Are you a stranger?" she says.

"Not anymore, right?"

"I'm Kirby. Kirby Mazrachi. But I'm gonna change it to Lori Star as soon as I'm old enough."

"When you go to Hollywood?"

She draws the cup across the ground towards her, stirring the bug under it to new heights of outrage, and he can see he's made a mistake.

"Are you sure you're not a stranger?"

"I mean, the circus, right? What is Lori Star going to do? Flying trapeze? Elephant rider? Clown?" He wiggles his index finger over his top lip. "The mustachioed lady?"

To his relief, she giggles. "Noooo."

"Lion tamer! Knife thrower! Fire-eater!"

"I'm going to be a tightrope walker. I've been practicing. Wanna see?" She moves to get up.

"No, wait," he says, suddenly desperate. "Can I see your lion?"

"It's not really a lion."

"That's what you say," he prods.

"Okay, but you gotta be real careful. I don't want him to fly away." She tilts the cup the tiniest fraction. He lays his head down on the ground, squinting to see. The smell of crushed grass and black earth is comforting. Something is moving under the cup. Furry legs, a hint of yellow and black. Antennae probe towards the gap. Kirby gasps and slams the cup down again.

"That's one big old bumblebee," he says, sitting back on his haunches.

"I know," she says, proud of herself.

"You got him pretty riled."

"I don't think he wants to be in the circus."

"Can I show you something? You'll have to trust me."

"What is it?"

"You want a tightrope walker?"

"No, I—"

But he's already lifted up the cup and scooped the agitated bee into his hands. Pulling off the wings makes the same dull pop sound as plucking the stem off a sour cherry, like the ones he spent a season picking in Rapid City. He'd been up and down the whole goddamn country, chasing after the work like a bitch in heat. Until he found the House.

"What are you doing?" she shouts.

"Now we just need some flypaper to string across the top of

two cans. Big old bug like this should be able to pull his feet free, but it'll be sticky enough to stop him falling. You got some fly-paper?"

He sets the bumblebee down on the rim of the cup. It clings to the edge.

"Why did you *do* that?" She hits his arm, a fluster of blows, palms open.

He's baffled by her reaction. "Aren't we playing circus?"

"You ruined it! Go away! Go away, go away, go away, go away." It becomes a chant, timed with each slap.

"Hold on. Hold on there," he laughs, but she keeps on whacking him. He grabs her hand in his. "I mean it. Cut it the fuck out, little lady."

"You don't swear!" she yells and bursts into tears. This is not going like he planned—as much as he can plan any of these first encounters. He feels tired at the unpredictability of children. This is why he doesn't like little girls, why he waits for them to grow up. Later, it will be a different story.

"All right, I'm sorry. Don't cry, okay? I've got something for you. Please don't cry. Look." In desperation, he takes out the orange pony, or tries to. Its head snags on his pocket and he has to yank it free. "Here," he jabs it at her, willing her to take it. One of the objects that connects everything together. Surely this is why he brought it? He feels only a moment of uncertainty.

"What is it?"

"A pony. Can't you see? Isn't a pony better than some dumb bumblebee?"

"It's not alive."

"I know that. Goddammit. Just take it, okay? It's a present."

"I don't want it," she sniffs.

"Okay, it's not a present, it's a deposit. You're keeping it safe for me. Like at the bank when you give them your money." The sun is beating down. It is too hot to be wearing a coat. He is barely able to concentrate. He just wants it to be done. The bumblebee falls off the cup and lies upside down in the grass, its legs cycling in the air.

"I guess."

He is feeling calmer already. Everything is as it has to be. "Now keep this safe, all right? It's real important. I'll come to get it. You understand?"

"Why?"

"Because I need it. How old are you?"

"Six and three-quarters. Almost seven."

"That's great. Really great. Here we go. Round and round, like your Ferris wheel. I'll see you when you're all grown-up. Look out for me, okay, sweetheart? I'll come back for you."

He stands up, dusting his hands against his leg. He turns and walks briskly across the lot, not looking back, limping only slightly. She watches him cross the road and walk up towards the railroad until he disappears into the tree-line. She looks at the plastic toy, clammy from his hand, and yells after him. "Yeah? Well I don't want your dumb horse!"

She chucks it onto the ground and it bounces once before coming to land beside her bicycle Ferris wheel. Its painted eye stares blankly at the bumblebee, which has righted itself and is dragging itself away over the dirt.

But she goes back for it later. Of course she does.

HARPER

20 November 1931

———

The sand gives way beneath him, not sand at all, but stinking icy mud that squelches into his shoes and soaks through his socks. Harper curses under his breath, not wanting the men to hear. They're shouting to each other in the darkness: "You see him? You got him?" If the water wasn't so goddamn cold, he'd risk swimming out to make his escape. But he is already shivering violently from the wind off the lake that nips and worries at him right through his shirt, his coat abandoned behind the speakeasy, covered in that shit-heel's blood.

He wades his way across the beach, picking a path between the garbage and the rotting lumber, mud sucking at his every step. He hunkers down behind a shack on the water's edge, assembled out of packing boxes and held together with tar-paper. Lamplight seeps through the cracks and the cardboard patching, making the whole thing glow. He doesn't know why people build so close to the lake anyways—like they think the worst has already happened and there's no downhill from here. Not like people shit in the shallows. Not like the water might swell with the rains and wash the whole goddamn stinking Hooverville away. The abode of forgotten men, misfortune saturated deep down into their bones. No one would miss them. Like no one's going to miss Jimmy fucking Grebe.

He wasn't expecting Grebe to gush like that. Wouldn't have come to it if the bastard had fought fair. But he was fat and drunk and desperate. Couldn't land a punch, so he went for Harper's balls. Harper had felt the sonofabitch's thick fingers grabbing at his trousers. Man fights ugly, you fight uglier back. It's not Harper's fault the jagged edge of the glass caught an artery. He was aiming for Grebe's face.

None of it would have happened if that dirty lunger hadn't coughed up on the cards. Grebe had wiped the bloody gob off with his sleeve, sure, but everyone knew he had consumption, hacking his contagion into his bloody kerchief. Disease and ruin and the cracking nerves of men. It's the end of America.

Try telling that to "Mayor" Klayton and his bunch of vigilante cocksuckers, all puffed up like they own the place. But there's no law here. Like there's no money. No self-respect. He's seen the signs—and not just the ones that read "foreclosed." Let's face it, he thinks, America had it coming.

A pale streamer of light sweeps over the beach, lingering on the scars he trailed across the mud. But then the flashlight swings to hunt in another direction, and the door of the shack opens, spilling light out all over the place. A skinny rat of a woman steps out. Her face is drawn and gray in the kerosene glow—like everyone else's around here—as if the dust storms out there in the country blew away all traces of people's character along with their crops.

There's a dark sports coat three sizes too big for her draped over her scrawny shoulders, like a shawl. Heavy wool. It looks warm. He knows that he is going to take it from her even before he realizes that she is blind. Her eyes are vacant. Her breath smells like cabbage and the teeth rotting in her head. She reaches out to touch him. "What is it?" she says. "Why are they shouting?"

"Rabid dog," Harper says. "They're chasing it down. You should go back inside, ma'am." He could lift the jacket right off her and be gone. But she might scream. She might fight him.

She clutches at his shirt. "Wait," she says. "Is it you? Are you Bartek?"

"No, ma'am. Not me." He tries to pry her fingers off of him. Her voice is rising in an urgent way. The kind to draw attention.

"You are. You must be. He said you would come." She is verging on hysterical. "He said he would—"

"Shhhh, it's all right," Harper says. It is no effort at all to raise his forearm to her throat and push her back against the lean-to with his full weight. Only to quiet her, he tells himself. Hard to scream around a crushed windpipe. Her lips pout and pop. Her eyes bulge. Her gullet heaves in protest. She twists her hands in his shirt as if she's wringing out laundry, and then her chicken-bone fingers fall away and she sags against the wall. He bends with her, setting her down gently, even as he lifts the coat off her shoulders.

A little boy is staring at him from inside the hovel, his eyes big enough to swallow you whole.

"What you looking at?" Harper hisses at the boy, hooking his arms through the sleeves. It's too big for him, but no matter. Something jangles in the pocket of the coat. Loose change, if he's lucky. But it will turn out to be much more than that.

"Get inside. Get your mother some water. She's poorly."

The boy stares and then, without changing his expression, opens his mouth and lets out a screeching wail, drawing the goddamn flashlights. Beams lance across the doorway and the fallen woman, but Harper is already running. One of Klayton's cronies—or maybe it's the self-appointed mayor himself—shouts, "There!" and the men stampede down towards the beach after him.

He darts through the maze of shacks and tents put up without rhyme or purpose all tumbled on top of each other, with barely space for a pushcart to move between them. Insects have better judgment, he thinks as he veers in the general direction of Randolph Street.

He is not counting on people acting like termites.

He steps on a tarpaulin and falls straight through it into a pit the size of a piano box, but considerably deeper, hacked out of the earth where someone has set up a semblance of a home and simply nailed a cover into the ground across the top of it.

He lands hard, his left heel smacking the side of a wooden pallet bed with a sharp twang like a guitar string snapping. The impact slams him sideways into the edge of a home-made stove that catches him under his ribcage and knocks the breath out of him. It feels like a bullet has torn clean through his ankle, but he didn't hear a gunshot. He can't breathe to scream and he's drowning in the tarp, falling in on top of him.

They find him there, flailing against the canvas and cursing the sonofabitch human driftwood who didn't have the materials or the skills to build a proper shack. The men assemble at the top of the hidey-hole, malevolent silhouettes behind the glare of their flashlights.

"You can't come here and just do what you want," Klayton says in his best Sunday preacher voice. Harper can finally breathe again. Every inhalation burns like a stitch in his side. He's cracked a rib for sure, and he's done something worse to his foot.

"You have to respect your neighbor and your neighbor must respect you," Klayton continues. Harper's heard him using this line at the community meetings, talking about how they needed to try and get along with the local businesses across the way—the same ones that sent in the authorities to tack up warning notices on every tent and hovel, advising them that they had seven days to vacate the land.

"Hard to do respecting when you're dead," Harper laughs, although it's more of a wheeze and it makes his stomach tighten with pain. He thinks they might be holding shotguns, but that seems unlikely, and it is only when one of the flashlights shifts away from his face that he sees they are armed with pipes and hammers. His gut clenches again.

"You should turn me over to the law," he says, hopefully.

"Nah," Klayton replies. "They got no business here." He waves his flashlight. "Haul him out, boys. Before Chinaman Eng comes back to his hole and finds this d-horner garbage squatting in here."

And here is another sign, clear as dawn, which is starting to creep over the horizon past the bridge. Before Klayton's goons can climb down the ten feet to get to him, it starts to rain, slicing drops, cold and bitter. And there is shouting from the other side of the camp. "Police! It's a raid!"

Klayton turns to confer with his men. They sound like monkeys with their jibber-jabber and arm-waving, and then a jet of flame sears through the rain, lighting up the sky and putting paid to their conversation.

"Hey, you leave that—" A yell drifts across from Randolph Street. Followed by another. "They got kerosene!" someone yells.

"What you waiting for?" Harper says quietly, under the drumming rain and the uproar.

"You stay right there," Klayton jabs his pipe at him as the silhouettes disperse. "We're not done with you."

Ignoring the rasping sound his ribs make, Harper scoots up on his elbows. He leans forward, grabs hold of the tarp that is still clinging to its nails on one side, and tugs on it, dreading the in-evitable. But it holds.

Above, he can distinguish the dictatorial tone of the good mayor's voice, cutting through the melee, shouting at persons un-seen. "You got a court order for this? You think you can just come here and burn up people's homes after we've lost everything once already?"

Harper gets a thick fold of the material in his grip and, using the overturned stove for leverage with his good foot, heaves him-self up. His ankle bangs against the dirt wall and a bright flash of pain, clear as God, blinds him. He retches, coughing up only a long stringy amalgam of spit and phlegm tinged with red. He clings to the tarp, blinking hard against the black holes blossom-ing across his vision, until he can see again.

The shouts are dissipating under the drum of the rain. He is running out of time. He hauls himself up the greasy, wet tarp, hand over fist. He couldn't have done this even a year ago. But af-ter twelve weeks of driving rivets into the Triboro in New York, he's strong as the mangy orangutan he witnessed at a county fair, ripping a watermelon in half with its bare hands.

The canvas makes ominous brittle sounds of protest, threaten-ing to tumble him back into this goddamn hole. But it holds and he pulls himself gratefully over the edge, not even caring as he scrapes open his chest on the nails fastening the tarp. Later, ex-amining his wounds in safety, he will note that the gouges make it look like an enthusiastic whore has laid her mark on him.

He lies there, face in the mud, the rain pelting down on him. The shouts have moved away, although the air reeks of smoke, and the light from a half-dozen fires mixes with the gray of the dawn. A fragment of music drifts through the night, carrying from an apartment window, perhaps, with the tenants leaning out to enjoy the spectacle.

Harper crawls on his belly through the mud, lights flaring in his skull from the pain—or maybe they're real. It is a kind of a rebirth. He graduates from crawling to hobbling when he finds a heavy piece of timber the right height to lean on.

His left foot is useless, dragging behind him. But he keeps going, through the rain and the darkness, away from the burning shantytown.

Everything happens for a reason. It's because he is forced to leave that he finds the House. It is because he took the coat that he has the key.

KIRBY

18 July 1974

═══════

It's that time of the early morning when the dark feels heavy; after the trains have stopped running and the traffic has petered out, but before the birds start singing. A real scorcher of a night. The kind of sticky hot that brings out all the bugs. Moths and flying ants patter against the porch light in an uneven drumbeat. A mosquito whines somewhere near the ceiling.

Kirby is in bed, awake, stroking the pony's nylon mane and listening to the sounds of the empty house, groaning, like a hungry stomach. "Settling," Rachel calls it. But Rachel is not here. And it's late, or early, and Kirby hasn't had anything to eat since stale cornflakes at long-ago breakfast, and there are sounds that don't belong to "settling."

Kirby whispers to the pony, "It's an old house. It's probably just the wind." Except that the porch door is on a latch and it shouldn't bang. The floorboards shouldn't be creaking as if under the weight of a burglar tiptoeing towards her room, carrying a black sack to stuff her in and carry her away. Or maybe it's the living doll from the scary TV show she's not supposed to watch, tick-tacking on little plastic feet.

Kirby throws back the sheet. "I'm going to go see, okay?" she tells the pony, because the thought of waiting for the monster to come to her is unbearable. She tiptoes to the door, which her mother painted with exotic flowers and rambling vines when they moved in four months ago, ready to slam it in the face of whoever (whatever) comes up the stairs.

She stands behind the door as if it's a shield, straining to hear, picking at the rough texture of the paint. She has already stripped one tiger-lily to the bare wood. Her fingertips are tingling. The quiet rings in her head.

"Rachel?" Kirby whispers, too softly for anyone but the pony to hear.

There is a thump, very close, then a bang and the sound of something breaking. "Shit!"

"Rachel?" Kirby says, louder. Her heart is clattering like an early train.

There is a long pause. Then her mother says, "Go back to bed, Kirby, I'm fine." Kirby knows she's not. But at least it's not Talky Tina, the living killer doll.

She quits picking at the paint and pads across the hallway, sidestepping the broken bits of glass like diamonds between the dead roses with their crinkled leaves and spongy heads in a puddle of stinky vase water. The door has been left ajar for her.

Every new house is older and shabbier than the last one, although Rachel paints the doors and cupboards and sometimes even the floorboards to make it theirs. They choose the pictures together out of Rachel's big gray art book: tigers or unicorns or saints or brown island girls with flowers in their hair. Kirby uses the paintings as clues to remind herself where they are. *This* house has the melty clocks on the kitchen cabinet above the stove, which means the refrigerator is on the left and the bathroom is under the stairs. But although the layout of each house changes, and sometimes they have a yard, and sometimes Kirby's bedroom has a closet and sometimes she is lucky to have shelves, Rachel's room is the one thing that remains constant.

She thinks of it as a pirate's treasure cove. ("Trove" her mother corrects, but Kirby imagines it as a magic hidden bay, one you can sail into, if you're lucky, if your map reads right.)

Dresses and scarves are tossed around the room as if by a gypsy pirate princess throwing a tantrum. A collection of costume jewelry is hooked onto the golden curlicues of an oval mirror, the first thing Rachel puts up whenever they move in somewhere new, inevitably whacking her thumb with the hammer. Sometimes they play dress-up, and Rachel drapes every necklace and bracelet on Kirby and calls her "my Christmas tree girl," even though they are Jewish, or half.

There is a colored glass ornament hanging in the window that casts dancing rainbows across the room in the afternoon sun, over the tilted drawing table and whatever illustration Rachel is working on at the time.

When Kirby was a baby and they still lived in the city, Rachel would put the play-pen fencing around her desk, so that Kirby could crawl about the room without disturbing her. She used to do drawings for women's magazines, but now "my style is out of fashion, baby—it's fickle out there." Kirby likes the sound of the word. *Fickle-pickle-tickle-fickle.* And she likes that she sees her mother's drawing of the winking waitress, balancing two short stacks dripping with butter, when they walk past Doris's Pancake House on the way to the corner store.

But the glass ornament is cold and dead now, and the lamp next to the bed has a yellow scarf half-draped over it, which makes the whole room look sickly. Rachel is lying on the bed with a pillow over her face, still fully dressed, with her shoes on and everything. Her chest jerks under her black lace dress like she has the hiccups. Kirby stands in the doorway, willing her mother to notice her. Her head feels swollen with words she doesn't know how to say.

"You're wearing your shoes in bed," is what she manages, finally.

Rachel lifts the pillow off her face and looks at her daughter through puffy eyes. Her make-up has left a black smear across the pillow. "Sorry, honey," she says in her chipper voice. ("Chipper" makes Kirby think of chipped teeth, which is what happened to Melanie Ottesen when she fell off the climbing rope. Or cracked glasses that aren't safe to drink from anymore.)

"You have to take off your shoes!"

"I know, honey," Rachel sighs. "Don't shout." She pries the black-and-tan slingback heels off with her toes and lets them clatter to the floor. She rolls over on to her stomach. "Will you scratch my back?"

Kirby climbs onto the bed and sits cross-legged next to her. Her mother's hair smells like smoke. She traces the curly lace patterns with her fingernails. "Why are you crying?"

"I'm not really crying."

"Yes, you are."

Her mother sighs. "It's just that time of the month."

"That's what you always say," Kirby sulks, and then adds as an afterthought, "I got a pony."

"I can't afford to buy you a pony." Rachel's voice is dreamy.

"No, I already got one," Kirby says, exasperated. "She's orange. She has butterflies on her butt and brown eyes and gold hair and um, she looks kinda dopey."

Her mother peeks back at her over her shoulder, thrilled at the prospect. "Kirby! Did you steal something?"

"No! It was a present. I didn't even want it."

"That's okay then." Her mother rubs at her eyes with the heel of her hand, dragging a smudge of mascara across her eyes like a burglar.

"So I can keep it?"

"Of course you can. You can do almost anything you want. Especially with presents. Even break them into a million billion pieces." Like the vase in the hallway, Kirby thinks.

"Okay," she says, seriously. "Your hair smells funny."

"Look who's talking!" Her mother's laugh is like a rainbow dancing across a room. "When was the last time you washed yours?"

HARPER

22 November 1931

———

The Mercy Hospital does not live up to its name. "Can you pay?" the tired-looking woman in the reception booth demands through a round hole in the glass. "Paying patients go to the front of the line."

"How long is the wait?" Harper grunts.

The woman inclines her head towards the triage waiting area. It is standing-room only, apart from the people who are sitting or lying half-collapsed on the floor, too sick or tired or plain goddamn bored to stay on their feet. A few glance up with hope or outrage or some unsustainable mix of the two in their eyes. The others have the same look of resignation he's seen in farm horses on their last legs, ribs as pronounced as the cracks and furrows in the dead earth they strain the plow against. You shoot a horse like that.

He digs in the pocket of the stolen coat for the crumpled five-dollar bill he found there, together with a safety pin, three dimes, two quarters and a key, worn out in a way that feels familiar. Or maybe he has become accustomed to tarnish.

"Is this enough for *mercy,* sweetheart?" he asks, shoving the bill through the window.

"Yes." She holds his gaze, to tell him that she is not ashamed to charge, even though the very act of doing so says otherwise.

She rings a little bell and a nurse comes to collect him, her practical shoes slapping against the linoleum. E. Kappel it reads on her name-badge. She is pretty, in an ordinary sort of way, with rosy cheeks and carefully ironed cherry-brown curls under her white cap. Apart from her nose, which is turned up too much, so it looks like a snout. Little piggy, he thinks.

"Come with me," she says, irritated that he's there at all. Already cataloging him as so much more human trash. She turns and strides away so that he has to jolt after her. Each step sends pain shooting up to his hip, like a Chinese rocket, but he is determined to keep up.

Every ward they pass is crammed to capacity, sometimes with two people to a bed, laid head to foot. All the sickness inside spilling out.

Not as bad as the field hospitals, he thinks. Mangled men clustered on blood-stained stretchers among the stink of burns and rotting wounds and shit and vomit and sour fever sweats. The incessant moaning like a terrible choir.

There was that boy from Missouri with his leg blown off, he remembers. He wouldn't let up screaming, keeping them all awake, until Harper sneaked over, as if to comfort him. What he actually did was slide his bayonet in through the idiot boy's thigh above the bloody wreckage and neatly flick it up to sever the artery. Just like he'd practiced on the straw dummies in training. Stab and twist. A gut wound will drop a man in his tracks every time. Harper always found it more personal than bullets, getting right up into someone. It made the war bearable.

No chance of that here, he supposes. But there are other ways to get rid of troublesome patients. "You should break out the black bottle," Harper says, just to rile the chubby nurse. "They'd thank you for it."

She gives a little snort of contempt as she leads him past the doors of the private wards, tidy single-occupant rooms that are mostly vacant. "Don't you tempt me. Quarter of the hospital is acting as a pest-house right now. Typhoid, infection. Poison would be a blessing. But don't you let the surgeons hear you talking about no black bottle."

Through an open doorway, he sees a girl lying in a bed surrounded by flowers. She has the look of a film star, even though it's been over a decade since Charlie Chaplin upped and left Chicago for California and took the whole movie industry with him. Her hair is sweat-plastered in damp blonde ringlets around her face, made paler by the wan winter sunlight struggling through the windows. But as he falters outside, her eyes flutter open. She half sits up and smiles at him radiantly, as if she was expecting him, and he'd be welcome to come sit for a while and talk with her.

Nurse Kappel is having none of it. She grabs him by the elbow and escorts him away. "No gawping, now. The last thing that hussy needs is another admirer."

"Who is she?" He looks back.

"No one. A nudey dancer. Little idiot poisoned herself with radium. It's her act, she paints herself with it so that she glows in the dark. Don't worry, she'll be discharged soon and then you can see as much of her as you like. *All* of her, way I hear it."

She ushers him into the doctor's room, bright white with an antiseptic sting. "Now sit here and let's take a look at what you done to yourself."

He hops up unsteadily onto the examination table. She screws up her face in concentration as she cuts away the filthy rags he has tied as tight as he could bear in a stirrup under his heel.

"You're stupid, you know that?" The little smile at the corner of her mouth says she knows she can get away with talking to him like this. "Waiting to come here. You think this would get better all on its own?"

She's right. It doesn't help that he's been sleeping rough for the last two nights, camped out in a doorway with a cardboard box to sleep on and a stolen coat for a blanket because he can't go back to his tent, in case Klayton and his stooges are waiting with their pipes and hammers.

The neat silver scissor-blades go *snik-snik* through the rag binding which has cut white lines into his swollen foot, so that it looks like a trussed ham. Now who's the little piggy? What's stupid, he thinks bitterly, is that he came through the war without any permanent damage, and now he's going to be crippled from falling into some hobo's hidey-hole.

The doctor blusters into the room, an older man with comfortable padding round his belly and his thick gray hair swept around his ears like a lion's mane.

"And what's your complaint today, sir?" The question is no less patronizing for the accompanying smile.

"Well, I ain't been dancing in glow-in-the-dark paint."

"Nor will you have the opportunity, by the looks of it," the doctor says, still smiling, as he takes the swollen foot between his hands and flexes it. He ducks deftly, professionally even, when Harper roars in pain and swings at him.

"Keep that up, sport, if you want to get chucked out on your ear," the doctor grins, "paying or not." This time when he flexes the foot up and down, up and down, Harper grits his teeth and clenches his fists to stop himself from lashing out.

"Can you pull up your toes on your own?" he says, watching intently. "Oh, good. That's a good sign. Better than I thought. Excellent. You see here?" he says to the nurse, pinching the hollow indentation above the heel. Harper groans. "That's where the tendon should connect."

"Oh yes," the nurse pinches the skin. "I can feel it."

"What does that mean?" Harper says.

"It means you should spend the next few months on your back in hospital, sport, but I'm guessing that's not an option for you."

"Not unless it's free."

"Or you have concerned patrons willing to sponsor your convalescence, like our radium girl." The doctor winks. "We can put you in a cast, send you off with a crutch. But a ruptured tendon isn't going to heal itself. You should stay off your feet for at least six weeks. I can recommend a shoe-maker who specializes in medical footwear to raise the heel, which will help it along some."

"How am I supposed to do that? I gotta work." Harper is pissed at the whine that creeps into his voice.

"We're all facing financial difficulties, Mr. Harper. Just ask the hospital administrators. I suggest you do what you can." He adds, wistfully, "I don't suppose you have syphilis, do you?"

"No."

"Pity. There's a study starting in Alabama that would have paid for all your medical care if you did. Although you'd have to be a Negro."

"I'm not that, either."

"Too bad." The doctor shrugs.

"Will I be able to walk?"

"Oh yes," the doctor says. "But I wouldn't count on being able to audition for Mr. Gershwin."

Harper hobbles out of the hospital, his ribs bound, his foot in a cast, his blood full of morphine. He reaches into his pocket to feel how much money he has left. Two dollars and change. But then his fingers brush the jagged teeth of the key and something opens in his head like a receiver. Maybe it's the drugs. Or maybe it was always waiting for him.

He never noticed before that the streetlights hum, a low frequency that burrows in behind his eyeballs. And even though it is afternoon and the lights are off, they seem to flare as he steps under them. The hum skips ahead to the next light, as if beckoning him. *This way.* And he'd swear he can hear a crackling music, a faraway voice calling to him like a radio that needs to be tuned in. He follows the path of the humming streetlights, going as fast as he can manage, but the crutch is unwieldy.

He turns down State and it leads him through the West Loop into the canyons of Madison Street, with skyscrapers looming forty stories high on either side. He passes through Skid Row, where two dollars might buy him a bed for a while, but the humming and the lights lead him on, into the Black Belt where the shabby jazz joints and cafés give way to cheap houses stacked on top of each other, with ragged children playing on the street and old men with hand-rolled cigarettes sitting on the steps, watching him balefully.

The street narrows and the buildings crowd in on one another, casting chill shadows over the sidewalk. A woman laughs from one of the upstairs apartments, the sound abrupt and ugly. There are signs everywhere he looks. Broken windows in the tenements, handwritten notices in the empty shop windows below: "Closed for business," "Closed until further notice," and once, just "Sorry."

A clamminess comes in from the lake on the wind that cuts through the bleak afternoon and under his coat. As he gets deeper into the warehouse district, the people thin out, and then vanish altogether, and in their absence, the music swells, sweet and plaintive. And now he can make out the tune. "Somebody from Somewhere." And the voice whispers, urgently, *Keep on, keep on, Harper Curtis.*

The music carries him over the railroad tracks, deep into the West Side and up the stairs of a worker's lodging house, indistinguishable from the other wooden tenements in the row, shouldering in on each other, with peeling paint and boarded-up bay windows and a notice that reads "Condemned by the City of Chicago" pasted up on the planks that have been nailed across the front doors in Xs. Make your mark for President Hoover right here, you hopeful men. The music is coming from behind the door of 1818. An invitation.

He reaches under the crossed planks and tries the door, but it's locked. Harper stands on the step, full of the sense of a terrible inevitability. The street is utterly abandoned. The other houses are boarded up or their curtains are drawn tight. He can hear traffic a block over, a hawker selling peanuts. "Get 'em hot! Eat 'em on the trot!" but it sounds dulled, as if coming through blankets wrapped around his head. Whereas the music is a sharp splinter that drives right through his skull: *The key.*

He sticks his hand in the pocket of the coat, suddenly terrified that he has lost it. He is relieved to find that it is still there. Bronze; printed with the mark Yale & Towne. The lock on the door matches up. Trembling, he slides it home. It catches.

The door swings open into darkness, and for a long, terrible moment, he stands paralyzed by possibilities. And then he ducks under the boards, negotiating his crutch, awkwardly, through the gap, and into the House.

KIRBY

9 September 1980

It's that kind of day, crisp and clear, on the cusp of fall. The trees have mixed feelings about it; leaves showing green and yellow and brown all at the same time. Kirby can tell Rachel is stoned from a block away. Not just by the sweet smell hanging over the house (dead giveaway), but by the agitated way she is pacing the yard, fussing over something laid out in the overgrown grass. Tokyo is leaping and barking around her in excitement. She isn't supposed to be home. She's supposed to be away on one of her sojourns or "so-johns" as Kirby used to call it when she was little. Okay, a year ago.

For weeks, she wondered if this So-John guy was her dad, and if Rachel was working up to take her to meet him, when Grace Tucker at school told her that a john was a word for a man who uses a prostitute, and that's all her mother was. She didn't know what a prostitute was, but she gave Gracie a blood-nose, and Gracie pulled out a clump of her hair.

Rachel thought it was hysterical, even though Kirby's scalp was red and sore where the hair was gone. She didn't mean to laugh, really, "but it *is* very funny." Then she'd explained it to Kirby the way she did everything, in a way that didn't explain anything at all. "A prostitute is a woman who uses her body to take advantage of the vanity of men," she'd said. "And a sojourn is a revitalization of your spirit." But it turned out that wasn't even close. Because a prostitute has sex for money, and a sojourn is a vacation from your real life, which is the last thing Rachel needs. Less vacationing, more real life, Mom.

She whistles for Tokyo. Five short sharp notes, distinctive enough to separate it from the calls everyone else uses for their dogs at the park. He comes bounding over, happy as only a dog can be. "Pure-bred mutt" is how Rachel likes to describe him. Scrappy, with a long snout and patchwork sandy-and-white fur and creamy rings around his eyes. "Tokyo" because when she grows up she's going to move to Japan and become a famous translator of haiku poetry and drink green tea and collect samurai swords. ("Well, it's better than Hiroshima" is what her mother said.) She's already started writing her own haiku. This is one:

Rocket ship lift-off
take me far away from here
the stars are waiting.

This is another:

She would disappear
folded like origami
into her own dreams.

Rachel applauds enthusiastically whenever she reads her a new one. But Kirby has begun to think she could copy down the wording from the side of the Cocoa Krispies box, and her mother would cheer just as loudly, especially when she's stoned, which is more and more often these days.

She blames So-John. Or whatever his name is. Rachel won't tell her. As if she doesn't hear the car pull up at 3 a.m. or the hissed conversations, unintelligible but fraught, before the door slams and her mother tries to tiptoe in without waking her. As if she doesn't wonder where their rent money comes from. As if this hasn't been going on for *years*.

Rachel has laid out every single one of her paintings—even the big one of Lady Shalott in her tower (Kirby's favorite, not that she'd admit it), which is normally stowed at the back of the broom cupboard with the other canvases her mother starts, but never quite manages to finish.

"Are we having a yard sale?" Kirby asks, even though she knows the question will irritate Rachel.

"Oh, honey," her mother gives her a distracted half-smile, the way she does when she's disappointed in Kirby, which she seems to be all the time these days. Usually when she says things Rachel insists are too old for her. "You're losing your child-like wonder," she'd told her two weeks ago, with a sharpness in her voice like it was the worst thing in the world.

Weirdly, when she gets into real trouble, Rachel doesn't seem to mind. Not when she gets in fights at school or even when she set fire to Mr. Partridge's mailbox to pay him back for complaining about Tokyo digging up his sweetpeas. Rachel told her off, but Kirby could tell she was delighted. Her mother even put on a big pantomime, the two of them yelling at each other loud enough for that "self-righteous windbag next door" to hear them through the walls, her mother screeching "Don't you realize it's a federal crime to interfere with the US mail service?" before they collapsed in giggles, clamping their hands over their mouths.

Rachel points to a miniature painting positioned squarely between her bare feet. Her toenails are painted a bright orange that doesn't suit her. "Do you think this one is too *brutal?*" she asks. "Too red in tooth and claw?"

Kirby doesn't know what that means. She struggles to tell her mother's paintings apart. They're all pale women with long flowing hair and mournful bug eyes too big for their heads in muddy landscapes of greens and blues and grays. No red at all. Rachel's art reminds her of what Coach said to her in gym class, when she kept messing up the approach to the vaulting horse. "For Pete's sake, stop trying so hard!"

Kirby hesitates, not sure what to say in case she sets her off. "I think it's just fine."

"Oh, but fine isn't anything!" Rachel exclaims and grabs her hands and pulls her into a stepping foxtrot over the paintings, twirling her round. "Fine is the very definition of mediocrity. It's what's polite. It's what's socially acceptable. We need to live brighter and deeper than just *fine,* my darling!"

Kirby squirms out of her grasp and stands looking down at all the beautiful sad girls with their skinny limbs reaching out like praying mantises. "Um," she says. "Do you want me to help you move the paintings back inside?"

"Oh, honey," her mother says with such pity and scorn that Kirby can't bear it. She runs inside, clattering up the porch stairs, and forgets to tell her about the man with the mousy hair and jeans pulled up too high and a skew nose like a boxer, who was standing in the shade of the sycamore next to Mason's Filling Station, sipping a bottle of Coke through a straw and watching her. The way he looked at her made Kirby's stomach flip like when you're on the tilt-a-whirl, and it feels like someone has scooped out your insides.

When she waved vigorously, over-cheerful at him, like, *Hey, mister, I see you staring at me, jerk-wad,* he raised one hand in acknowledgment. And kept it up (super creepy) until she turned the corner up Ridgeland Street, skipping her usual shortcut through the alley, hurrying to get out of his sight.

HARPER

22 November 1931

It's like being a boy again, sneaking into the neighboring farm-houses. Sitting at the kitchen table in the quiet house, lying between the cool sheets of someone else's bed, going through the drawers. Other people's things tell their secrets.

He could always tell if someone was home; then and all the times he's broken into abandoned houses since, to scrounge for food or some overlooked trinket to pawn. An empty house feels a certain way. Ripe with absence.

This House is full of expectation that makes the hair on his arms rise. There is someone in here with him. And it is not the dead body lying in the hallway.

The chandelier above the stairs casts a soft glow over dark wooden floors, gleaming with fresh polish. The wallpaper is new, a dark green and cream diamond pattern that even Harper can tell is tasteful. To the left is a bright modern kitchen, straight out of the Sears catalog, with melamine cupboards and a brand-new toaster oven and an icebox and a silver kettle on the stove, all laid out. Waiting for him.

He swings his crutch wide over the blood seeping like a carpet across the floorboards and limps around to get a better look at the dead man. He's gripping a half-frozen turkey, the gray-pink flesh pimpled and smeared with gore. The fellow is thickset, in a dress shirt with suspenders, gray pants and smart shoes. No coat. His head has been pulped like a melon, but there is enough left to make out jowly cheeks with stubble and bloodshot blue eyes staring out of the mess of his face, wide in shock.

No coat.

Harper limps past the corpse, following the music into the parlor, half-expecting to find the owner, sitting in the upholstered chair in front of the fireplace, the poker he used to bash the man's head in laid across his lap.

The room is empty. Although the fire is lit. And there *is* a poker beside the wood rack, stacked full, as if in anticipation of his arrival. The song spills from a gold-and-burgundy gramophone. The label on the record reads "Gershwin." Of course. Through a crack in the curtains, he can see the cheap plywood nailed up over the windows, blocking out the daylight. But why hide this behind boarded-up windows and a condemned sign? *To prevent other people finding it.*

A crystal decanter filled with a honey-colored liquor has been set out next to a single tumbler on the side table. It's on top of a lace-doily tablecloth. That will have to go, Harper thinks. And he will have to do something about the body. Bartek, he thinks, recalling the name the blind woman had said before he choked her.

Bartek never belonged here, the voice in his head says. But Harper does. The House has been waiting for him. It called him here for a purpose. The voice in his head is whispering *home*. And it feels like it, more than the wretched place he grew up or the series of flophouses and shacks he's moved between all his adult life.

He props his crutch up against the chair and pours himself

a glass of liquor from the decanter. The ice clinks as he swirls it. Only half-melted. He takes a slow draft, rolling it round his mouth, letting it burn down his throat. Canadian Club. Finest smuggled import, he toasts the air. It's been a long time since he had anything to drink that didn't have the bitter homebrew after-taste of formaldehyde. It's a long time since he sat on a chair that had cushioning.

He resists the chair, even though his leg is aching from the walking. Whatever fever propelled him is still burning. *There's more, right this way, sir,* like a carnie barker. *Step up, don't miss out. It's all waiting for you. Keep on, keep on, Harper Curtis.*

Harper hauls himself up the steps, hanging on the balustrade that is so polished that he leaves handprints on the wood. Oily ghost impressions—already fading. He has to swing his foot up and round every time, his crutch dragging behind him. He is panting through his teeth at the effort.

He limps along the hallway, past a bathroom with a basin spat-tered with runnels of blood to match the towel in a soggy twist on the floor beside it, leaking pink across the shining black-and-white tiles. Harper pays no heed to this, nor to the stairs leading from the landing up to the attic, nor the spare room with the bed neatly made up, but the pillow dented.

The door to the main bedroom is closed. Shifting light stripes the floorboards through the gap underneath it. He reaches for the handle, half-expecting it to be locked. But it turns with a click and he nudges the door with the tip of his crutch. It opens onto a room bathed, inexplicably, in the glare of a summer afternoon. The furnishings are paltry. A walnut closet, an ironwork bed.

He squints against the sudden brightness outside and watches it change to thick rolling clouds and silvered dashes of rain, then to a red-streaked sunset, like a cheap zoetrope. But instead of a gal-loping horse or a girl saucily removing her stockings, it's whole seasons whirring past. He can't stand it. He goes to the window to pull the curtains shut, but not before he glimpses the tableau outside.

The houses across the way *change*. The paint strips away, re-colors itself, strips away again through snow and sun and trash tangled with leaves blowing down the street. Windows are broken, boarded over, spruced up with a vase of flowers that turn brown and fall away. The empty lot becomes overgrown, fills over with cement, grass grows through the cracks in wild tufts, rubbish congeals, the rubbish is removed, it comes back, along with aggressive snarls of writing on the walls in vicious colors. A hopscotch grid appears, disappears in the sleeting rain, moves elsewhere, snaking across the cement. A couch rots through seasons and then catches fire.

He yanks the curtains closed, and turns and sees it. Finally. His destiny spelled out in this room.

Every surface has been defaced. There are artifacts mounted on the walls, nailed in or strung up with wire. They seem to jitter in a way that he can feel in the back of his teeth. All connected by lines that have been drawn over again and again, with chalk or ink or a knife tip scraped through the wallpaper. *Constellations*, the voice in his head says.

There are names scrawled beside them. Jinsuk. Zora. Willy. Kirby. Margo. Julia. Catherine. Alice. Misha. Strange names of women he doesn't know.

Except that the names are written in Harper's own handwriting.

It's enough. The realization. Like a door opening up inside. The fever peaks and something howls through him, full of contempt and wrath and fire. He sees the faces of the shining girls and knows how they must die. The screaming inside his head: *Kill her. Stop her.*

He covers his face with his hands, dropping the crutch. He reels backwards and falls heavily onto the bed, which groans under his weight. His mouth is dry. His mind is full of blood. He can feel the objects thrumming. He can hear the girls' names like the chorus of a hymn. The pressure builds inside his skull until it's unbearable.

Harper takes away his hands and forces himself to open his eyes. He hauls himself to his feet, using the bedpost for balance, and hobbles over to the wall where the objects pulse and flicker, as if in anticipation. He lets them guide him, reaching out his hand. There is one that seems sharper somehow. It nags at him, the way an erection does, with incontrovertible purpose. He has to find it. And the girl who comes with it.

It is as if he has spent his entire life in a drunken blur, but now the veil has been whipped away. It is the moment of pure clarity, like fucking, or the instant he opened up Jimmy Grebe's throat. *Like dancing in irradiated paint.*

He picks up a piece of chalk that is lying on the mantel and writes on the wallpaper beside the window, because there is a space for it and it seems he must. He prints "Glowgirl" in his jagged sloping script, over the ghost of the word that is already there.

KIRBY

30 July 1984

She could be sleeping. At first glance. If you were squinting into the sun dappled through the leaves. If you thought her top was supposed to be a rusty brown. If you missed the flies thick as midges.

One arm is flung casually above her head, which is tilted fetchingly to one side, as if listening. Her hips are twisted the same way, her legs folded together, bent at the knee. The serenity of the pose belies the gaping wreck of her abdomen.

That carefree arm that makes her look so romantic lying amongst the tiny blue and yellow wildflowers, bears the marks of defensive wounds. The incisions on the middle joint of her fingers, down to the bone, indicate that she probably tried to grab the knife from her attacker. The last two fingers on her right hand are partially severed.

The skin on her forehead is split from the impact of multiple blows by a blunt object, possibly a baseball bat. But equally possibly the handle of an axe or even a heavy tree branch, none of which have been found at the scene.

The chafe marks on her wrists would indicate that her hands

were tied, although the restraints have been removed. Wire probably, by the way it has bitten into her skin. Blood has formed a black crust over her face, like a caul. She has been slit sternum to pelvis in an inverted cross, which will lead certain factions among the police to suspect Satanism before they pin it on gangbangers, particularly as her stomach has been removed. It is found nearby, dissected, the contents spread on the grass. Her guts have been strung from the trees like tinsel. They are already dry and gray by the time the cops finally cordon off the area. This indicates that the killer had time. That no one heard her shouting for help. Or that no one responded.

Also entered into evidence:

A white sneaker with a long streak of mud down the side, as if she skidded in the dirt as she was running away and it came off. It was found thirty feet from the body. It matched the one she was wearing, which was spattered with blood.

One ruched vest, spaghetti straps, sliced up the center, formerly white. Bleached denim shorts, stained with blood. Also: urine, feces.

Her book bag containing: one textbook (*Fundamental Methods of Mathematical Economics*), three pens (two blue, one red), one highlighter (yellow), a grape lipsmacker, mascara, half a packet of gum (Wrigley's spearmint, three sticks left), a square gold compact (the mirror is cracked, possibly during the attack), a black cassette tape, "Janis Joplin — Pearl" handwritten on the label, the keys to Alpha Phi's front door, a school diary marked with assignment due dates, an appointment at Planned Parenthood, her friends' birthdays and various phone numbers that the police are going through one by one. Tucked in between the pages of the diary is a notice for an overdue library book.

The newspapers claim that it is the most brutal attack in the area in fifteen years. The police are pursuing all leads and urgently encourage witnesses to come forward. They have high hopes that the killer will be quickly identified. A murder this ugly will have had a precedent.

Kirby missed the whole thing. She was a little preoccupied at the time by Fred Tucker, Gracie's older brother by a year and a half, trying to put his penis inside her.

"It won't fit," he gasps, his thin chest heaving.

"Well, try *harder*," Kirby hisses.

"You're not helping me!"

"What more do you want me to do?" she asks, exasperated. She's wearing a pair of Rachel's black patent heels, together with a filmy beige-gold slip she'd lifted straight off the rail from Marshall Field's three days ago, shoving the discarded coat hanger deep into the back of the rack. She'd stripped Mr. Partridge's roses for petals to scatter on the sheets. She'd stolen condoms from her mother's bedside drawer, so that Fred wouldn't have to risk the embarrassment of buying them. She'd made sure Rachel wouldn't be coming home for the afternoon. She's even been practising making out with the back of her hand. Which was about as effective as tickling yourself. It's why you need other fingers, other tongues. Only other people can make you feel real.

"I thought you'd done this before." Fred collapses onto his elbows, his weight on top of her. It's a good kind of weight, even though his hips are bony and his skin is slick with sweat.

"I just said that so you wouldn't feel nervous." Kirby reaches past him to Rachel's cigarettes lying on the bedside table.

"You shouldn't smoke," he says.

"Yeah? You shouldn't be having sex with a minor."

"You're sixteen."

"Only on the eighth of August."

"Jesus," he says and climbs off her in a hurry. She watches him fluster around the bedroom, naked, apart from the socks and the condom—his dick still bravely erect and good to go—and takes a long drag on the cigarette. She doesn't even like cigarettes. But cool is all about having props to hide behind. She has worked out the formula: two parts taking control without making it look like you're trying to, and three parts pretending it doesn't matter anyway. And hey, it is no big deal if she loses her virginity today to Fred Tucker or not. (It is a *really* big deal.)

She admires the lipstick print she has left on the filter, and swallows down the coughing fit that is trying to erupt. "Relax, Fred. It's supposed to be fun," she says, playing smooth, when what she wants to say is, *It's okay, I think I love you.*

"Then why do I feel like I'm having a heart attack?" he says, clutching at his chest. "Maybe we should just be friends?"

She feels bad for him. But also for herself. She blinks hard and stubs out the cigarette, three drags in, as if it was the smoke making her eyes water.

"You want to watch a video?" she says.

So they do. And they end up fumbling around on the couch, kissing for an hour and a half, while Matthew Broderick saves the world on his computer. They don't even notice when the tape runs out and the screen turns to bristling static, because his fingers are inside her and his mouth is hot against her skin. And she climbs on top of him and it hurts, which she expected, and it's nice, which she'd hoped, but it's not world-changing, and afterwards they kiss a lot and smoke the rest of the cigarette, and he coughs and says: "That wasn't how I thought it would be."

Neither is being murdered.

The dead girl's name was Julia Madrigal. She was twenty-one. She was studying at Northwestern. Economics. She liked hiking and hockey, because she was originally from Banff, Canada, and hanging out in the bars along Sheridan Road with her friends, because Evanston was dry.

She kept meaning to sign up to volunteer to read textbook passages for the blind students association's study tapes, but never quite got round to it, the same way she'd bought a guitar but only mastered one chord. She *was* running for head of her sorority. She always said she was going to be the first woman CEO of Goldman Sachs. She had plans to have three kids and a big house and a husband who did something interesting and complementary— a surgeon or a broker or something. Not like Sebastian, who was a good-time guy, but not exactly marriage material.

She was too loud, like her dad, especially at parties. Her sense of humor tended to be crass. Her laugh was notorious or legendary, depending on who was telling. You could hear it from the other side of Alpha Phi. She could be annoying. She could be narrow-minded in that got-all-the-answers-to-save-the-world way. But she was the kind of girl you couldn't keep down. Unless you cut her up and caved in her skull.

Her death will send out shockwaves among everyone she knew, and some people she didn't.

Her father will never recover. His weight drops away until he becomes a wan parody of the loud and opinionated estate agent who would pick a fight at the barbecue about the game. He loses all interest in selling houses. He tapers off mid-sales pitch, looking at the blank spaces on the wall between the perfect family portraits or worse, at the grouting between the tiles of the ensuite bathroom. He learns to fake it, to clamp the sadness down. At home, he starts cooking. He teaches himself French cuisine. But all food tastes bland to him.

Her mother draws the pain into herself: a monster she keeps caged in her chest that can only be subdued with vodka. She does not eat her husband's cooking. When they move back to Canada and downsize the house, she relocates into the spare room. Eventually, he stops hiding her bottles. When her liver seizes up twenty years later, he sits next to her in a Winnipeg hospital and strokes her hand and narrates recipes he's memorized like scientific formulas because there is nothing else to say.

Her sister moves as far away as she can, and keeps moving, first across the state, then across the country, then overseas to become an au pair in Portugal. She is not a very good au pair. She doesn't bond with the children. She is too terrified that something might happen to them.

After three hours of questioning, Sebastian, Julia's boyfriend of six weeks, has his alibi corroborated by independent witnesses and the grease-stains on his shorts. He was tinkering with the 1974 Indian motorbike he'd been restoring, the garage door open, in full view of the street. Moved by the experience, he takes Julia's death as a sign that he has been wasting his life studying business science. He joins the anti-apartheid student movement, has sex with anti-apartheid girls. His tragic past clings to him like pheromones that women find impossible to resist. It even has a theme song: Janis Joplin's "Get It While You Can."

Her best friend lies awake at night feeling guilty because, even through her shock and grief, she has worked out that the statistical significance of Julia's murder is that she is 88 percent less likely to be murdered herself.

In another part of town, an eleven-year-old girl who has only read about the case, only ever seen Julia's valedictorian photograph from her school yearbook, takes out the pain of it—and life in general—very precisely with a boxcutter on the tender skin inside her upper arm, above the line of her T-shirt sleeves, where the cuts will not be seen.

And five years later, it will be Kirby's turn.

HARPER

24 November 1931

———

He sleeps in the spare room, with the door closed tight against the objects, but they burrow their way into his brain, insistent as flea bites. After what seems like days of fractured fever dreams, he hauls himself out of bed and manages to limp down the stairs.

His head feels as thick as bread soaked in turpentine. The voice is gone, subsumed in that moment of searing clarity. The totems reach out to snag him as he limps past the Room. Not yet, he thinks. He knows what has to be done, but right now his stomach is clenching around the emptiness inside.

The sleek Frigidaire is empty, apart from a bottle of French champagne and a tomato that is slowly going to mulch, just like the body in the hall. It's turned greenish with the first hints of a high, rotten smell. But the limbs that were stiff as wood two days ago have softened and gone limp. It makes it easier to shift the corpse over to get at the turkey. He doesn't even have to break any fingers to pry it loose from the dead man's grip.

He washes the scab of blood off the bird with soap. Then he

boils it up with two old potatoes that he finds in a drawer in the kitchen. Mr. Bartek obviously did not have a wife.

The only record he can find is the one that is already on the gramophone, so he winds it up and starts it playing the same set of show tunes to keep him company. He eats ravenously, sitting in front of the fire, forgoing cutlery to tear chunks of meat off with his hands. He washes it down with whiskey, filling the tumbler to the brim, not bothering with ice. He is warm and there is food in his gut and the pleasant fuzz of liquor in his head and the gaudy music seems to quiet the objects.

When the crystal decanter is empty, he goes to fetch the champagne and swigs it straight from the bottle, until that's gone too. He sits sullenly drunk, the picked-apart husk of the bird tossed on the floor beside him, ignoring the ticking of the gramophone, the needle scratching uselessly without a groove, until the urge to take a piss forces him, reluctantly, to get up.

He staggers against the couch on his way to the commode and the clawed feet scrape across the floorboards and catch on the carpet, revealing a corner of battered blue luggage tucked underneath the couch.

He leans down on the armrest and hooks the suitcase out by the handle, trying to haul it up onto the cushions to get a better look. But between the booze and his greasy fingers, it slips and the cheap catch snaps apart, disgorging the contents onto the floor: bundles of money, a scattering of yellow and red Bakelite betting chips and a black ledger, bristling with colored papers.

Harper swears and drops to his knees, his first instinct being to shovel it back in. The bundles are thick as decks of cards: $5, $10, $20, $100 banknotes, bound up with rubber bands, and a set of five $5,000 bills, tucked down the side of the torn lining of the suitcase. It's more money than he's ever seen. No wonder someone bashed Bartek's brains out. But then why didn't they search for this? Even through the blur of alcohol, he knows this doesn't make sense.

He examines the banknotes more carefully. They're arranged by denomination, but separated into variations, all subtly different. It's the size, he reckons, fingering them. The paper, the color of the print, tiny shifts in the arrangement of the images and the wording about legal tender. It takes him a while to figure out the most peculiar thing. The dates of issue are wrong. *Like the view outside the window,* he thinks and immediately tries to un-think it. Perhaps this Bartek was a forger, he rationalizes. Or a prop-maker for the theater.

He turns to the colored papers. Betting slips. With dates that skip around from 1929 to 1952. Arlington Racetrack. Hawthorne. Lincoln Fields. Washington Park. Every one a winner. Nothing too outrageous—score too big, too often, and you draw the wrong kind of attention, Harper reckons, especially in Capone's city.

Each slip has an accompanying entry in the black accounts ledger, the amount and date and source printed in block capitals in a neat hand. All of them are listed as profits, $50 here, $1,200 there. Except one. An address. The house number, 1818, set against a figure written in red: $600. He hunts through the ledger for the corresponding document. The deed of ownership for the House. It is registered to Bartek Krol. April 5, 1930.

Harper sits back on his heels, flicking his thumb over the edge of a bundle of tens. Perhaps *he* is the madman. Either way, he has found something remarkable. It explains why Mr. Bartek was too busy to get real groceries. Too bad his winning streak was cut short. Lucky for Harper. He's a gambling man himself.

He glances across at the mess in the hallway. He will have to do something about it before it turns to mush. When he returns. It's an itch, to get outside. To see if he's right.

He dresses in the clothes he finds hanging in the wardrobe. A pair of black shoes. Workman's denim. A button-up shirt. Exactly his size. He glances at the wall of objects again, to make sure. The air around the plastic horse seems to twitch and shiver. One of the girls' names reads more clearly than the rest. Practically glowing. She'll be waiting for him. Out there.

Downstairs, he stands by the front door, flicking out his right hand with nerves, like a boxer warming up to throw a punch. He has the object in mind. He has triple-checked that he has the key in his pocket. He is ready now, he thinks. He thinks he knows how it works. He will be like Mr. Bartek. Conservative. Wily. He won't go too far.

He lunges for the handle. The door swings open on to a flash of light, sharp as a firecracker in a dark cellar, ripping through the guts of a cat.

And Harper steps in to sometime else.

KIRBY
3 January 1992

=======

Y ou should get another dog," her mother says, sitting on the
wall looking out at Lake Michigan and the frosted beach.
Her breath condenses in the air in front of her like cartoon speech
bubbles. They predicted more snow on the weather report, but
the sky isn't playing.

"Nah," Kirby says, lightly. "What'd a dog ever do for me anyway?" She is idly picking up twigs and breaking them into smaller
and smaller pieces until they won't break anymore. Nothing is in-
finitely reducible. You can split an atom but you can't vaporize it.
Stuff sticks around. It clings to you, even when it's broken. Like
Humpty Dumpty. At some point you have to pick up the pieces.
Or walk away. Don't look back. Fuck the king's horses.

"Oh, honey." It's the sigh in Rachel's voice that she can't stand
and it provokes her to push it further, always further.

"Hairy, smelly, constantly jumping up to lick your face. Gross!"
Kirby pulls a face. They always end up stuck in the same old loop.
Contemptuously familiar, but also comforting in its way.

She tried running for a while, after it happened. Dumped her studies—even though they offered her a sympathetic leave of absence—sold her car, packed up and went. Didn't get very far. Although California felt as strange and foreign as Japan. Like something out of a TV show, but with the laugh track out of sync. Or she was; too dark and fucked up for San Diego and not fucked up enough, or in the wrong ways, for LA. She should have been tragically brittle, not broken. You have to do the cutting yourself, to let out the pain inside. Getting someone else to slice you up is cheating.

She should have kept moving, gone to Seattle or New York. But she ended up back where she started. Maybe it was all that moving when she was a kid. Maybe family exerts a gravitational pull. Maybe she just needed to return to the scene of the crime.

There was a fluster of attention around the attack. The hospital staff didn't know where to put all the flowers she received, some of them from total strangers. Although half of those were condolence bouquets. No one expected her to pull through and the newspapers got it wrong.

The first five weeks after were full of rush and people desperate to do things for her. But flowers wilt and so do attention spans. She was moved out of intensive care. Then she was discharged. People got on with their lives and she was expected to do the same, never mind that she couldn't roll over in bed without waking up from the jagged spike of pain. Or she'd be paralyzed with agony, terrified that she'd torn something when the painkillers suddenly wore off as she was reaching for the shampoo.

The wound got infected. She had to go back in for another three weeks. Her stomach bulged, like she was going to give birth to an alien. "Chestburster got lost," she joked to the doctor, the newest in a series of specialists. "Like in that movie, *Alien?*" No one got her jokes.

Along the way, she misplaced her friends. The old ones didn't know what to say. Whole relationships fell into the fissures of awkward silence. If the horror show of her injuries didn't stun them into silence, then she could always talk about the complications from the fecal matter that leaked into her intestinal cavity. It shouldn't have surprised her, the way conversations veered away. People changed the subject, played down their curiosity, thinking they were doing the right thing, when actually what she needed more than anything was to talk. To spill her guts, as it were.

The new friends were tourists, come to gawk. It was careless, she knows, but oh so horribly easy to let things slip. Sometimes all it took was not returning a phone call. With the more persistent ones, she had to stand them up, repeatedly. They would be baffled, angry, hurt. Some left shouty messages, or worse, sad ones, on her answering machine. Eventually she just unplugged it and threw it away. She suspects it was a relief for them in the end. Being her friend was like going to a tropical island for a little fun in the sun, only to be kidnapped by terrorists. Which was something real that she saw a news piece about. She reads a lot about trauma. Survivor's stories.

Kirby was doing her friends a favor. Sometimes she wishes she had the same options on an exit plan. But she's stuck in here, a hostage in her head. Can you give yourself Stockholm Syndrome?

"So how about it, Mom?" The ice on the lake shifts and cracks musically like wind chimes made of broken glass.

"Oh, honey."

"I can pay you back in ten months, max. I figured out a schedule."

She reaches into her backpack for the folder. She worked up the spreadsheet at a copy shop, in color and with a fancy font that looks like script. Her mother is a designer, after all. Rachel gives it due diligence, reading carefully down the rows as if she's examining an art portfolio instead of a budget proposal.

"I've paid off most of my credit card from traveling. I'm down to a hundred and fifty a month plus one thousand dollars on my student loan, so it's totally do-able." Her school did not give her a sympathetic leave of absence on her debt. She's babbling, but she can't stand the tension. "And it's not that much, really, for a private investigator." Normally $75 an hour, but he said he would do it for $300 a day, $1,200 a week. Four grand for the month. She's budgeted for three months, although the PI says he'll be able to tell her whether it's worth pursuing after one. A small price to pay for knowing. For finding the fucker. Especially now that the cops have stopped talking to her. Because apparently it's not healthy or helpful to take too much interest in your own case.

"It's very interesting," Rachel says politely as she closes it up and tries to hand it back. But Kirby won't take it. Her hands are too busy, breaking up sticks. Snap. Her mother sets the folder down on the wall between them. The snow immediately starts soaking into the cardboard.

"The damp in the house is getting worse," Rachel says, closing the subject.

"That's your landlord's problem, Mom."

"You know what Buchanan is like," she laughs, wryly. "He wouldn't come out if the house was falling down."

"Maybe you should try knocking out some walls and see." Kirby can't keep the bitterness out of her voice. It's an internal barometer of putting up with her mother's crap.

"And I'm moving my studio space to the kitchen. There's more light there. I find I need more light these days. Do you think I have Robles' disease?"

"I told you to get rid of that medical book. You can't self-diagnose, Mom."

"It seems unlikely. It's not like I've come in to contact with river parasites. It could be Fuchs' dystrophy, I suppose."

"Or you're just getting older and you need to deal with it," Kirby snaps. But her mother looks so sad and lost that she relents. "I could come and help you move it. We could go through the basement, find things to sell. I bet some of that stuff is worth a fortune. That old printmaking kit must be worth two thousand dollars on its own. You'd probably make a heap of cash.

"You could take a couple of months off. Finally finish *Dead Duck*." Her mom's work-in-progress is, morbidly, a story of an adventurous duckling who travels the world asking dead things how they came to be dead. Actual sample:

> —*And how did you die, Mr. Coyote?*
> —*Well, Duck, I was hit by a truck.*
> *I wasn't looking when I crossed the street*
> *Now I'm a snack for hungry crows to eat.*
> *It's too bad. I'm so sad.*
> *But I'm glad for what I had.*

It always ends the same way. Every animal dies in a different gruesome way but has the same answer, until Duck himself dies and reflects that he too is sad, but glad for what he had. It's the kind of dark pseudo-philosophical whimsy that would probably do very well in children's publishing. Like that bullshit book about the tree that self-sacrifices and self-sacrifices until it's so much graffiti-ed rotting wood on a park bench. Kirby always hated that story.

This has nothing to do with what happened to her, according to Rachel. It's about America and how everyone thinks that death is something you have to fight, which is weird for a Christian country that believes in an afterlife.

She's just trying to show that it's a normal process. No matter how you go, the end result is always the same.

That's what she says. But she started it when Kirby was still in ICU. And then ripped it all up, pages and pages of adorably grisly illustrations, and started again. Over and over with these stories of the cute dead animals, but never finishing it. It's not like a kid's picture book even needs to be very long.

"I take it that's a no, then?"

"I just don't think it's the best use of your time, honey," Rachel pats her hand. "Life is for living. Do something useful. Go back to college."

"Sure. That's useful."

"Besides," Rachel says, her gaze dreamy, looking over the lake. "I don't have the money."

It's impossible to push her mother away, Kirby thinks, letting the crumble of sticks fall from her numbed fingers onto the snow. Her default state of being is absent.

MAL

29 April 1988

═══════════

Malcolm spots the white boy straight away. Not that a lack of melanin is wholly unusual round these parts. Usually they driving, the car barely pausing long enough to make their score. But you get your walk-ups too, from the far-gone fiends with their yellow eyes and chicken skin and hands shaking like old folk through to miss lady lawyer in her expensive suit, coming up from downtown to wait patient with the rest of them every Tuesday and, lately, Saturdays too. The street's egalitarian that way. But they don't tend to hang around after.

This man just standing there, right on the steps of them abandoned tenements, looking about like he owns the joint. Maybe he does. Rumors going round that they aiming to gentrify Cabrini, but you'd have to be one crazy motherfucker to try that shit out in Englewood with *these* rundown shitholes.

Mal doesn't know why they even bother boarding them up no more. They all been long stripped of any pipe or brass handles or other Victorian whatnot. Broken windows, rotten floors, and whole generations of rat families living on top of each other;

granny and gramps and mammy and pappy and baby-boo rat. So only the really hard-up tweakers would try their luck using 'em as a shooting gallery. Those places a wreck. And in this neighborhood, that's saying something.

Not a realtor, he figures, watching as the man steps down onto the cracked concrete, his shoes scuffing the faded hopscotch grid. Mal has already had his hit, the dope sitting in his guts, slowly turning them to cement. It takes the teeth off his day, so he's got all the time in the whole world to watch some white man acting weird.

The cracker crosses the lot, skirting the wreck of an old couch, walking under the rusting pole that used to have a basketball hoop attached 'til kids yanked it down. Self-sabotage, that's what that is. Fucking your own shit up.

Not police neither, way he's dressed. Which is badly, in floppy dark-brown pants and an old-fashioned sports coat. That crutch under his arm speaks to a sure sign of someone who has gone spiked up in the wrong place and done themselves some damage. Must have traded his hospital cane to the pawn shops already to have ended up with that clunky old thing. Or maybe he didn't go to hospital at all 'cos he got something to hide. There's something wack about him.

He's interesting. A prospect, even. Could be the guy's hiding out. Ex-mob. Hell, ex-wife! Good place for it. Could be he's got some cash stashed in one of those old rat nests. Mal peers at the row houses, speculating. He could sniff around while the white boy's out about his business. Alleviate him of any valuables that might be troubling him. No one the wiser. Probably doing him a favor.

But looking at the houses, trying to figure which one he mighta stepped out of, makes Mal feel strange. Could be the heat rising off the asphalt giving everything the shimmers. Not quite the shakes, but close. He should have known better than to buy product off Toneel Roberts. That boy been dipping, for sure, which means he been cutting too. Mal's stomach cramps like someone's got their hand right up in there. A little reminder that he hasn't eaten in fourteen hours and an indication, oh yes, that the dope's been cut. Meantime, Mr. Prospect is heading down the street, smiling and waving away the corner kids shouting out to him. He gives it up for a bad idea. Least for the time being. Better to wait 'til the white boy comes back and he can check it out properly. Right now, nature calling.

He catches up with him a couple of blocks down. Luck plain and simple. Although it helps that the guy is staring at the TV in the window of the drug store, so hypnotized that Mal is worried he had a seizure or something. Not even aware he's obstructing people's way. Maybe it's some big news. World war fucking three broke out. He sidles up to see, innocent as you please.

But Mr. Prospect is watching commercials. One after the other. Creamette's pasta sauce. Oil of Olay. Michael Jordan eating Wheaties. Like he's never seen someone eating Wheaties before.

"You okay, man?" he says, not willing to lose sight of him again, but not quite steeled up enough to tap him on the shoulder. The guy turns with such a ferocious smile that Mal almost loses his nerve.

"This is amazing," the guy says.

"Shit, man, you should try Cheerios. But you blocking traffic. Make some room for the people, you know?" He gently guides him out of the way of a kid on rollerblades barreling down on them. His man stares after him.

"Dreads on a white boy," he agrees, or he thinks he does. "Just can't do it. How's about that one?" He pretends to nudge him with his elbow, not making actual contact, to indicate the girl with tits that God himself must have sent down from on high, barging up against each other under her tank top. But the guy barely looks at her.

Mal senses he's losing him. "Not your type, huh? That's all right, man." And then, because the jonesing is already beginning to gnaw at him: "Say, you got a dollar to spare?"

The guy seems to see him for the first time. Not like the normal white-man-glance-you-over neither. Like he gets him right to his core. "Sure," he says and reaches into the inside pocket of his jacket to pull out a bundle of banknotes held together with a rubber band. He peels one off and hands it over, watching him with the intensity of some rookie trying to pass off baking soda as the real thing, putting Mal on his guard even before he looks at the note.

"You fuckin' kidding me?" he scowls at the $5,000 bill. "What am I supposed to do with this?" He has his doubts now about this whole damn enterprise. Cracker is crazy.

"Is this better?" he says, and flicks through the bills to hand him a C-note, looking for his reaction. Mal is tempted not to give him the satisfaction, but hell, who to say he won't give him another if he gets what he's looking for. Whatever that is.

"Oh yeah, this'll do fine."

"Is the Hooverville still down by Grant Park?"

"I don't even know what you talking about, man. But give me another one of those and I'll walk you up and down the whole park 'til we find it."

"Just tell me how to get there."

"Hop on the green line. Take you all the way downtown," he says, pointing to the El tracks visible between the buildings.

"You've been a great help," the man says. To Mal's dismay, he tucks the bundle back into his jacket and starts limping away.

"Hey now, wait up." He breaks into a little jog to catch up with him. "You from out of town, right? I can be your tour guide. Show you the sights. Get you some pussy. Whatever flavor you like, man. Look out for you, know what I'm saying?"

The guy turns to him, all friendly, like he's giving him the weather report. "Leave off, friend, or I'll gut you here in the street."

Not ghetto bluster. Matter of fact. Like tying your shoelaces. Mal stops dead and lets him go. Doesn't fucking care no more. Crazy cracker. Better off not getting involved.

He watches Mr. Prospect limping down the street and shakes his head at the ridiculous fake bill. He'll keep it as a memento. And maybe he'll go back to those broke-down houses to have a poke around, while the guy's gone. His stomach clenches at the thought. Or maybe not. Not while he's still flush. He'll treat himself. Blue caps. No more of Toneel's inferior shit. He might even buy for his boy, Raddison, if he sees him. Why not? He's feeling generous. He'll make it last.

HARPER
29 April 1988

═══════

It is the noise that bothers Harper the most—worse than being huddled in the sucking black mud of the trenches, dreading the high whine that precipitated the next round of artillery fire, the dull thud of distant bombs, tanks grating and rumbling. The future is not as loud as war, but it is relentless with a terrible fury all its own.

The sheer density is unexpected. Houses and buildings and people all crammed on top of each other. And cars. The city has been reshaped around them. There are entire buildings built to park them in, rising layer on layer. They rush past, too fast and too loud. The railroad tracks that brought the whole world to Chicago are quiet, subdued by the roar of the expressway (a word he will only learn later). The churning river of vehicles just keeps coming, from where he can't imagine.

As he walks, he catches glimpses of the shadow of the old city underneath. Painted signs that have faded. An abandoned house that has turned into an apartment block, also boarded up. An overgrown lot where a warehouse stood. Decay, but also renewal. A cluster of storefronts sprung up where an empty lot used to be.

The shop windows are baffling. The prices are absurd. He wanders into a convenience store and retreats again, disturbed by the white aisles and fluorescent lights and the glut of food in cans and boxes with color photographs that scream the contents. It makes him feel nauseous.

It's all strange, but not unimaginable. Everything extrapolates. If you can catch a concert hall in a gramophone, you can contain a bioscope in a screen playing in a store window, something so ordinary it doesn't even attract an audience. But some things are wholly unexpected. He stands entranced by the whirling and flaying brush strips of a car wash.

The people remain the same. Hustlers and shit-heels, like the homeless boy with the bulging eyes who mistook him for an easy mark. He saw him off, but not before he was able to confirm some of Harper's suppositions about the dates on money or where he is. Or when. He fingers the key in his pocket. His way back. If he wants to go.

He takes the boy's advice and gets on the Ravenswood El, which is practically the same as in 1931, only faster and more reckless. The train skelters through the corners so that Harper clings to the pole, even sitting down. Mostly, the other passengers avert their eyes. Sometimes they move away from him. Two girls dressed like whores giggle and point. It's his clothes, he realizes. The others are wearing brighter colors and fabrics that are somehow shinier and tackier, like their lace-up shoes. But when he starts moving across the carriage towards them, their smiles wither and they get off at the next stop, muttering to each other. He has no interest in them anyway.

He ascends the stairs onto the street, his crutch clanging against the metal, drawing a pitying look from a uniformed colored woman who nevertheless does not offer him assistance.

Standing under the metal pylons of the railroad, he sees that the neon of the Loop has intensified ten-fold. *Look here, no, here,* those flashing lights say. Distraction is the order and the way.

It takes only a minute to figure out how the lights work at the crosswalk. The green man and the red. Signals designed for children. And aren't all these people exactly that with their toys and noise and haste?

He sees that the city has changed its color, from dirty whites and creams to a hundred shades of brown. Like rust. Like shit. He walks down to the park to see for himself that the Hooverville has indeed gone, leaving no trace.

The view of the city from here is unnerving. The profile of the buildings against the sky is wrong, shining towers so high the clouds swallow them up. Like a vista of hell.

The cars and the crush of people makes him think of woodborer beetles eating their way through a tree. Trees riddled with those wormy scars die. As this whole pestilential place will, collapsing in on itself as the rot sets in. Perhaps he'll see it fall. Wouldn't that be something?

But now he has a purpose. The object burns in his head. He knows where to go, as if he has been this way before.

He gets on another train, descending into the bowels of the city. The clattering of the tracks is louder in the tunnels. Artificial lights slice past the windows, shearing people's faces into fragmented moments.

It leads him, ultimately, to Hyde Park, where the university has created a pocket of pink-faced wealth among the working-class rubes, who are overwhelmingly black. He feels edgy with anticipation.

He gets a coffee from the Greek diner on the corner, black, three sugars. Then he walks up past the residences until he finds a bench to sit on. She's here, somewhere. As it is meant to be.

He slits his eyes and tilts his face as if he is enjoying the sunshine, so that it doesn't seem that he is examining the faces of all the girls who pass him. Glossy hair and bright eyes under heavy make-up and fluffy hairstyles. They wear their privilege like it's something they pull on with their socks in the morning. It blunts them, Harper thinks.

And then he sees *her,* getting out of a boxy white car with a dent in the door, which has pulled up at the entrance to a residence barely ten feet from his bench. The shock of recognition goes all the way through to his bones. Like love at first sight.

She's tiny. Chinese or Korean, in mottled blue-and-white jeans with black hair that has been fussed up like cotton candy. She pops the trunk and starts unloading cardboard boxes onto the ground, while her mother laboriously clambers out of the car and comes round to help. But it is obvious, even as she struggles, laughing in exasperation, with a box that is splitting at the bottom under the weight of books, that she is a different species to the empty husks of girls he's seen. Full of *life,* that lashes out like a whip.

Harper has never limited his appetites to one particular kind of woman or another. Some men prefer girls with wasp waists or red hair or heavy buttocks you can dig your fingers into, but he has always taken whatever he could get, whenever he could get it, paying for it most of the time. The House demands more. It wants *potential*—to claim the fire in their eyes and snuff it out. Harper knows how to do that. He will need to buy a knife. Sharp as a bayonet.

He leans back and starts rolling a cigarette, pretending to watch the pigeons fighting the seagulls for a scrap of sandwich yanked from a dustbin, every bird for himself. He doesn't look at the girl and her mother fussing and fretting as they carry the boxes inside. But he can hear everything, and if he stares down contemplatively at his shoes while he's rolling, he can see them out the side of his eye.

"Okay, that's the last one," the girl—Harper's girl—says, lugging a half-open box out of the back of the car. She spots something inside and reaches in to pull out a doll, shockingly naked, holding it by the ankle. "Omma!"

"What now?" her mother says.

"Omma, I told you to drop this off at the Salvation Army. What am I supposed to do with all this junk?"

"You love that doll," her mother reprimands her. "You should keep it. For my grandkids. But not yet. You find a nice boy first. A doctor or a lawyer, seeing as you are studying sociopathy."

"Sociology, Omma."

"And that's another thing. Going into these bad places. You're looking for trouble."

"You're overreacting. It's where people live."

"Sure. Bad people, with guns. Why can't you study opera singers? Or waiters? Or doctors. Good way to meet a nice doctor, I think. Aren't they interesting enough for your degree? Instead of these housing projects?"

"Maybe I should study the similarities between Korean mothers and Jewish ones?" She tangles her fingers absently in the doll's long blonde hair.

"Maybe I should slap your face for being rude to the woman who raised you! If your grandmother heard you talking like this..."

"Sorry, Omma," the girl says, sheepish. She examines the doll's locks twirled around her fingers. "Remember that time I tried to dye my Barbie's hair black?"

"With shoe polish! We had to throw that one away."

"Doesn't that bother you? The homogeneity of aspiration?"

Her mother waves her hand impatiently. "Your big college words. It bothers you so much, you take the kids you working with in the projects black Barbies, then."

The girl tosses the doll back in the box. "That's not a bad idea, Omma."

"But don't use shoe polish!"

"Don't even joke." She leans over the box in her arms to kiss the older woman on the cheek. Her mother bats her away, embarrassed by the show of affection.

"Be good," she says, climbing into the car. "You study hard. No boys. Unless they're doctors."

"Or lawyers. I got it. Bye, Omma. Thanks for your help."

The girl waves and waves as the woman drives off, up towards the park, then drops her arm as the car executes a reckless U-turn to come all the way back. Her mother rolls down the window.

"I nearly forgot," she says. "Lots of important things. Remember dinner on Friday night. And drink your Hahn-Yahk. And call your grandmother to let her know you're all moved in. You'll remember all that, Jin-Sook?"

"Yes, okay, I got it. Bye, Omma. Seriously. Go. Please."

She waits for the car to leave. Once it turns the corner, she looks helplessly at the box in her arms and then sets it down next to the trash can before disappearing into the residence.

Jin-Sook. Her name sends a flush of heat through Harper. He could take her now. Strangle her in the hallway. But there are witnesses. And, he knows this deep down, there are rules. Now is not the time.

"Hey, man," a sandy-haired young man says, in a not quite friendly way, standing over him with the casual overconfidence of his size. He's wearing a T-shirt with a number on it, and shorts that have been cut off at the knee, leaving white fraying threads. "You gonna be here all day?"

"Finishing my cigarette," Harper says, dropping his hand to his lap to hide his half-erection.

"Think you better hurry it up. Campus security don't like people hanging around."

"Free city," he says, although he has no idea if that's true.

"Yeah? Well don't be here when I get back."

"I'm going." Harper takes a long drag, as if to prove it, without moving an inch. It's enough to placate the young bull. He jerks his head in acknowledgment and strolls off towards the strip of shops, glancing back once, over his shoulder. Harper drops the cigarette to the ground and ambles up the way, as if he's leaving. But he stops at the trash can where *Jin-Sook* left the box.

He crouches down beside it and starts pawing through the jumble of toys. It's why he's here. He is following a map. All the pieces must be put into place.

He finds the pony with the yellow hair as *Jin-Sook* (the name sings in his head) emerges from the building, hurrying back to the box, looking guilty.

"Hey, sorry, um, I changed my mind," she starts apologizing, then cocks her head, confused. Up close, he can see that she's wearing a single earring, a dangly shower of blue and yellow stars on silver chains. The motion makes the stars shiver. "That's my stuff," she says, accusing.

"I know." He gives her a mocking little salute as he starts

limping away on his crutch. "I'll bring you something else instead."

He does, but only in 1993, when she is a fully fledged social worker for the Chicago Housing Authority. She will be his second kill. And the police won't find the gift he leaves her. Or notice the baseball card he takes away.

DAN

10 February 1992

The *Chicago Sun-Times'* typeface is ugly. So is the building it sits on, a low-rise eyesore that squats on the bank of the Chicago River on Wabash, surrounded by soaring towers. It is, in fact, a shithole. The desks are all still heavy old metal things from World War II with wells for typewriters that have been plugged with computers. There is aerated ink caked in the air vents from the printing presses that shake the whole building when they run. Some reporters have ink in their veins. The *Sun-Times* staff have ink in their lungs. Once in a while someone will complain to OSHA.

There's a pride in the ugliness. Especially in comparison to the Tribune Tower across the way with its neo-Gothic turrets and buttresses, like some cathedral of news. The *Sun-Times* has an open sprawling office with all the desks butting up against one another, arranged around the city editor. Features and sports are shunted off to the side. It's messy, it's noisy. People are shouting over each other and the squawking police radio. There are televisions going and phones ringing and the fax machines bleeping as they churn out incoming stories. The *Tribune* has *cubicles*.

The *Sun-Times* is the working-class paper, the cop's paper, the garbage collector's paper. The *Tribune* is the broadsheet of millionaires and professors and the suburbs. It's South Side vs. North Side, and never the twain shall meet—until the start of intern season, when the rich college brats with connections descend.

"Incoming!" Matt Harrison yells in a sing-song, marching between the desks with the bright-eyed young people following in his wake like baby ducks behind their momma. "Warm up the copy machine! Get your messy filing prepped! Have your coffee orders ready!"

Dan Velasquez grunts and slumps down deeper behind his computer, ignoring the little ducklings quack-quacking in excitement at being in a real live newsroom. He shouldn't even be here. There is no reason for him to come into the office. Ever.

But his editor wants a face-to-face about plans for covering the coming season, before he jets off to Arizona for spring training. Like that's going to make a difference. Being a Cubs fan is about being an optimist against all odds or rationale. True believer stuff. Maybe he can say that. Get away with a bit of editorializing. He's been nagging for Harrison to let him write a column instead of gamers all the time. That's where great writing is: opinion pieces. You can use sports (or, heck, movies) as an allegory for the state of the world. You can add meaningful insight to the cultural discourse. Dan searches himself for meaningful insight. Or at least an opinion. He finds himself lacking.

"Yo, Velasquez, I'm talking to you," Harrison says. "You got your coffee order ready?"

"What?" He peers over his glasses, new bifocals that confound him as much as the new word processor does. What was wrong with Atex? He *liked* Atex. Hell, he liked his Olivetti typewriter. And his old fucking glasses.

"For your intern," Harrison makes a ta-da gesture at a girl barely out of kindergarten, surely, with crazy kindergarten hair sticking up all over the place, a multicolored striped scarf looped around her neck with matching fingerless gloves, a black jacket with more zips than is conceivably practical, and worse, an earring in her nose. She irritates him on principle.

"Oh no. Nuh-uh. I don't do interns."

"She asked for you. By name."

"All the more reason not to. Look at her, she doesn't even like sports."

"It's a real pleasure to meet you," says the girl. "I'm Kirby."

"That's not relevant to me because I'm never going to talk to you again. I'm not even supposed to be here. Pretend I'm not."

"Nice try, Velasquez." Harrison winks. "She's all yours. Don't do anything litigiously offensive." He walks away to drop off the other interns with various reporters eminently more qualified and willing to have them.

"Sadist!" Dan yells after him and then turns grudgingly to the girl. "Great. Welcome. Pull up a chair, I guess. I don't suppose you happen to have an opinion on the Cubs line-up this year?"

"Sorry. I don't really do sports. No offense."

"I knew it." Velasquez glares at the blinking cursor on his screen. It's mocking him. At least with paper you could doodle on it or write notes or crumple it up and toss it at your editor's head. His computer screen is unassailable. So is his editor's head.

"I'm much more interested in crime."

He spins slowly in his wheelie chair to face her. "Is that so? Well, I got real bad news for you. I cover baseball."

"But you used to be on homicide," the girl insists.

"Yeah, like I used to be able to smoke and drink and eat bacon and not have a fucking stent in my chest. All a direct result of working the homicide beat. You should forget about it. It's no place for a nice wannabe hardcore punk girl like you."

"They don't offer internship positions on homicide."

"For a very good reason. Can you imagine you kids running around a crime scene? Christ!"

"So you're the closest I can get." She shrugs. "Besides. You covered my murder."

He is thrown, but only for a moment. "All right, kid, if you're serious about covering crime, the first thing you gotta do is get the terminology right. You would have been an 'attempted murder.' As in, not successful. Right?"

"That's not the way it feels."

"*Qué cruz.*" He mimes pulling out his hair. Not that he has much left. "Remind me again which of Chicago's very many homicides you're supposed to be?"

"Kirby Mazrachi," she replies, and it all comes back to him, even as she's unwinding her scarf to reveal the raw ridge across her throat where the maniac cut her, nicking the carotid, but not severing it, if he recalls the ME's report.

"With the dog," he says. He'd interviewed the witness, a Cuban fisherman whose hands shook the whole way through the interview, although, Dan thought cynically, he pulled himself together by the time the TV news people got to him.

He described how he saw her stumble out of the woods with blood pulsing from her throat, a loop of gray-pink intestine protruding under the ripped remains of her T-shirt, carrying her dog in her arms. Everyone thought she was going to die for sure. Some of the papers even reported it that way.

"Huh," he says, impressed. "So, you want to crack the case? Bring the killer to justice? You want a sneak peek at your files?"

"No. I want to see the others."

He leans back, his chair creaking precariously, *very* impressed. And not a little intrigued.

"Tell you what, kiddo. You phone Jim Lefebvre for a quote about these rumors that they're going to fly Bell from the Cubs line-up, and I'll see what I can do about these *others*."

HARPER

28 December 1931

━━━━━

CHICAGO STAR
Glow Girl Caught In Death's Dance
By Edward Swanson

CHICAGO, IL. — At this writing, the police are scouring the city for the murderer of Miss Jeanette Klara, also known as the Glow Girl. The little French dancer gained a level of notoriety in the city for cavorting unclad behind feathered fans, diaphanous veils, oversized balloons and other trifles. She was found in the early hours of Sunday morning, gruesomely dispatched in an alleyway at the back of Kansas Joe's, one of several specialty theaters catering to patrons of dubious moral tastes.

Her untimely death might nonetheless be a mercy, compared to the inevitable alternative of a slow and painful one. Miss Klara was under observation by doctors who suspected that she was a victim of radium poisoning from the powder that lit her up like a firefly, anointed before every feature performance.

"I am tired of hearing about zee radium girls," she said in an interview with the press conducted from her hospital bed last week, cheerfully dismissing the story she's been regaled with scores of times, of the young women who were poisoned by radioactive substances while painting luminous undark watch dials in a New Jersey factory. Five young women who were destroyed by the irradiation infecting first their blood and then their bones sued US Radium for $1,250,000. They were paid out a settlement of $10,000 each and a $600 yearly pension. But they died, one by one, and there is no record to show that any of them considered that she was well paid for dying.

"Razz-ber-eeees," sniffed Miss Klara, tapping her pearly whites with one red nail. "Do my teeth look like zey are falling out to you? I am not dyeeing. I am not even seeck."

She did cop to getting "leetle bleesters" that would come up on her arms and legs, and told her maid to hurry with her bath after every show, because of the sensation that her skin was "on fire."

But she did not want to talk about "such theengs" when I visited her in her private ward filled with bouquets of winter blooms, apparently from admirers. She'd paid for the best medical care (and, rumors in the ward persisted, some of the bouquets too) with her earnings from shimmying on stage.

Instead she showed me a pair of gossamer butterfly wings she had sewn with sequins and painted with radium as part of a new costume and a new routine she was working on.

To understand her, you must know her species. The ambition of every performer is to originate a specialty, something that is impregnable against the legions of imitators, or at least, that will be deferred to you as being the first of its kind. For Miss Klara, becoming the Glow Girl was a way of rising above the competitive mediocrity that confounds even the most lithe and harmonized of dancers. "And now I will be zee Glow Butterfly," she said.

She bemoaned the lack of a boyfriend. "Zey hear zees stories about ze paint and they theenk I will poison them. You tell zem, please, in your newspaper zat I am only intox-zicating, not poisonous."

Despite being warned by doctors that the radiation had penetrated her blood and her bones and that she might even lose a leg, the petite provocateur who once performed at Folies Bergère in Paris and (somewhat more clothed) at the Windmill in London before coming to take America by storm, said she would "keep danceeng until the day I die."

Her words proved miserably prophetic. The Glow Girl capered her last on Saturday night at Kansas Joe's, returning for one encore. The last anyone saw of the unfortunate girl was when she blew her traditional farewell kiss to Ben Staples, the club's bouncer, who guarded the back door against overly enthusiastic fans.

Her body was found in the early hours of Sunday morning by a machinist, Tammy Hirst, on her way home after the night shift, who said she was attracted by a strange glow in the alleyway. On seeing the mutilated corpse of the little dancer, still wearing her paint under her coat, Miss Hirst fled to the nearest police precinct, where she tearfully reported the body's location.

———

There were plenty of witnesses who saw him at the bar that night. But Harper is not surprised at the fickleness of people. They were largely high society folk slumming it for the night. They had a bored off-duty cop with them, earning a little on the side to play minder, show them the sights, give them a taste of sin and debauchery in the Black and Tan belt. Funny how *that* didn't make the papers.

It was easy for him to be unobtrusive in that crowd, but he left the crutch outside. He'd found it was a good prop. People's eyes slid away from it. They underestimated him. But inside the bar, it would have been a detail to hang your memory on.

He stood at the back, nursing what passed for gin under the Volstead Act, served in a porcelain teacup so the bar could claim innocence in a raid.

The rich folk clustered around the stage, thrilled to be rubbing shoulders with the hoi polloi, as long as they didn't rub too close, or not without express permission. That's what the cop was for. They were whooping and hollering for the show to start already and only got more aggressive when, instead of *Miss Jeanette Klara—Radiant Wonder Of The Night, Brightest Star In The Firmament, Luminous Mistress Of Delight, This Week Only,* a small Chinese girl in modest embroidered silk pajamas stepped out from the wings and sat down, cross-legged on the edge of the stage, behind a wood and wire instrument. But when the lights dimmed, even the most drunk and boisterous of the fancy folk hushed up in anticipation.

The girl started plucking the strings of the instrument, creating a twanging oriental melody, sinister in its strangeness. A shadow slipped out among the coils of white fabric artfully arranged on the stage, dressed top-to-toe in black like an Arab. Her eyes glinted once briefly, catching the light from outside as a late arrival was grudgingly allowed entry by the thickset doorman. Cool and feral as an animal's eyes caught in the headlights, Harper thought, like when he and Everett used to drive to Yankton before dawn to pick up farm supplies in the Red Baby.

Half the audience didn't even realize anyone was there, until, cued by some undetectable shift in the music, the Glow Girl slid off one long glove, revealing an incandescent disembodied arm. The onlookers gasped and one woman near the front screamed in shrill delight, startling the cop, who craned his neck to see if there had been any impropriety.

The arm unfurled, the hand at the end twisting and turning in a sensual dance all its own. It teased its way around the black sack, exposing, briefly, a girlish shoulder, a curve of belly, a flash of painted lips, firefly bright. Then it moved to tug off the other glove and throw it into the crowd. Now there were two glowing arms, exposed from the elbow down, sensually contorting, beckoning the audience: *Come closer*. They obeyed, like children, clustering around the stage, jostling for the best view and tossing the glove up into the air, passing it hand-to-hand, like a party favor. It landed near Harper's feet—a wrinkled thing, with radium paint streaks showing like innards.

"Hey, now, no souvenirs," the huge doorman said, snatching it out of his hands. "Give it here. That's Miss Klara's property."

On stage, the hands crept up to the veiled hood and unclasped it, letting loose a tumble of curls and revealing a sharp little face with a bow mouth and giant blue eyes under fluttering lashes, tipped with paint so they glowed too. A pretty decapitated head floating eerily above the stage.

Miss Klara rolled her hips, twisting her arms above her head, waiting for the suspense of a dip in the melody and the sharp clang of the cymbals she held between her fingers before she removed another piece of clothing, like a butterfly shrugging out of the folds of a black cocoon. But the movement reminded him more of a snake wriggling out of its skin.

She wore dainty wings underneath, and a costume beaded with insect-like segments. She fluttered her fingers and winked her big eyes, dropping into a contorted pose among the coils of fabric like a dying moth. When she re-emerged, she had slipped her arms into sleeves in the gauze and was swirling it around her. Above the bar, a projector flickered to life, casting the blurry silhouettes of butterflies on the gauzy cloth. Jeanette transformed into a swooping, diving creature among a whirlwind of illusory insects. It made him think of plague and infestation. He fingered the folding knife in his pocket.

"Zank you! Zank you!" she said at the end of it, in her little girl voice, standing on stage wearing only the paint and a pair of high heels, her arms crossed over her breasts, as if they hadn't already seen all there was to see. She blew the audience a grateful kiss, in the process revealing her pink nipples to roaring approval. She widened her eyes and gave a coquettish giggle. She quickly covered up again, playing at modesty, and skipped off stage, kicking up her heels. She returned a moment later and wheeled round the stage, her arms held up high and wide in triumph, chin raised, eyes glittering, demanding that they look at her, take their fill.

All it cost him was a penny's worth of caramels, the box slightly battered from being under his coat all night. The doorman was distracted, dealing with a society lady who was vomiting copiously on the front steps, while her husband and his friends jeered.

He was waiting for her when she emerged from the back door of the club, dragging her suitcase of props. She was hunched against the cold in a thick coat buttoned up over the spangled costume, her face streaked with sweat through the glow paint which she had only made a cursory attempt to wipe off. The light of it cast her features into sharp relief, hollowing out her cheekbones. She looked fraught and exhausted, with none of the verve she'd had on stage, and for a moment Harper doubted himself. But then she saw the treat he'd brought her and a brittle hungriness lit her up. She'd never been more naked, Harper thought.

"For me?" she said, so charmed that she forgot the French accent. She recovered quickly, glossing over the broad Boston vowels. "Iz zat not *so* sweet? Did you zee ze show? Did you like eet?"

"It wasn't to my taste," he replied, just to see the disappointment flicker before the pain and surprise took over.

It was no great thing to break her. And if she screamed — he wasn't sure because the world had narrowed to this, like looking through the lens of a peepshow — no one came running to see.

Afterwards, when he bent to wipe his knife on her coat, his hands shaking with excitement, he noticed that tiny blisters had already formed on the soft skin under her eyes and around her mouth, her wrists and thighs. Remember this, he told himself through the buzzing in his head. All the details. Everything.

He left the money, the pathetic ream of her takings, all in one- and two-dollar bills, but he took the butterfly wings, wrapped in a chemise, before limping away to retrieve his crutch where he had stashed it behind the trash cans.

Back at the House, he showered upstairs for a long time, washing his hands again and again until they were pink and raw, afraid of the contamination. He left the coat soaking in the bathtub, grateful that it was dark enough for the blood not to show.

Then he went to hang the wings on the bedpost. Where the wings were already hanging on the bedpost.

Signs and symbols. Like the flashing green man that gives you permission to cross the street.

No time but the present.

KIRBY

2 March 1992

The axles of corruption are greased with donut glaze. Or that's what it costs Kirby to get access to files she really doesn't have any good excuse to be looking at.

She's already exhausted the microfilm at the Chicago Library, ratcheting the machine's whirring shutter through twenty years' worth of newspapers, all the spools individually boxed and cataloged in drawers.

But the *Sun-Times* archive library goes back deeper and is staffed by people with lateral skills for finding information that borders on the arcane. Marissa, with her cat's-eye glasses and swishy skirts and secret fondness for the Grateful Dead, Donna, who avoids eye contact at all cost, and Anwar Chetty, also known as Chet, who has stringy dark hair flopping over his face, a silver bird's-skull ring that covers half his hand, a wardrobe built on shades of black and a comic book always close at hand.

They're all misfits, but she gets on best with Chet, because he is so utterly unsuited to his aspirations. He is short and slightly tubby and his Indian complexion is never going to be the fishbelly white of his chosen pop-culture tribe. She can't help wondering how tough the gay goth scene must be.

"This isn't sports." Chet points out the obvious, lolling with both elbows on the counter.

"Yeah, but donuts..." Kirby says, flipping the box and turning it to face him. "And Dan said I could."

"Whatever," he says, picking one out. "I'm doing it for the challenge. Don't tell Marissa I took the chocolate."

He goes into the back and returns a few minutes later with clippings in brown envelopes. "As requested. All of Dan's stories. The every-single-femicide-that-involved-a-stabbing-in-the-last-thirty-years is gonna take me a little longer."

"I'll wait," Kirby says.

"As in it's going to take me a few days. It's a big ask. But I pulled the most obvious stuff. Here."

"Thanks, Chet." She shoves the donut box towards him and he helps himself to another. Due tribute. She takes the envelopes and disappears into one of the meeting-rooms. There's nothing scheduled on the whiteboard by the door, so she should have some privacy to go through her haul. And she does for half an hour, until Harrison walks in and finds her perched cross-legged in the middle of the desk, the clippings spread out around her in all directions.

"Hey there," the editor says, unfazed. "Feet off the table, intern. Hate to break it to you, but your man Dan's not in today."

"I know," she says. "He asked me to come in and look something up for him."

"He's got you doing actual research? That's not what interns are for."

"I thought I could scrape the mold off of these files and use it in the coffee machine. Can't taste worse than the stuff they have in the cafeteria."

"Welcome to the glamorous world of print journalism. So what's the old blowhard got you digging up?" He glances over the files and envelopes spiraling around her. "Denny's Waitress Found Dead," "Girl Witnesses Mother's Stabbing," "Gang Link to Co-Ed Killing," "Grisly Find in Harbor"...

"Little morbid, don't you think?" He frowns. "Not exactly your beat. Unless they're playing baseball very differently to how I remember."

Kirby doesn't flinch. "It's linked to a piece on how sport is a useful outlet for youths in the projects who might otherwise turn to drugs and gangsterism."

"Uh-huh," Harrison says. "And some of Dan's old stuff too, I see." He taps the story on "Cop Shooting Cover-up."

That does make her squirm a little. Dan probably wasn't counting on her digging up the details on the story of how he made his name mud with the cops. Turns out the police don't like it when you report on one of their own who accidentally discharges his weapon into a hooker's face while coked up to the eyeballs. Chet said the officer got early retirement. Dan got his tires slashed every time he parked at the precinct. Kirby is happy to discover she's not the only one with the ability to alienate the whole of the Chicago PD.

"It wasn't this that finished him, you know." Harrison sits down on the table next to her, his previous injunction forgotten. "Or even the torture story."

"Chet didn't give me anything on that."

"That's because he never filed it. Got three months into investigating it in 1988. Heavy stuff. Murder suspects making pitch-perfect confessions, only they're coming out of this one particular Violent Crimes interrogation room with electric-shock burns on their genitals. *Reportedly*. Which, by the way, is the most important word in a journalist's vocabulary."

"I'll remember that."

"There's a long tradition of roughing up suspects a little. The cops are under pressure to get results. And they're scumbags anyway, is the attitude. Must be guilty of *something*. It seems like the Department is going to turn a blind eye. But Dan keeps at it, trying to get more than "reportedly." And hey, what do you know? He's making inroads, got a good cop willing to talk about it, on the record and everything. And then his phone starts ringing late at night. First it's silence. Which most people would understand. But Dan's stubborn. He needs to be *told* to back off. When that doesn't work, they move to death threats. Not him, though, his wife."

"I didn't know he was married."

"Well, he's not anymore. It had nothing to do with the phone calls. *Reportedly*. Dan doesn't want to let it go, but it's not only him they've been threatening. One of the suspects who says he was burned and beaten changes his mind. He was high, he says now. Dan's cop buddy doesn't just have a wife, he's got kids too and he can't handle the thought of something happening to them. All the doors are slamming in Dan's face and we can't run a story without credible sources. He doesn't want to drop it, but there's no other choice. Then his wife leaves him anyway and he has that heart thing. Stress. Disappointment. I tried to reassign him after he came out of hospital, but he wanted to stay on the corpse count. Funnily, enough, I think you were the last straw."

"He shouldn't have given up," Kirby says, and the ferocity in her voice surprises both of them.

"He didn't give up. He got burned out. Justice is high-concept. It's a good theory, but the real world's all practicality. When you see that every day . . ." He shrugs.

"Telling stories out of class again, Harrison?" Victoria, the pictures editor, is leaning against the doorframe, arms folded across her chest. She's wearing her usual uniform of a button-up men's shirt and jeans with heels, a little bit shlumfy, a little bit fuck-you.

The editor hunches guiltily. "You know me, Vicky."

"Boring people to tears with your long stories and deep insights? Oh yes." But the glint in her eye says something else and Kirby suddenly realizes that the blinds are closed in here for a reason.

"We were done here, anyway, right, intern?"

"Yeah," Kirby says. "I'll get out of your way. Let me just pack up this stuff." She starts shuffling the files together. "Sorry," she mutters, which is probably the worst thing she could say because it acknowledges that there is something to be sorry about.

Victoria frowns. "It's all right, I have a mountain of layouts to check anyway. We can reschedule for later." She makes a smooth but swift exit. They both watch her go.

Harrison sniffs. "You know you should really pitch me before you go to all this trouble researching a story."

"Okay. So, can this be my pitch?"

"Keep it on ice. When you've got a little more experience under your belt? Then we can talk. In the meantime, you know what the other most important word in journalism is? Discretion. Meaning, don't tell Dan I said anything."

Or mention that you're screwing the pictures editor, she thinks.

"Gotta run. Keep it up, worker bee." He skips out, no doubt hoping to catch up to Victoria.

"Sure thing," Kirby says under her breath as she slides several files into her backpack.

HARPER

Anytime

════════

He relives it in his head, again and again, lying on the mattress in the master bedroom where he can reach out and trace the whorls of sequins on the wings while he tugs at his cock, thinking of that flicker of disappointment in her face.

It's enough to satisfy the House. For now. The objects are quiet. The thick pressure in his head has retreated. He has time to adapt and explore. And get rid of the Polack's body still rotting in the hall.

He tries out other days, careful that no one sees him coming or going after the encounter with the homeless boy with the bulging eyes. The city changes every time. Whole neighborhoods rise and fall, put on pretty faces, peel them away to reveal the disease. The city manifests symptoms of dilapidation: ugly markings on the walls, broken windows, garbage that congeals. Sometimes he can trace the trajectory, sometimes the landscape becomes wholly unrecognizable and he has to reorient himself by the lake and landmarks he has memorized. The black spire, the rippled twin towers, the loops and bends of the river.

Even when he is wandering, he walks with purpose. He starts by buying meals from delis and fast-food restaurants where he can be anonymous. He avoids talking so that he won't make an impression. He stays friendly but unobtrusive. He watches people closely and steals appropriate behaviors to echo. It's only when he needs to eat or use the restroom that he will engage, and then only long enough to get what he wants.

Dates are important. He is careful to check his money. Newspapers are the easiest to gauge by, but there are other hints for the observant. The number of cars that clot the roads. Street name signs that have changed from yellow with black type to green. The surplus of things. The way strangers respond to each other on the street, how open or defensive they are, how much they keep themselves to themselves.

He spends two whole days at the airport in 1964, sleeping on the plastic seats in the viewing area, watching the planes take off and land; metal monsters gorging on people and suitcases and spewing them out again.

In 1972, his curiosity gets the better of him and he shoots the breeze with one of the construction workers on a break from building the skeleton frame of the Sears Tower. And goes back a year later when it's finished, to ride the elevator to the top. The view makes him feel like a god.

He tests the limits. He only has to think of a time and the door will open onto it, although he can't always tell if his thoughts are his own or if the House is deciding for him.

Going backwards makes him uneasy. He worries about becoming trapped in the past. And he can't push past 1929 anyway. The furthest he can go into the future is 1993, when the neighborhood has gone to utter ruin, vacant houses all around and no one to bother him. Maybe it's Revelations, the collapse of the world into fire and brimstone. He would like to see that.

Certainly it's the end of the line for Mr. Bartek. Harper decides it's safest to leave the fellow as far from his own lifetime as possible. The disposal is a laborious process. He ties a rope around the body, under the armpits and between the legs. The liquefying insides are starting to seep through the clothing, so that as he drags the body to the front door, leaning heavily on his crutch, it leaves a trail of slime across the floorboards.

Harper concentrates on far away and he steps out into the predawn of summer 1993. It's still dark, before the birds are stirring, although somewhere a dog is barking, a harsh *hak-hak-hak* that breaks through the stillness. Harper stands on the porch for a long minute anyway, just to make sure there is no one around, and then yanks the corpse untidily down the steps.

It takes another twenty minutes of sweating and heaving for him to drag it to a dumpster he has scouted out in an alleyway two blocks away. But when he flips open the heavy metal lid, there is a corpse already in there. The face is swollen and purple from strangulation, the pink tongue protruding between the teeth, eyes bloodshot and froggy, but the mane of hair is instantly recognizable. The doctor from Mercy Hospital. This should surprise him. But there are limits to his imagination. The man's body is here because it's supposed to be, and that is enough.

He hefts Bartek in on top of the doctor and pulls some trash over them. They'll keep each other company, feeding the maggots.

He always returns home. The House feels like a no-man's land, but when he steps outside, thinking about his own time, it is to find that the days have passed as usual.

He accidentally misses New Year, 1932, but on the day after he takes himself out for a steak dinner. On the way home, he comes across a young colored girl and is hit with the unmistakable lightning jolt of recognition and inevitability. One of his.

She's sitting on the steps with a little boy beside her, both of them bundled up in jackets and scarves, tearing pages out of a newspaper and folding them into little darts.

"Hello, there, sweetheart," Harper says, real neighborly. "What are you doing? I thought newspapers were for reading."

"I c'n read just fine, mister," the girl says, meeting his eyes, brazen. The kind of look to get you slapped. She's much older than he first thought. Practically a young woman.

"You shouldn't be talking to no white man, Zee," the boy hisses.

"It's all right, we don't have to stand on all those formalities," Harper soothes. "Besides, I talked to her first, right? No disrespect there, huh, little man?"

"We're makin' airplanes." She flicks out her wrist, sending one of the darts swooping through the air for long graceful seconds before it nose-dives and plummets into the frosted sidewalk in front of him.

He is about to ask if he can have a go, anything to prolong the interaction, when a neighbor comes out from one of the adjoining houses, holding a potato peeler, the screen door banging behind her. She glares at Harper.

"Zora Ellis! James! You get inside now."

"Told you," the boy says, equal parts smug and bitter.

"Well, see you again soon, sweetheart," Harper says.

She gives him that cool look again. "I don't think so, mister. My daddy wouldn't like it."

"Wouldn't want to make your daddy mad. You give him my regards, you hear."

He walks away, whistling, his hands jammed in his pockets to stop them from shaking. It's no matter. He'll find her again. He has all the time in the world.

But his head is so full of her, Zora-Zora-Zora-Zora, that he makes a mistake and opens the House to find the goddamn corpse back in the hallway, the blood wet on the floorboards and the turkey still frozen. He stares at it, shocked. And then ducks back over the threshold, under the wooden X of the planks and pulls the door shut.

His hands are shaking as he fumbles the key back in the lock. He concentrates intently on today's date. Second of January 1932. To his relief, when he bumps the door open with his crutch, it's to find Mr. Bartek gone. Now you see him! Now you don't! A sideshow magic trick.

It was a misstep, like the gramophone needle skipping a groove on the record. Natural that he should be drawn back to this day. The beginning of everything. He wasn't concentrating. He will have to be more focused.

But the urge is still on him. And now that he is returned to the correct day, he can feel the objects thrumming like a hornet's nest. He drops the fold-out knife into his pocket. He will go find Jin-Sook. Fulfill the promise he made to her.

She's the kind of girl who wants to soar. He'll take her a pair of wings.

DAN
2 March 1992

===

What Dan *should* be doing is packing for Arizona. Spring training starts tomorrow and he's on the early flight because it's cheapest, but honestly, the thought of packing his single guy's carry-on suitcase is too depressing.

He's just settled in to watch the highlights from the Winter Olympics on replay when his doorbell makes that sickly electronic wheeze it's been reduced to. Another thing to fix. Not like he doesn't already have to swap out the batteries from the VCR remote for the TV remote. He hauls himself out of the couch and opens up to find Kirby standing on the other side of the screen, holding a trio of beer bottles.

"Hey, Dan, can I come in?"

"Oh, I gotta choice now?"

"Please? It's fucking freezing out here. I brought beer."

"I don't drink, remember?"

"It's non-alcoholic. Unless you'd prefer me to run down to the store to get some carrot sticks instead."

"Nah, you're good," he says, even though calling Miller Sharp's alcohol-free brew "beer" is optimistic. He shoves open the screen door. "As long as you don't expect me to tidy up."

"I would never," she says, darting under his arm. "Hey, nice place."

Dan snorts.

"Well, nice to have a place then."

"You living with your mom?" He's done his homework, looked up her news story and his notes to reacquaint himself with the salient details. On the typed-up transcript of the interview with the mother, Rachel, he'd written: *Beautiful woman! Distracted. (distracting). Kept asking about the dog. Ways of dealing with grief?*

His favorite quote from the interview with her was: "We do this to ourselves. Society is a poisonous hamster wheel." Of course the sub-editor slashed it on the first pass.

"I have an apartment in Wicker Park," Kirby says. "Gets noisy between the bands and the crack addicts, but I like it. Having people around."

"Safety in numbers, sure. So why'd you say that? 'Nice to have a place'?"

"Making conversation, I guess. Because some people don't."

"You stay alone?"

"I don't really play well with others. And I get nightmares."

"I can imagine."

"You can't."

Dan shrugs agreeably. No denying that. "So what did you get from our friends at the library?"

"A boatload of stuff." She takes a beer for herself before she hands off the other two. She sits down, tucking the bottle under her armpit so she can lever off her big black boots. She folds herself into the couch in her socks, which somehow seems terribly forward to Dan.

She shoves aside the clutter on his coffee table—bills, more bills, a *Reader's Digest* sweepstake announcement with the gold foil scratch-off sticker (You're already a winner!) and, cringingly, a *Hustler* he bought on a whim, feeling lonely and horny, which seemed like the least embarrassing choice *then*. But she doesn't seem to notice. Or is too polite to comment. Or she's sorry for him. God.

She pulls a folder out of her bag and starts laying out the clippings on the table. Originals, Dan notices, and he wonders how the hell she sneaked that past Harrison. He puts on his glasses to have a better look. Gruesome stabbing deaths aplenty. All the kind of uniformly depressing stuff he used to write about. It makes him feel tired.

"So what do you think?" Kirby challenges.

"*Ay bendito,* kiddo," he says, picking out a few of the clippings. "Look at your victim profile. It's all over the place. You got a black prostitute dumped in a playground through to a housewife stabbed in her driveway, which is obviously a carjacking. And this one, 1957? Seriously? It's not even the same MO. Her head was found in a barrel. Besides, your statement said your guy was in his early thirties. You got nothing here."

"Not yet." She shrugs, unmoved. "Start wide, narrow it down. Serial killers have a type. I'm trying to figure out what his was. Bundy liked college girls. Long hair, middle parting, wearing pants."

"I think we can eliminate Bundy," Dan says, without thinking about how crass that sounds until it's out of his mouth.

"Bzzzt," Kirby says in imitation of an electric chair, absolutely dead-pan, which makes it more inappropriately funny. It rocks him. How easily they're able to talk about this, make stupid jokes. Not like he and the cops didn't crack wise with the gallows humor when he was reporting on equally horrible crimes every other week. Frogs in boiling water. You can get used to anything. But that wasn't personal.

"Okay, okay, hilarious. Let's assume your guy is not going for the usual easy targets of prostitutes, junkies, runaways and homeless men. Who else has traits in common with you?"

"Julia Madrigal. Same age range, early twenties. College student. Secluded forested area."

"Solved. Her killers are rotting in Cook County. Next?"

"Oh please, you don't buy that."

"Are you sure you don't want to believe it because Julia's killers are black and the guy who hurt you was white?" Dan asks.

"What? No. It's because the cops are incompetent and under pressure. She's from a nice middle-class family. It was an excuse to wrap it up."

"What about the MO? If this was the same killer, how come he didn't use your insides to re-decorate the forest, huh? Don't these guys get *more* violent as they go? Like that cannibal freak they just caught in Milwaukee?"

"Dahmer? Sure. It's all about the escalation. They get more elaborate because the rush wears off. You have to keep upping the game." She gets up and paces, waving her bottle, eight and a half steps across his living-room and back again. "And he *would* have, Dan, with me. I'm sure he would, if he hadn't been interrupted. He's a classic mix of disorganized, organized and delusional."

"You've been reading up on this."

"I kinda had to. I couldn't scrape the money together to hire a PI. And I figure I'm more motivated anyway. So: disorganized killers are impetuous. Kill 'em when you can. It means they get caught quicker. The organized guys come prepared. They have a plan. They carry restraints. They take more care to dispose of the bodies, but they like to play headgames. They're the ones that'll write to the newspapers to brag, like the Zodiac with his cryptograms. Then you get the lost-the-plot freaks who think they're possessed or whatever, like BTK—who is still on the loose, by the way. His letters are all over the place. He swings from bragging about his crimes to terrible regret and blaming the demon in his head who makes him do it."

"All right, Miss FBI. Here's a hard question. Do you know for sure it's a serial killer? I mean, the guy who did . . ." he falters and waves his beer in her direction, unconsciously echoing the motion of an attempted disembowelment, until he realizes what he's doing and shoves the bottle against his lips instead, wishing the fucking thing was alcoholic, even two percent. ". . . He was a sick fuck, no mistake. But it could have been random opportunistic violence. Isn't that the prevailing theory? Hopped up on PCP?"

In his practically illegible shorthand, his interview with Detective Diggs states it more baldly: "Most likely drug-related." "Victim shouldn't have been alone." As if that was an invitation to be gutted, for Chrissake.

"You interviewing me now, Dan?" She raises her beer and takes a long slow sip. He notices that unlike the pale imitation he's drinking, hers is the real deal. "Because you didn't before."

"Hey, you were in the hospital. Practically comatose. They wouldn't let me near you." This is only partly true. He could have Prince Charminged his way in, the way he'd done a hundred times before. Nurse Williams at the front desk could have been persuaded to turn a blind eye if he'd flirted with her enough, because people need to feel wanted. But he was so over all of it—already burned out, even if it took another year to hit for real.

He found the whole thing depressing. Detective Diggs's insinuations, the mother who snapped out of her initial numbness and started phoning him in the middle of the night because the cops couldn't find the guy and she thought maybe he might have the answers, and then started screaming at him when he didn't. She thought it was personal for him, like it was for her. But it was just another fucked-up story of the fucked-up shit that people do to each other, and he didn't have any other explanation for her. And he couldn't tell her that the only reason he'd given her his number was because he thought she was hot.

So that by the time Kirby was out of critical care, he was sick of the whole affair, and didn't want to do a follow-up. And he appreciated that there was a dog, thank you, Mr. Matthew Harrison, and that was a nice angle because everyone loves dogs, especially brave ones who die trying to save their mistresses, making this story *Lassie* meets *The Texas Chainsaw Massacre,* but it wasn't like there was any new information or leads or any fucking movement from the cops on finding, let alone catching the twisted bastard who had done this to her, and who was still out there waiting to do it to someone else. So fuck the dog and fuck the fucking story.

Which meant that Harrison sent Richie to do the follow-up, but by then the mom had decided all journalists were assholes, and refused to talk to anyone. Dan was made to do penance by covering a series of shootings in K-Town, which was textbook thug-life stupid.

And this year, the murder rate is even worse. Which makes him even happier he's not stuck doing homicide. Sports is theoretically more stressful, with all the travel. But it gives him an excuse to get away and not to have to think about being stuck in a lonely apartment. Sucking up to managers is much the same as sucking up to cops, and baseball isn't as tediously repetitive as murder.

"That's such an easy scapegoat," Kirby complains, dragging him back to the present. "Drugs. He wasn't on drugs. Or not any I'm familiar with."

"Expert, huh?"

"Have you met my mom? You would have taken drugs too. Although I was never terribly good at it."

"It doesn't work, what you're doing, Deflecting with humor. Just tells me that there's something you need to deflect from."

"Years on the homicide beat had made him a keen-eyed observer of humanity, a philosopher of life," she intones in a movie-trailer voice, two octaves down.

"Still doing it," says Dan. His cheeks are hot. She gets to him in a way that's infuriating. Like when he started out as a kid fresh out of college, working the society pages with that old bat Lois, who was so annoyed by him being in her department that she only ever referred to him in the third person. As in: "Gemma, tell *that boy* that's not how we write wedding announcements."

"I had a rough patch as a teenager. I started going to church, Methodist, which drove my mom nuts because at least it should have been Shul, right? I'd come home overflowing with piety and forgiveness and I'd flush her weed down the toilet, and then we'd have a screaming match for three hours and she'd storm out and only come back the next day. It got so bad that I moved in with Pastor Todd and his wife. They were trying to start a halfway house for troubled youth."

"Let me guess, he tried to put his hand in your pants?"

"Jeez, dude." She shakes her head. "Not every church leader has to be a kiddie fiddler. They were sweet people. They just weren't my kind of people. Too fucking earnest. It was fine that they wanted to change the world, but I didn't want to be their pet project. And you know, daddy issues, whatever."

"Sure."

"Which is what religion is based on, really. Trying to live up to the expectations of Big Sky Dad."

"Now who's the amateur philosopher?"

"Theologian, please. My point is that it didn't work out. I thought I craved stability, but it turned out it was boring as hell. So I swung one-eighty."

"Started hanging with the wrong crowd."

"I *was* the wrong crowd." She grins.

"Punk music will do that." He toasts her with the almost-empty bottle.

"No doubt. I've seen a lot of drugged-up people. This guy wasn't one of them." She stops. But Dan knows this species of pause. It's the glass teetering on the edge of the desk, fighting against gravity. The thing about gravity is that it wins every single time.

"There's something else. It's in the police report, but not in the papers."

Bingo, Dan thinks. "They often do that. Leave out important details so they can flush out the crazies phoning in from any real tips." He downs the last dregs of the bottle, unable to meet her eyes, afraid of what she's going to say, feeling a churning of guilt that he never read the follow-up articles.

"He threw something at me. After he'd . . . A cigarette lighter, black and silver, sort of vintage art nouveau. It was engraved. 'WR.'"

"That mean anything to you?"

"No. The cops cross-referenced it with possible suspects, and victims too."

"Fingerprints?"

"Sure, but too smudged to be any use. Fucking typical."

"Or some decrepit fence, if they had his prints on record."

"They couldn't track him down. And before you ask, I've already gone through the phonebook and called every 'WR' in the greater Chicagoland area."

"And that's all they know about it?"

"I described it to a collector at a roadshow, and he said it's probably a Ronson Princess De-Light. Not the rarest lighter out there, but maybe worth a couple of hundred bucks. He had a similar one he showed me, from around the same time, 1930s, 1940s. Offered to sell it to me for two hundred and fifty dollars."

"Two hundred and fifty bucks? I'm in the wrong business."

"The Boston Strangler tied his girls up with nylon stockings. The Night Stalker left pentagrams on the scene."

"You know *way* too much about this stuff. It's not good for you to spend so much time in these people's heads."

"Only way to get him out of mine. Ask me anything. Typical starting age is twenty-four to thirty, although they'll keep killing long as they can get away with it. They're usually white, male. Lack of empathy, which can manifest as antisocial behavior or extremely egotistical charm. History of violence, breaking and entering, torturing animals, messed-up childhoods, sexual hang-ups. Which doesn't mean they're not functioning members of society. There have been some fine upstanding community leaders, married with kids even."

"Where the neighbors are just so shocked, even though they smiled and waved over the picket fence while the nice guy next door was digging a hole for his torture dungeon." Dan has a special place of loathing reserved for the none-of-my-business types. Comes with seeing one too many domestic violence cases. Which number, for the record, is one.

She stops pacing and sits down on the couch next to him, causing the springs to groan in complaint. She half-reaches for the last beer until she remembers that it's non-alcoholic. Then she takes it anyway.

"Split?" she offers.

"I'm good."

"He said it was to remember him by. He didn't mean me, obviously. The dead don't remember shit. He meant the families or the cops or society in general. It's his signature fuck-you to the world. Because he thinks we'll never catch him."

For the first time there is a splinter in the way she says it, which makes Dan tread extra carefully with his next words. He tries not to think about how weird it is talking about this with ski-jumpers flying off the end of the ramp on the muted television.

"I'm just going to say this, okay?" he tries, because he feels like he has to. "It's not your job, kiddo, to go around catching killers."

"I'm supposed to let this go?" She tugs down the black-and-white spotty kerchief she's tied round her neck to reveal the scar across her throat. "Really, Dan?"

"No." He says it simply. Because how could you? How could anyone? Put it behind you. Move on, people say. But there's been enough fucking coming to terms with this kind of shit in the world already every single fucking day, and it is time they called fucking bullshit.

He tries to get back on track. "All right, so that's one of the things you're looking for when you're digging through the clippings. Antique lighters."

"Actually," she says, tucking her scarf back in place, "it's not technically antique because it's less than a hundred years old. It's vintage."

"Don't be a smart-ass," Dan grumbles, relieved to be back on safe ground.

"Tell me it's not a good headline."

" 'The Vintage Killer'? It's fucking brilliant."

"Right?"

"Oh no. Just because I'm helping you doesn't mean I'm going to open that can of worms. I cover sports."

"I've always thought that was an interesting expression. Worms being bait and all."

"Yeah, well, I'm not biting. In nine hours I am flying to Arizona for a few weeks to watch men swat at balls. But here's what *you're* going to do. Keep going through old stories. Try to give the librarians more specific stuff to search for. Unusual items on the bodies, things that seem out of place—sounds like a plan. They find anything similar on Madrigal?"

"Not in any of the stories I read. I tried to get hold of the parents, but they've moved, changed their phone number."

"All right. The case is closed, so the files will be a matter of public record. You should go down to the courthouse and check them out. Try and talk to her friends, witnesses, maybe track down the prosecutor."

"Okay."

"And you're going to put an ad in the paper."

" 'Single White Male serial killer wanted for good times and life sentence'? I'm sure he'll respond to that."

"You're being obstreperous."

"Word of the day!" she teases.

"The ad is for victims' loved ones. If the cops aren't paying attention, the families will be."

"That's all great, Dan. Thank you."

"Don't think that gets you off the hook on actual intern stuff. I expect updated player stats faxed to my hotel room. And I expect you to get up to speed on how baseball actually works."

"Easy. Ball. Bats. Goals."

"Oof."

"I'm kidding. Anyway, it can't be stranger than this."

They sit in companionable silence watching a man in a shiny blue jumpsuit and a helmet hurtling down a near-vertical slope crouched on carbon planks, straightening out as the curve tips him up to shoot into the air.

"Who comes up with this stuff?" Kirby says. She's right, Dan thinks. The grace and absurdity of human endeavor.

ZORA

28 January 1943

The ships rise up in steel edifices above the prairies, all set to sail out of their berths and away over the frozen cornfields. Where they are actually going is down the Illinois River, into the Mississippi, out past New Orleans and into the Atlantic, chugging over the sea to hostile beaches on the other side of the world, where the big bay doors cut into the bow will crank open and the ramp will lower like a drawbridge to discharge men and tanks into the icy surf and the line of fire.

They build them well, the Chicago Bridge & Iron Company, with the same attention to detail as they did the water towers before the war, but they push them out so quick they don't bother to name them. Seven ships a month with space for 39 Stewart Light tanks and 20 Shermans in their hull. The shipyard operates twenty-four hours a day, clanking, grinding industry, pushing out Landing Ship Tanks as fast as they can make them. They work straight through the night: men and women, Greeks and Poles and Irish, but no other Negroes. Jim Crow is still alive and well in Seneca.

They're launching one of the ships today. A lady dignitary from the USO in a dainty hat bashes a bottle of champagne against the bow of LST 217, its mast laid flat on the deck. Everyone applauds and whistles and stamps their feet as 5,500 tons slides sideways down the ramp, because the Illinois is so narrow. It hits the river port side, sending up individual plumes like cannon shots that turn into a monster wave, setting the LST to rocking crazily in the water before it rights itself.

It's actually the second launch for LST 217, because it ran aground on its way down the Mississippi and had to be towed back for repairs. But no matter. Any excuse for a party. You can raise morale like a flag up a pole if there's drinking and dancing after.

Zora Ellis Jordan is not among the work crew that have "abandoned ship" for the night shift to go out and celebrate. Not with four kids at home to feed and a husband who is never coming home from the war, his ship blown out of the water by a skulking U-boat. The navy sent his papers back to her as a keepsake, together with his pension. They didn't issue him with a medal, because he was black, but they did include a letter from the government expressing their deepest condolences and praising his valor for dying in the service of his country as ship's electrician.

She'd been working at a laundry in Channahon before this, but when a woman brought in a man's shirt with burn marks on the collar, she'd asked her about it. When she applied, she was given the choice between welder or bucker. She asked which paid more.

"Mercenary, huh?" the boss said. But Harry was dead and the condolence letter hadn't specified how she was supposed to feed and clothe and school Harry's children all on her own.

He didn't think she'd last the week: "None of the other coloreds did." But she's tougher than they were. Maybe it's because she's a woman. Dirty looks and ugly words slide right off; meaningless compared to the empty space next to her in the bed.

But it means there is no official housing for coloreds, let alone colored families, and she rents a small house, two rooms with an outside latrine, on a farm three miles away on the outskirts of Seneca. The hour it takes her to walk there and back every day is worth it to be able to see her kids.

She knows it would be easier in Chicago. Her brother, who has epilepsy, works for the postal service. He could get her a job, he says. His wife could help with the kids. But it's too painful. The city is haunted with memories of Harry. At least here, among the sea of white faces, she doesn't catch glimpses of her dead husband and rush to catch up, to take his arm, only to have him turn towards her to reveal himself a stranger. She knows she's punishing herself. She knows it's stupid pride. So? It's ballast—the one thing holding her up.

She earns $1.20 an hour and an extra five cents on top of that for overtime. So by the time the launch is done and another hull is being hauled in to 217's berth, Zora is already back on the deck of another LST, with her helmet on and her torch sparking, and little Blanche Farringdon crouched nearby, meekly handing up new rods whenever she asks for them.

They complete the ships in phases, different crews with different specialties doing their thing and then passing the ship along to the next team. She prefers to work above decks. She used to get claustrophobic deep in the ship, welding the curb plates, like a baseboard for the wiring or the wheel valves that would flood the ballast tanks with water to weigh the flat-bottomed ship down for ocean crossing. It felt like she was hunching down in the husk of some giant, frozen metal insect. She'd taken her overhead welding exam a few months back. This pays better and lets her work in the open air, but, more importantly, it means she gets to weld the gun turrets that will tear those Nazi shits into mincemeat.

Snow is falling, big powdery flakes that settle on their thick men's overalls and melt, leaving little damp patches that eventually soak in, the same way the sparks from the welding torch singe through. The mask protects her face, but her neck and chest are pockmarked with tiny burns. At least she has her work to keep her warm. Blanche is shivering pathetically, even with the spare torches arranged around her and burning.

"That's dangerous," Zora snaps. She's angry with Leonore and Robert and Anita for taking off to go dancing, leaving the two of them on their own.

"I don't care," Blanche says, miserable. Her cheeks are flushed with cold. Things are still off-kilter between them. Blanche tried to kiss her last night in the shack where they store their communal gear, standing up on tiptoes to press her mouth against Zora's as she pulled off her helmet. Little more than a chaste peck on the lips really, but the intent was clear.

She appreciates the sentiment. Blanche is a lovely girl, even if she is skinny and pale with a weak chin, and once let her hair catch on fire because she was vain. She tied it back after that, although she still wears make-up to work and sweats it off. But even if she'd had time between nine-hour shifts and trying to look after her kids, Zora simply isn't engineered that way.

She's tempted. Of course. No one has kissed her since Harry left for the Merchant Marines. But having arms like a wrestler from building ships doesn't make Zora a lesbian, any more than a nationwide shortage of men does.

Blanche is only a child. Barely eighteen. And white. She doesn't know what she's doing and besides, how would Zora explain it to Harry? She talks to him on the long walk home every morning, about the children, about the grueling labor of constructing ships, which is not only useful work, it keeps her mind occupied so she doesn't miss him so much. Although "much" doesn't describe the aching emptiness that she drags around with her.

Blanche scurries across the deck to haul back the thick cable for Zora. She thumps it down at her feet and says "I love you," quickly into her ear. Zora pretends not to hear. The helmet is thick enough that she might not have.

They work in silence for the next five hours, communicating only perfunctorily, Hand me this, Can you get me that, Blanche holding the anchor pad for Zora to get a bead on it, and then using the hammer to knock off the slag. Her blows are clumsy today, mis-timed. She can't bear it.

Finally, the whistle blows for end of shift, releasing them from their mutual agony. Blanche bolts down the ladder and Zora clambers after her, slower in her helmet and the men's work boots that she has stuffed with newspaper to fit her size-eight feet after seeing a woman in loafers get the bones of her foot crushed by a falling crate.

Zora jumps down onto the dry dock and walks between the crowds of the shift change. Music is blaring from the speakers mounted on poles beside the spotlights playing cheerful radio hits to keep spirits high. Bing Crosby segues into the Mills Brothers and Judy Garland. By the time she has stashed her gear and is walking out between the ships in various stages of assembly and the trenches cut to accommodate the crawler cranes, the speakers are playing Al Dexter. "Pistol-packin' Mama." Hearts and guns. Lay them down, mama. She never meant to mislead little Blanche.

The crowd thins as women head off to their car pools or towards the cheap workers' housing nearby, its wooden beds stacked up as high as the bunks they weld into the berth of the LSTs.

She heads north up Main Street through Seneca proper, which has swelled from a tiny township with no movie theater or school to a bustling labor camp of 11,000. War is good for enterprise. The official family housing for workers is at the high school, but that doesn't extend to her sort.

Her boots crunch on the gravel as she steps over the thick sleepers of the Rock Island line that helped civilize the West, carrying hope in every railcar packed with migrants, white, Mexican, Chinese, but especially black folk. You wanted to get the hell out of the South, you hopped on a train for Charm City and the jobs advertised in the *Chicago Defender,* or sometimes, as in her daddy's case, *at* the *Defender,* working as a linotype operator for thirty-six years. The railroad brings in prefabricated parts now. And her daddy's been in the ground for long years already.

She crosses over Highway 6, spookily quiet at this time of night, and up the steep hill that climbs past Mount Hope Cemetery on the way to the farm. She *could* be further away. But not by much. She is halfway up the slope when the man steps out from the shadows of the trees to meet her, leaning on a crutch.

"Good evening, ma'am, may I walk with you for a bit?" he says.

"Oh no," she says, shaking her head at this white man who has no business here at this time. It is a byproduct of her job that she thinks "saboteur" before she thinks "rapist." "No thank you, sir. I've had a long day and I am going home to my kids. And besides, I think you'll find it's morning." It's true. It's just gone six, although it's still dark and cold as a witch's tit.

"Come on, Miss Zora. Don't you remember me? I said I'd see you again."

She stops dead, not really believing that she has to deal with this shit, now. "Mister, I am tired and I am sore. I have worked a nine-hour shift, I have four kids waiting for me at home, and you are giving me the willies with your talk. I suggest you limp away and leave me the hell alone. Because I *will* drop you."

"You can't," he tells her. "You shine. I need you." He is smiling like a saint or a madman and, perversely—wrongly—this puts her at ease.

"I am in no mood for compliments, sir, nor religious conversions if you're one of those Jehovah types," she dismisses him. Even in daylight, she wouldn't have recognized him as the man who lingered on the steps outside their apartment block twelve years ago. Although the talking-to her daddy gave her that evening about being careful filled her with such dread and defiance that it stayed with her for years. Even once earned her a cuffing from a white shopkeeper because she was staring. But she hasn't thought about that in a very long time, and it's dark and exhaustion has sunk into her bones. Her muscles ache, her heart is sore. She doesn't have time for this.

The weariness drops away when she sees him, from the corner of her eye, pull out the knife from his sports coat. She turns, surprised, giving him the perfect opening to punch the blade into her stomach. She gasps and doubles over. He pulls it out and her legs collapse like a shoddy weld.

"No!" she yells, furious, with him and her body for betraying her. She grabs his belt, pulling him down with her. He struggles to raise the knife again and she punches him so hard in the side of his head that she dislocates his jaw and breaks three of her fingers, the knuckles crunching like popped corn on the stove.

"Yew unt!" he screams, his consonants mangled, jaw already swelling up like an orange. She grabs hold of a handful of his hair and smashes his face into the gravel, trying to get up on top of him.

Panicked, he stabs her under her armpit. It's a clumsy blow, not deep enough to reach her heart, but she cries out and pulls away, instinctively, clutching at her side. He seizes the opportunity and rolls onto her, pinning her shoulders down with his knees. Zora might be built like a wrestler, but she has never been in the ring.

"I got kids," she says, crying in pain from the wound in her side. He has nicked a lung and there is blood bubbling on her lips.

She has never been so afraid. Not even when she was four years old with the whole city at war with itself in the race riots, and her daddy running with her bundled into his coat because they were pulling black folk off the trams and beating them to death right there in the streets.

Not even when she thought Martin, who was so little and five weeks early, was going to die, and she locked herself in the room with him and sent everyone away, enduring it the only way she could, minute to minute for nine weeks, until she brought him through.

"They'll just be waking up now," she gasps through the pain. "Nella will be making breakfast for the little ones . . . getting them dressed for school . . . even though Martin will be trying to do it himself—putting his shoes on the wrong feet." She manages a half-sobbing cough. She's hysterical, she knows, rambling. "And the twins . . . they live a secret life, those two." She can't seem to get control of her thoughts. "It's too much responsibility for Nella on her own . . . She won't manage. I'm only . . . twenty-eight . . . I have to see them grow up. Please . . ."

The man shakes his head, mutely, and brings down the knife.

He leaves the baseball card tucked into the pocket of her overalls. Jackie Robinson, outfield Brooklyn Dodgers. Taken recently from Jin-Sook Au. Shining stars linked together through time. A constellation of murder.

He trades it for the metal Cooper Black letter "Z" from an old printers tray she carried around like a talisman, that her daddy brought home for her from his work at the *Defender*. "Fighting the good fight," he'd told the kids, dropping a letter for each of them, stamped with Barnhart Brothers & Spindler at the bottom. Defunct now. "But you can't stop progress," her daddy had said.

The war is over for Zora. Progress will go on without her.

KIRBY

13 April 1992

Hey, intern." Matt Harrison is standing over the desk with an elderly gentleman in a blue suit like somebody's dapper hep-cat grandfather.

"Hey, ed." Kirby casually slides a file over the letter she's been writing to the lawyer of Julia Madrigal's supposed teen murderers. Joint defense, which tells you something—that they didn't turn on each other to try to get a shorter sentence.

She's squatting at one of the culture writer's desks because Dan is away so much he doesn't actually have a desk, let alone one she can share. She's supposed to be compiling all the information she can on Sammy Sosa and Greg Maddux after the Cubs' win.

"You want to do a *real* story?" Matt asks. He's in a remarkably good mood, kicking back on his heels. She knew she shouldn't have brought herself to his attention. Dammit.

"You think I'm ready?" she says in a way that means *it depends*.

"You heard about the flooding this morning?"

"Hard to miss half the Loop being evacuated."

"They're estimating billions in damages. There've been reports of fish in the basement of the Merchandise Mart. We're calling it The Great Chicago Flood, like the Great Chicago Fire."

"Historical in-jokes. I like it. They punched through an old coal tunnel by accident, right?"

"Brought the whole river gushing in. If you believe that. But Mr. Brown here," he indicates the dressed-to-the-nines old man, "has a different take on it and I was hoping you might be willing to interview him about it. If you have the time."

"Seriously?"

"Normally I wouldn't want you to write outside your beat, but this thing is a big, soggy mess and we're struggling to cover every angle."

"Sure." Kirby shrugs.

"Attagirl. Mr. Brown, please have a seat." He swings a chair round and stands by, his arms folded. "Don't mind me. I'm supervising."

"Hold on, let me find a pen." Kirby scrabbles in the desk drawer.

"I hope you're not going to waste my time." The old man scowls up at Matt. He has very thin eyebrows, barely there at all, which makes him look more fragile. His hands are trembling slightly. Parkinson's or just old age. He must be in his eighties. She wonders if he dressed up especially to come down here.

"Not at all." Kirby paws out a ballpoint and poises it over the pad of paper. "I'm ready when you are. Should we start with what you saw?" she says. "Were you there when they busted through the tunnel?"

"I didn't see it."

"Okay. So tell me why you're here. The bridge repair company? I heard Mayor Daley put it out for tender to the lowest bidder."

"You *do* pay attention," Matt says.

"Don't sound so surprised," Kirby snaps, with just enough smile in her voice to avoid alarming sweet Mr. Brown.

"I don't know anything about that," the old man says, his voice quavering.

"Interview technique 101. You should probably let him speak," Matt advises. "Does Velasquez teach you nothing?"

"I'm sorry. Why don't you tell me what you wanted to talk about? I'm listening."

Mr. Brown looks to Matt for reassurance, and he nods tightly to say *she's okay*. The old man chews on his lip and gives a heavy sigh, then he leans forward across the desk and hisses: "Aliens."

In the second it takes for it to sink in, Kirby realizes how quiet the rest of the newsroom has been this whole damn time.

"Aaaaand I think you can handle it from here," Matt says with a grin, walking away. Abandoning her with the crazy old man, who is nodding so hard his entire head judders on the stalk of his neck.

"Oh yes. They don't like it when we go delving in to the river. They live under there. They're hydrogen-based, obviously."

"Obviously." Behind her back, Kirby gives the finger to the rest of the newsroom, who are falling around trying not to laugh.

"If it wasn't for the aliens, we would never have been able to reverse the flow of the river. Engineering, they say—don't you believe it, my girl. We struck a bargain with them. But we don't want to provoke them. If they can reverse the river and flood the city, what else do you think they're capable of?"

"What else indeed?" Kirby sighs.

"Well, write it down," Mr. Brown gestures impatiently, triggering a fresh round of intently suppressed sniggers.

The bar is a dive. It smells like stale cigarettes and expired chat-up lines.

"That was really shitty," Kirby says, smacking the white ball as hard as she can. Tried and true tactic when you don't have a decent shot lined up. "I had real work to do!"

It was Matt's suggestion to go play pool with some of the gang after the shift shut down. It turns out to be her, Victoria, Matt and Chet, because Emma has gone to cover the *actual* flooding.

"Rite of passage, intern." Matt is leaning against the counter, drinking a vodka lime, half-watching CNN on the TV in the corner. He's supposed to be partnered up with Chet, but he keeps forgetting to take his turn.

"Brown's one of the regulars," Victoria explains. "He shows up every time there's a water-related story. But we have a bunch of them. What's the collective for insane people?"

"A gabble of crazies?" Kirby offers.

"There's a homeless woman who delivers notebooks full of illegible poetry bound up in rubber bands every October. A psychic who phones in offering to help with every single murder story *and* lost pet in the classifieds. Thank God I only have to deal with faked photos of kiddie porn."

"Lot of sports cranks." Matt turns away from the news long enough to chip in. "You haven't had to field that yet? Your man Dan refuses to answer the phone when he's in the office. They call to complain about lousy refs. Lousy managers. Lousy players. Lousy pitch. General lousy."

"My favorite is the racist old lady who brings us cookies," Chet interrupts.

"Why doesn't anyone stop them?"

"Let me tell you a story, intern," Matt proclaims. On the TV, the news has looped itself. As if fifteen minutes of headlines sums up all the world.

"Oh boy," Victoria rolls her eyes affectionately.

Matt ignores her. "You been over to the *Tribune*?"

"In passing, sure," Kirby says. She clips the white ball on the side and it goes cracking across the table, dispersing the cluster by the left corner pocket.

"Here. You're just chasing them round the table," Victoria says. She corrects Kirby's grip. "Now, lean down over the cue, line it up, and when you're ready, breathe out steadily as you make the shot."

"Thanks, Professor Pool." But this time, she sinks the fourteen, sending the white ball on a smooth trajectory to tap it gently into the corner pocket. Kirby straightens up, grinning.

"Nice work," Victoria says. "Now you need to concentrate on sinking your color."

The realization sinks in. "We're solids. Dammit." She drops her head in disgrace and shoves the cue at her partner.

"Is *anyone* listening to my story?" Matt complains.

"Yes!" they shout simultaneously.

"Good. Now. If you go to Trib Tower, you'll see that they have pieces of historic rock cemented into the wall outside on the pavement. A bit of brick from the Great Pyramid, the Berlin Wall, the Alamo, the British Houses of Parliament, a piece of Antarctic rock, they've even got a chunk of moon in there. You've seen it?"

"Why haven't they been pried out and stolen?" Kirby says, ducking out of the way as Chet nearly smacks her with his draw-back.

"I don't know. That's not the point."

"The point is that it's a symbol," Chet says, failing to sink his ball. "Of the global reach and power of print. It's a romantic ideal, because that hasn't been true since Charles Dickens's time. Or not since television."

Kirby stares down the cue, willing the ball to go where she wants it. It doesn't. She stands up, annoyed. "How did they even get a piece of the pyramid? Isn't that illegal artifact smuggling? How did that not cause an international diplomatic scandal?"

"That is not the point either!" Matt swishes his glass at them for emphasis, and Kirby realizes that he is fairly drunk. "The *point* is that the *Tribune* attracts tourists. And *we* attract crazy people."

"That's because they have actual security. You have to sign in at reception. Folk come to us and they can walk out the elevator straight into the newsroom."

"We're the people's paper, Anwar. We have to be accessible. It's the principle."

"You're drunk, Harrison," Victoria steers the news editor away to a booth. "Come on, I'll buy you something caffeinated. Leave the young people alone."

Chet waves his cue at the abandoned game. "Want to carry on playing?"

"Nah. I suck. Want to come outside with me for some air? The smoke in here is killing me."

They stand around uneasily on the curb. The Loop is emptying out, the last of the business crowd heading home via whatever detours the flooding has forced them to take. Chet fiddles with his bird-skull ring, suddenly shy.

"So yeah," he starts, "you'll learn to spot them. The cranks. Whatever you do, avoid eye contact, and if you make the mistake of engaging, dump them on somebody else as soon as possible."

"I'll remember that," Kirby says.

"Do you smoke?" Chet says, hopefully.

"No, that's why I had to get out of the bar. I can't do it any-more. It hurts my stomach too much when I cough."

"Oh. Yes. I read about that. I mean, I read up on you."

"Thought you might."

"Being a librarian."

"Yeah." She asks as casually as she can, trying not to let the hope shine through: "Learn anything I don't already know?"

"No. I don't think so." He laughs nervously. "I mean, you were *there*."

She recognizes the note of reverence in his voice and feels the old familiar despair.

"Sure was," she says, chirpy. She's not helping, she knows, but she's pissed that he's in awe of what happened to her. It's not that great, she wants to say. Girls get murdered all the fucking time.

"I was thinking, though?" he says, helplessly trying to bridge the gap. Too late, Kirby thinks.

"Yeah?"

He rushes in, headlong. "There's this graphic novel I think you should read. It's about this girl, she's had something horrible hap-pen to her, and she creates this whole magical dreamworld in her head, and there's this homeless guy who becomes her protector superhero, and spirit animals. It's amazing. Really amazing."

"It sounds . . . great." She'd thought he'd be cooler about it. But that's her problem, not his. It's not his fault. She should have seen it coming a mile off.

"I guess I thought you'd find it interesting." He looks miserable. "Or useful. It sounds really dumb when I say it now."

"Maybe you can lend it to me when you're done," she says in a way that says *please don't. Please just forget it and never bring it up again because my life is not a fucking comic book.* She changes the sub-ject to try to save them from themselves and the sucking hole of awkwardness opening up between them. "So, Victoria and Matt?"

"Oh God!" he brightens. "On-and-off for years. Worst-kept se-cret ever."

Kirby tries to muster enthusiasm for office gossip, but she doesn't actually give a shit. She could ask him about his love-life, but that would only open up questions about her own. The last guy was someone from her philosophy of science class, spiky and smart and good-looking in an interesting way. But in bed, he turned out to be unbearably tender. He kissed her scars as if he could magic them away with the ministrations of his tongue. "Hey, I'm up here," she'd had to say after enduring him kissing over her stomach, gently working his way across every inch of scar tissue. "Or a little further down. Your call, baby." Needless to say, it didn't last.

"It's really cute the way they pretend," she manages now, which only serves to drop them into stunted silence again.

"Oh." Chet digs in his jeans pocket. "Is this yours?" He hands over a piece cut from the classifieds on Saturday:

Wanted: Info on Chicagoland female murder cases 1970–1992 with unusual artifact left on body.
All queries pvt & confidential.
Mail KM, Box 786, Wicker Park, 60622

Of course she put it in the *Sun-Times,* but also all the other pa-pers and local community broadsheets, as well as posting flyers on noticeboards in grocery stores and women's centers and head-shops from Evanston to Skokie.

"Yeah. It was Dan's idea."

"Cool," he says.

"What?" Kirby is annoyed.

"Just be careful."

"Yeah, okay, anyway. I have to go."

"Right. Me too," Chet says. It's plainly a relief for both of them. "Should we say goodbye to them?"

"I think they'll be fine. Which way are you heading?"

"Red line."

"I'm the other way." This is a lie. But she can't stand the thought of trying to continue conversation on the walk to the station. She should know better by now than to try and connect with people.

HARPER
4 January 1932

═══════

Y ou hear what happened to the Glow Girl?" the little piggy
nurse says. She has given him her first name this time round,
like it's a gift tied up with a bow. Etta Kappel. It's amazing what a
difference money in your pocket makes. Being whisked past the
wards packed tighter than cattle in the stockyards to a private
room with linoleum floors and a dresser with a mirror and a view
overlooking the courtyard, for example. This is something the
rich know: money talks, so you don't have to. Five dollars a night
gets you treated like an emperor in the palace of the sick.

"Mmmmnghff," Harper says, gesturing impatiently at the morphine in its glass vial on the tray beside the bed, which has been
inclined forty-five degrees so he can sit up.

"Murdered in the night," she says in a thrilled stage whisper,
pushing the rubber tube down his throat between the wires holding his teeth together, screwed right into his jaw so it will be
impossible to shave.

"Nggghkk."

"Oh, don't whine. You're lucky it's only dislocated. Still. Not like that dancer didn't have it coming. Little hussy." She taps the vial with her fingernail to dissipate any errant bubbles, then slices off the glass nipple with a scalpel and draws the liquid up into the syringe.

"You ever go to that kind of show, mister?" she says, off-hand.

Harper shakes his head. He's interested in the change in her tone. He knows her type. Up on their moral high horse, so they can get a better view. He sinks back onto the bed as the drug takes its hold.

It took two days of agony to get back here. Hiding out in barns, sucking on icicle shards, greasy with soot from the shipping yards, until he was able to hop a train from Seneca to Chicago among the hobos and drifters who wouldn't pass comment on his purple bulging face.

The wiring around his teeth will curtail his ability to find the girls. He needs to be able to talk. He will have to lay low. He will have to reassess the way he does things.

He's not going to get hurt again. He will need to find a way to restrain them.

At least the pain is mostly gone, drowned in a morphine glaze. But the goddamn nurse is still fussing around his bed, unnecessarily as far as he can tell. He can't figure out why she is hanging around. He wishes she would go away. He gestures tiredly at her. "Wht?"

"Just making sure you're all settled. You call me if you need anything else, all right? You ask for Etta." She squeezes his thigh under the sheet and sweeps briskly out of the room.

Oink, oink, he thinks as the drugs sweep up and swallow him whole.

They keep him in the hospital three days for observation. Observation of his wallet, he suspects. Lying in bed has made him itchy with impatience, so as soon as he gets back to the House he goes out, jaw wired-up and all. He won't be caught unawares again.

He goes back to read about her murder, which is widely covered until it becomes clear that it was just homicide and not an act of war. The only paper that publishes an obituary is the *Defender,* which also prints the details of her funeral. This is not at the cemetery where he killed her, which is for white folk only, but at Burr Oak in Chicago. He cannot resist the urge to attend. He hangs at the back, the lone white man present. When someone asks him, inevitably, why he is there, he mutters around the wiring, "Knw hrr," and the fools rush to fill in the gaps themselves.

"Did you work with her? Come to pay your respects? All the way from Seneca?" They seem amazed.

"Wish there were more like you, sir," a lady in a hat says, and they nudge him to the front so that he is standing looking down at the coffin six feet deep in the hole and laid with lilies.

The children are easy to spot: the three-year-old twins, playing a game between the headstones, not really understanding, until a relative cuffs them and drags them back to the graveside, bawling; a twelve-year-old girl who glares at him like she *knows,* her little brother holding her hand, too shell-shocked to cry, although he keeps taking deep shuddering breaths.

Harper throws in his handful of earth on top of the coffin. *I did this to you,* he thinks, and the wires around his teeth make it look like his terrible rictus grin is something he cannot help.

The pleasure of seeing her laid in the ground and no one suspecting keeps him going. Reliving it almost makes up for the pain in his jaw. But eventually he gets restless. He can't stay inside the House too long. The objects are starting to hum again, driving him out. He has to find another. And *the finding,* surely, can be done without employing his charm?

He goes past the war, which is tiresome, with the rationing and the fear in people's faces, to 1950. He tells himself he is only looking around, but he *knows* one of his girls is here. He always does.

It's the same tug in his stomach that brought him to the House. That sharp edge of awareness when he walks into someplace he's meant to be—and recognizes one of the talismans from the Room. It's a game. To find the girls through different times and places. They're playing along, ready and waiting for the destiny he's writing for them.

As *she* is, sitting at a café in Old Town with a sketchbook, a glass of wine and a cigarette. She's wearing a tight-fitting sweater with a pattern of rearing horses. She's half-smiling to herself as she draws, her black hair falling forward, catching fleeting impressions of faces, other patrons or people walking past. Caricatures that take seconds to sketch, but clever, he sees, catching a glimpse over her shoulder.

He takes his opportunity when she frowns and rips the sketch out, squashes it in her fist and drops it. It falls close enough to the sidewalk that he can make as if he notices it in passing. He stoops to pick it up and unfolds the crumpled ball.

"Oh, don't do that," she says, half-laughing, mortified, like she's been caught with her skirt tucked into her pantyhose, but she falls into startled silence when she sees the metal around his face.

The drawing is good. It's funny. She's caught the vain haughtiness of the pretty woman with the brocade jacket rushing across the street, with a v-dash of a sharp chin and pointy little breasts to match and a little dog as angular as she is. Harper sets the sketch on the table in front of her. There is a smear of ink across her nose where she has rubbed it absently.

"Yw drppd ths."

"Yes. Thank you," she says, and then half gets to her feet. "Wait, can I draw you? Please?"

Harper shakes his head, already walking away. He has seen the black and silver art deco lighter on her table, and he is not sure he can control himself. *Willie Rose.*

It is not time yet.

DAN

9 May 1992

———

He's gotten used to her already. It's not just the easy access to the irritating bits of research that he'd otherwise have to look up himself while on the road, or being able to delegate phone calls for soundbite quotes. It's having her around in general.

He takes her for lunch at the Billy Goat on Saturday, so she can "acclimatize to the culture" before he takes her into the press box at an actual live game. There are big-screen TVs and sports memorabilia, green and orange vinyl chairs and old-time regulars, including journalists. The booze is reasonable and the food is good, even if it's becoming more touristy. Ever since the cheezborger *Saturday Night Live* skit with John Belushi, which it turns out she's seen.

"Yes, but it was infamous long before that," he says. "This was Cubs history—1945, the owner of this tavern tried to take a real live billy goat to the game at Wrigley Field. Bought the goat a ticket and everything, but he got turfed out because Mr. Wrigley decided the animal was too smelly. He was so mad about it that he made a solemn promise on the spot that the Cubs would never win the World Series. And they never have."

"So it's not just because they suck?"

"See, that's exactly the kind of thing you can't say in the press box."

"I feel like the Eliza Doolittle of baseball."

"Who?"

"*My Fair Lady*? You're giving me the makeover so that I can be presentable in public."

"And I have *so* much work to do."

"You could do with some finessing yourself, you know."

"Oh really?"

"The whole scruffy-almost-handsome thing is a good look for you, but you need better clothes."

"Wait, I'm confused. Are you flirting with me or insulting me? And you're one to talk, kiddo. Your entire wardrobe consists of T-shirts of bands no one has ever heard of."

"*You've* never heard of. You should let me school you sometime. Take you to a gig."

"That is not going to happen."

"Oh, and talking about school, do you think you could proofread these assignments for me before the game starts and I have to pay attention?"

"You want me to do your homework for you? Here?"

"It's already done. I just want you to play copy-editor. Besides, you try interning and studying *and* trying to hunt down a serial killer."

"How's that going?"

"Slowly. No replies to the ad, yet. Although I have a meeting with the defendants' lawyer in the Madrigal case."

"You were supposed to talk to the prosecutor."

"He hung up on me. I think he thinks I'm trying to get the case reopened."

"Well, you are. On some half-baked theory you've got."

"Give it more time in the oven. So, can you read these essays while I get us drinks?"

"You're taking advantage," he grumbles, half-heartedly, but takes out his glasses anyway.

The essays veer wildly from whether free will exists (apparently it doesn't, he's disappointed to discover) to the history of erotica in popular culture. Kirby plops back down in the chair with a Diet Coke for him and a beer for her, and sees him raising his eyebrows at the content.

"It was that or 'propaganda war films of the twentieth century' and I've already seen *Bugs Bunny vs. the Nazis,* which is the master-work of its time."

"You don't have to explain your choices to me, but it's obvious that whoever is teaching this stuff is just using it as an excuse to get his students into bed."

"Actually, it's a female lecturer and, no, she's not a lesbian. Although, come to think of it, she did mention a sideline in cater-ing for orgies."

He hates how easily she can make him blush.

"All right, shut up. We need to talk about your enthusiasm for commas. You can't stick them anywhere you like."

"That's what my gender studies professor said."

"I'm ignoring that. You need to get to grips with the mysteries of punctuation. And lose the formal academic style. All this 'one must contextualize this within the strictures of the postmodern framework' crap."

"You know, academic kinda comes with the territory."

"Sure, but it's going to kill you when you have to write jour-nalism. Keep it simple. Say what you mean. Otherwise, it's fine. Some of the ideas are stale, but you'll grow into original think-ing." He looks at her over his glasses. "And I'm just saying, as much fun as it is for me to read about stag films from the 1920s through to blaxploitation pornos, you might want to consider doing this in a study group with other actual students."

"Yeah, no," she dismisses him. "It's bad enough going to class."

"Don't be silly. I'm sure you could—"

She interrupts. "If you're about to say 'make friends if you tried,' fucking don't, okay? It's like being the train-wreck celebrity without the limo rides or free designer clothes. Every single day, everyone stares. Everyone knows. Everyone's talking about it."

"I'm sure that's not true, kiddo."

"There's this amazing thing I can do, which is condense clouds of silence around me. It's like magic. I'll walk through a conversation and it'll stop, dead. And resume again the moment I'm gone. In slightly lower tones."

"It'll wear off. They're young and stupid. You're a fad."

"I'm a *grotesque*. There's a difference. I shouldn't have survived. And if I absolutely had to, I should have been different. Like the tragic damsels my fucking mother's always painting."

"You're no shrinking Ophelia, that's for sure." And in response to her raised eyebrow, "Hey, I had a college education too, you know. But I didn't waste mine sitting around drinking Diet Coke with sports hacks."

"It's not a waste. It's an invaluable part of my internship, which is worth a college credit."

"And you forgot to add that I'm not a hack."

"Uh-huh."

"Well," Dan says cheerily, "now that our afternoon's off to a miserable start, you want to watch some ball?"

The bar is well and truly packed out, the fans wearing rival colors, "like gangs," Kirby whispers during the anthem. "Crips and Bloods."

"Shhh," he says.

He finds that he enjoys explaining the game to her, not only the blow-by-blow, but the nuances.

"Thanks. My personal commentator." She snarks.

The whole bar leaps to its feet in a roar, half elation, half disappointment. Someone spills their beer, the splash barely missing Kirby's shoes.

"And that's a home run." Dan nudges her, pointing at the screen. "Not a *goal*."

She punches him playfully in the arm, but hard, with her knuckle out, and he retaliates without really thinking about it, punching her back with about the same amount of force. Give as good as you get, his sisters taught him. They threw some mean punches. Also wrist burns. Wrestling him to the ground and pulling his hair. Affectionate violence. For when a hug just won't do. That's a Hallmark card for you.

"Ow, you ass!" Her eyes widen. "That hurt."

"Oh shit, I'm sorry, Kirby," he panics. "I didn't mean to. I wasn't thinking." Nice fucking work, Velasquez, hitting the girl who survived the most horrific assault he's ever heard of. Next up: beating old ladies and kicking puppies.

"Yeah, right. Give me some credit." She snorts, but she's staring intently at the screen mounted above the bar—at the MilkBoy commercial, which has already aired twice during the game. He realizes it's not the play-fighting that has upset her, but his reaction.

And it's that easy. He reaches out and taps her knee softly with his knuckle. "Tough cookie, huh?"

She gives him a side-eyed smile, pure mischief. "So hardcore even Girl Scouts can't sell me."

"Wow. Your jokes are feeble," he says, grinning, leaving himself wide open.

"Not as feeble as your punches," she retorts.

"*Almost* handsome?" He shakes his head.

WILLIE

15 October 1954

The first nuclear reactor went critical under the University of Chicago's overgrown football stadium in 1942. It was a miracle of science! But it didn't take long for it to twist into a miracle of propaganda.

Fear festers in the imagination. It's not fear's fault. That's just the way it's made. Nightmares breed. Allies become enemies. Subversives are everywhere. Paranoia justifies any persecution, and privacy is a luxury when the Reds have the bomb.

Willie Rose makes the mistake of thinking it's a Hollywood thing. Mr. Walt Disney testifying to the Motion Picture Alliance for the Preservation of American Ideals that commie cartoonists want to turn Mickey Mouse into a Marxist rat! How absurd.

Of course she's heard about the ruined careers and people blacklisted for not taking the oath of loyalty to the United States of America and all it stands for. But she's no Arthur Miller. Nor Ethel Rosenberg, for that matter.

So it's a shock when she gets into work on Wednesday at Crake & Mendelson, third floor at the Fisher Building, to find the pair of comics sitting on her drafting table like an accusation.

Fighting American: Don't Laugh—They're not funny! POISON IVAN *and* HOTSKY TROTSKI. A superhero dressed in the American flag and a golden boy sidekick prepare to take on the hideous weirdo pinko mutants creeping out of a tunnel below. On the cover of the other comic, a handsome secret agent wrestles a gun-wielding dame in a red dress while a Russki soldier with a big beard bleeds to death on the carpet. There's a snowy landscape hanging above the fireplace with a streaked red sky and the silhouette of distinctive minarets visible through the window. *Admiral Zacharias' Secret Missions: Menace! Intrigue! Mystery! Action!* The woman looks a bit like her, same pitch-black hair. Hardly subtle. Risible. Except it's not.

She sits down in her swivel chair with the loose wheel that cants precariously to the side, and flips through the comics, looking serious. She half-spins in her seat to catcall at the giant with the thinning hair in the blue shirt with the white collar watching her from the water cooler. Six foot eight and all asshole. The same guy who told her the only reason they hired a woman architect was so that she could also answer the phones. Number of times she's answered the phone since she started here eight months ago: zilch.

"Hey, Stewie, your funny books aren't funny." She dumps them dramatically in the waste-paper basket at her feet, two-handed, as if they weigh a ton. The tension she didn't even know was there breaks, and several of the guys chuckle. Good old Willie. George fakes a one-two punch at Stewart's jaw. K.O. The asshole puts up his hands in mock defeat and everyone more or less gets back to work.

Is it her imagination or are things slightly out of place on her desk? Her .25 Rapidograph is on the right of her T-square and the slide rule, but she usually leaves it on the other side because she is left-handed.

For God's sake, she's not even a socialist, let alone a member of the Communist Party. But she's artistic. And these days that's bad enough. Because artists socialize with all kinds of people. Like blacks and left-wing radicals and people with opinions.

That she finds William Burroughs incomprehensible and all the brouhaha over the *Chicago Review* daring to publish his over-the-top pornography equally so is beside the point. She's never been much of a reader. But she has friends down at the 57th Street colony—writers and artists and sculptors. She's sold her sketches down at the art market. Female nudes. Friends who pose for her. Some of them more intimately than others. It doesn't make her red, dammit. Even if there are things she'd prefer not to come out in the wash. To most people, it's all equivalent anyway. Pinkos. Subversives. Homos.

To keep her hands from shaking, she fiddles with the cardboard model she's been working on for the new Wood Hill bungalows. She's done fifty sketches of the same, but she finds it easier to imagine in three dimensions. She's already built five of them based on the most promising ideas, in varying degrees from the original concept sketch George gave her, trying to find the opportunity. It's hard to have an original thought when you've been briefed very specifically by the firm's principal. Can't reinvent the wheel. But you can put your own spin on it.

They're working-class homes, part of an insular development blatantly based on Park Forest and its self-contained downtown with a bank and a Marshall Field's. He's letting her handle it on her own, down to cabinetry and lighting fixtures. She won't get to present, but he's said she can manage the project on site. It's only because the rest of the office is tied up with office blocks for the government project they're pitching on that everyone is treating very hush-hush.

Wood Hill is not to her personal taste. She'd never give up her

Old Town apartment, the hustle and vibrancy of the city, or the ease with which she can smuggle a beautiful girl up the stairs. But she finds it fulfilling, designing these utopian model homes. In an ideal world, she'd want them to be more modular, in the Kecks' style, so you could switch things up and make them different, with a flow between the interior and exterior spaces. She's been looking at books on Morocco recently, and she thinks an enclosed central courtyard might work with Chicago's brutal winters.

She's got ahead of herself and already done a watercolor artist's impression of her favorite of the designs. It's filled in with a happy family, mom and dad, two kids and a dog and a Cadillac in the driveway. It looks cozily uncomplicated, and is it her fault if the dad seems a little fey, with high cheekbones?

When she started here, she was peeved that she was having to make modifications to these shake'n'bake homes. But Willie is a woman who has come to terms with her ambitions. She'd tried to get into Frank Lloyd Wright's colony and been rebuffed. (Rumors were he was broke anyway and was never going to finish another building, so boo to him.) And she was never going to be a Mies van der Rohe. Which was probably a good thing, because Chicago has a surplus of would-be van der Rohes. Like the Three Blind Mies over the way. Not her description. That Wright's a funny, bitter old guy.

She would have liked to do public buildings. A museum or a hospital, but she had to fight for this job like she fought to get a place at MIT. Crake & Mendelson were the only firm who invited her back for a second interview, and she made it count, wearing her tightest pencil skirt, armed with her brassiest humor and a portfolio that showed she was more than that, even if they hired her for those other reasons. You take whatever advantages nature and wile afford you.

This latest stuff is her own fault. Running off her smart mouth about how suburban developments are going to transform the lives of working-class families. She likes that they're building communities around people's workplaces, that blue-collar guys can have white-collar dreams and get to move out of the city where ten families are squashed into an apartment meant for one. She can see now how that might be seen as being pro-worker, pro-union. Pro-commie. She should have just shut up about it.

Anxiety poisons her, like too much coffee. It's the way Stewart keeps darting her little wounded looks. She's made a dreadful mistake, she realizes. He'll be the first to put her up against the wall. Because that's what people do now. Neighbors twitching curtains, teachers ratting out the kids in their class, colleagues making statements on subversives one desk over.

It's because she laughed at him when they all went for drinks in her first week and he got a little tipsy and followed her into the ladies' room. He tried to kiss her with those thin dry lips, pressing her against the sink with its gold-plated faucets and black tiles, trying to hike up her skirt while reaching into his pants. The ornate nouveau mirrors reflected endless iterations of his fumbling. She tried to push him away and when he didn't give, she reached into her purse, propped on the sink because she'd been applying a fresh coat of lipstick when he'd come in, and grabbed her silver-and-black deco cigarette lighter—the present she bought herself on getting into MIT.

Stewart screeched and pulled away, sucking at the blister already rising on the knobbly bone on the back of his wrist. She didn't tell the other guys. She might have a fast mouth, but occasionally she knew when to keep it shut. Someone must have seen him coming out, still burning with humiliation, because word got around. Ever since, he's been dead set against her.

She works through lunch, so she doesn't have to run into him on the way out, even though her stomach is growling like a tiger.

Only when Stewart goes into a meeting with Martin does she grab her bag and head for the door.

"Not lunchtime now?" George says, affably checking his watch.

"I'll be so quick, I'll be back at my desk before you see me leave," she says.

"Like the Flash?" he says. And that's it right there. Good as a confession.

"Just like," she says, even though she's never read the darn comic book. She gives him a heavy, saucy wink and sashays out the door, across the shimmering mosaic tiles that look like fish scales to the elevator with its ornate gold doors.

"You all right, Miss Rose?" the doorman at the front desk says as she steps out, the dome of his bald head as polished and shiny as the fixtures.

"Dandy, Lawrence," she replies. "And you?"

"Got the flu, ma'am. Might have to pop out to the drugstore later. You look pale. Hope you're not coming down with it too. It's a bad 'un."

On the street outside the Fisher Building, she leans against the arch of the doorway, feeling the ornately carved dragon fish pressing against her back. Her heart is thudding like it's trying to bash its way right out her chest.

She wants to go home and curl up in her unmade bed. (The sheets still smell like Sasha's cunt from Wednesday night.) Her cats would be delighted to have her home in the middle of the afternoon. And she still has half a bottle of Merlot in the fridge. But how would that look, taking off in the middle of the day? Especially to *George*.

Act normal, for God's sake, she thinks. Get yourself together. She's already drawing stares and, worse, kindly intentions. She launches herself away from the archway before the interfering old lady with wrinkles cutting down her neck can come over to ask if she's okay. She walks purposefully up the street, heading for a bar several blocks away where she's unlikely to run into any of her colleagues.

It's one of those basement numbers, where all you can see from the window are people's shoes going by. The bartender is surprised to see her. He's still setting up, taking the battered chairs down from equally battered tables. "We're not open—"

"Whiskey sour. Neat."

"I'm sorry, miss—"

She puts a twenty on the bar. He shrugs, turns to the cluster of bottles above the bar and starts mixing her drink, more laboriously than necessary. "You from Chicago?" he says, grudgingly.

She taps the note on the bar counter. "I'm from where there's more of that if you shut the hell up and make me my drink." In the thin slice of mirror behind the bar, she watches reflected legs go by. Black brogues. Tan Mary Janes. A girl in bobbysocks and lace-ups. A man on a crutch shuffling past. It triggers something in her memory, but when she turns to look, he's already gone. And so what? At least her drink is served.

Willie downs it and then another. By the third, she's feeling like she's ready to go back. She slides the twenty across the counter.

"Hey, what about the other one?"

"Nice try, champ," she says, and swims back to the office through a pleasant floatiness. By the time she reaches the door of the building, the light-headedness is turning queasy. It weighs down, like a thunderstorm gathering right on top of her. She can feel the barometric pressure rising with each step, so that it takes every ounce of willpower to turn on a happy face when she opens the door into the office.

God, how could she have been so wrong about who her enemies are? Stewart looks at her with concern, not contempt.

Maybe he knows he was out of hand that night. She realizes he's been nothing but a gentleman since. Martin is irritated that she wasn't here when he was looking for her. And George... George grins and raises his eyebrows. Like, *What took you so long? And also: I'm watching you*.

The plans on the vellum are blurry in front of her. She jabs angrily at the kitchen walls with her blotting powder; they're all wrong and will need to be reconfigured.

"You all right?" George says, putting a hand on her shoulder, overly familiar. "You look a little out of sorts. Maybe you should go home."

"I'm just peachy, thanks." She can't even come up with a witty retort. Dear George. Cuddly, furry, harmless George. She thinks about the night they both stayed late working on the Hart's project and he broke out the bottle of scotch Martin kept in his office, and they sat up talking until two in the morning. What did she say? She scours her brain to remember. She talked about art and growing up in Wisconsin and why she wanted to become an architect, her favorite buildings, the ones she wished she'd built. Adler and Sullivan's soaring towers and sculpted details. Which got her on to Pullman and how the workers who lived in his housing were forced to live by these ridiculously patronizing rules. And he said barely a word, just let her ramble. Let her incriminate herself.

She feels paralyzed. She could wait it out. Stay at her desk until everyone else has gone home for the day and she can try to make sense of this. She could go back to the bar. Or straight home to destroy anything deviant and subversive.

Five o'clock comes and goes and her colleagues start peeling away one by one. Stewart is one of the first to go. George one of the last. He hangs around, as if waiting for her.

"You coming or should I leave you with the keys?" His teeth

are too big for his mouth, she notices for the first time. Great big slabs of white enamel.

"You go ahead. I'm going to crack this bastard if it kills me."

He frowns. "You've been working on that all day."

She can't stand it anymore. "I know it was you."

"Huh?"

"The comics. It's stupid and it's not fair." To her fury, her eyes are welling up. She keeps them wide, refusing to blink.

"Those things? They've been circling the office for days. Why you so wound up about it?"

"Oh," she says. The sheer enormity of how wrong she's been crashes down on her and takes her breath away.

"Guilty conscience?" He squeezes her shoulder and slings his briefcase over his arm. "Don't worry, Willie, I know you're not a Red."

"Thank you, George, I—"

"Pink at most." He's not smiling. He puts the keys down on the desk in front of her. "I don't want anything coming between the firm and this government project. I don't care what you do in your private life, but you clean up after yourself. All right?" He cocks his finger like a gun at her and slides out the door.

Willie sits there, stunned. You can bury your radical magazines and tear up your sexually perverse sketches and burn your sheets. But how do you erase who you are?

She's startled nearly out of her skin by knuckles rapping on the door. She can see a man's profile through the fluted glass hand-lettered with the name of the firm. She's ashamed that her first thought is *FBI!* Which is ridiculous. It has to be one of the guys, probably forgotten something. She glances round the office and sees Abe's jacket hanging on the back of his chair. Just Abe. His wallet is probably in it, with his bus pass. She unhooks it from the chair. She might as well leave at the same time.

She opens the door to find that it's not Abe standing outside, but a horribly thin man leaning on a crutch. He turns the corners of his lips up around the wires between his teeth and screwed into his jaw in something that is supposed to be a smile. She pulls back in revulsion and tries to close the door on him. But he jabs the rubber foot of his crutch in the gap and shoves through. The door slams into her, bouncing off her forehead and cracking the glass. She falls backwards against one of the heavy Knoll desks. The metal edge catches her in the small of her back and she slides down onto the floor. If she can make it to Stewart's desk, she could throw the big lamp at him . . .

But she can't get up. There's something wrong with her legs. She whimpers as he limps in, grimacing around the wires in his mouth, and closes the door softly behind him.

DAN

1 June 1992

Dan and Kirby are taking advantage of journalists' privilege, sitting in the dugout looking out over the field, which is impossibly green against the warm red of the dirt and the crisp white lines cutting through it and the Boston ivy growing up the brickwork. The friendly confines are still empty, although the party has already started on the rooftops around the stadium.

The other reporters are setting up in the press box that floats high above the curves of gray plastic seating lining the stadium. But it's still a good forty minutes before the punters start streaming in. The vendors have rolled up their shutters. The smell of hot dogs is percolating in the air. It's one of Dan's favorite times, when the whole place is full of potential. He'd be happier if he weren't half-annoyed with Kirby.

"I'm not just your access pass to the *Sun-Times* library. You have to do some real work," he snaps. "Especially if you actually want that college credit."

"I was working!" she sparks with indignation. She is wearing some incomprehensible punky vest-top with a high turtleneck that covers her scar, like a priest's cassock with the sleeves cut off. Which is not exactly going to fit in with the button-up-shirt-and-sports-jersey brigade in the press box. He was nervous about bringing her here. And now it seems with good reason. He ignores the distraction of the fine blonde hairs on her bare arms.

"I gave you a list of approved questions. All you had to do was read them and add a question mark. Instead, I got Kevin and the guys telling me that while I'm busting my ass trying to get a useful soundbite out of Lefebvre, you're in the Padres locker room playing cards and flirting."

"I *did* ask all your questions. And *then* I sat down to play poker. It's called laying the groundwork. Solid journalistic principle, my lecturers tell me. It wasn't even my idea. Sandberg dealt me in. I won twenty bucks."

"You reckon you can get away with playing the cute naïve girl? That act's going to let you get away with stuff your whole life?"

"I think I can get away with being interested and interesting. I think curiosity trumps ignorance. I think comparing scars helps."

Dan smirks, just a little. "I heard about that. Sammy Sosa really showed you his butt?"

"Wow. Talk about sensationalizing the news. Who told you that? It was his lower back, just above his hip. Besides, it's not like they don't get naked in the showers right in front of you. He had this huge bruise from walking into one of those big metal trash cans. He didn't see it, he was saying goodbye to a friend and half-turned around and wham! He said he's clumsy sometimes."

"Huh. If he drops the ball, that quote is so going in."

"I even wrote it down for you. And I got something else that was interesting. We were chatting about travelling, being away all the time. I told them that funny story about how I was crashing on the couch of a girl I met in a video store in LA and she tried to get me into a threesome with her boyfriend and I ended up on the street at four a.m., walking around until the sun came up. It was really beautiful, watching the whole city come alive."

"I haven't heard that story."

"That was it. *Anyway.* I said it was good to come back to Chicago, and I asked Greg Maddux how he felt living here, and he got a bit weird."

"Weird how?"

Kirby checks her notebook. "I wrote it down when I got outside. He said: 'Why would I want to go anywhere else? The people are so friendly. Not just the fans, but the cabbies, hotel porters, folks on the street. In other cities people act like they are doing you a favor.' And then he winked and started telling me about his favorite swear words."

"You didn't follow up?"

"He railroaded me. I wanted to. I thought it would make a good piece, ballplayer's Chitown. Top five recommendations, restaurants, parks, clubs, hang-outs, whatever. And then Lefebvre came back in and I got chucked out so they could get ready for the game, and I started thinking it was a peculiar thing to say out of nowhere."

"I'll give you that."

"You think he's planning a move?"

"Or considering it. Mad Dog's a control freak. He likes to push things as far as he can. He was definitely playing you. Which means we should keep an eye on it."

"Little rough on the Cubs if he's planning to bail."

"No, I get it. You gotta go where your best chances are to play ball like you mean it. He's hot stuff right now."

"Oh really? You go that way?"

"You know what I mean, obstreperous girl."

"Yeah." She shoulders him, affectionately. Her skin is so warm from the sunshine that he can feel it right through his shirt, like she's burned him.

"Anything else up your sleeve?" he says, moving away, trying to be casual about it. Thinking, *You're being ridiculous, Velasquez. What are you, fifteen?*

"Give me a chance," she says. "There'll be more poker games."

"Sooner you than me. I'm a terrible bluffer." Really terrible. "Come on, we should be heading up."

"Can't we watch from there?" Kirby points out the green scoreboard that looms over the centerfield bleachers. He's thought the same thing. It's beautiful. Real Americana, with its clean white font and windows that open between the slats where the numbers go.

"You and every other punter. It's not going to happen. That's one of the last hand-turned score-boards in the country. They're very protective. No one gets in."

"But you have."

"I earned the right."

"Bullshit. How did you do it?"

"I did a profile on the guy who turns the score. He's been doing it for decades. He's a legend."

"Do you think he'd let me flip one?"

"I think your chances are minimal. Besides, I know how your mind works by now. You only want to go because no one else is allowed to."

"I think it's really a secret gentleman's club where the most powerful men in America plan the future of the country, with cocktails and strippers, while an innocent baseball game plays out below."

"It's a bare room with a battered floor, and it gets as hot as hell."

"Sure. That's exactly what someone who was trying to protect the secrets of the club would say."

144 • Lauren Beukes

"All right, I'll try to get you up there sometime. But only after you've gone through initiation and mastered the secret handshake."

"Promise?"

"Swear to the man upstairs. But only on condition that when we get up to the press box in front of my colleagues, you pretend that I chewed you out for being unprofessional, and you feel real remorse."

"So much remorse." She grins. "But I'm holding you to that, Dan Velasquez."

"Believe me, I know."

His anxiety about her not fitting in turns out to be pointless. She doesn't and is all the more charming for it.

"It's like the United Nations in here. With a better view," Kirby cracks, looking around at the rows of phones and men, mostly, sitting behind the nametags of whichever media outlet they're representing, already taking notes or jabbering pre-game blather into the handsets.

"Yeah, but this is *much* more serious," Dan says. She laughs, and that's really all he wants.

"Sure, what's world peace compared to baseball?"

"This your intern?" Kevin says. "I should get me one. Does she do laundry?"

"Oh, I wouldn't trust her with that," Dan shoots back. "But she gets good quotes."

"Can I borrow her?"

Dan is about to bristle on Kirby's behalf, but she has a comeback already lined up. "Sure, but I'll need a raise. What's double of free?"

That draws a laugh from half the room, and why shouldn't it? The game is underway. The Cubs' bats are starting to make some noise. The tension in the press box ramps up, everyone suddenly very focused on the action playing out on the diamond below. They might actually win this. And he's happy to see her getting caught up in it too. The magic.

Afterwards, Dan phones it in among the hubbub of other reporters doing the same, reading from his notebook and his scrawled handwriting that is so illegible, Kirby says, that he might as well be writing prescriptions. The Cubs took it in the seventh inning after the game slowed into a vicious pitchers' duel, largely thanks to brand-new golden boy Mad Dog Maddux.

He claps Kirby across her shoulders. "Nice work, kiddo. You might even be cut out for this."

HARPER

26 February 1932

━━━━━

Harper buys a new suit to fit at the Baer Brothers and Prodie Store (where they treated him like shit until they saw the color of his money) and takes Nurse Etta and her roommate from the woman's boarding house out to dinner. The other girl, Molly, is a teacher from Bridgeport, a bit rough and tumble compared to her tight-wound friend. She's going to chaperone, she says, with a wicked smile, as if he doesn't know she is only along for the free food. Her shoes are worn and the dark wool on her coat is forming little balls, like a sheep. The piggy and the lamb. Maybe he'll have chops for dinner.

Mostly he's happy to be eating real food again instead of white bread soaked in milk and mashed potatoes. He's lost a lot of weight waiting for his jaw to heal. The wire came off after three weeks, but he's been unable to chew until recently. His shirts hang baggy, and he can count his ribs like he hasn't been able to since he was a boy and the bruises from his father's belt made the calculations easier.

He collects the girls from the station and they walk up La Salle in the snow, past the new soup kitchen where the line extends halfway down the block. The men are so deep in their shame they can't raise their eyes above their shoes, stamping their feet against the cold and shuffling forward. A pity, Harper thinks. He's hoping that miserable wretch Klayton will look up and see him, a girl on each arm, a new suit, with a roll of money in his pocket, along with his knife. But Klayton keeps his gaze on the ground, as they walk right past him, gray and shriveled up into himself like a cock with the drip.

Harper could come back and kill him. Find him sleeping rough in a doorway. Invite him back to the house to get warm. No hard feelings. Put a glass of whiskey in his hand in front of the fire, and then beat him to death with the claw end of a hammer, like Klayton wanted to do to Harper. Start by knocking out his teeth.

"Tsk," Etta clucks. "It's just getting worse."

"You think they got it bad?" her friend says. "The school board is talking about putting us all on scrips. We gotta get paid in vouchers now instead of real money?"

"Rather be paid in booze. All that stuff they're confiscating. No use to anyone. That would keep you warm and toasty." Etta squeezes Harper's arm, distracting him from the fantasy he's wrapped himself up in. He glances back to see Klayton staring after him, hat in his hands, mouth hanging open to catch flies.

Harper spins the girls around. "Give my friend a hello," he says. Molly complies with a flirtatious wriggle of her fingers, but Etta frowns. "Who is he?"

"Someone who tried to undo me. He's getting a taste of that remedy now."

"Speaking of remedies..." Molly prods Etta, and she fumbles in her purse and pulls out a small glass bottle with a label that reads "rubbing alcohol."

"Yes, yes, I got us a nip." She takes a swig and hands it to Harper first, who wipes the rim on his coat before letting it touch his lips.

"Don't worry, it's not actual rubbing alcohol. The factory that supplies the hospital has a side-trade."

The booze is potent and Molly is greedy with it, so that by the time they get to Mme Galli's on East Illinois, the lambkin is well on her way to being shit-faced.

Inside the restaurant, there is a large caricature of an Italian opera singer and photographs of various theater people from downtown hung on the walls, their signatures scrawled across beaming faces. This doesn't mean anything to Harper, but the girls coo appreciatively and, for his part, the waiter does not comment on the shabbiness of the coats that he takes to be hung up on the hooks beside the door.

The establishment is half-full already, lawyers and bohemians and actor types. The converted double parlor is warm from the fireplaces on either side, and the hubbub of people as it starts to fill up.

The waiter shows them to a table near the window, Harper on one side and the girls roosted next to each other opposite, looking over the cheery fruit bowl that forms the centerpiece. Evidently, Mme Galli has the law in her pocket because the waiter brings them a bottle of Chianti from a bookcase especially converted into a liquor cabinet without any special fussing.

Harper orders lamb chops for the entrée and Etta follows suit, but Molly orders the filet with a defiant sparkle in her eye. Harper doesn't care. It's all the same to him, $1.50 per mouth for five courses, so the conniving wench can have whatever she wants.

The girls eat the spaghetti with gusto, twirling their forks like they were born to it. But Harper finds the pasta slippery to handle, and the taste of garlic is overwhelming. The curtains are grubby from smoke. At the next table, the young woman who smokes cigarettes between every course, aiming for cosmopolitan, is as vacuous as her companions, who talk too loudly. Every cocksucker in here, all putting on a show, dressed up in their clothes and manners.

It's been too long, he realizes. He hasn't killed anyone in almost a month. Not since Willie. The world becomes washed out in the gaps. He can feel the tug of the House like string tied between each vertebrae. He's been trying to avoid the Room, sleeping downstairs on the couch, but lately he's found himself going up the stairs as if dreaming, to stand in the doorway and watch the objects. He will need to go again soon.

And in the meantime the livestock across the table from him are batting their eyelashes and trying to out-simper each other.

Etta excuses herself to "touch up her lipstick," and the Irish girl slides round the table to sit beside him. She presses her knee against his.

"You're quite a find, Mr. Curtis. I want to hear all about you."

"What do you want to know?"

"Where you grew up. Your family. Were you ever married or engaged? How you made your money. The usual."

He can't deny that he's intrigued by how bald her enquiry is. "I have a House." He's feeling reckless, and she is so deep in her cups, she'll be lucky if she can remember her own name tomorrow, never mind his strange declarations.

"A property owner," she trills.

"It opens on to other times."

She looks confused. "What does?"

"The House, sweetheart. It means I know the future."

"Fascinating," she purrs, not believing him in the slightest, but letting him know she's willing to play along. With much more than a story, if he's inclined. "So, tell me something amazing."

"There's another big war coming."

"Oh really? Should I be worried? Can you tell *my* future?"

"Only if I open you up."

She takes it the wrong way, as he knew she would, slightly flustered, but excited too. It is so predictable. She brushes her finger back and forth over her lower lip and the half-smile dwelling there. "Well, Mr. Curtis, I might be amenable to that. Or can I call you Harper?"

"What are you doing?" Etta interrupts, blotchy with anger.

"We're just talking, sweetie," Molly smirks. "About the war."

"You hussy," Etta says, and dumps her bowl of spaghetti over the lady teacher's head. It glops down into her eyes, chunks of tomato and ground beef congealed in her hair with damp strands of spaghetti. Harper laughs in surprise, at the slapstick violence.

The waiter rushes over with napkins and helps wipe Molly off. "*Caspita!* Is everything all right?"

The girl is shaking in rage and humiliation. "Are you going to let her do that?"

"Looks to me like it's already done," Harper says. He tosses the linen napkin at her. "Go clean yourself up. You're a joke." He presses a five-dollar bill into the waiter's hand before he can ask them to leave, tipping because his mood has brightened. He holds out his arm for Etta to take. She smiles with smug triumph, and Molly bursts into tears, as Harper and Etta breeze out of the restaurant into the night.

The streetlamps form greasy spotlights along the street, and it seems natural to walk down to the lake, despite the cold. The pavements are thick with snow, the bare branches of the trees like lace against the sky. The low buildings shoulder together along the shore in a brace against the water. The tiers of Buckingham Fountain are white-crusted, the huge bronze seahorses striving against the ice, going nowhere.

"It's like icing," Etta says. "Looks like a wedding cake."

"You're just sour that we skipped out before dessert," Harper replies, trying for banter.

Her face darkens at the reminder of Molly. "She had it coming."

"Of course she did. I could kill her for you." He is testing her.

"I'd like to kill her myself. Hussy." She rubs her bare hands together and blows on her chapped fingers. Then she reaches out to take his hand. Harper startles, but she's only using him for leverage to climb onto the fountain.

"Come with me," she says. And after a moment's hesitation, he clambers up after her. She picks her way across the snow, skidding on the ice, to one of the verdigris seahorses and leans against it, posing. "Want a ride?" she says, girlishly, and he sees that she is even more devious than her friend. But she intrigues him. There's something marvelous about her greed. A woman of selfish appetites who sets herself above the rest of miserable humanity, deservedly or not.

He kisses her then, surprising himself. Her tongue is quick and slippery in his mouth, a warm little amphibian. He pushes her back against the horse, one hand groping up under her skirt.

"We can't go back to my apartment," she pulls back. "There are rules. And Molly."

"Here?" he says, trying to turn her round, fumbling with his flies.

"No! It's freezing. Take me home with you."

His erection caves in and he lets her go abruptly.

"Impossible."

"What is it?" she calls after him, hurt, as he jumps down off the fountain, hobbling back towards Michigan Avenue. "What did I do? Hey! Don't you walk away! I'm not some whore, you know! Screw you, buddy!"

He doesn't respond, not even when she takes off her shoe and throws it at his back. It falls woefully short. She will have to go hopping across the snow to retrieve it. The idea of her humiliation pleases him.

"Screw you!" she screams again.

KIRBY
23 March 1989

There are clouds scudding low over the lake like puffy boats in the gray light of morning. Barely 7 a.m. There's no way Kirby would be up at this time normally, if not for the Damn Dog.

Before she's even managed to turn off the car, Tokyo is climbing over from the back seat of her fourth-hand Datsun, crushing her arm with his big galumphing paws as she reaches to pull up the handbrake.

"Ooof, you galoot," Kirby says, shoving him off her and onto the seat, a service he rewards by farting in her face. He has the decency to look guilty for all of one second before he starts pawing at the door and whining to be let out, his tail thumping against the sheepskin cover that hides how badly cracked the seat is.

Kirby reaches past him and manages to flick the catch. Tokyo barges the door open with his head and slips through the gap into the parking lot. He bounds round to her side of the car and jumps up with both paws against the window, tongue-lolling, his breath fogging up the window, as she's trying to get out.

"Hopeless, you know that?" Kirby grunts, shoving the door

open against his weight. He gives a bark of delight and runs to the grassy verge and back again, urging her to hurry up, in case the beach ups and leaves. The way she's about to bail on him.

She's feeling pretty cut up about it. But she's been saving so she can move out of Rachel's house, and the junior dorms are gestapo-strict on the no furry roommates clause. She tells herself that she'll be only a few hops away on the El. She'll be able to take him for walks on the weekends and she's persuaded the kid across the road to take him round the block once a day for a dollar. Still, that's five bucks a week, twenty a month. That's a lot of Ramen.

Kirby follows Tokyo down the path to the beach through the rustling corridor of overgrown grass. She should have parked closer to the actual beach, but she's used to coming here at weekend lunchtimes, when you can't find an empty bay for money or love. It's a totally different place without the crowds. Ominous even, with mist and a cold wind off the lake scything through the grass. The chill will have put off all but the most dedicated joggers.

She takes the grimy tennis ball out of her pocket. It's cracked and balding and squidgy from being chewed on. She sends it arcing in a high parabola over the skyline across the lake, aiming for the Sears Tower, as if she could knock it over.

Tokyo has been waiting for this, ears pricked, mouth snapped shut in concentration. He turns and pelts after the ball, anticipating its trajectory with mathematical precision and snatching it out of the air on its way down.

And this is the thing that drives her nuts, when he gets all coy with the ball. Skipping forward like he's going to drop it into her hand and then ducking to one side as she reaches for it, with a delighted rumble in the back of his throat.

"Dog! I'm warning you."

Tokyo hunches down, butt in the air, tail thwacking from side to side. "Owwwwwrrrr," he says.

"Give me that ball or I'll...have you turned into a rug." She feints at him and he bounds away two steps, just out of range, and assumes the position again. His tail is helicoptering wildly.

"It's all the rage, you know," she says, ambling down the beach, thumbs in the pockets of her jeans, playing it cool, definitely not aiming for him. "Polar bears and tigers are so passé. But a dog-skin rug—especially a troublesome dog? That's class, baby."

She lunges for him, but he's been wise to her all along. He yips in excitement, the sounds muffled by the ball clamped between his teeth, and bolts down the beach. Kirby lands on one knee on the damp sand as he bounds into the freezing surf, with a doggy grin so big she can see it from here.

"No! Bad dog! Tokyo Speedracer Mazrachi! You get back here, now!" He doesn't listen. He never does. Wet dog in the car. One of her favorite things.

"Come on, boy." She whistles for him, five sharp notes. He obeys, sort-of. He wades out of the water at least and drops the ball onto the bleached sand, shaking himself out like a doggy sprinkler. He barks once, happily, still playing.

"Oh for God's sake," Kirby says, her purple sneakers sinking into the mud. "When I catch you—"

Tokyo suddenly whips his head in the other direction, barks once and races across the grass near the pier.

A man in a yellow fisherman's weatherproof is standing at the water's edge, beside a cart contraption with a bucket and a fire extinguisher. Some kind of weird fishing technique, she realizes, as he pops his sinker into a metal pipe and then uses the pressure of the extinguisher to send it flying out into the lake further than he could have ever cast it.

"Hey! No dogs!" he shouts agreeably, pointing at the faded sign in the overgrown grass. As if whatever he's doing with that fire extinguisher is legal.

"No! Really? Well, you'll be glad to know it's not a dog anyway, it's a rug-in-waiting!" Her mother calls it her sarcasm force field, keeping boys at bay since 1984—if only she knew. Kirby scoops up the scuffed tennis ball and shoves it in her pocket. Infernal animal.

She will be glad to move into the dorms, she thinks, fiercely. The neighbor is welcome to the dog. She'll do weekends if she has time: inclination. But who knows? She might be stuck in the library. She might be hungover. Or have a hot boy to entertain to sweet/awkward morning-after breakfast now that Fred has gone off to NYU and film school, as if that wasn't her dream that he kind of acquired and ran with, and worst of all, was able to pay for. Even if she'd been accepted (and she should have been, dammit—she has more talent in her left earlobe than he has in his whole central nervous system), there's no way she could have paid for it. So she's doing English and history at DePaul, two years and a lifetime of debt to go, assuming she can get a job after graduating. Of course, Rachel has been nothing but encouraging. Kirby almost considered doing accounting or business sciences to spite her.

"Tokyooooooo!" Kirby yells into the brush. She whistles again. "Stop messing around." The wind nips through her clothes, bringing goosebumps up on her arms all the way to the back of her neck—she should have worn a proper jacket. Of course he's gone into the bird sanctuary, where he can snag her a really stiff fine for letting him off the leash. Fifty dollars or two weeks' worth of walking fees. Twenty-five packets of Ramen. "Decor, dog!" Kirby yells down the empty beach. "That's what you're gonna be when I'm done with you."

She sits on a bench carved with names—"Jenna + Christo

4eva"—by the entrance to the sanctuary and pulls her shoes back on. The sand chafes in her socks, wedged between her toes. There is a Peewee calling in the bushes somewhere. Rachel was always into birds. She knew all their names. It took Kirby years to figure out that she was making them up, that there was no such thing as a Riding Hood Woodpecker or a Crystal Rainbow Malachite. They were just words Rachel liked to put together.

She stomps into the sanctuary. The birds have stopped singing. Silenced, no doubt, by the presence of a wet and troublesome dog blundering around here somewhere. Even the wind has died, and the waves are a dull shushing in the background, like traffic. "Come on, damn dog." She whistles again, five notes, ascending.

Someone whistles back, exactly the same.

"Oh, that's really cute," Kirby says.

The whistle comes again, mocking.

"Hello? Jerkwad?" She ups the sarcasm in proportion to how badly unnerved she is. "Have you seen a dog?" She hesitates for a second before she steps off the path, pushing through the dense underbrush towards the general vicinity of the whistler. "You know, furry animal, teeth to rip your throat out?"

There's no reply, save for a rasping, hacking noise. A cat with a hairball.

She has time to yelp in surprise as a man steps out from the shrubs, grabs her arm and swings her to the ground with quick and incontestable force. She wrenches her wrist as she automatically sticks it out to catch herself. Her knee hammers into a rock so hard that her vision goes briefly white. When it clears, it's to see Tokyo lying heaving on his side in the bushes.

Someone has wrapped a wire coathanger round his neck so that it cuts into his throat, leaving the fur around it soaked with blood. He's twisting his head, squirming his shoulders, trying to get away, because the wire is looped to a branch sticking out of a fallen tree. Every time he moves, it cuts in deeper. The hacking sound is him trying to bark with his vocal cords severed. At something behind her.

She forces herself up on to her elbows, in time for the man to swing the crutch into her face. The impact shatters her cheekbone in an explosion of pain that arcs through her skull. She crumples onto the damp earth. And then he's on top of her, his knee in her back. She writhes and kicks under him, as he wrests her arms behind her, grunting while he wires her wrists together. "Fuckyougetoffme" she spits into the mulch of dirt and leaves. It tastes of damply rotting things, soft and gritty between her teeth.

He rolls her over roughly, panting through his teeth and rams the tennis ball into her mouth before she can scream, splitting her lip and chipping a tooth. It compresses as it goes in, expands to force her jaw open. She chokes on the taste of rubber and dog spit and blood. She tries to push it out with her tongue only to encounter a shard of enamel from a broken tooth. She gags at this piece of *her skull* in her mouth. The vision in her left eye has gone hazy and purple. Her cheek bone, pushing up against the socket. But everything is contracting anyway.

It's hard to breathe around the ball. He's wound the wire so tight around her hands, pinned beneath her, that they've gone numb. The edges are digging into her spine. She churns her shoulders, trying to get traction to wriggle away from him, sobbing. No destination in mind. Away, please God, just away. But he's sitting on her thighs, clamping her down with his weight.

"I've got a present for you. Two," he says. The tip of his tongue is sticking out from between his teeth. He's making a high-pitched wheezing sound as he reaches into his coat.

"Which would you like first?" He holds out his hands to show her. A small shiny silver-and-black case. Or a folding knife with a wooden handle.

"Can't decide?" He flicks the catch on the lighter, the flame springing up like a jack-in-the-box, and snaps it off again. "This: to remember me." Then he unhasps the blade of the folding knife. "This is just what needs to be done."

She tries to kick out, to dislodge him, screaming in fury against the ball. He lets her, watching her. Amused. Then he sets the lighter against her eye socket and digs the hard edge in against her broken cheekbone. Black spots bloom in her head, pain arcing through her jaw, down her spine.

He pulls up her T-shirt, exposing her skin, winter-pale. He drags his hand across her stomach, his fingertips digging into her skin, clutching, greedy, leaving bruises. Then he punches the knife into her abdominal wall and twists and pulls it across in a jagged cut, following the trajectory of his hand. She bucks up against him, screaming into the ball.

He laughs. "Easy there."

She is sobbing something incoherent. The words don't make sense in her head, let alone in her mouth. Don't-please-don't-don't-you-fucking-dare-don't-don't-please-don't.

Their breathing is evenly matched, his excited wheezes, her rabbit inhalations. The blood is hotter than she would have ever imagined, like pissing yourself. Thicker. Maybe he is done. Maybe it's over. He only wanted to hurt her a little. Show her who's boss before—her mind blanks at the possibilities. She can't bring herself to look at him. She's too afraid of seeing his intention in his face. So she lies there, looking up at the pallid morning sun glancing through the leaves, listening to their breathing, hard and fast.

But he's not done yet. She groans and tries to twist away before the tip of the blade even touches her skin. He pats her shoulder, grinning savagely, his hair plastered down and sweaty from the exertion. "Scream louder, sweetheart," he says hoarsely. His breath smells like caramel. "Maybe someone will hear you."

He slides the knife home and twists it across. She screams as loudly as she can, the sound muffled by the ball, and instantly despises herself for obeying him. And then grateful that he let her. Which makes the shame worse. She can't help it. Her body is a separate animal to her mind, which is a shameful, bargaining thing, willing to do anything to make it stop. Anything to live. Please, God. She closes her eyes, so she doesn't have to see his look of concentration or the way he tugs at his pants.

He yanks the knife down and then up in a pattern that seems predetermined. Like being here is, surely, trapped beneath him. Like this is the only place she has ever been. Under the sharp sear of the wounds, she can feel the blade catching on the fatty tissue. Like carving fucking sirloin. An abattoir smell of blood and shit. Please-please-please.

There is a terrible noise, worse even than his breathing or the meaty tearing sound of the knife. She opens her eyes and turns her head to see Tokyo, shaking and twisting his head, like he's having a fit. He's snarling and growling through the wreck of his throat. His lips pulled back to reveal the red foam on his teeth. The whole log shakes with the movement. The wire saws into the branch it's been looped around, bits of bark and lichen flaking away. Bright bubbles of blood bead his fur like an obscene necklace.

"Don't," she manages. It comes out "Ownt."

He thinks she's talking to him. "It's not my fault, sweetheart," he says. "It's yours. You shouldn't shine. You shouldn't make me do this." He moves the knife to her neck. He doesn't see Tokyo yank himself free until the dog is right on top of him. The dog launches itself at him, clamping his teeth into his arm through the coat. The blade jerks across her throat, too shallow, only nicking the carotid, before he drops it.

The man howls in fury and tries to shake the animal off, but Tokyo's jaws are locked tight. The weight drags him down. He feels around for the knife with his other hand. Kirby tries to roll over it. She's too slow and uncoordinated. He grabs it out from under her and then Tokyo gives a long rasping sigh and he's prying her dog away from his arm, yanking at the knife stuck in his neck.

Any fight she had left goes out of her. She closes her eyes and tries to play dead, the act belied by the tears running down her cheeks.

He crawls over to her, cradling his arm. "You're not fooling me," he says. He pokes his finger diagnostically into the wound in her throat and she screams again, blood pulsing out.

"You'll bleed out quick enough."

He reaches into her mouth and yanks the tennis ball out, squashing it between his fingers. She bites him as hard as she can, grinding her teeth into his thumb. More blood in her mouth, but it's his this time. He punches her in the face and she blacks out for a moment.

It's a shock coming back. The pain slams down as soon as she opens her eyes, like Wile E. Coyote's anvil on her head. She starts weeping. The fucker is limping away, holding his crutch loosely in one hand. He stops, his back to her, digging in his pocket. "Almost forgot," he says. He tosses the lighter at her. It lands in the grass near her head.

Kirby lies there, waiting to die. For the pain to stop. But she doesn't and it doesn't, and then she hears Tokyo give a little grunt, like he's not dead either, and she starts getting seriously pissed off. *Fuck* him.

She shifts her weight onto her hip and swivels her wrists experimentally, reawakening the nerves that blast her brain with a shrieking Morse code. He's been sloppy. It's a short-term measure, to hold her, not keep her, especially with her weight off.

Her fingers are too numb to work properly, but the blood makes it easier. WD40 for bondage, she thinks and laughs, bitterly, surprising herself.

Fuck *this*.

She painstakingly works one hand free and then passes out when she tries to sit up. It takes her four minutes to get up onto her knees. She knows because she counts the seconds. It's the only way she can force herself to stay conscious. She wraps her jacket round her waist to try to staunch the blood. She can't tie it. Her hands are shaking too much, her fine motor skills shot. So she tucks it into the back of her jeans as best she can.

She kneels next to Tokyo, who rolls his eyes at her and tries to wag his tail. She lifts him up, levering him onto her forearms and then hefting him up to her chest. And almost drops him.

She staggers towards the path and the sound of the waves, her dog in her arms. His tail thuds weakly against her thigh. "It's okay, boy, we're nearly there," she says. Her throat makes a horrible gargling sound when she speaks. Blood pulses down her neck, soaking into her T-shirt. Gravity feels terrible. Increased a millionfold. Not the weight of her dog, his fur matted with blood. The weight of the world. She feels something come loose from her middle, hot and slippery. She can't think about it.

"Nearly there. Nearly there."

The trees open out onto a cement path that leads to the pier. The fisherman is still there. "Help," she rasps, but too soft for him to hear.

"HELP ME," she screams and the fisherman turns and gapes, misfiring the sinker from the pipe so that the red ball bounces off the cement between the husks of discarded shad. "What in hell?" He drops his rod and yanks a wooden baton from the cart. He runs towards her, brandishing it above his head. "Who did this to you? Where is he? Help! Somebody! Ambulance! Police!"

She buries her face in Tokyo's fur. She realizes he's not wagging his tail. Hasn't been this whole time.

It was physics. The jolt of every step. Equal and opposite reaction.

The knife is still sticking out the side of his neck. It's so deeply wedged in his vertebrae, the vet will have to remove it surgically, rendering it almost unusable for forensics. It's what saved her from the man pulling it out and finishing the job.

No please, but she's crying too hard to say it.

DAN

24 July 1992

———

It's absurdly hot inside Dreamerz. And loud. Dan hates the music before the band has even started. What kind of a name is Naked Raygun? And when did looking dirty on purpose become a thing? Scruffy guys with weird facial hair and black T-shirts mill around the stage endlessly before the actual band comes on, ironically more neatly dressed, fiddling with guitars and plugs and pedals. Also endlessly.

His shoes keep sticking. It's a spilled-drink-cigarette-stump type of floor. Better than the upstairs balcony, which is paved with actual headstones like the bathroom is wallpapered with photocopied flyers. The weirdest one is for a play featuring a woman in a gas mask and heels. The boys on the stage look positively mainstream in comparison.

He has no idea what he's doing here. He only came because Kirby asked him, because she thought it might be awkward seeing Fred. And, boy, is it ever. First love, she told him. Which made him sound even *less* like someone Dan would want to meet.

Fred is so very, very young. And stupid. Childhood sweethearts should not come back, especially from film school. Especially if that's all they're going to talk about. Movies he's never heard of. He's not an uncultured lunk, whatever his ex-wife might think. But the kids have moved on from talking art-house to totally obscure experimental shit. It's worse because Fred keeps trying to involve him in the conversation, like the good guy he is, which still, please note, does not make him worthy of her.

"Do you know Rémy Belvaux's work, Dan?" Fred says. His hair is shaved so short it's not much more than dark fuzz over his skull. The look is finished with a goatee and one of those annoying piercings under his lip that looks like a giant metal zit. Dan has to restrain himself from leaning forward to try and pop it. "No budget, he's stuck in Belgium. But his work is so self-aware. It's so real. He really lives it."

Dan thinks about living *his* work by applying a baseball bat to someone's face, just for example.

It's a blessing when the band starts up, rendering conversation, and the momentum towards him murdering Fred, impossible. Mr. First Love whoops in demented enthusiasm and hands off his beer to Dan, shoving through the crowd towards the front of the stage.

Kirby leans in and shouts in his ear. Something-something-venge, he hears.

"WHAT?" he yells back. He's holding his lemonade like a crucifix. (Of course, the bar doesn't sell low-alcohol.)

Kirby presses her thumb down over the little knob of cartilage above Dan's ear canal and shouts again: "Think of it as revenge for all the games you've dragged me to."

"THAT'S WORK!"

"So's this." Kirby grins happily, because somehow she has managed to convince Jim in the lifestyle section of the *Sun-Times* to try her out on a gig review. Dan glowers. He should be happy for her that she's getting to write about something she's actually interested in. The reality is that he's jealous. Not *that* way, that would be ridiculous. But he's got used to having her around. If she starts writing for lifestyle, she won't be on the other end of the phone line when he's halfway across the country at an away game, giving him the scoop on a rumored injury or a batting record, never mind sitting on his couch with her feet curled under her, watching old videotapes of classic games and throwing in basketball or ice hockey terms just to annoy him.

His buddy Kevin was teasing him about her the other day. "You gotta thing for this girl?"

"Nah," he said. "I feel sorry for her. It's more protective, you know. Paternal."

"Ah. You want to rescue her."

Dan snorted into his drink. "You wouldn't say that if you met her."

But that doesn't explain why her face flashes through his head when he is taking out his frustrations in his lonely double bed, imagining a consortium of naked women, which makes him feel so guilty and confused that he has to stop. And then resume, feeling shifty and awful, but thinking about what it would be like to kiss her and hold her tucked against his chest with his arm around her and her breasts against him and stick his tongue . . . Jesus.

"You should probably just fuck her and get it out of your system," Kevin said, philosophically.

"It's not like that," Dan replied.

But this *is* work. She's on assignment, which means it's *not* a date with Fred. It just so happens that the smug little prick is in town, and this is the most convenient night for her to see him. And he can take comfort in that. Assuming he survives the aural assault of the band.

Dan eyes a plate of nachos being carried over to a table by an adorable red-headed waitress with tattoos up both arms and a lot of piercings.

"I wouldn't," Kirby says, doing the ear trick again. Tragus, it suddenly comes to him, like a crossword clue, that's what that little bit of cartilage is called. "They're not known for their food."

"How do you know I wasn't checking out the waitress?" Dan shouts back.

"I know. She has more piercings than a stapler convention."

"You're right, that doesn't do it for me!" He realizes he hasn't had sex in—he does the arithmetic—fourteen months. A blind date with a restaurant manager called Abby that went well. At least, he thought so, but she didn't return his calls afterwards. He's done a post-mortem on the experience a thousand times, trying to figure out what he did wrong. Analyzing every word because the sex *was* good. He may have talked too much about Beatriz. Maybe it was too soon after his divorce. Wishful thinking to put himself out there. You'd think all the traveling would give him plenty of opportunity, but it turns out women like to be wooed, and being single is harder than he remembers.

He still drives past Bea's house sometimes. She's in the phonebook, it's not exactly a crime to have looked her up, even if he can't bring himself to press dial after tapping the numbers into his cordless phone he can't even count how many times.

He's been trying, he really has. And maybe she'd be proud of him, out, at a club, listening to a band, drinking lemonade with a twenty-three-year-old attempted murder victim and her childhood sweetheart.

It would be something they could talk about. God knows they ran out of things to talk about. His fault, he knows. It was an exorcism for him, compulsively sharing the stuff that Harrison wouldn't let him print. The grisliest details—and worse, the saddest. The lost causes, the cases that never got solved or went nowhere, the kids with drug-addict single moms who tried to stay in school but ended up on the corners, because honestly, where else were they supposed to go? But how many horrible crimes can any one person stand to hear about? It was a mistake, he realizes now. All a terrible cliché. You don't share that shit. Let alone drag your loved ones into it. He should never have told her that some of the threats were aimed at her. He shouldn't have told her he'd bought a gun, just in case. That's what really freaked her out.

He should have gone for proper therapy (yeah, right). He should have tried listening for once. Maybe he would have really heard her about Roger, the carpenter, who was making them a new TV cabinet. "You'd think he was Jesus, the way you go on about him," he'd said at the time. Well, he worked miracles all right. Made her disappear right out of Dan's life. Got her pregnant at forty-six. Which means it was Dan's problem all along. His swimmers didn't have the mettle. But he thought she'd given up on the idea years ago.

Maybe it would have been different if they'd gone out more. He could have brought her here to Club Dreamerz. (God, that "z" drives him crazy.) Or maybe not here, exactly, but somewhere nice. Blues at the Green Mill. Or walks along the lakefront, picnics in the park, hell, they should have taken the Orient Express across Russia. Something romantic and adventurous instead of getting stuck in the everyday.

"What do you think?" Kirby yells into his ear. She's bouncing on the spot, like a demented bunny on a pogo stick, in time to the beat, if the noise emanating from the stage could be said to have a beat.

"Yeah!" he shouts back. In front of them, a group of people are literally pinballing off each other.

"Is that a good yeah or a bad yeah?"

"I'll let you know when I can make out the lyrics!" Which is not likely to be anytime soon.

She gives him a thumbs-up and throws herself into the mosh. Occasionally her crazy hair or Fred's zero buzzcut surfaces above the crowd.

He watches, sipping his lemonade, which had too much ice in it to start with, and is now a diluted, flat and only vaguely lemony water.

After the band has played forty-five minutes and an encore, the two emerge, sweaty and grinning and—Dan's heart sinks— holding hands.

"Still want to eat?" Kirby says, helping herself to what's left in his glass, mostly melted ice.

They end up at El Taco Chino along with the last dregs from other clubs and bars, eating some of the best Mexican food he's ever had.

"Hey, you know what, Kirbs," Fred says, as if the thought just popped into his head. "You should make a documentary. About what happened to you. And you and your mom. I could help you with it. Borrow some of NYU's equipment, maybe move back here for a couple of months. It'd be fun."

"Oof," Kirby says. "I don't know—"

"That's a terrible fucking idea," Dan jumps in.

"Sorry—remind me what your qualifications on filmmaking were again?" Fred says.

"I know criminal justice. Kirby's case is still open. If they ever catch the guy, the film could be prejudicial in court."

"Right, maybe I should do a film about baseball instead. Why it's such a big deal. Maybe you can tell me, Dan?"

And because he's tired and irritated and not interested in

playing alpha male, Dan rolls out the glib answers. "Apple pie. Fireworks on the Fourth of July. Playing catch with your old man. It's part of what makes this country."

"Nostalgia. The great American pastime," Fred sneers. "What about capitalism, greed and CIA assassination hit squads?"

"That's the other part," Dan agrees, refusing to let this boy with the dumb facial hair rile him. God, how could she have had *sex* with him?

But Fred is still spoiling for a fight, trying to prove something. "Sports is like religion. An opiate for the masses."

"Except you don't have to pretend to be a good person to be a sports fanatic. Which makes it a lot more powerful. It's the club anyone can join, the great unifier, and the only hell is when your team is losing."

Fred is barely listening. "And so predictable. Don't you get bored to death writing about the same thing over and over? Man hits ball. Man runs. Man gets caught out."

"Yeah, but it's the same as movies or books," Kirby says. "There are only so many plots in the world. It's how they unfold that makes them interesting."

"Exactly." Dan is unreasonably pleased that she's come out on his side. "A game can play out any way. You've got heroes and villains. You're living through the protagonists, loathing the enemy. People extend the stories to themselves. They live and die by their team, friends and strangers right there with them on this mass scale. You ever watch guys getting emotional about sports in public?"

"It's pathetic."

"It's grown men having fun. Getting caught up in something. Like being a kid again."

"That's a sad indictment of masculinity," Fred says.

Dan manages to restrain himself from saying, "Your face is a sad indictment," because he's supposed to be the grownup here. "All right. How about it's because there's a science and a music to it? The strike zone changes every game and you have to use every bit of intuition and experience to predict what's coming at you. But what I really like? It's that failure is built in. The greatest hitter in the world is only ever going to succeed, what, thirty-five percent of the time?"

"Lame," Fred complains. "Is that all? Best hitters of all time can't even hit the ball?"

"I appreciate that," Kirby says. "It means it's okay to fuck out."

"As long as you're having fun." Dan toasts her with a forkful of refried beans.

Maybe it means he's in with a chance. Maybe it means the least he can do is try.

KIRBY

24 July 1992

━━━━━

It feels really good to have someone's warm breath on her neck, someone's hands under her shirt. It's sweet teenage fumbling, making out in his car. The safety of familiarity. *Nostalgia, the national pastime.* "You've come a long way, Fred Tucker," Kirby whispers, arching her back to make it easier for him to unclip her bra.

"Hey! That's not fair," he says, pulling away at the reminder of that first long-ago awkward attempt at sex. It must be nice to have the space for small humiliations to hurt so much, she thinks, and immediately rebukes herself for being ungenerous.

"Stupid joke, I'm sorry. Come back." She draws his mouth to hers. She can tell he's still a little cross, but the bulge in his jeans doesn't give a damn about his once-upon-a-time wounded pride. He leans over the handbrake to kiss her again and slips his hands under the loosened cups of her bra to graze his thumb over her nipple. She gasps against his mouth. His other hand slips down her stomach, exploratory, heading towards her jeans, and she feels him freeze at the raised spiderweb of scars.

"Did you forget?" It's her turn to pull back. Every time. The rest of her life. Talking someone through it.

"No. I guess I wasn't expecting it to be so . . . dramatic."

"Do you want to see?"

She raises her shirt to show him, leaning back so that the streetlight catches on her skin and the network of angry pink ridges across her stomach. He traces them with his fingers.

"It's beautiful. You're beautiful, I mean." He kisses her again. They make out for a long time, which feels really fucking nice and uncomplicated.

"Do you want to come up?" she says. "Let's do that now."

He hesitates as she is reaching for the car door handle. His mom's, while he is in town.

"If you want to," she says, more cautious.

"I do."

"There's a but there." She is already on the defensive. "Don't worry. I'm not looking for a relationship, Fred. That whole thing about taking a girl's virginity and she'll love you forever? I don't even know you. But I used to. And this feels good, and that's really all I want."

"I'd like that too."

"There's still a but." A spike of impatience pierces up through what has been, up until now, some very lovely and all-consuming lust.

"I need to get something out the trunk."

"I have condoms. I bought them earlier. In case."

He laughs, softly. "You bought them the last time too. It's not that. It's my camera."

"No one's going to break in for it. My neighborhood's not *that* rough. If you left it in full view lying on the back seat, maybe."

He kisses her again. "Because I want to film you. For the documentary."

"We can talk about that later."

"No, I mean, while we're..."

She shoves him away. "Fuck off."

"Not in a bad way! You won't even notice."

"Oh, I'm sorry. Maybe I misunderstood. I thought you said you wanted to film me while we were having sex."

"I do. To show how beautiful you are. Confident and sexy and strong. It's about reclaiming what happened to you. What's more powerful and vulnerable than showing you naked?"

"Are you even hearing yourself?"

"It's not exploitative. You'll have full agency. That's the whole point. It'll be as much your film as mine."

"That's *so* thoughtful."

"You'll obviously have to get the stuff with your mother, at first, till I can win her over, but I'll help you. I'll come back for a few months to do the filming."

"Isn't this unethical? Sleeping with your documentary subject?"

"Not if that's part of the film. All filmmakers are complicit anyway. There's no such thing as objectivity."

"Oh my God. You are such an asshole. You had this planned the whole time."

"No, I just wanted to propose it to you, as an idea. It would be astounding. Award-winning."

"And you happened to bring the camera in your car."

"You seemed open to the idea at the Mexican place."

"We didn't even start to get into it. And you definitely didn't mention making a home porno."

"Is this about the sports guy?" Fred whines, turning it around.

"Dan? No. It's about you being a colossal insensitive moron who is no longer getting laid, which is a tragedy, because I thought, maybe, for once, I could have uncomplicated sex with someone I kinda liked."

"We can still have sex."

"*If* I still kinda liked you." She slams out the car, gets halfway to the door and then turns back to lean in the window. "Hot tip, stud: next time bring up the stupid movie idea that's pretty much guaranteed to piss off your date *after* you've been to bed with her."

MAL

16 July 1991

———

Getting clean is easy. You fuck off for a few months to some-where you haven't burned anyone yet, where they might take you in and look after you, feed you up some, maybe even put you to work. Mal has a second cousin or step-aunt in Greensboro, North Carolina, he forgets which. Families are messy to deal with anyways, even before you start getting into that twice-removed shit. But blood calls to blood.

Aunt Patty, however she fits in, cuts the boy some slack. "Only on account of your mama," she is at pains to remind him regularly. Same mama who introduced him to dope and checked out at the ripe old age of thirty-four with a bad hit in her arm, but he knows better than to bring that up. And maybe that's why she's helping him in the first place. Guilt is a great human motivator.

The first few weeks are recurring death. He gets the sweats and the shakes and begs Aunt Patty to get him to the hospital for methadone. She takes him to church instead, and he sits and shivers in the pews and she drags him to his feet every time there's a hymn. But it feels better than he could have imagined to have a whole bunch of people praying for you. Really invested in your future and calling out to God on your behalf for you to be healed of the sickness, praise Jesus.

Maybe it's divine intervention or maybe he's still young enough to be able to shrug off the bad shit or maybe the dope was cut so much it wasn't that bad in the first place, but he gets through the withdrawal and pulls himself together.

He gets a job packing groceries at the Piggly Wiggly. He's sharp and friendly and people like him. This comes as a surprise. He upgrades to working the cash register. He even starts dating a nice girl, a coworker, Diyana, who already has a baby by another man, and is working hard and studying part-time so she can move up to manager or maybe even head office, and make a better life for her child.

It doesn't bother Mal. "Long as we don't make one of our own," he tells her, making sure they always have protection. Because he's done with stupid mistakes.

"Not yet," she says, all smug, like she knows she has him hooked. And he don't mind that either, because maybe she does. And that wouldn't be a bad life at all. Him and her and a family, working their way up. They could open up their own franchise.

Staying clean? That's another thing. You don't even have to go looking. Trouble calls out its own. The corner finds you, even in Greensboro.

One bump for old times' sake.

Shortchanging old Mr. Hansen, who is half blind and can't make out the numbers anyway. "I was sure it was a fifty, Malcolm," he says in that quavering voice.

"No, sir." Mal is full of good-natured concern. "Definitely a twenty. Want me to pop the register and show you?"

It's too easy. Old habits mix up with new ones, and next thing you know you're on the next Greyhound back to Chitown with nothing but bad feelings behind and a $5,000 banknote burning in your pocket.

He took the bill to a pawn shop two years ago, just to find out. The man behind the counter told him it was worthless, Monopoly money, but offered to buy it off him for $20 (for "novelty value"), which tells Mal it's worth a lot more than that.

Walking back through Englewood without a cent to his name and boys calling out Red Spiders, Yellow Caps, twenty bucks is looking mighty fine right now. Mighty fine. But the only thing worse than not getting a hit is getting taken for a ride, and Mal ain't getting swindled by no pawn dealer.

It takes him a couple of weeks to settle back in and get something going. He hits up his boy Raddisson, who still owes him, and puts out feelers for his Mr. Prospect.

He gets reports now and again from the tweakers who know he has an interest, and demand a dollar, or a bump, for the intel. Which Mal will happily pony up if they can prove that they ain't just inventing it. He wants the details. How the guy limps, which side his crutch is on, what it looks like. Soon as they describe metal, he knows they lying. But he's sneaky enough not to tell them when they getting it wrong. You can't hustle a hustler.

Mainly, he watches the house. He thinks he's got it figured out which one. He knows there's something inside. Even though he's prowled past those houses up and down, looking in the windows at the wreckage inside, already plundered to shit. But he figures his guy is clever. He'll have hidden his stash. Drugs or money. Maybe under a floorboard or inside the walls. Somethin' like that.

But what's that other great human motivator? Oh yeah. Greed. He sets up in one of the houses across the way. Drags in an old mattress and tries to make sure he's high enough by the time he goes to sleep so's that the rat bites won't bother him none.

And one rainy day he sees him come out. Yes, he does. Mr. Prospect limps out, no crutch today, although he still dresses funny. He checks out the scene, left and right and left again, like crossing the street. He thinks no one's looking, but Mal is. He's been waiting for him for months. Keep the house in your head, he thinks. Keep it locked in.

The moment his mark is round the corner, Mal is out of his rat-infested bolthole with an empty backpack, darting across the street and up the porch stairs of that rotten old wooden tenement. He tries the door, but it's locked, the boards nailed across the front just for show. He skips round the back and picks his way over the barbed wire across the stairs that's supposed to keep people like him out, and through the broken window into the house.

There is some Vegas-level David Copperfield shit going on in here. Must be mirrors and shit. Because what looks like a picked-over ruin from the outside is a decked-out crib when you get in. Old-fashioned, though, like something out of a museum. But who cares, long as it's worth something. Mal pushes away the thought that maybe it's hoodoo for real. And maybe the $5,000 bill in his pocket is a one-way ticket. Junkie paranoia.

He starts stuffing his backpack with everything he can find. Candlesticks, silverware, a bundle of banknotes lying on the kitchen counter. He does a quick mental calculation as he shoves it into his backpack: $50 bills, thick as a pack of cards. Gotta be an easy 2k.

He'll have to make a plan with the bigger items. It's decrepit shit, but some of it has to be worth real dough, like that gramophone or the couch with the claw feet. He'll have to make a few enquiries with genuine antiques dealers. And then figure a way to get it out. It's ripe for the picking.

He's about to venture upstairs, when he hears footsteps on the front porch and reconsiders. He's had about all the fun he can take for one day. And truth is, the place gives him the dreads.

Someone is at the front door. Mal goes for the window. But his heart is skipping like he's had a bad hit because what if he can't get out? The devil comes for his own. Sweet Jesus take me home, he thinks, even though he doesn't believe in that church crap.

But he scrambles out into summer 1991, just the way he left it. Rain pourin' down, so he has to dash across the road for shelter. He looks back at the house, which is a dead wreck. He'd think he was trippin' if he didn't have the bag of goodies as evidence. Fuck me, he breathes, looking back. It's trickery and special effects. Hollywood shit. Stupid to get so worked up about it.

But he ain't going back. Not for nothing, he tells himself. Knowing already that of course he will.

Soon as he's spare again. Soon as he's jonesing again. Dope don't have no sympathy, not for love or family, definitely not for fear. Put dope and the devil up against each other in the ring, and dope will win out. Every single time.

KIRBY

22 November 1931

———

She doesn't know what she is looking at. A monument, of sorts. A shrine that takes up the whole room. There are mementoes in incomprehensible configurations pinned to the walls, lined up on the mantel above the fireplace, on the dresser with its cracked mirror, the windowsill, arranged on the exposed metal frame of the bed (the mattress is on the floor, a dark stain showing through the sheet). They've been circled with chalk or black pen or the tip of a knife gouged into the wallpaper. There are names written beside them. Some of them she knows by heart. The others are strangers to her. She wonders who they were. If they managed to fight back. She must try to remember. If only she could hold on to the words long enough to read them. If only she had a fucking camera. It's hard to concentrate. Everything has a hazy quality, flickering in and out of focus like a strobe.

Kirby trails her hand through the air, not quite able to bring herself to touch the costume butterfly wings dangling from the bedpost or the white plastic ID badge with a barcode for Milkwood Pharmaceuticals.

Of course, she thinks, the pony is here. Which means the lighter will be too. She's clinging to cold rationality, trying to take in the details. Just the facts, ma'am. But the tennis ball undoes all that. It drops her into freefall like an elevator with its cables cut. It's hooked onto a nail by its split seam. Her name is written in chalk on the wallpaper next to it. She can make out the shape of the letters. He has spelled it wrong: Kirby Mazrackey.

She feels numb. The worst has already happened. Isn't this what she was looking for? Doesn't this prove everything? But her hands start shaking so hard that she has to press them against her stomach. The old scars ache reflexively under her T-shirt. And then a key jiggles in the lock downstairs.

Jesusfuckshit. Kirby looks round the room. There is no other exit, no potential weapon. She yanks at the sash window to climb out on to the staircase that runs up the back of the house, but it's wedged shut.

She could make a break for it, try to barge past him as he comes in. If she can get downstairs, she could hit him with the kettle.

Or hide.

The key stops scrabbling. She takes the coward's way out. She shoves aside the hanging shirts and identical pairs of jeans, and clambers into the wardrobe, tucking her legs in under her, perched on top of his shoes. It's cramped, but at least it's solid walnut. She can kick the door so it smashes into his face if he tries to open it.

It's what the self-defense instructor told them, after her psychiatrist insisted she go, to take back control. "All you're aiming for is to give yourself enough time to get away. Get him down and run." Always a "him," these perpetrators of terrible violence upon women. As if women were incapable of evil. The instructor demonstrated various methods. Gouge the eyes, hit him under his nose or in the throat with the palm of your hand, smash his instep with your heel, rip off his ear (cartilage tears easy) and throw it at his feet. Never go for the balls, it's the one attack men anticipate and guard against. They practiced throws and strikes and how to get out of a hold. But everyone in the class treated her as if she would break. She was too real for them.

Downstairs she can hear a man struggling to get in the door. *"Co za wkurwiające gówno!"* Polish maybe. He sounds drunk.

It's not him, she thinks and she's not sure if what she's feeling is giddy relief or disappointment. She hears the man stumble inside, towards the kitchen, from the sound of ice clattering into a tumbler. He stomps into the parlor and fumbles around. A moment later music starts playing, scratchy and tender-sweet.

She hears the front door open again, furtive this time. But even though he's drunk, the Pole has heard it too.

The wardrobe smells of mothballs and maybe the faintest trace of *his* sweat. The possibility makes her feel sick. She picks at the paint on the back of the door. All the old nervous habits come back. For a while, after it happened, she used to pick at the skin around her nails until they bled. But she's bled enough for him. Enough for a lifetime. The door can take it though, especially if it'll keep her from doing something rash like bursting out, because the darkness in here has a weight and a pressure like being in the deep end of the swimming pool.

"Hej!" the Pole shouts at the person entering the house. *"Coś ty za jeden?"* He clomps through to the hallway. She can hear the pitches and falls of a conversation, but she can't make out the words. Wheedling. Abrupt responses. Is it his voice? She can't tell. There is a meaty smack. A cow being staple-gunned in the head. Squealing, high-pitched and undignified. There is another abattoir smack. And another. Kirby can't contain it anymore. A

low animal sound wrenches through her, and she clutches her jaw with both hands pressed over her mouth.

Downstairs, the squealing cuts off suddenly. She strains to hear, biting her palm to keep from crying out. A muffled thump. A one-sided struggle, heaving and swearing. And then the sound of someone coming up the stairs, swinging a crutch that goes *tok-tok* on every step.

HARPER

22 November 1931

─────

The door swings open into the past and Harper hobbles through carrying a filthy tennis ball, but without his knife, practically into the arms of a bear of a man in the hallway. He is drunk and gripping a frozen turkey by one goose-pimpled pink leg. The last time Harper saw him, he was dead.

The man lurches towards him, bellowing and waving the bird around like a cudgel. *"Hej! Coś ty za jeden? Co ty tu kurwa robisz? Myślisz, że możesz tak sobie wejść do mojego domu?"*

"Hello," Harper says, friendly, already knowing the outcome. "If I was a betting man, I would gamble on you being Mr. Bartek."

The man turns shifty and breaks into English. "Did Louis send you? I have explained this. There is no cheating, my friend! I am an engineer. Luck has mechanics just like anything else. You can calculate it. Even horses and faro games."

"I believe it."

"I can help you, if you like. Place a bet. My method is fool-proof, my friend. Guaranteed." He looks hopefully at Harper. "You are a drinking man? Have a drink with me! I have whiskey.

And champagne! And I was going to cook this turkey. There is more than enough for two. We can be congenial together. No one needs to get hurt. Am I right?"

"I'm afraid not. Take off your coat, please."

The man considers this. He realizes that Harper is wearing the same coat. Or a future variation of it. His bluster sags and puckers like a cow's stomach when you punch a knife through it. "You are not from Louis Cowen, are you?"

"No." He recognizes the gangster's name even if he's never had any truck with him. "But I am grateful. For all of this." Harper gestures at the hallway with his crutch and as Bartek involuntarily follows the motion, he brings it singing down onto the back of his neck. The Polack drops, squealing, and Harper leans against the wall for balance and smashes the crutch down on his head. Again and again. With practiced ease.

It takes him a long time to tug off the coat. Harper wipes his face with the back of his hand and it comes away bloody. He will need to take a shower before he goes to do what is required, setting the gears in motion for something that has already happened.

HARPER

20 November 1931

———

It's the first time he has been back to the Hooverville since he left, returning *before* he left. It is diminished by his experience. The people are meaner and lower. Gray skin sacks swung around by a numbed puppeteer.

He has to remind himself that no one is looking for him. Not yet. But he avoids his old haunts and takes a different route through the park, clinging to the water's edge. He finds the woman's shack easily. She is taking down the washing outside, her blind fingers feeling down the wire to pluck away the stained petticoat, the blanket infested with lice that resist being washed away in cold water. She deftly folds each garment and hands it to the boy standing beside her.

"Mami. Someone. Someone is here."

The woman turns her face towards him, full of trepidation. He guesses she has always been blind, oblivious to the need to arrange the muscles in guile. It makes the task at hand all the more tiresome. There is no game here. He has no interest in this dull woman who is already dead.

"Begging your pardon, ma'am, for disturbing you this fine evening."

"I ain't got no money," the woman says, "if you've come to rob me. You ain't the first, you know."

"The opposite, ma'am. I have a favor to ask. No big thing, but I can pay you for it."

"How much?"

Harper laughs at the nakedness of her need. "Straight to haggling? You don't even want to know what I want you to do."

"You'll be wanting the same as the others. Don't worry. I'll send the boy to beg at the station. He won't get in the way of your taste of cunny."

He crushes the bills into her hand. She flinches. "A friend of mine will be passing by here in an hour or so. I need you to give him a message and this coat." He drapes it over her shoulders. "You need to wear it. That's how he will know you. His name is Bartek. Will you remember that?"

"Bartek," she repeats. "And what's the message?"

"That'll be enough, I think. There'll be a commotion. You'll hear it. You only need to say his name. And don't think of taking anything from the pockets. I know what's in there, and I'll come back to kill you."

"You needn't say such things in front of the boy."

"He'll be my witness," Harper says, pleased by the truth of it.

KIRBY

2 August 1992

———

Dan and Kirby walk up the driveway past the neatly clipped lawn, which sports a yard sign: "Vote Bill Clinton." Rachel used to put up signs for all of the political parties, just to be difficult. She also used to tell campaigners that she was voting for the lunatic fringe. But when she busted Kirby making prank calls to an old lady, convincing her to wrap all her appliances in tinfoil to stop the radiation from the satellites penetrating the house, she told her to stop being childish.

There is the muffled sound of kids shouting inside the house. It could do with a fresh lick of paint, but there are orange geraniums in flowerpots on the porch. Detective Michael Williams's widow opens the door, smiling but harried.

"Hi, sorry, the boys . . ." There is a scream behind her.

"Moo-ooom! He's using hot water."

"Excuse me one second." She disappears into the house and comes back, hauling two kids with water pistols by the arms. Six or seven, Kirby's not great at judging children's ages. "Say hello, boys."

"'Lo," they mutter, staring at their feet, although the younger one sneaks a look up at her through crazily long lashes, which makes Kirby glad she wore a neck scarf today.

"Good enough. Outside, please, thank you. And use the garden hose." Their mother thrusts them into the yard. They gain momentum like loosed missiles, whooping and hollering.

"Come in. I just made iced tea. You must be Kirby? I'm Charmaine Williams." They shake hands.

"Thanks for this," Kirby starts, as Charmaine leads them into a house as neatly kept up as the garden. It's an act of defiance, Kirby thinks. Because this is the problem with death, be it murder or heart attacks or car accidents: life continues.

"Oh, I don't know if it will be any use, but it's lying around taking up space, and the guys at the station don't want it. You're doing me a favor, honestly. The boys will be glad to have their own rooms."

She opens the door onto a small study with a window overlooking the alley behind the house. It's been colonized by cardboard boxes that creep across the floor and pile up against the walls. Opposite the window is a felt bulletin board pinned with family photos and a Bulls pennant and a blue ribbon for Chicago PD Bowling League Championships 1988 and a collection of old lottery tickets framing the edge; a bad-luck border.

"Played his badge number?" Dan says, examining the board. He does not comment on the photograph of the dead man lying sprawled in a flowerbed with his arms thrown out like Christ, or the Polaroid of a bag of housebreaking tools, or the *Tribune* article "Prostitute Found Dead" that are pinned up, disturbingly, among the happy domestic memorabilia.

"You know it," Charmaine says, frowning at the desk, a K-Mart kit job, which is barely visible underneath the spread of papers, and specifically at the striped coffee mug that's grown a fine fuzz of mold in the bottom.

"I'll just get you that iced tea," she says, sweeping up the mug.

"This is weird," Kirby says, looking around the room at the painfully exposed detritus of investigations past. "It feels haunted." She picks up a glass paperweight with a hologram of a soaring eagle and puts it down again. "I guess it is."

"You said you wanted access. This is access. Mike investigated a lot of femicides and he kept all his old case notes."

"Don't they normally go into evidence?"

"The critical investigative stuff does: the bloody knife, witness testimony. It's like math, you have to show all your workings, but there's a lot of messing around before you get there; interviews that don't seem to go anywhere, evidence that seems irrelevant at the time."

"You're killing whatever remaining faith I had left in the justice system, Dan."

"Mike was one of the cops campaigning to get the system changed. To force detectives to file absolutely everything. There was a lot he thought needed revamping in the police department."

"Harrison told me about your torture investigation."

"Big mouth. Yeah, this guy Mike was the whistleblower on that until they started threatening Charmaine and the boys. I don't blame him for backing down. He took a transfer to Niles, stayed out of their way. But in the meantime he kept every piece of paper that crossed his desk from every murder he worked, and any others he could lay his hands on. There was a damp problem at one of the precincts. He rescued a lot of files, brought them here. Some of the stuff is impossible to identify. I think he had this idea that he was going to retire and sort through it and solve cold cases. Maybe write a book. Then the car crash."

"No foul play?"

"It was a drunk driver. Hit him head-on, killed them both pretty much instantly. Sometimes bad shit happens. Anyway, he was a bit of a homicide hoarder, Mike. There'll be stuff in here that you won't find in the *Sun-Times* archives or at the library. Probably nothing. But you know, like you said. Wide net."

"Just call me Pandora," Kirby says, trying not to be daunted by the sheer number of boxes, every single one packed tight with grief. This would be the moment to call it quits.

Like hell.

DAN
2 August 1992

It takes them ten trips to haul twenty-eight boxes of old case files up the three flights of stairs to Kirby's apartment above the German bakery.

"You couldn't live somewhere with an elevator?" Dan complains, nudging open the door with his foot and heaving a box on to an old door set up on trestles that's doing a shoddy impression of a desk.

Her place is a dump. The parquet floors are faded and scratched up. There are clothes scattered all over the room. And not like sexy underwear either. T-shirts, turned inside out, and jeans and sweatpants and one big black boot lying on its side in a tangle of laces from half-under the couch, no sign of its partner. Dan recognizes the bleak symptoms of don't-give-a-damn-single life. He was hoping to get some hint of whether or not she'd taken that idiot boy Fred to bed last weekend, or if she had started seeing him again, but there's too much mess to infer anything about possible sexual encounters, let alone the hidden routings of her heart.

The mismatched furniture speaks to a demented DIY ingenuity, crap that's been recycled off the street and repurposed, and not just your average student-pad milk-crate bookshelves either. The coffee table in the tiny space in front of the couch that does for a living-room, for example, is an old gerbil cage with a round glass top balanced on it.

He shrugs off his jacket and throws it over the couch, where it instantly blends with an orange sweater and a pair of cut-off shorts, and bends down to see the diorama she's created inside with dinosaur toys and fake flowers.

"Oh, never mind that. I was bored," she squirms.

"It's . . . interesting."

The wooden stool next to the kitchen counter, which cants at an alarming angle, has been hand-painted with tropical flowers. There are plastic goldfish stuck to the bathroom door and fairy lights strung up above the kitchen curtains, blinking like Christmas.

"No elevator, sorry. Not for this price. And I'd go for the smell of fresh bread over that any day. I get a discount on yesterday's donuts."

"I wondered where you got the cash to spread them around like that."

"Spreading my waistline!" She lifts up her T-shirt to pinch at her belly.

"You'll work it off on the stairs," Dan says, not looking, definitely not, at the way her waist curves in from the hard knob of her hip above her jeans.

"The evidence workout. We'll need more boxes. You got any more dead cop friends?" She sees his face. "Sorry, I guess that was too dark, even for me. You want to stick around for a bit? Help me sort through some of this?"

"I got somewhere better to be?"

Kirby opens up the first box and starts spreading it out on the table. Michael Williams has been anything but systematic. It seems to be three decades' worth of assorted crap. Photographs of cars, clearly from the seventies, from the golds and beiges and the heavy boxy shapes. Mug-shots of creeps, various, all sporting a case number, a date. Front, side-on, left, right. A guy with huge glasses oozing cool, Mr. Handsome with his hair slicked up, a man with jowls so deep you could use them to smuggle drugs in.

"How old *was* this cop friend?" she raises an eyebrow.

"Forty-eight? Fifty? Been in the force since forever. Old-school police. Charmaine's his second wife. Divorce rates among cops are higher than the national average. But they were doing okay. I think they might even have lasted, if not for the accident."

He nudges the boxes on the floor with his boot. "I'm thinking we should separate out the ancient stuff. Anything before . . . 1970? Gets filed in the not helpful pile."

"Okey-dokey," she agrees, opening up one of the boxes marked 1987–1988, while Dan starts shoving aside the boxes with dates that are too early.

"What's this?" she says, holding up a Polaroid of a row of men with bushy beards and tiny red shorts. "A bowling alley?"

Dan squints at the picture. "Police shooting range. That's how the cops used to do identity line-ups, with a spotlight shining in the guys' eyes so they couldn't see the person ID-ing them. Little uncomfortable, I'd guess. The whole one-way glass set-up is strictly for the movies and police departments with an actual budget."

"Wow," Kirby says, studying the men's hairy legs. "History isn't kind to fashion."

"You hoping to see your guy?"

"Wouldn't that be nice?" The mix of wistfulness and bitterness in her voice kills him. He's setting her up on a hiding to nothing. It's busy work to keep her occupied, because the reality is that she has no chance of catching the psycho. Certainly not by digging through boxes. But it makes her happy, and he felt sorry for Charmaine, and he thought maybe they could help each other out and get it out of their systems.

Poison shared is poison halved. Or maybe it just poisons everyone equally.

"Listen," he says, hardly knowing what he's saying. "I don't think you should do this. It was a stupid idea. You don't want to see all this shit, and it's not going to go anywhere and—fuck!"

He nearly kisses her, then. A way of shutting his own darn fool mouth and because she's so close. So *here*. Looking at him with all that bright hungry curiosity beaming out of her face.

He stops himself in time. Being relative. In time to save himself from being a deluded idiot. From her rebuffing him like a pinball bumper, with the same automatic elastic snap. In time that she didn't even notice. Christ, what was he thinking? He's already standing up, making for the door, in such a rush to get out of there that he forgets his jacket.

"Shit. Sorry, it's late. I gotta get up early. I've got copy due. I'll see you. Soon."

"Dan," she says, half laughing in surprise and confusion.

But he's already closed the door, too hard, behind him.

And the mug shot labeled "Curtis Harper 13 CHGO PD IR 136230 16 October 1954" stays where it is, buried in a box that has been set aside.

HARPER

16 October 1954

─────

He goes back too soon is what lands him in trouble. The day after Willie Rose. Of course it doesn't feel like that for him. For Harper, it has been weeks.

He's killed twice since: Bartek in the hall (a joyless obligation) and the Jew girl with the crazy hair. But he is feeling unsettled. He had hoped when he lured her into the bird sanctuary that she would have the pony he gave her as a child, to complete the circle. The way killing Bartek and returning the coat to the woman in the Hooverville completed a circle. The toy is a loose thread apt to snag on something. He doesn't like it.

He rubs at his bandaged arm where the goddamn dog bit him. Like mistress, like mongrel. Another lesson. He was sloppy. He will have to go back to check that she's dead. He will have to buy another knife.

There is something else jangling his nerves. He would swear there are trinkets missing from the House. A pair of candlesticks gone from above the fireplace. Spoons from the drawer.

Reassurance. That's all he needs. Killing the architect was perfect. He wants to revisit it. An act of faith. He feels a flush of anticipation. He is confident no one will recognize him. His jaw is all healed up and he's grown a beard over the scars left by the wire. He leaves his crutch behind. It's not enough.

Harper tips his hat at the black doorman of the Fisher Building and takes the stairs up to the third floor. He's thrilled to see that they have not been able to get all the blood out of the glassy tiles outside the door of the architecture firm. It makes him achingly hard and he grips himself through his pants, stifling a little moan of pleasure. He leans against the wall, pulling his coat around him to obscure the unmistakable jerky movements of his hand, remembering what she was wearing, how red her lipstick was. Brighter than blood.

The door of Crake & Mendelson crashes open, and a bear of a man with thinning hair and red eyes confronts him. "What the hell do you think you're doing?"

"Excuse me," Harper covers, reading one of the names off the doors opposite. "I'm looking for the Chicago Dentistry Society."

But the doorman has followed him upstairs and is pointing his finger at him. "That's the one! That's the bastard! I saw him leaving the building covered in Miss Rose's blood!"

Harper is interrogated for seven hours at the police station by a rangy flyweight of a cop, who punches out of his class, and a rotund detective with a bald patch, who sits and smokes. They alternate between talking and hitting. It does not help that he has no appointment to see the Chicago Dentistry Society and that the Stevens Hotel, where he claims to be a registered guest, has not been called that for years.

"I'm from out of town, fellas," he tries, smiling, before a fist slams into the side of his head, making his ears ring and his teeth ache, threatening to pop his jaw out all over again. "I told you. I'm a traveling salesman." Another punch, this time below his sternum, driving the breath out of him. "Dental hygiene products." The next blow knocks him to the floor. "I left my sample case on the El. How about it, fellas? If you would let me file a lost baggage report—" The paunchy balding officer kicks him in the kidney, a glancing blow. He should leave the violence to his more qualified friend, Harper thinks, still grinning.

"Is this amusing to you? What's so funny, shitbird?" The thin cop leans down and exhales his cigarette in Harper's face. How does he explain that he knows this is just something he has to endure? He knows he will make it back to the House because there are still girls' names on the wall, their destinies unfulfilled. But he has made a mistake and this is his punishment for it.

"Only that you got the wrong guy," he huffs through his teeth.

They take his fingerprints. They make him stand against the wall, holding a number for a mug shot. "Don't you fucking smile, or I will wipe it right off your face. A girl is dead and we know you're the one who did it."

But they don't have enough evidence to keep him. The doorman is not the only witness who saw him come out the building, but they all swear that yesterday he was clean-shaven with a wire contraption round his mouth. And now he has two weeks' worth of beard that they've yanked at with their fat policemen's fingers to make sure it's not glued on. Add to this that there is not a spot of blood on him and no sign of the murder weapon—which would normally be in his pocket—because it is buried in the neck of a dead dog thirty-five years from now.

He has made the dog bite part of his alibi. A mutt attacked him when he was running for the train to retrieve his sample case. Right at the time this poor lady architect was getting murdered.

There is no doubt, the detectives agree, that he is some kind of degenerate pervert, but they do not have enough to prove that he is a danger to society or a real suspect in the death of Miss W. Rose. They charge him with public indecency, file the mug-shot and set him loose.

"Don't go too far," the detective warns him.

"I won't leave the city," Harper promises, limping worse than usual from the beating. It's a promise he keeps, more or less. But he never comes back to 1954, and he loses the beard.

After that he only revisits the scenes years later or before, skipping decades, to jerk off over the place a girl died. He likes the juxtaposition of memory and change. It makes the experience sharper.

There are at least two other photographs of him in police records from the last sixty years, although he gives a different name each time. Once for public indecency in 1960, touching himself obscenely at what will become a construction site, another in 1983, when he broke a cab driver's nose for refusing to drive him to Englewood.

The one pleasure he is not prepared to surrender is reading the newspapers, reliving the murders from other perspectives. That has to be done in the days immediately after the killing. Which is how he finds out about Kirby.

KIRBY
11 August 1992

═══════

She is sitting in the waiting-room of Delgado, Richmond & Associates, a firm which only sounds impressive, flipping through a three-year-old *Time* magazine that screams "Death By Gun" on the cover. She felt compelled to pick it up given that her other choices are "The New USSR" or "Arsenio Hall," even though her field of interest is actually "death by knife" and firearms are not much use to her.

The magazines are not the only things out of date. The leather couch has seen better decades. The plastic rubber tree has a fine coating of dust on its leaves and more than one cigarette has been stubbed out in its base. Even the receptionist's hairstyle is unfashionably eighties. Kirby wishes she had dressed up a bit more for the occasion. She is pushing the limit even by slovenly newsroom standards with a Fugazi T-shirt under a checked shirt and a wool-lined brown leather bomber jacket that she picked up for cheap down on Maxwell Street.

The lawyer, Elaine Richmond, comes to collect her personally, a soft-spoken middle-aged woman in black pants and a blazer, with sharp eyes and a bobbed weave. "*Sun-Times?*" she smiles and pumps Kirby's hand with too much enthusiasm, like a lonely maiden aunt in an old folks' home glomming on to other people's visitors. "Thank you so much for coming."

Kirby follows her down the passage into a boardroom cramped with cardboard boxes nudging out the legal books on the shelves and making incursions across the floorspace too. She thunks down an assortment of pink and blue folders stuffed with paperwork, but doesn't actually open them.

"Well," she says, "you're a little late to the party, you know."

"Uh?" Kirby manages.

"Where were you a year ago when Jamel tried to kill himself? We sure could have done with a little press back then." She laughs ruefully.

"I'm sorry," Kirby says, wondering if she's in the wrong law firm altogether.

"Tell that to his family."

"I'm just an intern, I thought this would make a good story on, uh," she ad-libs, "miscarriages of justice and the terrible after-effects? Human interest stuff. But actually I'm a little bit out of the loop with the latest developments."

"There aren't any. As far as the district attorney is concerned, that's a wrap! But see here. Do these boys look like the murdering type to you?" She flips open the file and spreads out the pages to show her the mug shots of four young men staring sulkily into the lens with flat eyes. It's amazing, Kirby thinks, how easily "teen apathy" can translate into "stone-cold killer."

"Marcus Davies, fifteen at the time they were arrested. De-shawn Ingram, nineteen. Eddie Pierce, twenty-two, and Jamel Pelletier, seventeen years old. Accused of the murder of Julia Madrigal. Found guilty on 30 June 1987. Sentenced to death row, apart from Marcus, who went down to juvenile detention. Jamel attempted suicide on . . ." she peers at the date, "September 8 last year, on hearing that the latest appeal had been overturned. He was a volatile kid anyway, but it just crushed the soul of him. Did it straight after we got back from court. He twisted his pants into a noose and tried to hang himself in his cell."

"I didn't know about that."

"It got some press. Usually buried on page three, if we were lucky. A lot of the papers didn't report it at all. I think most people believe they're guilty as the devil's own."

"But you don't."

"My clients were not very nice young men." Elaine shrugs. "They sold drugs. They broke into cars. Deshawn had an assault rap for beating up his drunk father when he was thirteen years old. Eddie's had several charges dropped against him, from rape to breaking and entering. They were joyriding in a stolen car in Wilmette, which makes them stupid because a bunch of black boys in a nice ride in the lily-white burbs draws the wrong kind of attention. But they didn't kill that girl."

Kirby feels a shot of ice go down her spine hearing her say it. "That's what I think too."

"It was a high-pressure case. Sweet white college girl with top marks is horribly murdered. It becomes a community issue. The whole ward gets up in arms. Parents are upset, talking about campus security, getting blue-light phones installed or pulling their daughters out of school altogether."

"Any ideas on who did do it?"

"Not Satanists. The police were ringing on the crazy-town doorbell with that one. Took them three weeks to stop chasing that wild goose, though."

"A serial killer?"

"Sure. We couldn't pull anything to corroborate the theory in court. You want to tell me what you're thinking? If you have a lead on something that could help these boys, you need to tell me right now."

Kirby squirms, not quite ready to lay it all out. "I thought you said they weren't good people."

"I'd say that about eighty percent of the clients I represent. Doesn't mean you shouldn't do right by them."

"Can you put me in touch with them?"

"If they want to talk with you. I might advise them not to. It depends what you're going to do with it."

"I don't know yet."

HARPER

24 March 1989

He is still bruised from the beating by the zealous detectives when he goes back to 1989 to buy a full set of papers from a newsagent to cheer himself up. He sits in the window of the Greek diner on 53rd Street. It's cheap and bustling, serving up food from the counter, with a line that sometimes snakes round the corner. As close to a routine as he comes.

He makes a point of making eye contact with the chef, a man with a thick mustache that varies between solid black and shot through with gray, depending on whether he is the son or the father or the granddad this go-around. If the man ever recognizes him, he makes no show of it.

The murder has been pushed out by a ship running aground and pouring oil into a bay somewhere in remote Alaska. *Exxon Valdez,* the name of the tanker is in huge capitals on every front page. He eventually finds two columns in the metro section. "Brutal attack," it reads. "Saved by her dog." "Little hope of survival" says one. "Not expected to live out the week."

The words are not right. He reads them again, willing them

to jitter and shift like the ones on his wall to spell out the truth. Dead. Murdered. Gone.

He's become adept at navigating wonders. The phone directory, for example. He looks up the hospital where she is either in intensive care or the morgue, depending on which paper you read, and calls from the payphone at the back of the diner, near the restrooms. But the doctors are occupied and the woman he speaks to is "unable to give out personal information about a patient, sir."

He smarts for hours, until he realizes that he has no choice. He has to go see for himself. And finish it if need be.

He buys flowers at the gift shop downstairs, and, because he still feels empty-handed (it burns him that he does not have his knife), a purple teddy bear with a balloon that says "Get Well Beary Soon!"

"For a little one?" asks the shop assistant, a big warm woman with an air of permanent sadness. "They always like the toys."

"It's for the girl who was murdered." He corrects himself. "Attacked."

"Oh, that was so awful. Just terrible. There have been a lot of people sending her flowers. Total strangers. It's the dog. It was so brave. Such an amazing story. I've been praying for her."

"How is she doing, do you know?"

The woman tightens her lips and shakes her head.

"I'm sorry, sir," says the nurse at the front desk. "Visiting hours are over. And the family has requested that no one should disturb them."

"I'm a relative," Harper says. "Her uncle. Her mother's brother. I came as soon as I could."

There is a stripe of sun across the floor like yellow paint, a woman's shadow across it as she stares out over the parking lot.

There are flowers everywhere, like another hospital room from another time, Harper remembers. But the bed is empty.

"Excuse me," he says and the woman at the window looks over her shoulder, guilty, fanning the cigarette smoke out. He recognizes the resemblance to her daughter, the jut of her chin, the wide eyes, even if her hair is dark and smooth, held back by an orange scarf. She's wearing dark jeans and a chocolate brown turtleneck, with a necklace made of mismatched buttons that click together as she fiddles with them. Her eyes are glittering from crying. She exhales a puff of smoke and waves, irritated. "Who the fuck are you?"

"I'm looking for Kirby Mazrachi," Harper says, holding up the flowers and the bear. "I was told she was here."

"Another one?" She gives a bitter laugh. "What bullshit story did you spin them to get in? Fucking useless nurses." She crushes the cigarette against the windowsill, harder than necessary.

"I wanted to see if she was all right."

"Well, she's not."

He waits, while she glares at him. "Do I have the wrong room? Is she somewhere else?"

She flies across the room, furious, and jabs him in the chest with her finger. "You have the wrong everything. Fuck you, mister!"

He falls back under her wrath, holding up his offerings in innocent protest. His heel clips against one of the buckets of flowers. Water sloshes onto the floor. "You're upset."

"Of course I'm upset!" Kirby's mother screams. "She's dead. All right? So just fucking leave us alone. There's no story here, you vulture. She's dead. Will that make you happy?"

"I'm sorry for your loss, ma'am." This is a lie. He's overwhelmed with relief.

"And tell the others too. Especially that Dan prick who can't be bothered to call me back. Tell them to fuck right off."

ALICE
4 July 1940

"Will you sit your toches down?" Luella says through the hairpin clenched between her teeth. But Alice is too excited to keep still, prancing up from her seat at the mirror every two minutes to peek through the caravan door at the rubes pouring into the fairground, grinning and happy, already arming themselves with popcorn and cheap beer in paper cups.

Crowds gather in pockets of interest; at the hoop toss and the tractor show or to gawp at the rooster who plays tic-tac-toe. (Alice lost two out of three games to that chicken this morning, but she has it figured now, just you wait.)

The women veer towards the pitchmen reciting the merits of domestic wares that will "transform your kitchen *and* your life." Rich men in stetson hats and expensive boots that have never set heel on a range amble over towards the auction to bid on steers. A young mother dangles a baby over the fence to see the enormous prize sow, Black Rosie, with a white snub nose and a low-hanging spotted belly and nipples like pinky fingers.

A pair of teenagers, a girl and a boy, are standing admiring the butter cow, which is supposed to have taken three days to carve. It is already suffering in the sun, and Alice can detect a whiff of rancid dairy among the tumult of hay bales and sawdust and tractor smoke and cotton candy and sweat and animal dung.

The boy makes a joke about the butter cow, something everyone else would have said already, Alice imagines, about the number of flapjacks you could eat with that, and the girl giggles and responds with something equally clichéd, maybe that he's just trying to butter her up. And he takes her words as his cue to dart forward to kiss her, and she pushes his face away with one hand, teasing, only to reconsider and dip back to peck him on the lips. Then she slips away, towards the Ferris wheel, laughing and looking back for him. And it's so lovely, Alice could just die.

Luella lowers the brush and tuts, irritated: "You want to do your own damn hair?"

"Sorry, sorry!" Alice says, and flings herself back into the chair so that Luella can resume the unenviable task of trying to iron and pin her mousy blonde hair, which is too short and too unruly to do what it is told. "Very modern," is what Joey said at her audition.

"You should try a wig," Vivian says, smacking her lips together, to spread the lipstick evenly. Alice has practiced the same maneuver in the mirror, trying for that brazen little pop of a kiss-off. Vivacious Viv, the feature attraction. It's her likeness painted on the pictorials on the ornately carved front, with her shining coal hair and those enormous blue eyes that manage to look salacious and naïve at the same time. It's a good look for the new act that has impressed ministers and schoolteachers in going on six different towns now. A girly show unlike any other that got them specially invited to appear.

"B-a-l-l-y, ladies! Five minutes 'til bally." Joey the Greek throws open the door of the already cramped trailer, a bumblebee of a man stuffed into a jade green sequinned waistcoat and shiny black pants that are starting to wear around the seams. Alice gives a little squeal of surprise, her hand fluttering to her chest.

"Well, you're skittish as a filly, Miss Templeton," Joey says and tweaks her cheek. "Or a schoolgirl. You keep that up."

"Or a colt 'bout to get gelded," Vivian snipes.

"What's that supposed to mean, Vivi?" he frowns.

"Only that you get more than you bargained for with Alice," Vivian says, pulling on one of her curls to test its bounce. Dissatisfied, she re-subjects it to her iron.

"Like actually being able to remember my dance steps?" Alice retorts, feeling a bright burst of hate.

"Now now," Joey claps his hands, "there'll be no cat-fighting in my girly show. Not unless it's on the billing and we charge extra for it."

There have been extras in the past, Alice knows. Luella used to do torch shows with men peering between her legs like a gynecological exam. But there is a new prudishness in the air lately and Joey has cunningly adapted the act to suit.

It feels like family, this gilly show, packing everything up into railcars to move on to another showground, a new fair. A million miles removed from Cairo (that would be Kay-ro, Illinois, not Egypt, even if Joey says she has "Nefertiti cheekbones") and everyone who knew her. She would have simply expired if she'd stayed there. Of sheer boredom, if not in actuality at the hands of Uncle Steve. When they evacuated people with the '37 floods, Alice evacuated right out of Cairo *and* her old life. God bless the Ohio River, she thinks.

Joey grabs Eva's ass through her costume as she steps into her heels, and gives it a fond little shake. He winks at Alice. "Curves, princess! That's what men like. You need to earn more dollars so you can buy more cake so you can get more curves so you can earn more dollars!"

"Yes, Mr. Malamatos." Alice gives him a nervous curtsey in her green-and-white cheerleader skirt. Joey susses her out, leaning on his cane topped with a fist-sized emerald he swears is real, eyebrows bobbing up and down, up and down in a vaudeville leer. "Like humping caterpillars," he once put it.

And then he goes for her crotch. For a gut-wrenching moment, she is terrified he is going to grope her, but he only tugs her pleated skirt down.

"Much better," he says. "Remember, princess, this show is wholesome family fare."

He ducks out the front, clumping up the stairs to the bally, framed by the carved marquee with its suggestive paintings of Vivian to ignite patrons' imaginations, already launching into his patter. "Step up, gents and ladies, step up, and let me tell you about our performance today. But first, let me warn you. This is no cooch show! We don't have diving girls or hula girls or forbidden Oriental dancers!"

"What do ya got then?" someone heckles from the crowd.

"Why, sir, I'm glad you asked!" Joey turns to him, beaming. "For you, sir, I have something far more valuable. For you, sir, I have an education!"

There is a smattering of boos and jeers, but Joey has them hooked before any of the girls have set so much as a toe on the bally steps. "Look here, sir. Come closer. Don't be shy, sir. May I draw your attention to this lovely specimen of innocence, Miss Alice!"

The curtain twitches to allow Alice through, blinking against the sunlight. She's wearing a cheerleader's outfit: a pleated wool skirt with green insets, a white jersey embroidered with the motif of a green megaphone and a collegial "V" (for "virgin"

Joey teased when he presented it to her), bobby socks and shoes.

"Why don't you come on up here and say hello, sweetheart?"

She waves cheerfully at the smattering of people gathering, drawn in like kids to a shooting gallery, and skips up the stairs. As she reaches the top, she flips neatly into a cartwheel that brings her up standing right beside Joey.

"Wowsers!" he says, impressed, "Give her a hand, folks. Isn't she lovely? The all-American girl. Sweet sixteen and never been kissed. Until . . . well."

"Well, what?" It's the skeptics that are easiest to play. Get their buy-in and you've hooked the crowd. Alice knows that the candy butchers will have marked the loudmouth to work on him the moment he's inside the tent.

Joey prowls down the bally. "Well? Well, well, well." He takes Alice's hand, as if to waltz, and swings her round to face the crowd. She looks down in sham modesty, one hand on her cheek, but peeking at the onlookers through her lashes to gauge the response. She spots the young couple from earlier hanging on the fringe of the crowd, the girl grinning, the boy wary.

Joey lowers his voice, conspiratorial, so that the audience has to edge closer to hear. He circles Alice on the bally. "It's true, isn't it, that there is a certain kind of man who likes to destroy innocence? To *pluck* it, like you might a ripe cherry from a tree." He reaches out to draw a pretend fruit to his mouth and pretends to take a sensual bite. He hangs on to the moment, drawing it out and then snaps round, pointing to the base of the stairs with his stick.

"Or what about the young housewife plagued by unnatural, un-*controllable* desires?" Eva brushes through the curtain, wearing a belted-up housecoat and a beaded mask over her eyes and makes her ascent, her hand poised on her chest. Joey shakes his head, apparently not noticing that her hand has started to fret at her clothing, rubbing over her bosom.

"This poor young woman, who wears a disguise to protect what remains of her dignity, is that most pathetic of creatures, wholly at the mercy of her depraved fantasies. A nymphomaniac, ladies and gentlemen!" At this point, Eva tugs open her coat to reveal the lacy negligee she is wearing underneath and Joey, horrified at this display, quickly goes to cover her up.

"Fair ladies, good gentlemen. This is *not* one of those *low* carnie shows designed to titillate and inflame you. This is a warning! About the dangers of decadence and desire and how easily the fairer sex may be led astray. Or do the leading . . ."

"Pre-sen-ting . . ." Vivian throws open the curtain and struts out wearing bright red lipstick and a pencil skirt, her hair tied up in a bun. "The strumpet! The hussy. The harlot. The wicked temptress! The ambitious young office girl with her eye on the boss. Intent on coming between husband and wife. Women, learn how to spot her. Men, learn how to resist her. This lascivious predator in lipstick is a danger to society!"

Vivian stares into the crowd, hand on hip, reaching up to unpin her hair so that it cascades down over her shoulders. Unlike poor suffering nympho Eva, Vivian wears her lust the way other women would strut a mink coat.

Joey ramps up the spiel. "All this and more, inside! Instruction in avoiding moral *turpi*tude. Come see for yourselves just how far and how *easily* a good woman may fall. Prostitutes and drug addicts! Women victim to their own quivering desires! Insatiable black widows and sweet young innocence tainted!"

It all proves too much for the teenage couple, and the boy tugs the girl away to other pursuits, cleaner ones to judge by the stink-eye he gives them. The other girls have developed an immunity to contempt, but Alice still feels shame like a hot bead in her throat.

She flushes and looks down, not pretending this time, and when she looks up again, she sees *him*.

A lean, rakish man, well dressed, handsome if not for his bent nose. He's standing at the back, staring at her—and not the way men usually do, with a wolfish hunger full of jokey bravado. He's riveted. As if he knows her. As if he can see deep down into her secret self. Alice is so startled by the pure fervor of his attention that she stares back, barely hearing Joey's wrap-up. The man breaks into a smile that makes Alice feel warm and sick and dizzy. She cannot look away.

"Ladies and gentlemen, this show will *mesmerize* you!" Joey swings his cane to point at a young woman in the audience who grins in embarrassment. "It will *hypnotize* you!" He swings it again, stabbing at the loudmouth from before. "It will *paralyze* you!" And here he raises the cane up, stiff and quivering. But only for a brief moment before he sweeps the stick, and indeed his entire portly body, towards the tent entrance down below. "But only if you buy a ticket! Three shows only, ladies and gents. Step up, step inside and let us educate you!"

Joey bustles the girls down the other set of stairs as the crowd sweeps towards the ticket booth, primed to go. "No cartwheels down the stairs?" he chides Alice, but she is too busy looking over her shoulder for the stranger. To her relief, he's still there, pressing forward with the rest of them to buy a ticket. She stands on the back of Eva's heel going down the stairs and nearly causes them all to go skeltering over like milk bottles at One Ball when the carnie loads the heavy bottle on top of the pyramid to demonstrate that there's no trickery here, folks.

"Sorry, sorry," she whispers.

She only gets more flustered when she peeks through the curtain to see that he's standing still as stone among the tide of punters scrambling for good seats. The candy butchers are already working the short con. "Get some candy, win a prize!" Bobby is chatting up an older couple, but Micky spots the man standing all by himself and moves in for the kill: "Hey, fella, you want to win something? We got a new confection, Anna Belle Lee, brand new on the market. And tell you what, we're so convinced you'll love it, we've sweetened the deal with surprise gifts in some of the packages. We got men's and ladies' watches, lighters, pen sets and five-dollar bill-folds! Take a chance, you might get lucky! Only fifty cents! It's a sweet deal. Whaddaya say?" But the guy brushes him off without even looking at him, his face tilted up towards the stage. He is waiting for her. Alice knows this with absolute certainty.

It's so unnerving that she almost blows her vignette. The spot blinds her, so she can't see the audience, but she can feel his gaze. She misses her cue, then she mistimes her flick-flack and nearly tumbles off the stage. Luckily, it fits in well with her act, the cheerleader who is plied with drugs and promises by Micky in a zoot suit, so that in the final scene she is leaning against a street pole in heels and a skimpy dress, innocence lost, having succumbed, as Joey's breathless narration says, "to the ultimate corruption." The spotlight dips dramatically and she slips off stage to make way for the next scene, as the incognito nympho is carried on stage, lounging decadently on a couch carried by two strapping young stagehands.

"Someone's got an admirer," Vivian jeers. "Does he know that there's a dud prize in his candy box?"

And like that, Alice is on top of her, scratching at her face, yanking at those perfect curls, knocking her glasses right off. Vivian goes down hard enough for the sound to be heard out front, forcing Joey to speak louder: "... Who would have thought that the most intimate, most loving moment between husband and wife on their wedding night would have unleashed this dark insatiable hunger, throbbing inside her?"

Luella and Micky pull her off. Vivian gets to her feet, smiling as she touches the scratches on her cheek. "That all you got, Alice? No one ever teach you to fight like a lady?" And while Luella and Micky are holding her, limp and sobbing, Vivian backhands her, her fistful of rings slicing into her face.

"Jesus, Viv!" Micky hisses. But she's already moving to take her position. Just in time, as Eva drops her negligee on stage and the lights snap off, giving the rubes only a moment's ogling, which is still enough to set off gasps of shock and outrage from the well-intended, and whistles and cheers from the peanut gallery. Vivian struts on as Eva walks off, naked, grinning. "Heck, you'd think they'd never seen two seconds of a naked lady . . . Oh hell's bells, Alice, are you all right?"

Luella and Eva take her back to the dressing-room to wash off the blood and rub in some ointment from Luella's collection. She's practically an apothecary with all the lotions and oils she collects. But Alice can tell it's bad because they won't say anything about it.

The worst is still to come.

Joey calls her into the caravan right after the show, with his serious face on, no waggling eyebrows now. "Take off your clothes," he says, cold as she's ever seen him. She's still wearing her Fallen Woman outfit, the red high heels and the slinky dress.

"I thought it wasn't that kind of show," Alice protests with a half laugh that doesn't even fool her.

"Now, Alice."

"I can't."

"You know why."

"Please, Joey."

"You think I don't know? Why you get dressed in the toilet all by yourself? Why you carry rubber bands around wherever you go?"

Alice gives a tight little shake of her head.

Gentler this time: "Let me see."

Trembling, Alice peels off the dress, lets it slip to the floor, revealing her flat chest, the elaborate bondage of tape and elastic around her genitals. Joey's eyebrows furrow.

She has fought against this her whole life. Against Lucas Ziegenfeus, who lives inside her. Or she lives inside him, resenting his physical body, the despicable hateful thing dangling between her legs that she straps down but doesn't have the courage to cut off.

"Yeah, all right." Joey indicates for her to get dressed. "You're wasted here, you know. You should go to Chicago. There are specialty shows in Bronzeville. Or join a carnival. Some of them still do he-she-it. Or be a bearded lady. Can you grow a beard?"

"I'm not a freak."

"You are in this world, princess."

"Let me stay. You didn't know. No one else has to find out. I can pull it off, I know I can, Joey. Please."

"What do you think will happen to us if someone sees you? Or Miss Magpie spills the beans? You've got her riled enough that she will, you know."

"We hightail it to the next town. Same as when Micky screwed the treasurer's daughter in Burton."

"This is different, princess. People like being fooled only up to a point. We'd be run out of town. Lynched, probably. All it takes is one rube to spot you wrapping up, one punter to get a hand up your dress before Bobby can intervene to protect your modesty."

"Then I won't perform. I can do candy. I could clean up, do the cooking, help the girls with their costume changes, their make-up."

"I'm sorry, Alice. It's a family show."

She can't bear it. She bursts from the caravan like a dove from a magician's sleeve, weeping. And runs straight into his arms.

"Hey there, sweetheart, careful. Are you all right?"

She can't believe it's him. That he's been waiting for her. She tries to speak, but her breath is coming in jerky sobs. She covers her face with her hands and he hugs her tight against his chest. She's never felt like she so utterly belonged somewhere before. She looks up into his face. His eyes are wet as if he's about to start crying himself.

"Don't," she says, filled with a desperate sympathy, touching her long, narrow fingers (girl's hands, her uncle always said) to his cheek. Everything in her wants this. She could fall away into him.

She is moved to see that he is just as overwhelmed. She intercepts him with her lips. His mouth is hot against hers, she can smell caramels on his breath before he pulls away, full of shock and wonder.

"Astonishing girl," he says. He is struggling against some torment inside, she can see by his face. *Let go,* she thinks. *Kiss me again. I'm yours.*

Maybe he's got some of the psychic gift Luella claims to have, because it's like he hears her and the resolve settles on him. "Come away with me, Alice. We don't have to do this."

Yes, the word is on her lips. And then Joey ruins everything. A torpid beetle silhouetted at the top of the stairs of the caravan. "Hey, what the fuck do you think you're doing?"

The stranger releases his hold on her. Joey lumbers down the stairs, waving that absurd jewel-topped cane. "This isn't that kind of show, my friend. Hands off, please."

"This has nothing to do with you, mister."

"Well pardon me. Did I not make myself fucking clear? Hands off, *now*."

"Go back inside, Joey," Alice says, filled with a calm so pure it leaves her giddy.

"Sorry, princess. Can't let it slide. Next thing you know, every rube's gonna want a piece."

"It's all right," her lover says, casually straightening his hat in defiance of Joey's bluster. But he is going, Alice realizes. She grabs at his arm, filled with panic.

"No! Don't leave me."

He chucks her lightly under the chin. "I'll come back for you, Alice," he says. "I promise."

KIRBY

27 August 1992

Kirby has been running the ad the first Saturday of every month, and every Thursday she clears out the mailbox. Sometimes there are only one or two. The most she got in one month was sixteen and a half, if you count the postcard scrawled with obscenities.

If Dan's in town, she goes to his place so they can go over them together. Today he's making her catfish and mash potatoes, bustling round his bachelor's kitchen while she goes through the haul.

The first mission of any mail day is to sort the replies into categories: sad but not useful, possibly interesting, and cranks.

A lot of them are heartbreaking. Like the one from a man whose sister had been shot. Eight pages, double-sided, written by hand, detailing how she caught a stray bullet in a drive-by. The only unusual object at the scene wasn't exactly out of place. Bullet casings.

Some of them are borderline. The woman who saw her mother's spirit lingering after a burglary gone wrong, to make sure to tell her to feed the cat. The boyfriend who blamed himself—if he'd just let the muggers take his watch, the gun wouldn't have gone off, she'd still be alive, and now he sees the same watch everywhere. In magazines and shop windows and billboard advertisements and on other people's wrists. Do you think it's God's way of punishing me? he wrote.

Kirby deals with these and the others that are clearly non-starters by sending back a brief and sincere letter thanking them for taking the time to write, and including information on free counseling and local victim support groups that Chet dug up for her.

In all these months, only two seemed worth following up on. A girl stabbed outside a nightclub, who was found with an antique Russian cross around her neck. But the letter was from her Russian mobster boyfriend, who wanted Kirby to negotiate with the police on his behalf to get it back, because it was his mother's and he couldn't exactly approach them directly given that it was his business dealings that got her killed in the first place.

The other was a teenage boy (wide net, she thought to herself at the time) found in a tunnel where the skater kids hung out, beaten to death, with a lead toy soldier inserted in his mouth. The parents were distraught, sitting in their living-room on a couch with a Peruvian throw over it, their hands clasped together as if their fingers had fused, asking if she had answers for them. Please, that's all they wanted. Why? What did he do to deserve this? It was excruciating.

"Any pictures from J today?" Dan says, looking over her shoulder. J is their regular, who sends photographs of artfully arranged death scenes of a girl with heavy kohl make-up and red hair. She could be either J herself, if you assumed J was a woman, or J's girlfriend. Drowned in a fishpond in a floaty white dress with her hair drifting out around her. Dead in a black lace number with elbow-length gloves, clutching a white rose in a pool of blood that looked suspiciously like paint.

Today's picture in the black envelope is of J sitting in a leather chair with her legs spread, in hold-up stockings and army boots, with her head tilted back and a spatter of red on the wall behind her, a revolver dangling from her limp fingers with perfectly manicured nails.

"I bet you it's an art student," Kirby complains. They never reply to J. And yet she keeps sending the kinky pictures.

"Better than film students," Dan says, casually, filleting the fish.

"It's still killing you, isn't it?" she grins.

"What?"

"If I slept with him."

"Of course you did. He was your first love. Not exactly a news flash, kiddo."

"You know what I mean."

"None of my business," he shrugs, like it's nothing, which gets to her, quite a lot, if she is honest with herself.

"All right. I won't tell you then."

"I still don't think you should do a documentary."

"Are you kidding? I already turned down Oprah."

"Ow, shit!" he says, burning himself on the steam as he drains the potatoes. "Seriously? I didn't know that."

"My mom did. I was still in the hospital. She got hectic with journalists. She said they were all assholes, either they were basically breaking into my hospital room to get an interview, or they never called her back."

"Ah," Dan says, feeling guilty.

"We had a lot of talk shows wanting me to come on. But it felt so voyeuristic. You know? It was part of why I had to take off. Just get away from all of that."

"I can understand."

"So don't worry. I told Fred where to shove his documentary."

Kirby holds a peach envelope up to her nose. "This one even smells good. That has to be a bad sign, right?"

"Hope you're not going to say the same thing about my cooking."

Kirby snickers and tears open the envelope. The return address reads: St. Helen's Retirement Village. She pulls out two pages of old-fashioned stationery. The writing goes over the front and back of both pages. "Well, read it," Dan says, mashing the potatoes. He takes a particular pride in getting all the lumps out.

Dear Mr. KM,

This is a peculiar letter to find myself writing and I confess that I hesitated, but your (rather obtuse) advertisement in the newspaper demands a response because it ties in with a family mystery that I have long been obsessed with even if it falls outside of your specified time-frame.

It feels a little alarming to be sharing this information with you when I have no idea of what your intentions are. What was the purpose of your ad? Academic or some morbid curiosity? Are you a detective with the Chicago PD or a conman who trades on people's hurt for whatever satisfaction it gives you?

I'll spare you further speculation because, I suppose, this is an opportunity that, like all opportunities, carries its own risk, but I trust that once you have read this, you will reply, if only to clarify your interest in this subject.

My name is Nella Owusu, nee Jordan. My father and mother were both killed during World War Two, he abroad in the course of duty, she in Seneca, in a horrifying unsolved murder in the winter of 1943.

My siblings — we were moved around between various orphan-

*ages and foster homes, but in adulthood were able to reconnect—
think that I am inappropriately absorbed with this. But I was the
oldest. I remember her best.*

*Your ad specified that you were particularly interested in "out of
place artifacts."*

*Well, when my mother's body was consigned to the earth and the
possessions found on her body released to us, the "artifacts" included
a baseball card.*

*I mention this because my mother had no interest in the game. I
cannot imagine why she would possibly have had a card on her person at the time of her death. We can discuss this further, if you can
tell me more about the nature of your inquiry, and if I am up to it.
I must warn you that I have been unwell of late.*

*I trust that you will reply and not keep me guessing as to your
motive.*

Kind regards,

N. Owusu

"Crank file," Dan declares, setting the plate down in front of
her on the coffee table.

"I don't know. I think it might be worth checking out."

"If you're bored, I can find you stuff to do. I need background
for the St. Louis game coming up."

"Actually, I was thinking about trying to write something about
all this. Call it the Murder Diaries."

"*Sun-Times* would never run it."

"No, but maybe a zine would. *The Lumpen Times* or *Steve Albini
Thinks We Suck.*"

"Sometimes you speak a foreign language," Dan says, through a
mouthful of food.

"Get with the program, dude," she shrugs, pitch-perfect Bart
Simpson.

"Do. You. Speak. English?" Dan shouts in the manner of tourists traveling abroad.

"Small press alternative magazines."

"Oh, that reminds me. Talking about not-so-small and alternative. Chet asked me to pass this on. He said he knows no one got stabbed, but he says you're the only other person in the newsroom who would appreciate the weirdness." He goes to get a cutting out of his battered leather briefcase. It's barely more than a line item.

Drug Bust Turns Up Old-Fashioned Cash

Englewood: A police raid on a local drug den turned up more than crack vials and caps of heroin. Several handguns were recovered from the apartment of Toneel Roberts, a known drug dealer, as well as $600 in expired currency dating back to 1950, originally called Silver Certificates. The bills can be easily identified by the blue seal on the front. Police have speculated that the money most likely came from an old stash and have warned local business owners that it is not legal tender.

"That's really sweet of him," she says and means it.

"You know, when you've wrapped up your degree, there's a chance I could get you a real job with the paper," Dan offers. "Maybe even in lifestyle, if that's where you wanted to be."

"That's really sweet of *you,* Dan Velasquez."

He blushes and looks down at his fork with great purpose. "Assuming you don't want to go to the *Trib* or one of those underground zine things."

"I haven't really thought about it."

"Yeah, well, best you start. You're going to crack the case and then what are you going to do?"

But she can tell by the way he says it that he doesn't believe it'll ever happen.

"The fish is lovely," she says.

HARPER

10 April 1932

═════

For the first time he is almost reluctant to go and make a kill. It was the way the showgirl kissed him. Full of love and hope and desire. Is it so bad to want that? He knows he is putting it off, delaying the inevitable. He should be hunting for the future version of her, instead of strolling down State Street like he doesn't have a care.

When who should he see but his little piggy nurse, window-shopping and all tucked up nice and tight under another man's arm. She is plumper, in a better coat. The padding suits her, he thinks, and recognizes the thought as covetous. Her gentleman friend is the doctor from the hospital, with his mane of hair and a fine cashmere scarf. He last saw him, Harper recalls, staring up sightlessly from a dumpster in 1993.

"Hello, Etta," Harper says, moving in too close, almost stepping on their toes. He can smell her perfume. Too-sweet citrus. It smells whoreish. It suits her.

"Oh," Etta says, her expression racing through seasons: recognition, dismay, a sharp glee.

"Is this someone you know?" The doctor gives an uncertain half-smile.

"You fixed my leg," Harper says. "I'm sorry you don't remember me, Doc."

"Oh yes," he blusters, as if he knows exactly who Harper is. "And how *is* your leg, sport?"

"Much better. I barely need the crutch. Although it still comes in useful sometimes."

Etta snuggles in tighter to the doctor, clearly aiming to get under Harper's skin. "We were just off to a show."

"You've got both your shoes today," Harper points out.

"And I am going dancing in them," she sniffs.

"Well, I don't know if we're going to manage that as well," the doctor says, thrown by the exchange. "But if you like. Hang it all, why not?" He looks to Etta for his cue. Harper knows his kind exactly. Twisted round a woman's fingers like a cat's cradle. He thinks he's in control, which lets him defer to her because he's trying to impress. He thinks he's safe in the world, but he doesn't know its reaches.

"Don't let me interrupt you. Miss Etta. Doctor." Harper nods respectfully, and moves on before the man can recover himself enough to take offense.

"It was very nice to see you, Mr. Curtis," Etta calls over her shoulder. Hedging her bets. Or egging him on.

He follows the good doctor home from the hospital the next night, after his shift. Tells him that he wants to take him out for dinner to thank him for seeing him right. When the man politely tries to decline Harper's invitation, he is forced to get out his knife, a new one, to convince him to come back with him to the House.

"Just popping in and out," he says, pushing the man's head

down to duck under the planks barring the door, closing it behind them, and re-opening it sixty years into the future, where the doctor's fate is already awaiting him. He doesn't even struggle. Not very much. Harper leads him to the dumpster and then strangles him with his own scarf. The hardest part is tipping him in after.

"Don't worry," he tells the puce-faced corpse, "you'll have company soon."

DAN

11 September 1992

―――――

This is perspective. Being on planes. The world teeny tiny beneath you and far away from a girl somewhere below, as unreal as the flotsam of clouds washed up on the blue of the sky.

This is a whole other universe, with very explicit rules about how things work. Like sensible instructions on what to do in case of disaster. Inflate life vest. Fit the mask to your face. Assume the brace position. As if any of that would make a difference if the plane went down in flames. If only the rest of life had such facile placebos.

Keep your seatbelt buckled. Return your tray table to the upright position. Do not try to flirt with the flight attendants unless time is on your side and you still have all your hair and ideally also a seat in business class and a pair of shiny loafers slipped off and neatly set to one side in all that extra leg room, the better to show off your cotton-rich designer socks, my dear.

This is the last time he gets a seat at the front of economy, where he's in ear-shot of the champagne being offered behind the curtain and the smell of real food instead of soggy turkey rolls. Especially on the red-eye.

"Now they're just rubbing it in," he mutters to Kevin. But Kevin doesn't hear him because he's plugged into his Discman, the earbuds leaking bass-heavy fragments that come out uglier and more distorted than the actual music even, and flipping through travel stories about impossibly out-of-reach hotels in the inflight magazine. It leaves Dan alone in his head, which is, frankly, the last place he wants to be. Not with her in there.

Distraction is temporary. Oh, he can write out notes, lose himself in player statistics (whoever said sport was stupid never worked through the algebra of batting averages and RBI), but his thoughts loop back like a dog gnawing at a sore on its flank. Worst of all—and *this* is how pathetic he's become—pop songs make sense.

None of which makes his chances any better than Kevin's of holidaying at a five-star ski resort in the French Alps with Hollywood starlets. It's like his divorce all over again. The hardest part of which was not the despair and the betrayal and the horrific things they said to each other, but that splinter of unreasonable hope.

It's completely inappropriate. He's too jaded, she's too young, they're both too fucked up. He's confusing sympathy with infatuation. If he waits it out, it will numb itself. It will go away. He just has to be patient and avoid being a reckless idiot. Time heals. Crushes let up. Splinters work their way out. Doesn't mean they don't leave scars that itch.

There's a phone message waiting for him at the hotel in St. Louis when he gets in. Another pleasantly anonymous room with offensively inoffensive wall art and a view over a parking lot. The only difference between this room and every other one he's ever stayed in is the red flashing light on the telephone. It's her, his heart says. And he says back, Shuddup. But it is. Breathless, excited. "Hey, Dan, it's me. Please call me back as soon as you get this."

Press one to replay. Press three to call back. Press seven to delete. Press four to save.

"Hi," she says, sounding fresh and wide-awake at 2 a.m. "What took you so long?"

"Me? You're the one who hasn't been answering the phone." He doesn't tell her that he tried her from outside the press room, during the yawn-inducing ninth inning. And again from a payphone outside the bar where the guys went for drinks after the presser, where he sipped a Diet Coke and tried to muster enthusiasm for the conversational highlights replay of Ozzie Smith stealing another base or Olivares' crazy inning. "Did you see the way he plinked Arias in the second?" Kevin raved.

Or that he's listened to her message six times in between. One-four-one-one-one-one. You'd think he'd be more excited that his team won.

"Sorry," she says. "I went for a drink."

"With Fred?"

"No, dumbass. Let that go already. With one of the editors of *Screamin'* magazine. She's interested in the Murder Diaries story."

"Do you think that's a good idea? On top of everything else you've got going on?" Are there degrees of neutral? He tries to gear-shift up. He's seen television reporters do it. Politely disengaged but with an arched eyebrow.

"It's a long-term thing. I can send it in when it's ready. If it's ready. If I feel like it."

"So, tell me how it went with the baseball card lady."

"It was very sad, actually. It's not really a retirement village. More of a nursing home. Her husband was there to meet me. He owns a Ghanaian restaurant in Belmont. He says she has early-on-set Alzheimer's, even though she's only in her sixties. It's genetic. Her mind comes and goes. Some days she's really clear and others she's not there at all."

"And when you saw her?"

"Not so much. We had tea and she kept calling me Maria, who was a girl in one of the adult literacy classes she used to teach."

"Ouch."

"But her husband was great, we talked for about an hour afterwards. It's like the letter said. Her mom was murdered in 1943, really horrible case, and when the cops finally got round to returning her possessions to the family, there was a baseball card in with the stuff they said they found on her body. It was with her aunt and uncle for a long time and when they passed, it came to her."

"So which card was it?"

"Hang on, I convinced the woman in the front office to make a copy for me." There is the sound of paper being dug out of a bag. "Here. Jackie Robinson. Brooklyn Dodgers."

"Impossible," he says automatically.

"That's what it says." She's defensive.

"And she died in 1943?"

"Yes. I got a copy of the death certificate too. I know what you're going to say. I know how unlikely it is. But hear me out. There have been killing partners before, right? The Hillside Stranglers were cousins who raped and strangled women in LA together."

"If you say so."

"Trust me. I think this is part of it. My case. It could be a father-and-son team. An older psychopath who mentored a younger one. Not necessarily related, I guess. He might be ninety years old now, he might be dead. But his partner's carrying on the tradition of leaving something on the body. Vintage killers *plural,* Dan. It's the younger one who attacked me and Julia Madrigal and who knows who else. I'm gonna go back to the early boxes we set aside. This could go way back."

"I'm sorry, Kirby. It's wrong," he says, as gently as he can.

"What are you talking about?" she demands.

Dan sighs. "Do you know what a ghost ballplayer is?"

"I'm guessing it's not the obvious. No horror-movie hauntings of the dugout. The skull-faced fielder, the devil who pitched the flaming hell-ball—"

"Correct," he cuts her off.

"I don't think I want to hear what you have to say."

"You probably don't, and that's too bad. The most famous one is a guy called Lou Proctor. He was a Cleveland telegraph operator who inserted his own name into the Indians' box score in 1912."

"But he didn't exist."

"As a real person, but not as a ballplayer. It was a hoax. They picked it up in '87 and expunged it from the records. Seventy-five years' worth of his fifteen minutes. There've been others that weren't premeditated. Sloppy record-keeping, somebody gets a name wrong, makes a typing error."

"This is not a fucking *typo,* Dan."

"It's a mistake. She's wrong. You said it yourself, the poor woman has Alzheimer's, for God's sake. Listen to me. Jackie Robinson only started playing in the major leagues in '47. First black player to do so. Had a shitty time of it. His own team tried to sabotage him. The other teams used to try to gouge his legs with their shoes as they slid into base. I'll look it up, but I promise you, no one had even heard of him in '43. He didn't even exist as a ballplayer yet."

"You're so damn sure of your statistics."

"It's baseball."

"She might have got it mixed up with another card."

"That's what I'm saying. Maybe the cops did. Maybe it was sitting in somebody's attic for years. Didn't she say she was raised in foster care? And it got thrown together with a bunch of other junk up there."

"You're saying there was no card."

"I don't know. Was it in the police report?"

"They weren't great at keeping records in 1943."

"Then I'd say you've got your hopes pinned on something that doesn't exist."

"Crap." She throws it off, lightly.

"Sorry."

"Whatever. No big deal. Back to the drawing-board. Give me a shout when you get home. I'll see what new looney-tunes idea I can come up with to entertain you."

"Kirby—"

"You think I don't know you're just indulging me?"

"Someone fucking has to," he says, losing his temper right back at her. "At least I'm not trying to exploit you for my third-rate film project."

"I can do this on my own."

"Yeah, but then who would listen to your crazy theories?"

"The librarians. They love crazy theories." He can hear the smile in her voice. It makes him grin back.

"They love *donuts!* There's a difference. And there aren't enough day-old baked goods in the world to put up with your crap, trust me."

"Not even glazed?"

"Or cream-filled or double-dipped in chocolate with rainbow sprinkles!" he shouts into the phone, waving his arms, as if she could see him.

"I'm sorry for being a jerk."

"You can't help it. You're in your twenties. It comes with the territory."

"Nice. An age diss."

"I don't even know what that means," he grumps.

"You think there might have been another baseball card?"

"I think you should take it as interesting, but not helpful. Start a wild-card box where you can keep your crazy theories, and don't let them get in the way of what's real." Like this, he thinks.

"Okay, you're right. Thank you. I owe you a donut."

"Or a dozen."

"Good night, Dan."

"G'night, whippersnapper."

HARPER
No Time

═══════

There was a bantam cockerel on the farm that used to have seizures. You could bring them on by flashing a light in its eyes. Harper would lie on his stomach in the long grass that made his head feel ripe in summer, and use a bit of broken mirror to stun the rooster. (The same shard he used to cut the legs off one of the chicks, pressing down on the back of the silvered glass with his hand wrapped in an old shirt.)

The cock would be scratching in the dirt and twitching its head in that stupid way chickens have, then suddenly it would go blank and stand frozen and glassy eyed: a vacant thing. A second later it would be back, wholly oblivious. A stutter in its brain.

That's what the Room feels like: stuttering.

He can sit in here for hours, perched on the edge of the bed looking at his assembled gallery. The objects are always here, even when he takes them away.

The names of the girls have been traced over again and again until the letters have started to fray. He remembers doing it. He has no recollection of doing it. One of these things must be true.

It tightens something in his chest, like a gear in a watch that's been wound up too far.

He rubs his fingertips together and finds them silky with chalk dust. It doesn't seem clear anymore. It feels like doom. It makes him feel defiant, like doing something just to see what will happen. Like with Everett and the truck.

His brother caught him with the little chick. Harper was crouched on his haunches over it as it flapped its stubby wings and dragged itself forward, peeping-peeping-peeping. Its stumps left thick snail-trails of blood in the dust. He heard Everett coming, the slap-slap of shoes that would get passed down to him, the heel already peeling off. He squinted up at the older boy, who stood watching him without saying anything, the morning sun behind his head so he couldn't make out his expression. The chick squeaked and fluttered, making broken passage across the yard. Everett disappeared. He came back with a shovel and smashed the bird to a pulp with one blow.

He tossed the crush of feathers and gluey innards over-arm into the long grass behind the coop, then cuffed Harper hard enough to knock him on his ass. "Don't you know where our eggs come from? Stupid." He bent to pull him up, dusted off his front. His brother never stayed angry with him. "Don't tell Da," Everett said.

The thought hadn't occurred to Harper. The same way it didn't occur to him to pull up the handbrake the day of the accident.

Harper and Everett Curtis drove into town to pick up feed. Like the start of a nursery rhyme. Everett let him drive. But Harper, maybe eleven years old, took a corner too hard in the Red Baby and clipped the edge of the ditch. His brother grabbed the wheel and yanked the truck back into the road. But even Harper could tell the tire was punctured, by the flap of rubber and the way the steering went flabby in his hands.

"Brake!" Everett yelled. "Harder!" He braced himself against the steering wheel and Harper rammed his foot down on the pedal. Everett's head bounced off the side window, splintering the glass. The truck slewed sideways, the trees spinning and blurring together, before it came to a juddering stop across the middle of the road. Harper turned off the ignition. The engine clicked and tutted.

"It's not your fault," Everett said, holding the side of his head, where a knot was already swelling. "It's my fault. I shouldn't have let you drive." He swung the door open into the hazy morning, already humid. "Stay here."

Harper turned in the cab to see Everett digging around in the back for the spare. A breeze rippled through the cornfields, too slight to do anything but move the heat around.

His brother walked round to the front with the jack and the wheel spanner. He grunted as he levered it under the truck and cranked it up. The first nut came off easy, but the second one was stuck fast. His scrawny shoulders strained with the effort. "Just stay there, I can do it," he shouted to Harper, who wasn't planning to move.

He started kicking at the handle of the spanner. And that's when the truck slipped off the jack. It started rolling slowly forward towards the ditch again.

"Harper!" Everett yelled, irritated. And then, higher-pitched, panicky as the truck kept coming, "Pull the handbrake, Harper!"

But he didn't. He sat tight as Everett tried to push the truck back, his hands on the bonnet. The weight of it knocked him off his feet before it went over him. His pelvis made a sharp snapping sound, like a pinecone in the fireplace. It was hard to hear anything else over Everett screaming. It went on and on. Eventually, Harper got out to see.

His brother was the color of old meat, his face a purple-gray, the white of his eyes shot with blood. A shard of bone stuck out his thigh, shockingly white. There was a thick pool of grease around the tire where it was resting on his hip. Not grease, Harper realized. Everything looks the same when you turn it inside out.

"Run," Everett croaked. "Go get help. Run, dammit!"

Harper stared. He started walking, looking back over his shoulder. Fascinated.

"Run!"

It took two hours to fetch someone from the Crombie farm up the way. Too late for Everett to be able to walk again. Their father tanned Harper raw. He would have beat Everett too, if he weren't a goddamn cripple. The accident meant they had to hire a man. Harper had to do extra chores, which made him mad.

Everett refused to acknowledge him. He went sour like potato mash left too long in the still, lying in bed, staring out the window. A year after that, they had to sell the truck. Three years later, the farm. Don't let anyone tell you the Depression was the beginning of farmers' troubles.

The windows and doors got boarded up. They loaded everything onto a truck they borrowed from a neighbor to go and sell whatever they could. Everett was so much luggage.

Harper jumped off at the first town. He went to war, but he never went back to where he came from.

That's a possibility, he supposes. To leave the House and never come back. Take the money and run. Set up with a nice girl. No more killing. No more feeling the knife twist and the hot slip of a girl's insides spilling out, watching the fire die in her eyes.

He looks at the wall, at the stuttering objects. The cassette tape leaps out at him, urgent, demanding. There are five names left.

He doesn't know what happens after that, but he does know that hunting them through time is no longer enough for him.

He thinks he would like to switch it up a bit. To play within the loops he's already discovered, courtesy of Mr. Bartek and the good doctor.

He would like to try to kill them first and then go back and find them before, when they are innocent of what is going to befall them. That way he'll be able to converse politely with their younger and sweeter selves, setting them up for what he has already done to them, with the images of their deaths playing in his head. A reverse hunt, to make things more interesting.

And the House seems willing. The object that shines most brightly now, willing him to *take it,* is a pin-on button, red and white and blue with a flying pig.

MARGOT

5 December 1972

Natch, Margot has spotted the guy following them. All the way from the 103rd Street station, five blocks away. That's one block too far to be a coincidence, if you ask her. And okay, maybe she's over-cautious because she's Jane-ing today. Or maybe it's being in Roseland at this time of night that sets her nerves twanging like a banjo. But there's no way she's going to let Jemmie go home alone in her condition. They try to make it easy on the women. But it still hurts and it's still scary and it's still illegal.

She supposes that it's possible that the guy could, perfectly reasonably, just happen to be strolling along the exact same route at this exact same time of the evening in the pouring rain, tra-la-la-la-la.

Gangster-Pervert-Undercover-Gangster-Pervert-Undercover she sings in her head, running through the options in time to Jemmie's steps. Shuffle-shuffle like an old lady, leaning heavily on her arm and holding her stomach. Long sportscoat could mean cop. Or pervert. But he's been in a fight, which probably means pervert or mobster. The Outfit seem to have finally cottoned on that Jane don't make money. Not like the "respectable" doctors who charge $500 and more to have someone pick you up on the street corner and blindfold you so you can't identify them, and scrape your womb out and dump you back after it's done without so much as a how-do-you-do-ma'am-have-a-nice-day. Or maybe he's just some guy. Some pie-in-the-sky kinda guy.

"Say again?" Jemmie's breath catches from the pain.

"Oh jeez, sorry, thinking out loud. Don't pay me any mind, Jemmie. Oh, hey, see, we're nearly home."

"He wasn't, you know."

"Wasn't what?" Margot is only half-listening. The man has picked up his pace, skip-running across the street against the light to keep up with them. He steps ankle-deep into a puddle, curses and shakes out his shoes, then shoots her a goofy smile that's meant to be disarming.

Jemmie is angry with her. "Some pie-in-the-sky, like you was suggestin'. We engaged. Gonna get married when he gets back. Soon as I turn sixteen."

"That's swell," Margot says. She is not on top form. Normally she would have called Jemmie on this, a grown man shacking up with a minor before he ships off to Vietnam, promising her the world when he can't even manage to put on a rubber. Fourteen years old. Only slightly bigger than the kids she subs at Thurgood Marshall Middle School. It makes her heart hurt, man. But she is distracted from going into full lecture mode, because she is turning the uncomfortable thought over in her head that this guy dogging their steps looks familiar. Which brings her back to her litany. Gangster-pervert-undercover-cop. Or worse. Her stomach flip-flops. A disgruntled partner. They've had them before. Isabel Sterritt's husband who bust up her face and broke her arm when he found out what she'd done. Which was exactly the reason she didn't want to have another baby with him.

Oh please, let it not be a maniac partner.

"Can we . . . can we stop for a moment?" Jemmie has gone the color of stale chocolate that's melted in your purse. Sweat and rain shine on her forehead through the acne. Broken-down car. No umbrella. Could this day get worse?

"We're nearly there, okay? You're doing so well. Keep it up. Just one more block. Can you do that?"

Jemmie reluctantly lets her tug her along. "Are you going to come in with me?"

"Won't your mom think it's weird? A white girl bringing you home with stomach cramps?"

Margot is memorable. It's her height. Six foot tall with strawberry-blonde hair parted down the middle. She played basketball in high school, but she was too laid back to take it seriously.

"But can't you come in anyway?"

"If you want me to, I will," she says, trying to find some enthusiasm. Explaining to family members doesn't always go down well. "Let's see how we do, okay?"

She wishes Jemmie had found them earlier. The service is listed in the phone book, under "Jane How," but how would you know if you didn't? Ditto the ads in the alternative newspapers or pasted up at the laundromat. There's no way for a girl like Jemmie to find them except by personal referral, and that took three and a half months and a replacement social worker who was sympathetic to the cause. Sometimes she thinks it's the substitutes who make the real difference. Substitute teachers and social workers and doctors. Fresh eyes. Big picture. Stepping up. Even if it's only temporary. Sometimes temporary is all you need.

Fifteen weeks is borderline. You just can't take a chance.

Twenty women a day and they haven't lost one yet. Unless you count the girl they turned away because she had a terrible infection, telling her to go see a doctor, to come back when it cleared up. They found out later she died in the hospital. If only they'd seen her sooner. Like Jemmie.

Jemmie's was one of the last cards to get claimed. The easy cases go fast, all the volunteers sitting in Big Jane's cozy living-room in Hyde Park with the photographs of her kids on the bookshelf and "Me and Bobby McGee" on the record player, drinking tea and haggling over which patients to take, like they're trading horses.

Twenty-year-old co-ed, five weeks along, lives in Lake Bluff burbs? That 3×5 card is snapped up in the first go-around. But the forty-eight-year-old housewife worn down by seven kids who just can't go through it again? The farm manager whose twenty-two-week old baby is so deformed the doctor says he (or she) won't live more than an hour after birth, but insists she carry it to term? The fourteen-year-old from the West Side who rocks up with a jar full of pennies because that's all she has and begs you not to tell her ma? Those cards come up again and again until Big Jane growls in exasperation, "Well *somebody* has to take it." And in the meantime, the messages are still coming in on the answering machine, still being transcribed on to new cards for tomorrow and the day after. Leave your name and a number we can reach you on. We can help you. We'll call you back.

How many has Margot facilitated now? Sixty? A hundred? She doesn't do the actual D&C. She's clumsy at the best of times. It's her size. The world wasn't built to fit her, and she doesn't trust herself with a dainty curette. But she's real good at holding hands and explaining what's happening. Knowing helps. What's being done to you and why. Name that pain, she jokes. She gives the women a scale of reference. Is it better or worse than stubbing your toe? And compared to finding out that your crush is un-requited? A paper cut? Breaking up with your best friend? How about realizing you're turning into your mother? She gets actual laughs.

Most of the women cry afterwards, though. Sometimes be-cause they're sorry or guilty or scared. Even the most certain ones have doubts. Inhuman not to. But mainly it's out of sheer re-lief. Because it's hard and terrible, but now it's over and now they can get on with their lives.

It's getting tougher. Not just the mafia goons muscling in or the cops who've been coming down heavy since Yvette Coulis's self-righteous sister was so outraged that they dared give her an abortion, that she's been writing letters to the city council and generally sticking a bee up everyone's butt. The worst part was that she started hanging around at the Front, harassing the friends or husbands or boyfriends or moms and sometimes dads who the women brought along to support them. They had to move the Front to another apartment to get rid of her. The cops started sniffing around after that. The tallest men you ever saw, like that was a qualification to get into the homicide unit, in matchy-match trench coats and grumpy expressions that said this was a waste of their time.

But that's not even the biggest problem—which is that it's le-gal in New York now. Which should be a good thing, and maybe Illinois will follow, right? But it means that girls with money hop on a train or a bus or a plane and the ones who come to Jane are really desperate—the poor, the young, the old, the far-along.

Those are the ones she struggles with the most. Even the most hardline Janes do. For sure. Wrap up your first fetus in an old T-shirt for a burial shroud and toss it in a dumpster three miles from the Place and see how you like it. No one said it would be pretty, yanking despair out of a woman.

And then the man takes her by the arm. "Excuse me, ma'am. I think you dropped this," he says, offering her something in his hand. She has no idea how he caught up with them so suddenly. And she's certain she knows that lopsided smile.

"Margot?" Jemmie is frightened.

"You go along home, Jemmie," Margot says in her best, most authoritative school-marm voice, which is not particularly either, considering she's only twenty-five. "I'll be right behind you."

There shouldn't be any complications now. But if she does have to go to hospital, the doctors won't give her any trouble. Jane has started using Leunbach's paste. No pain, no blood, no problems, no way of proving the miscarriage was induced. She'll be just fine.

She checks to make sure that Jemmie is moving away and turns to face him, pulling back her shoulders and straightening up so she can look him direct in the eye.

"Can I help you, *sir?*"

"I've been looking all over for you, sweetheart. I wanted to return this."

She finally looks at the object he's shoving in her face. A protest button, home-made. She knows this because she drew it herself. A pig with wings. "Pigasus for President" it reads in her block capitals, sloping up, unevenly to the right. The Yippies' official candidate in '68 because a pig could hardly be worse than the real politicians.

"Do you recognize this? Can you tell me when you last saw it? Do you remember me? You must remember me." He asks it with terrible intensity.

"Yes," she gasps. "The Democratic Convention." It comes rushing back like a slap. The scene outside the Hilton, because their leader, Tom Hayden, had told them to get the hell out of the park as the police started laying into people, pulling them down off the statues they'd climbed up.

If they were going to be tear-gassed, the whole city would be tear-gassed, he was shouting. If blood was spilled in Grant Park, it would be spilled all over Chicago! Seven thousand people surging into the streets against the cops pushing back. Still angry about Martin Luther King, the whole of the West Side burning. The feeling of the concrete brick flying out of her hand like it was yanked on a string. She was aware of the cop barging into her, the baton glancing off her side, but she didn't feel any pain until afterwards, in the shower when she saw the bruising.

The news cameras and the lights on the steps of the hotel, chanting with the crowd at the top of her lungs, "The whole world is watching! The whole world is watching!" until the cops sprayed the entire crowd with mace. Yippies. Bystanders. Reporters. Everybody. She thought she heard Rob croaking, "The pigs are whores," but she couldn't find him in the crush of people crying and shoving, the spotlights glancing off the blue police helmets that were everywhere, batons slamming down mechanically.

Margot was leaning on the hood of a car on Balboa, her head down, spitting up saliva and rubbing her eyes with the hem of her T-shirt, which only made it worse. Something made her look up to see him, limping straight towards her, a tall man full of such ferocious intent. Like a brick on a string.

He stopped in front of her and gave her a skew smile. Inoffensive. Charming even. It was so out of place in this chaos that she moaned and tried to shove him away, suddenly terrified the way she hadn't been of the cops or the crowd or the burning that had threatened to collapse her chest.

He caught her wrists. "We've met before. But you won't remember." Such a weird thing to say, it stuck with her.

"Here," he grabbed hold of her lapel, as if to pull her to her feet, but instead he yanked off her button. "This is it." He let go so abruptly that she fell onto the car, sobbing in outrage and shock.

She staggered home, looking forward to showering for an hour before sinking onto the couch and smoking a jay to calm down. But when she unlocked the door and pushed past the beaded curtain, it was to find Rob in the middle of fucking some girl in their bed. "Oh hey, baby, this is Glenda," he said, not even pausing mid-thrust. "Want to join us?" She used her lipstick to write "asshole" on the mirror, pressing down so hard that she broke it in half.

They fought for five and a half hours after Glenda finally got the hint and took off. Made up. Had make-up sex that didn't turn out so well. (Turned out Glenda had crabs.) Broke up a week later. And then Rob slunk off to Toronto to avoid being drafted and she finished college and got into teaching because they hadn't managed to change the world, and she was disillusioned. Until she found Jane.

And the thing with the scary limping guy who so admired her button that he stole it in the middle of a riot became a funny anecdote she could break out at dinner parties or meetings, but then she got better stories, ones that actually went somewhere. She hadn't thought about any of that for ages. Until now.

He takes advantage of her shock. Slings his arm around her, pulling her close and slides the knife into her stomach. Right there, in the middle of the street in the rain. She can't believe it. She opens her mouth to scream, but only manages to gag as he twists the knife. A cab drives past, the light on, water spraying up from the tires, splashing against Margot's red pants, even as the blood starts welling up over her waistband, soaking into the ridges of corduroy, obscenely warm. She looks for Jemmie, but she's already disappeared round the corner. Safe.

"Tell me the future," he whispers, his breath warm against her ear. "Don't make me read it in your entrails."

"Screw you," she gasps, less strident than she imagined it in her head, and she tries to push him away. But all the strength has gone out of her arms and he has learned. Worse. He knows he is invincible. "Have it your way," he shrugs, still smiling. He wrenches her thumb backwards—it's unbearable—and uses it to shepherd her away to a construction site.

He pushes her down into the mud of the foundation pit and binds her up with wire and gags her and takes his time with the killing. When he is done, he tosses the tennis ball in after her.

He doesn't intend that she shouldn't be found. But the man operating the digger pushing the rubble into the pit next morning catches only a glimpse of reddish-blond hair in the mud and manages to convince himself that it's a dead cat, even though he sometimes lies awake at night and thinks it wasn't.

Her murderer takes the object he needs and then tosses her purse into an empty lot. The contents are picked over by various petty opportunists until a good citizen turns in the bag at the police station. But by that time all the useful stuff is gone. The cops can't identify someone from the cassette recordings she made. Copies of the music playing on Big Jane's player in that Hyde Park apartment, crackly and low-fi from the jerry-rigged connection of tapedeck to LP. The Mamas and Papas, Dusty Springfield, the Lovin' Spoonful, Peter, Paul & Mary, Janis Joplin.

Jemmie goes to bed early the night of her illegal abortion, complaining about something nasty she ate. Her parents don't question her, never find out the truth. Her guy does not come back from Vietnam, or maybe he does, but not to her. She gets good grades in school, goes to community college, but drops out to get married at twenty-one. She has three children, no complications. Goes back to school at thirty-four and ends up working for City Parks.

The women of Jane worry themselves sick, but there is nothing to show that Margot didn't just get tired and pack it all in, maybe to join that ex-boyfriend in Canada. And besides, they're preoccupied with their own troubles. A year later, Jane is raided. Eight women are arrested. Their lawyer keeps delaying the case for months and months, awaiting the outcome of a big trial that she says will change women's rights to be in control of their own bodies, forever.

KIRBY

19 November 1992

─────

Division 1 is the oldest part of the Cook County correctional facility, which is currently expanding with two new buildings to house the overflow of prisoners. Al Capone enjoyed a stay at the county's expense here back when there was direct access from the street. Now maximum security means that it's barricaded behind three layers of fences; you have to pass through one gate at a time, twirls of barbed wire double-stacked on top. The grass between the fences is patchy and yellow. The facade with its gothic lettering and lion heads and narrow rows of windows is dingy and discolored.

The historic building hasn't been afforded the same care and attention as the Field Museum or the Art Institute, although the prison has similar rules for visitors. No eating, no touching.

Kirby wasn't counting on having to take off her boots to go through the X-ray machine. It takes her five minutes on either side to undo them and lace them up again afterwards.

She is more freaked out than she wants to admit. It's culture shock. Because it's just like the movies, only tenser and smellier.

There's a fug of sweat and anger in here, and the dull noise of too many people cooped up together diffusing through the thick walls. The paint on the security gate is scuffed and scratched, especially around the lock, which makes a heavy kerlunk as the guard opens it to let her through.

Jamel Pelletier is already waiting for her at one of the tables in the visitors' room. He looks worse than the photographs of him in the *Sun-Times* clips Chet pulled for her. The cornrows are gone and his hair is short and neat, but his skin is greasy. He has a scattering of fine pimples across his forehead above wide eyes with thick lashes and scruffy eyebrows which make him look painfully young, even if he's in his mid-twenties now. Older than her. The tan prison uniform hangs on him like a sack, the number printed in bold letters down his chest. It's an automatic civility, moving to shake his hand, but he scrunches up his face with an amused huff and shakes his head.

"Crap. Already I'm breaking the rules," she says. "Thanks for meeting with me."

"You look different than I thought," he says. "You bring any chocolate?" His voice has a husky rasp. She guesses hanging yourself from the bars by your own pants and crushing your larynx will do that to you. The thought of another eight years in here would make that a conceivable option.

"Sorry. I should have thought of that."

"You gon' help me?"

"I'm gonna try."

"My lawyer said I shouldn't talk to you. She's plenty mad."

"Because I lied to her?"

"Yeah. Those people do that professionally. You don't try to out-bullshit a lawyer, man."

"It seemed like the best way to find out about the case. I'm sorry."

"You sorted it out with her?"

"I've left messages." Kirby sighs.

"Well, if it's not okay with her, then it's not with me neither," he says, getting up to go. He jerks his head at the guard, who looks annoyed, and starts to move toward him, reaching for the handcuffs at his belt.

"Wait. Don't you want to hear me out?"

"Your letter spelled it out pretty clear. You think it was some psycho killer did the same to you." But he hesitates all the same.

"Pelletier," the guard barks. "You coming or going?"

"Staying for a bit. Sorry, Mo. You know what bitches are like." He gives her a smug leer.

"Not cool," Kirby says, keeping her voice level.

"I give a fuck," he snarls. But he momentarily drops his front. Still young, still scared as hell, Kirby thinks. She has that T-shirt.

"Did you do it?"

"You serious? Anyone in here going to say different if you ask them that? I tell you what. You figure out what you're gonna do for me and I'll help you."

"I'll do a story on you."

He stares at her and then breaks into a grin so wide it could swallow you up. "Shit. You for real? You already tried that one."

"You play sports? I'll cover it." That would be a great piece, actually. Prison basketball. Harrison might even go for it.

"Nah. I do weights."

"All right. A profile interview on you. Your side of the story. Maybe for a magazine." She doesn't know how much currency he'll put in *Screamin',* but she's desperate.

"Huh," he says, like he's still not buying it. But Kirby knows the truth is everybody wants *someone* to hear them out. "What you want to know?"

"Where were you at the time of the murder?"

"With Shante. Banging that fine girl's ass up against the wall." He flaps his hand so that his fingers make a sloppy smacking sex sound against his palm. It sounds uncannily like the real thing. "You know it, baby."

"I can just as easily leave."

"Ooooh. Did I offend you?"

"It offends me when psychos get away with slashing up girls, jerk-wad. I'm trying to find the killer. Do you want to help me or not?"

"Relax, girl. I'm messing with you. I was with Shante, but she didn't want to testify 'cos she on parole and hanging with my ass is a violation 'cos of my priors, right? Better I go to jail than the mother of my child. We didn't think it was gonna stick anyhow. The charges were bullshit."

"I know."

"Stolen car, sure. Rest of it? Nah."

"But you were riding around the same day Julia was killed. Did you see anyone?"

"You gonna have to be more explicit. We saw a lot of people. Lot of people saw us was the problem. Should have stayed by the lakefront, no one woulda thought nothing of it. But we had to go north up Sheridan." He thinks about it. "We did stop for a piss near the woods. Probably right round there. Saw a guy. Acting funny."

Kirby's stomach flips. "Did he have a limp?"

"Sure," Jamel says, rubbing at the cracked skin on his lips. "Sure. Yeah. I remember that. He had a limp. That guy was a limping motherfucker. Kinda twitchy too. Kept looking all round."

"How close were you?" Her chest is tight. Finally. Fucking finally.

"Close enough. Across the road. I guess we didn't think much of it at the time. But he was limping. You could see that."

"What was he wearing?" she says, suddenly careful. You can want something to be true...

"One of those black puffy jackets and jeans. I remember because it was hot and it seemed odd. Guess he musta been wearing it to hide the blood—am I right?"

"Black guy? Really dark?" Also known as leading the witness.

"As night."

"You asshole." she says, furious with him. And herself for spoon-feeding him everything she wanted to hear. "You're making this up."

"You like it," he shoots back. "You think if I'd seen some suspicious motherfucker I wouldn't have told the polis?"

"Maybe they wouldn't have believed you. They already had you wrapped up for it."

"You're the one doing the wrapping. Hey, you know, maybe you *can* do a story on me."

"That's not on the table anymore."

"Shit. You tell a bitch what she wants to hear and she gets all up in your face. You know what I really want?" He leans forward and makes a little grabbing motion with his hand to get her to come closer so they won't be overheard. After a second's hesitation she does, even though she knows he's going to come out with some disgusting proposition. He gets his mouth right up against her ear. "You take care of my baby. Lily. She's eight years old now, going on nine. Got diabetes. You get her medicine and make sure her momma doesn't sell it for crack."

"I—" Kirby rocks back as Jamel starts laughing.

"You like that? We got a sob story going or what? You can do some of them heartbreak photos with my shorty with her fingers through the fence. Maybe one tear rolling down her chubby little cheek, her hair all done up in pigtails. All those different-colored hairbands. Get a petition going. Protesters outside the prison with them signs and everything. Get me an appeal in no time, right?"

"I'm sorry," Kirby says. She is so unprepared for his animosity, for the miserable fucked-upness of this place.

"You're sorry," he says flatly.

She pushes away from the table, taking the guard unawares. "You still got eight minutes," he says, glancing at the clock.

"I'm done. I'm sorry. I have to go." She shoulders her bag and the guard unlocks the door and jerks down the handle to let her out.

"Sorry don't mean shit!" Jamel calls after her. "Bring me chocolate next time you come. Reese's Peanut Butter Cups! And a pardon! You hear?"

HARPER
16 August 1932

Heavy tree-fern fronds curl over on either side of the florist's window in the Congress Hotel, like curtains on a stage. It makes the transaction a performance for the people passing through the foyer. He feels exposed. It's too hot. The smell of the flowers is too sweet. It crawls behind his eyeballs, heavy and stuffy. All of it makes him want to get out of here as quickly as he's able.

But the fat fairy in the apron insists on showing him all the possibilities, segregated by color and variety. Carnations for gratitude, roses for romance, daisies for friendship or loyal love. The man's rolled-up sleeves expose dark bristling curls like pubic hair that creep over his wrists halfway to his knuckles.

It's impetuous. A risk when he's been so careful with everything else. He has waited four months so as not to raise suspicion, nor appear too eager.

There's no light in her. Not like his girls. And yet she's more than the low dullards that trudge through the days, interchangeable in any of the Chicagos if you only look past their clothes. He likes her callow viciousness. He likes the sense that he is defying something.

Harper ignores the sprays of pale pinks and yellows and fingers the petal of a lily, splayed open obscenely. At his touch, the stamen drips powdery gold over the black and white tiles.

"Are you sending condolences?" the florist asks.

"No, it's an invitation."

He pinches the head of the flower closed and something inside bites him. His hand jerks, crushing the flower, knocking several long stems from the bucket. The sting quivers in his fingertip, the venom sac at the tip deflated and sapped out. From the mangle of petals on the floor, a bee crawls out, wings torn and legs dragging.

The florist stamps on it. "Gosh darn insect! I am so sorry, sir. It must have come in from outside. Can I get you some ice?"

"Just the flowers," Harper says, shaking his hand, brushing the sting away. The burn is ferocious. But it clears the heaviness in his head.

"Nurse Etta" the card reads, because he can't remember her last name. "Elizabethan Room, Congress Hotel. 8 p.m. Regards, Your Admirer."

On the way out, his hand still throbbing with the poison, he hesitates at the jeweler's and buys the silver bracelet in the window, hung with charms. A reward if she shows up. That it matches one already nailed up on his wall is a coincidence, he tells himself.

She's already sitting at the table when he arrives, peering round the room to see, her hands locked tight over her purse in her lap. She is wearing a beige dress that flatters her figure, even though it is a little tight around the arms, which makes him think it's borrowed. She's cut her cherry-brown hair and styled it in finger waves. She looks amused when she sees that it's him. A pianist tinkles a sweet and empty tune while the band sets up.

"I knew it was you," she says, her mouth twisting ironically.

"Did you?"

"I did."

"I thought I'd take a chance." And then, because he can't resist: "How is your gentleman friend?"

"The doctor? He disappeared. You didn't know?" Her eyes glint in the yellow light of the chandeliers.

"Do you think I'd have waited so long?"

"Rumors were he got some girl knocked up and ran off with her. Or got in trouble gambling."

"It happens."

"Bastard. Wish he was dead."

The waiter brings lemonade. With a twist, which Harper has paid extra for. It's too sharp. He has to stop himself from spitting it out over the tablecloth.

"I brought you something." He takes the jeweler's velvet box from his pocket and slides it across the table.

"Aren't I the lucky girl?" She makes no move to take it.

"Open it."

"All right." She reaches for the box. She takes the bracelet out and holds it up to the candlelight. "What's this for?"

"You're interesting to me."

"You only want me because you couldn't have me before."

"Maybe. Maybe I killed that doctor."

"Is that right?" She folds the bracelet around her wrist and extends it for him to fasten the clasp, bending back her hand so the tendons stand out in sharp relief among the fine network of veins under her skin. She makes him feel uncertain. His charisma doesn't work on her the way it does with others—she's wise to him.

"Thank you. Do you want to dance?" she says.

"No." The tables around them are filling up. The women are better and more dangerously dressed, in sequins and thin-strapped dresses. The men wear their suits with obscene confidence. This has been a mistake.

"Then let's go back to your house."

It's a test, he realizes. For her as well as him. "Are you sure?" he says. His hand throbs with remembered pain from the bee sting earlier.

He takes her the long way, so the streets will be emptier, even though she complains about her heels and eventually takes them off, along with her stockings, to walk in her bare feet. He leads her the last few blocks with a hand clamped over her eyes. An old man gives them a baleful look, but Harper kisses Etta on the head. *See,* he's saying, *it's just a lovers' game.* It is, in a way.

He keeps her eyes covered as he slides the key into the lock and helps guide her under the boards crossed over the door.

"What's going on?" she giggles. He can tell by her soft panting breath that she's excited.

"You'll see."

He locks the door behind them before he lets her see, guiding her towards the parlor, past the dark stain on the pocked and dented wood in the passage.

"This is fancy," she says, looking around at the fittings. She spies the decanter of whiskey, which he has refilled. "Should we have a drink?"

"No," he says, grabbing at her breasts.

"Let's go to the bedroom," she whispers as he steers her to the couch.

"Here." He pushes her down on her stomach and tries to pull up her dress.

"It's a zipper," she says, reaching to tug down the metal teeth. She wriggles, pulling it over her hips. He can feel himself starting to lose it. He wrenches her hands behind her back.

"Stay still," he hisses. He closes his eyes and summons images of the girls. Opening up under him. Their insides spilling out. The way they cry and struggle.

It's over too soon. He groans as he rolls off, his pants round his ankles. He wants to hit her. Her fault. Slut.

But she turns over to kiss him with that sly, darting tongue. "That was nice." She moves her mouth down to his lap and even though he can't stay hard, it proves more satisfying.

"Do you want to see something?" he says, absently rubbing at the lipstick smear on his testicles. She's sitting at his feet on the floor, her dress hanging off her shoulders, hand-rolling a cigarette.

"Seen it already," she leers.

He tucks himself away. "Get dressed."

"All right." The bracelet jangles around her wrist as she takes a long pull on the cigarette. She exhales a cloud of smoke between the neat bow of her lips.

"It's a secret." He feels a thrill at telling her. It's a violation and he knows it. But he needs to share it. His great and terrible mystery. The same goddamn thing if he was the richest man in the world and didn't have nothing to spend it on.

"All right," she says again, a knowing crease at the corner of her mouth.

"You can't look." He won't take her too far. He needs to see her limits.

He uses his hat this time to cover her face as he takes her out the door, but she still gasps at the light. They step out into a balmy afternoon with an insistent breeze and the spattering of spring rain. She catches on quick. Harper knew she would.

"What is this?" she says, her fingers digging into his arm, staring at the street. Her lips are parted, enough for him to see her tongue running over her teeth, back and forth, back and forth.

"You ain't seen nothing," he says.

He takes her downtown, which is not so different, but then they follow the crowds down to Northerly Island park, where the new World's Fair is underway. Spring of 1934. He's been here before in his wanderings.

"The Century of Progress," the banners proclaim. "The rainbow city." They walk through a corridor of flags among the throngs of people, excited and happy. She bugs her eyes at him, watching the red lights tick up the side of the narrow tower made to resemble a thermometer. "This isn't here," she says in wonder.

"Not yesterday."

"How did you do this?"

"I can't tell you," he says.

He quickly tires of the marvels, which seem quaint to him. The buildings are strange and, he knows, only temporary. She shrieks and clings to his arm at the dinosaurs that wag their tails and move their heads from side to side, but he is unimpressed by the crude mechanics.

There is a replica fort with Red Indians, and a golden Japanese building that looks like a broken umbrella—all jutting spokes. The House of the Future is not. The General Motors display seems laughable. A giant boy with a distorted puppet face sits astride an outsize red flyer wagon, riding it nowhere.

He shouldn't have brought her here. It is pathetic. The limits of the imagination, the future painted up all gaudy like a cheap whore, when he has seen the reality of it, fast and dense and ugly.

She picks up on his mood and tries to turn it around. "Will you look at that," she exclaims, pointing at the rocket-shaped gondolas of the Sky Ride scooting back and forth between two massive pylons on either side of the lagoon. "You want to go up? I bet the view is breathtaking."

He buys their tickets, grudgingly, and the elevator swoops them to the top with dizzying speed. And maybe the air is fresher up here or maybe it was only a matter of widening his outlook. The whole city is laid out before them, the entirety of the fair, strange and new from this height.

Etta takes his arm, pressing her body against his so he can feel the warmth and give of her breasts through her dress. Her eyes glitter. "Do you realize what you have?"

"Yes," he says. A partner. Someone who will understand. He already knows she's cruel.

KIRBY
14 January 1993

H̲ey, Kirsty, I'm so sorry. I completely forgot. Just lost track of time," Sebastian "call me Seb" Wilson launches in as he opens the door to her.

"It's Kirby," she corrects him. She'd been waiting in the lobby downstairs for half an hour before she got the receptionist to call his room.

"Yeah, sure, sorry. I don't know where my head's at. Well, actually I do. It's wrapped up in this deal. Come in, won't you? Excuse the mess."

His suite has to be one of the swankiest in the hotel; top-floor room with a view of the river and an adjoining lounge, the kind with a glass coffee table that would be marked with distinctive razor-blade scratches and the finest dusting of cocaine.

Right now, it's buried under a shuffle of spreadsheets and data forms. The bed is unmade. There is a collection of empty mini liquor bottles clustered around the over-sized statement lamp on the side table. He shoves his briefcase aside to make space for her to sit down on the white leather couch.

"Can I get you something? A drink? If there's anything left..." he glances at the empties, embarrassed, pushing his fingers through his immaculately tousled hair, revealing that it's starting to recede prematurely at the temples. Peter Pan all grown up and turned corporate, she thinks, but still trying to coast on the bad-boy persona from high school.

Even under the expensive suit, Kirby can make out that once rangy muscle is going soft, especially around his middle. She wonders when he last tinkered with a motorbike. Or if it's something he tells himself he's going to get back to as soon as he cracks that first million and retires at thirty-five.

"Thanks for taking the time to see me."

"Hey, sure. Anything to help Julia. It's tragic. I still haven't, you know... gotten over it." He shakes his head. "That day."

"It was a struggle to catch you."

"I know, I know. This big merger. Normally the firm wouldn't be interested in heartland stuff. We're more coast-centered. But farmers require mortgages, same as everyone else. You probably don't even know what I'm talking about. What did you say you were studying again?"

"Journalism. But actually, I just dropped out." It hasn't occurred to her that she's made the decision until the words are out in the open, confessed to this total stranger. But she hasn't been to class in over a month. Hasn't turned in an assignment in two. If she's lucky, they'll put her on probation.

"Hey, I get that. I got sucked into all those political demonstrations and shit. I thought it was something useful I could do with all the anger."

"You're very candid about it."

"I'm talking to someone who understands, right? Not a lot of people can."

"No kidding."

"I mean, you've been there."

The door opens and a Filipino maid sticks her head in. "Oh, sorry," she says, retreating quickly.

"An hour, okay?" Sebastian shouts, overly loud. "Come back and do the room in an hour!" He smiles vaguely at Kirby. "What was I talking about?"

"Julia. Politics. Being angry."

"Yeah. That's it. But what was I supposed to do? Stop my whole life? Jules would have wanted me to go on, make something of my future. And look at me now. I think she'd be proud, right?"

"Sure." Kirby sighs. Maybe death concentrates everything. Makes you more of a selfish fratboy ass, even if you're wounded and lonely underneath it all.

"So, you go round talking to victims' families? That must be depressing."

"Not as depressing as the murderer getting away with it. I know it's a long time ago, but can you remember if there was anything that struck you as strange about the police finding the body?"

"Are you kidding me? That it took two days for anyone to find her. That's injustice right there. When I think about her lying there in the woods, all alone."

The words are shop-soiled enough to irritate Kirby—he's said them so many times that they've lost all meaning. "She was dead. It wouldn't have mattered to her."

"That's cold, lady."

"It's true, though. That's why it's called having to *live* with it."

"Chill out. Damn. I thought we had a connection here."

"Was there anything out of the ordinary? Anything found on the body that was out of place, that didn't belong to her? A lighter. Jewelry. Something old."

"She wasn't into jewelry."

"Okay, thanks." Kirby feels tired. How many of these interviews has she done now? "You've been very helpful. I appreciate your time."

"Did I tell you about the song?" he throws in.

"I would have remembered."

"It has a lot of meaning to me now. 'Get It While You Can' — Janis Joplin."

"You don't strike me as the Joplin type."

"Neither was Julia. It wasn't even her handwriting."

"What wasn't?" Kirby clamps down on the spark of hope. Nothing, it's nothing. Just like Jamel.

"On the tape in her purse? I guess someone must have given it to her. You know what girls are like in dorms."

"Yeah, all that tape-swapping and pillow fights in their underwear," Kirby snipes, to hide her interest. "You tell the cops?"

"What?"

"That it wasn't her handwriting?"

"You think one of those assholes who killed her was a Joplin fan? I think it was more like . . ." He mugs drawing a gun sideways out of his pants. "Boom-boom! Fuck-tha-police, yo!" He laughs at his own bad parody, and then his face crumples into sadness. "Hey, you sure you don't want to stick around, have a drink with me?"

She knows what he means.

"It wouldn't help," Kirby says.

HARPER

1 May 1993

⸻

He is surprised to see how close they stay, despite cars and trains and the buzzing fury of O'Hare Airport. They are easy to track down, he's found. Mostly they're drawn to the city, which keeps expanding its reaches further and further into the countryside, like mold laying claim to a piece of bread.

The phone book is usually his starting point, but Catherine Galloway-Peck doesn't appear in the lists of names. So he phones her parents instead.

"Hello—" her father's voice comes through the instrument clear as if he were standing right beside him.

"I'm looking for Catherine. Can you tell me where to find her?"

"I've told you lot before, she doesn't live here and we have absolutely nothing, do you hear me, *nothing* to do with her debts." There is a hard click, followed by a sweet monotone hum. He realizes the man is no longer on the other end of the line, so he inserts another quarter into the little slot and goes through the whole process again, jabbing deliberately at the silver keys, the numbers grubby and weathered by other fingers. The handset trills for a long time.

"Yes?" Mr. Peck's voice is careful.

"Do you know where she is? I need to find her."

"For Pete's sake," the man says. "You need to get the message. Just leave us alone." He waits in vain for him to answer; long enough for the fear to manifest. "Hello?"

"Hello."

"Oh. I wasn't sure if you were still there." He is uncertain. "Is she all right? Has something happened? Oh God. Did she *do* something?"

"Why would Catherine do something?"

"I don't know. I don't know why she does anything. We paid for her to go to that place. We tried to understand. They said it's not her fault, but—"

"Which place?"

"New Hope Recovery Center."

Harper gently replaces the instrument.

He doesn't find her there, but he goes to one of the meetings affiliated with New Hope's halfway house, where he sits quietly and (as the name suggests) anonymously listening to sniveling sob stories until he is able to get her new address from a very helpful old-lady ex-junkie called Abigail, who is delighted that Catherine's "uncle" is reaching out to her.

CATHERINE

9 June 1993

———

Catherine Galloway-Peck paces in front of the blank canvas. Tomorrow she will take it down to Huxley and sell it for twenty bucks, even though that's what the stretching cost alone. But he'll feel sorry for her, and give her a hit too. She might have to throw in a blowjob. But she's not a whore. It's a favor. Friends help each other out. You can help a friend feel good.

Besides, art is supposed to be fueled by depression and substance abuse. Look at Kerouac. Or Mapplethorpe. Haring! Bacon! Basquiat! So how come when she looks at the blank canvas, the weave of it plinks in her brain like an out-of-tune piano stuck on one note?

It's not even a matter of starting. She has started a dozen times. Boldly, brilliantly, with a clear idea of where this will go. She can see the whole thing unfolding in her head. How the colors will layer over each other like bridges that will take her all the way to the end. But then it all becomes slippery. It skids away and she can't keep hold of it and the colors become muddy. She ends up doing half-baked collages of pages torn out of old trashy novels she got for a dollar a box, painting over them again and again, obliterating the words. The idea was to make a lightbox out of them with pinpricks spelling out new sentences that only she would know.

It's a relief to open the door and find him standing there. She'd thought it was Huxley, perhaps, pre-empting her need. Or Joanna, who sometimes drops off coffee and a sandwich, although she has been coming less often, and her eyes grow harder every time.

"Can I come in?" he asks.

"Yes," she says, and pulls open the door, even though he is holding a knife and a pink bunny hairclip from, what, eight years ago, if she does the math, but which looks like he bought it from the store yesterday. She realizes she has been anticipating him. Ever since she was twelve years old and he sat down next to her on the grass during the fireworks. She was waiting for her dad to come back from the portapotties because chili dogs never did agree with him. She said she wasn't allowed to talk to strangers and she would call the police, but actually she was flattered that he was interested in her.

He explained that she was brighter than the explosions that boomed in the sky above the buildings, reflected in the glass. He could see her shine from all the way over there. Which meant he would have to kill her. Not now, but later. When she was all grown-up. But she should watch out for him. He'd reached up and she'd flinched away. He didn't touch her, or only to take the clip from her hair. And it was that, more than the terrible inexplicable thing he'd said to her, that left her weeping inconsolably, to her father's consternation, when he finally returned, pale and sweaty and clutching his stomach.

And isn't that what set her on this course, this downward spiral? The man in the park who told her he was going to kill her.

That's a terrible thing to say to a child, she thinks, but what she says is, "Would you like a drink?" playing the polite hostess, as if she has anything to offer other than water in a paint-smeared glass.

She sold her bed two weeks ago, but she found a broken sofa on the sidewalk and inveigled Huxley to help her heft it up the stairs and then baptize it, because, c'mon, Cat, he wasn't going to do that shit for free.

"You told me I shone. Like fireworks. At the Taste of Chicago. Do you remember?" She does a pirouette in the middle of the room and almost falls over. When was the last time she had something to eat? Tuesday?

"But it's not true."

"No," she says. She sits down heavily on the sofa. The cushions are on the floor. She had started tearing the seams up, looking for crumbs. A scrap of rock she'd missed. She used to have a Dustbuster so she could vacuum the cracks between the floorboards and pick through the bag when she got really desperate. But she can't think what happened to it. She stares numbly at the discarded paperbacks with half the stories ripped out, scattered around the floor. It's been cathartic, tearing the pages out, even if she's not painting them. Destruction is a natural instinct.

"You don't shine anymore." He holds out the hair clip for her to take. "I'm still going to have to go back," he says, angry with her. "To close the loop."

She takes the clip, numbly. The pink bunny has her eyes closed, two little Xs and another for her mouth. Catherine thinks about eating it. A communion wafer for consumer society. That would be a good idea for a piece, actually. "I know. I'm sorry, I think it's the drugs." But she knows that's not true. It's the reason she takes the drugs. Like her vision for her artwork that skids away, she can't get a grip on the world. It's too much for her. "Are you still going to kill me?"

"Why would I waste my time." It's not even a question.

"You came. Didn't you? I mean, you're here. I'm not imagining this." She wraps her hand around the blade and he pulls it away. The burn in her palm makes her feel alive in a way she hasn't in a long time. It's clean and fierce. Not like the needle biting into the skin between her fingers, the crack mixed with white vinegar to make it injectable. "You promised."

She grabs his hand and he sneers, but momentary panic glances across his features mingled with distaste. She knows that look, she's seen it in people's faces when she spins them her story about needing bus fare because she was mugged and she has to get home. Isn't this what she's been waiting for? Killing time. Because she needs to get to the place where the pictures in her head make sense. She needs him to take her there. Blood spattered on the canvas. Take that, Jackson Pollock.

JIN-SOOK

23 March 1993

Chicago Sun-Times
**BRUTAL MURDER OF PASSIONATE
HOUSING WORKER ROCKS CITY**
by Richard Gane

CABRINI GREEN: A young social worker was found stabbed to death yesterday morning at 5 a.m. underneath the El line on the corner of West Schiller and North Orleans.

Jin-Sook Au (24) was a case worker for the Chicago Housing Authority (CHA) in one of the city's most notorious housing projects. But the police refuse to speculate if the murder was gang-related.

"We're not releasing details at this time, in the interest of investigating all possibilities," Detective Larry Amato said. "We'd like to encourage anyone who may have any information to come talk to us urgently."

Her body was discovered two blocks away from the trendy restaurant and comedy club district of Old Town. No witnesses have yet come forward.

CHA staff and residents of Cabrini Green have reacted with shock to the murder. CHA spokesperson Andrea Bishop said, "Jin-Sook was a bright young woman whose passion and insight made a real impact. We're deeply saddened and horrified by her loss."

Tonya Gardener, a Cabrini resident, said that Ms. Au would be sorely missed in the community. "She was real decent at explaining. You felt like you knew what was going on, even if she couldn't do nothing about it. She was good with the kids. Always bringing them little presents. Books and such, even though they asked for sweets. Inspirational things, you know. Martin Luther King's biography or Aretha Franklin CDs. Strong black role models the kids could look up to, you know?"

Ms. Au's parents were unavailable for comment. The Korean community has been rallying to support the family and will be holding a candlelit memorial at the Bethany Presbyterian Church on Thursday. All are welcome to attend.

The photograph accompanying the news story shows a body covered up by a blanket in the no-man's-land between a parking lot and a ramshackle house under the El support struts. The area is fenced off, but that hasn't stopped people using it as an impromptu dumping ground; a bag of rubbish that didn't make it to the corner for collection is cozied up next to a dead washing machine laid on its side.

An upset young beat cop is waving his hand towards the lens, hoping to obscure the shot or dissuade the photographer.

If the reporter's camera had panned left by an inch, the camera would have caught a pair of burlesque butterfly wings pinned against the fence by the wind, unrecognizably ripped, half-concealed by a plastic Walgreen's bag tangled up in the elastic, but still with a sheen of radium paint.

But then the red line El goes rattling overhead and the backdraft whips it away to join the rest of the city's jetsam.

It does not appear to have been a robbery. Her book bag has been tipped out next to her, but her wallet is untouched, still zipped up and with $63 and change inside. There is also a hair brush with several long black hairs that will be identified as hers, a pack of tissues, cocoa-butter lip balm, CHA case files on the families she was working with, a library book (*Parable of the Sower* by Octavia Butler), and a video tape "Live from All Jokes Aside," a local all-black comedy club. The kind of aspirational items she was known for. The cops do not realize that there is a baseball card missing—of a famous African-American player.

KIRBY
23 March 1993

─────────

G ive me everything you've got." Kirby goes straight to Chet.
   "Chill, dude, this isn't even your story," Chet says.

"C'mon, Chet. *Someone* must have done a human interest story on her. Korean-American girl working in one of the city's toughest neighborhoods? That's too good to resist."

"No."

"Why?"

"Cos Dan phoned this morning and said he'd hang me with my own balls after he'd cut them off with a pair of kiddy's safety scissors. He doesn't want you getting involved."

"That's very sweet of him, and also absolutely none of his beeswax."

"You're his intern."

"Chet. You know I'm scarier than Dan."

"Fine!" He throws up his hands, a movement hampered by the weight of his jewelry. "Wait here. And don't tell Velasquez." She knew he wouldn't be able to resist the temptation to practice his arcane arts in the stacks.

He comes back ten minutes later with various clippings about Cabrini and CHA's general blundering.

"I got you stuff on Robert Taylor Homes too. Did you know Cabrini's original residents were mainly Italian?"

"I did not."

"You do now. I got you an article on that, and white flight to the suburbs in general."

"You don't mess around."

He also produces a manila envelope with a flourish. "Ta-da. Korean Day 1986. Your girl came second in the essay competition."

"How did you do that?"

"If I told you, I'd have to kill you," he says, dipping his mussed-up-on-purpose head back behind *Swamp Thing*. Adding, without looking up: "No, really."

She starts with Detective Amato.

"Yes?" he says.

"I'm phoning about the murder of Jin-Sook Au."

"Yes?"

"I wanted to get some more information about how she was killed—"

"Get your sick kicks somewhere else, lady." He hangs up on her.

She phones back and explains to the duty officer that her call was cut off accidentally. She gets transferred back to his desk. He picks up immediately.

"Amato."

"Please don't hang up."

"You have twenty seconds to convince me."

"I think you're dealing with a serial killer. If you speak to Detective Diggs in Oak Park, he'll confirm my case."

"And you are?"

"Kirby Mazrachi. I was attacked in 1989. And I'm sure it's the same guy. Was there something left on the body?"

"No offense, miss, but we have procedures. I can't disclose that kind of information. But I will talk to Detective Diggs. You got a number I can reach you on?"

She gives him her number and the number at the *Sun-Times* for good measure. She hopes this will force them to take her seriously.

"Thanks. I'll get back to you."

Kirby goes through the articles Chet dug up for her. They don't give her anything about Jin-Sook Au, although she finds out more about unethical real-estate practices and the CHA's checkered history than she ever wanted to know. You'd have to be unreasonably stubborn and idealistic to try to work within the organization.

She fidgets. She's tempted to visit the scene, but she goes for the phonebook instead. There are four Aus in the directory. It's easy to track down the right one. It's the number that is permanently engaged because it's been left off the hook.

Finally, she catches a cab to Lakeview, to the home of Don and Julie Au. They do not answer the phone or the doorbell. She sits outside and waits, round the back of the house, never mind that it's freezing and her fingertips are going numb, even buried in her armpits. And ninety-eight minutes later, when Mrs. Au slips out the back door in a housecoat and a cream crocheted hat with a rose on the front, she is waiting for her. It takes the woman ages to walk down to the mini-market, like every step is a duty she has to remind herself of again. It's all Kirby can do to hang back out of sight.

In the store, she finds Mrs. Au standing in the tea and coffee aisle. Holding a box of jasmine tea and staring at it blankly, like it might have answers.

"Excuse me," she says, touching her arm.

The woman turns towards her, barely seeing. Her face is a mask of grief, all deep furrows. Kirby can't help herself, she's appalled.

"No reporters!" The woman comes to life, shakes her head frantically. "No reporters!"

"Please, I'm not, not technically. Someone tried to kill me."

The older woman looks terrified. "He's here? We must call the police."

"No, wait." This is spiraling out of control. "I think your daughter was killed by a serial killer who attacked me, years ago. But I need to know how she was stabbed. Did the killer try to disembowel her? Did he leave something behind on the body? Something that was out of place? That you know wasn't hers?"

"Are you all right, ma'am?" A cashier has come round from behind the counter to put a protective arm around Mrs. Au, because the old lady is flushed and shaking and crying. Kirby becomes aware that she's been shouting.

"You're sick!" Mrs. Au screams at Kirby. "Did the man who did this leave something on the body? Yes! My heart. Ripped right out of my chest. My only child! You understand?"

"I'm sorry, really sorry." Shitshitshit. How could she have got this so wrong?

"You get out of here, now," the cashier warns. "What is the matter with you?"

If she still had an answering machine, she might have been able to deflect it. As it is, she gets to the *Sun-Times* the next morning to find Dan waiting for her in the lobby. He grabs her by the elbow and sweeps her outside.

"Smoke break."

"You don't smoke."

"For once in your life, don't argue. We're going for a walk. Cigarettes optional."

"Okay, okay." She jerks her arm away from him as he walks her out the building and down to the riverbank. The buildings reflect in each other, an infinite city caught in the glass.

"Hey, did you know about blockbusting? Skanky real-estate agents moving a black family into an all-white neighborhood and then putting the fear into the other residents that it was all going to hell and getting them to sell out at a loss, and taking a fat commission?"

"Not now, Kirby."

The air off the water has a bite to it, the kind that sinks itself through your bones into your marrow. A cargo boat trundles along, churning the water in its wake, neatly sliding under the bridge.

Kirby gives in to his silent accusation. "Did Chetty rat me out?"

"For what? Accessing old clippings? That's not illegal. Harassing a murder victim's mother, however . . ."

"Crap."

"The cops called. They're unhappy. Harrison is apocalyptic. What were you thinking?"

"Don't you mean apoplectic?"

"I know exactly what I mean. As in, rain of fire on your ass."

"It's not exactly anything new. I've been doing this all year, Dan. I even tracked down Julia Madrigal's ex-boyfriend. Who was awful in a really sad way."

"*Bendito sea Dios, dame paciencia.* You do *not* make this easy." Dan rubs at the back of his head.

"Don't do that, you're going to make yourself bald," Kirby snipes.

"You need to calm down."

"Really? That's really what you're telling me?"

"Or at the very least be *reasonable*. Can't you see how crazy your behavior looks?"

"No."

"Fine. Do it your way. Harrison's waiting in the boardroom for you."

A detective, a city editor and a sports reporter walk into a room. There is no punchline. Just an epic shitstorm coming on her head.

Detective Amato is wearing full uniform, complete with bullet-proof vest, to let her know how serious this is. He has old acne scarring on his cheeks, like he's been sandpapering his face. It makes him look weathered, like a cowboy. A hint of gritty history gives you class, Kirby thinks. But the puffiness in his cheeks and the pouches under his eyes say he's not getting a whole lot of sleep. She can relate. She spends most of the lecture staring at his hands. It keeps her head down, which makes her seem more contrite.

His wedding ring is gold and scratched and pinches into his finger, which tells her he's been wearing it a long time. There's a trace of black ink on the back of his hand, the remnants of a phone number or a license plate he had to jot down in a hurry. She likes him more for that. The speech—she's not required to respond other than occasionally nod tightly—is all stuff she's heard before from Andy Diggs, back when he still took her calls and didn't fob her off to some junior officer to take a message.

It's not appropriate, Detective Amato says. He's spoken to Detective Diggs, who is working her case. Yes, *still*. He filled him in. No one appreciates what she's going through more than they do. They have to deal with this all the time. Wanting to nail the bad guys to the wall. Doing anything they can to find them. But there is a process.

She's distorting the evidence with all this speculation and getting witnesses mixed up. Yes, the victim was stabbed and slashed multiple times in the stomach and pelvic area. The cases do have that in common. But there was no object left on the body. The MO was completely different to the attack on her. No restraints. No indication that it was planned ahead. And he's sorry to speak so frankly, but the attack was amateur compared to what happened to her. Sloppy even. A killer just starting out. It was a horrible, opportunistic crime. They're not ruling out a copycat murder. Which is exactly why the police have been so tightlipped on all this, because they don't want to set off any more, and please appreciate that he's here in an informal capacity and this is all off the record.

It *is* a stabbing. But there are a lot of stabbings. She has to trust the police to do their job. And they will do their job. Please *trust* him.

Then Harrison apologizes for ten minutes while the detective fidgets, clearly wanting to get out of there now he's said his bit, about how she's not an official employee, and of course the *Sun-Times* has always been supportive of the efforts by the Chicago PD, and if there's anything they can do, here's his card, give him a call anytime.

The cop leaves, squeezing Kirby's shoulder as he goes. "We'll get him." But she doesn't see how that's supposed to comfort her when they haven't so far.

Harrison looks at her expectantly, waiting for her to say something. And then he lets rip.

"What the fuck were you thinking?"

"You're right, I should have prepared better. I wanted to get to her while it was still fresh. I didn't expect it to be so raw—" Her gut clenches. She wonders if Rachel looked the same way.

"This is not the time for you to answer me," Harrison rages. "You have brought this paper into disrepute. You have compromised our relationship with the police. You have possibly damaged a murder case. You have upset a grief-stricken old lady who did *not* need your shit. And you have *breached your mandate*."

"I wasn't writing about it."

"I don't care. You cover sports. You do not run around interviewing murder victims' families. That is why we have experienced, sensitive, actual crime reporters. You do not stick your nose one inch outside your beat. You get me?"

"You ran the article I did on Naked Raygun."

"What?"

"The punk band."

"Are you trying to make me insane?" Harrison is incredulous. Dan closes his eyes, his expression pained.

"It would be a good story," she says, unrepentant.

"What would?"

"Unsolved murders and the aftermath. With a tragic personal spin. Pulitzer material."

"Is she always this impossible?" Harrison asks Dan, but she can tell he's rolling the idea around, considering it.

But Dan isn't playing. "Forget it. No chance."

"It *is* interesting," Harrison says. "She'd have to do it together with an experienced reporter. Emma maybe, or Richie."

"She's not doing it," Dan says, his voice hard.

"Hey. You don't speak for me."

"You're *my* intern."

"What the fuck, Dan?" Kirby is nearly shouting.

"This is what I'm talking about, Matt. She's a train-wreck. You want a proper scandal? *Tribune* headline: Cub Reporter Loses Her Shit. City editor held responsible for emotional breakdown. Murder victim's mother hospitalized for shock. Korean-American community outraged. Homicide cases in the city set back twenty years."

"Okay, okay, I got it." Harrison waves his hand like he's shooing a fly.

"Don't listen to him! Why are you listening to him? Are you hearing this crap? That's not even plausible. C'mon, Dan." She's willing him to look at her. If he'll just meet her eyes, she'll be able to call him on this damn bluff. But Dan stares straight at Harrison and delivers the killing blow.

"She's emotionally unstable. She's not even going to classes anymore. I spoke to her professor."

"You did what?"

He meets her eyes. "I wanted her to write you a referral. To try and get you a real job here. Turns out you haven't been to class or turned in an assignment all semester."

"Fuck you, Dan."

"Enough. Kirby," Harrison says, with the same tone he uses for deadlines, "you've got a good sense for a story, but Velasquez is right. You're too wrapped up in this one. I'm not going to fire your ass."

"You can't fire me! I work for free."

"*But* you are going to take a break. Time out. Go back to school. I mean it. Get some thinking done. Go see a shrink, if that's what it takes. What you do not do is try to write a story about murders or go sniffing around the families, or set foot in this building again until I say so."

"I could go across the road. Or take it to *The Reader*."

"Good point. I'll phone them and let them know not to deal with you."

"You are being so unfair."

"Yeah, sure. Welcome to having a boss. I don't want to see you here 'til you've pulled yourself together, you get me?"

"Sir, yes, sir," Kirby says, not even trying to hold back the bitterness. She stands up to go.

"Hey, kiddo," Dan tries. "You want to get a coffee? Talk about it? I'm on your side."

He *should* feel bad, she thinks with a jagged spike of fury. He should feel like shit warmed up and slathered on a cheating ex's car windscreen.

"Not with *you*." She stalks out.

HARPER

20 August 1932

Harper collects Etta from the hospital after her shift and brings her back to the House. Always covering her eyes, always taking a different route. Escorting her back to the street where her boarding-rooms are afterwards. She has a new roommate. Molly moved out after the spaghetti incident, she tells him.

He takes his unease out on her. The grunting slipperiness that turns to hot relief banishes everything else. When he is heaving inside her, he doesn't have to think about how he misread the map and Catherine who didn't shine. He killed her quickly with no pleasure or ritual, driving the knife between her ribs into her heart. He didn't take anything, didn't leave anything behind.

It was purely mechanical going back and finding her younger self in the park with the fireworks booming against the night sky, taking the bunny clip from her. Little Catherine most certainly did shine. Should he have warned her that she would lose her gift? It's his fault, he thinks. He should never have tried to turn the hunt around.

They fuck in the parlor. He will not allow Etta upstairs. When she needs to pee, he tells her to do it in the kitchen sink and she hoists up her dress and squats there, smoking and chatting while she voids her bladder. She tells him about her patients. A miner from the Adirondacks who coughs up phlegm spotted with coal soot and blood. A stillbirth. An amputation today; a little boy who fell down into a broken grate in the street and caught his leg. "Very sad," she says, but she is smiling as she says it. She keeps up a prattle, talking so he doesn't have to. Bending over and hoisting her skirts without him having to ask.

"Take me somewhere, baby," she says as he puts himself away, afterwards. "Why won't you? You tease me." She slides her hand round to the front of his jeans, an irritating reminder that he owes her.

"Where would you like to go?"

"Somewhere exciting. You choose. Anywhere you like."

In the end it proves too tempting. For both of them.

He takes her on brief outings. Nothing like the first time. Half an hour, twenty minutes, which means staying in close vicinity. He ushers her to see the highway and she tucks her chin into his shoulder and hides her face at the roaring traffic, or claps her hands and bounces on her heels in calculated feminine delight at the tumble of the washing machines in the laundromat. The sham of her response is a conniving pleasure they share between them. She is playing at being the kind of woman who needs him. But he knows her rotten heart.

Maybe, he thinks, this is possible. Maybe Catherine was the end. Maybe *none* of the girls shine anymore, and he can be free of it. But the Room still hums when he goes up there. And the goddamn nurse will not relent with her pestering. She rubs her bare breast, flopped out of her uniform, against the skin of his arm where he's rolled up his shirtsleeves, and asks in that little girl voice: "Is it difficult? Is there a dial you turn upstairs, like on a furnace?"

"It only works for me," he says.

"Then it won't hurt for you to tell me how."

"You need the key. And the will to shift the time to where it needs to be."

"Can I try it?" she pesters.

"It's not for you."

"Like the room upstairs?"

"You shouldn't keep asking questions."

He wakes up on the floor of the kitchen, his cheek pressed against the cool linoleum and little men with hammers pounding behind his eyeballs. He sits up, groggily, wiping the saliva from his chin with the back of his hand. The last thing he recalls is Etta fixing him a drink. The same potent alcohol he had the first time they went out together, but with a bitter aftertaste.

Of course, she would have access to sleeping drugs. He curses himself for being so foolish.

She flinches when he walks through the door of the Room. But only for a moment. The suitcase is open on the mattress where he dragged it after he noticed that things were going missing. The money is arranged in stacks.

"This is beautiful," she says. "Look at this. Would you believe it?" She crosses the Room to kiss him.

"Why did you come up here? I told you not to come up here." He cuffs her, knocking her down.

She clutches her cheek with both hands, on the floor, her legs folded under her. She flashes him a smile, but for the first time there is uncertainty in it.

"Baby," she soothes, "I know you're peeved. It's okay. I had to see. You wouldn't show me. But now I have, and I can help you. You and me? We'll take this whole world."

"No."

"We should get married. You need me. You're better with me."

"No," he says again, even though it's true. He wraps his fingers in her hair.

It takes a long time of hitting her head against the metal bedframe before her skull splits open. Like he's trapped in this moment forever.

He doesn't see the homeless junkie boy with the bulging eyes, who has crept into the House again, burned by his last score and hoping for a better one, watching terrified from the passageway. He doesn't hear Mal turn and flee down the stairs. Because Harper is sobbing in self-pity, tears and mucus running down his face: "You made me do this. You made me. You fucking bitch."

ALICE
1 December 1951

A lice Templeton?" he says, not sounding sure.
      "Yes?" she turns.

It is the moment she has been waiting for her whole life. She has played it out in the cinema in her head, rewound the reel, played it again and again.

He steps into the chocolate factory and all the machines grind to a halt in mechanical sympathy, and all the other girls look up as he strides towards her and dips her low, and before he presses his mouth against hers and takes her breath away, he says, "I told you I'd come back for you."

Or he leans rakishly across the cosmetics counter, while she is applying rouge to some society lady who will spend more money on a lipstick than she earns in a week and say, "Excuse me, miss, I've been searching all over for the love of my life. Can you help me?" And he will reach out his hand for her and she will climb over the counter, past the tutting matron. He will spin her round in his arms and set her on her feet, looking at her in delight, and they will run through the department store, hand-in-hand and laughing, and the security guard will say, "But, Alice, you're still on shift," and she will unclip her gold name-tag and fling it at his feet and say, "Charlie, I quit!"

Or he will walk into the secretarial pool and say, "I need a girl! And she's the one."

Or take her hands and lift her gently from scrubbing the diner floors like Cinderella on her knees (never mind that she used a mop) and say, with terrible tenderness, "There's no need for that now."

She was not expecting him to come to her while she was tramping to work. She wants to weep with relief. But also frustration, because she is so awfully unglamorous at this moment. She has a scarf tied over her hair to hide that it's unwashed and limp. Her toes are frozen inside her boots. Her hands are chapped, her fingernails bitten. She's barely wearing any make-up. Having a job where you talk on the phone all day means people only judge her by her voice. "Sears Wish Book sales, what would you like to order?"

She once had a farmer phoning in to order a new tachometer for his John Deere who ended up proposing to her. "I could wake up to that in my ear," he declared. He begged her to see him when he next came up to the city, but she laughed him off. "I'm not all that," she said.

Alice has had bad encounters before with men who were expecting her to be more and less than what she is. Some good ones too, but usually when they already knew what they were letting themselves in for, and usually only for brief passionate clinches. She wants "A Sunday Kind of Love," as the song goes. One that lasts past the gin-flavored kisses of Saturday night. Her longest relationship was ten months and he kept breaking her heart and coming back. Alice wants more. She wants it all. She's been saving up to go to San Francisco where it's easier, the rumors say, for women like her.

"Where have you *been?*" She can't help herself. She hates the petulance that comes rushing into her voice. But it's been over ten years of waiting and hoping and reprimanding herself for pinning her dreams on a man who kissed her once at a county fair and then vanished.

He smiles, rueful. "I had things I had to do. They don't seem so important now." He links his arm in hers and turns her round in the other direction towards the lakefront. "Come with me," he says.

"Where are we going?"

"To a party."

"I'm not dressed for a party." She stops and wails, "I'm a frump!"

"It's a private affair. Just the two of us. And you look wonderful."

"So do you," she says, flushing, and lets him lead her down towards Michigan. She knows with a pure certainty that it won't matter to him. She could see that in the way he looked at her back then, all those years ago. And it's still in his eyes, bright desire and acceptance.

HARPER

1 December 1951

They swan into the lobby of the Congress past the non-func-
tioning escalators that have been covered like corpses under
burial cloth. No one spares the pair a second glance. The hotel is
renovating. The soldiers must have taken their toll on the rooms
during the war, Harper imagines. All that drinking and smoking
and whoring.

The rotary dial above the gold elevator doors adorned with ivy
wreaths and griffons lights up the floor numbers, counting down
to them. The minutes she has left. Harper clasps his hands in front
of his pants to hide his excitement. This is the most brazen he
has been. He fingers the white plastic disk of Julia Madrigal's pill
packet in his pocket. There is no undoing it. Everything is as it is
meant to be. As he determines it.

They step out onto the third floor and he pushes the heavy double doors open wide enough to guide her through into the Gold
Room. He fumbles for the lights. It hasn't changed so much as a
fitting since he drank spiked lemonade here with Etta a week ago,
twenty years ago, although the tables and chairs are stacked now
and the heavy curtains over the balconies are drawn shut. Renais-

sance arches with naked figures amid carved greenery stretch out
to each other across the room. Classically romantic, Harper supposes, although to him they look tortured, reaching for a comfort
denied them, lost without the music.

"What is this?" Alice gasps.

"The banquet room. One of them."

"It's beautiful," she says. "But there's no one else here."

"I don't want to share you," he says, swinging her round, to de-
fray that note of doubt in her voice. He starts humming, a song
he has heard that hasn't been written yet, and moves her across
the floor. Not quite a waltz, but something like it. He learned the
steps the way he does everything, watching other people and constructing a semblance.

"Did you bring me here to seduce me?" Alice asks.

"Would you let me?"

"No!" she says, but she means yes, he can tell. She looks away,
flustered, and glances up at him sidelong, her cheeks still pink
from the cold. It makes him angry and confused because maybe
he does want to seduce her. Etta has left him feeling wretched.

"I have something for you," he says, fighting through it. He
takes the velvet jewelry box out of his pocket and pops it to reveal
the charm bracelet. It glitters sullenly in the light. Hers all along.
It was a mistake to give it to Etta.

"Thank you," she says, a little shocked.

"Put it on." He is too aggressive. He grabs her wrist, too
tightly, he sees, by the way she winces. Something in her shifts.
She is aware, now, of being in a deserted ballroom with a stranger
from a decade ago.

"I don't think I want to," she says carefully. "It's been lovely to
see you again . . . Oh God, I don't even know your name."

"It's Harper. Harper Curtis. But never mind that. I have something to show you, Alice."

"No, really—" She twists her hand out of his grip and when he lunges for her, she pulls one of the chair stacks down in front of him. While he fights his way through the tangle of furniture, she runs for the side door.

Harper goes after her, shoving the door open to reveal a dim maintenance corridor with wiring dangling from a scaffolding of pipes above. He unfolds the knife.

"Alice," he calls, his voice full of friendly cheer. "Come back, darling." He walks slowly, unthreateningly down the corridor, his hand tucked slightly behind his back. "I'm sorry, sweetheart. I didn't mean to frighten you."

He rounds the corner. There is a quilted mattress with a brownish stain propped up against the wall. If she was clever, she might have hidden behind it, waited for him to go past.

"I was too eager, I know. It's been so long. Waiting for you."

Further along, there is a storage room, the door ajar to show more stacks of chairs. She could be hiding in there, crouched between them, peeking out between the legs.

"You remember what I said to you? You shine, sweetheart. I could see you in the dark." In a way, that's true. It is the light that gives her away—and the shadow it casts on the stairs leading up to the roof.

"If you didn't like the bracelet, you only had to say." He feints right as if he is going to walk away, deeper into the bowels of the building, and then darts up the rickety wooden stairs, three at a time, to where she's hiding.

The neon light is naked and unflattering. It makes her look even more afraid. He lashes out with the knife, but only catches the arm of her jacket, drawing a long graze along the sleeve as she shouts in terror, and flees further up, past the clanking boiler with its copper taps and the soot stains on the walls.

She yanks at the heavy door to the roof and bursts out into

blinding daylight. He is a second behind her, but she slams the door on his left hand. He shrieks and snatches it away. "Bitch!"

He emerges squinting into the sunlight, his injured hand tucked under his armpit. Only bruised, not broken, but it hurts like a bitch. He no longer bothers to try to hide the knife.

She is standing by the little lip of the wall at the edge between a row of round air vents, their fans spinning lazily. She has her fist clenched around a piece of brick.

"Come here." He motions with the knife.

"No."

"You want to make this hard, sweetheart? You want to die badly?"

She lobs the brick at him. It goes skeltering across the pitched tar, missing him by a mile.

"All right," he says. "All right. I won't hurt you. It's a game. Come here. Please." He holds out his hands and gives her his most guileless smile. "I love you."

She smiles back, brilliantly. "I wish that was true," Alice says. And then she turns and leaps off the edge of the roof. He is too shocked to even yell after her.

Pigeons burst into the air from somewhere below. And then it's just him and the empty rooftop. A woman screams from the street. Over and over, like a siren.

This is not the way it is supposed to be. He takes the contraceptive packet out of his pocket and stares at it, as if the circle of colored pills marked by the days of the week might be an omen he could read. But it tells him nothing. It is only a dull, dead object.

He squeezes it so tightly that the plastic cracks. Then he throws it after her in disgust. It drifts down, twirling like a child's toy.

KIRBY

12 June 1993

The temperature is brutal, even worse in the basement where Rachel's clutter seems to absorb the heat and swill it around with cloying nostalgia. One day her mother will be dead, and it will fall to Kirby to sort all this crap out. The more she can get rid of right now, the better.

She's started moving boxes out onto the lawn so she can go through them. It's bad on her back, hauling them up the rickety wooden ladder staircase, but it's an improvement on being cooped up in there with towers of stuff threatening to cave in on her. This is her whole life of late, going through boxes of remains. She suspects that these will be even more painfully evocative than the broken lives documented in Detective Michael Williams's defunct evidence files.

Rachel comes out onto the lawn and sits down cross-legged beside her, in a pair of jeans and a black T-shirt, like a waitress, her hair pulled back in a messy ponytail. Her long feet are bare, the nails painted with a glossy red polish so dark it's almost black. It's a sign of the times that she's taken to dyeing her own hair, so the brown, more chestnut than usual, is shot through with gray.

"Goodness, that's a lot of junk," she says. "We'd be better off setting fire to it." She digs her rolling papers out of her pocket.

"Don't tempt me," Kirby says. It comes out with more venom than she intended, but Rachel doesn't even notice. "If we were smart, we would set up a table for a yard sale and move it straight from the boxes onto display."

"I do wish you wouldn't dig into all this stuff," Rachel sighs. "It's so much easier to deal with when it's packed away." She tears the end off a cigarette and sprinkles the paper with half marijuana and half tobacco.

"Are you hearing yourself, Mom?"

"Don't play therapist. It doesn't suit you." She lights up the joint and absently hands it to Kirby. "Oh, sorry, I forgot."

"It's okay," she says, and takes a drag. She holds it in her lungs until it turns the inside of her head sweet and staticky, like switching the TV to white noise. If white noise turned out to be encoded signals from the CIA transmitted through treacle. She's never had her mom's tolerance for pot. It usually makes her paranoid and overanalytical. But then she's never got stoned *with* her mom before. Maybe she's been doing something wrong all these years, and she's been missing out on some secret mother-daughter knowledge that should have got passed along years ago, like how to do a French plait or keep boys guessing.

"You still banned from the paper?"

"I'm on probation. They let me compile a list of some college sports awards but I'm not supposed to come in until I've met my class requirements."

"They're looking out for you. I think it's sweet."

"They're treating me like a fucking child."

Rachel starts pulling a bunch of old board-game pieces and

Christmas tree decorations out of a box, all tangled up in a menorah. Brightly colored dots of plastic Ludo pieces scatter all over the lawn.

"You know, we never had a bat mitzvah for you. Would you like a bat mitzvah?"

"No, Mom. It's too late for that," Kirby says, yanking open the tape on another box that has lost its stick over the years but still makes a terrible tearing sound. Little Golden books and Dr. Seuss. *Dean's Treasury of Cowboys, Where the Wild Things Are, Revolting Rhymes.*

"I've been keeping those for you. For when you have kids."

"Not very likely."

"You never know. *You* weren't planned. You used to write your dad letters. Do you remember?"

"What?" Kirby fights through the drone in her head. Her childhood is slippy. Memory is curated. All this paraphernalia you collect to ward off forgetting.

"I threw them away, of course."

"Why would you do that?"

"Don't be ridiculous. Where was I going to send them? You might as well have been writing to Santa."

"I thought So-John was my dad for the longest time. You know. Peter Collier. I tracked him down."

"I know, he told me. Oh, don't look so surprised. We stay in touch. He said you went to see him when you were sixteen and impressed the hell out of him, demanding a paternity test and insisting that he pay child support."

Actually, Kirby remembers, she was fifteen. She figured out who he was by reassembling a passionately ripped-to-shreds magazine profile she'd found in Rachel's dustbin the day after her mother went on an all-time epic crockery-smashing crying jag for three days.

Peter Collier, creative genius at a major Chicago agency, according to the puff piece, responsible for ground-breaking campaigns over the last three decades, loving husband to a wife tragically crippled with multiple sclerosis, and, the article did *not* mention, notable motherfucker (literal definition) who had haunted much of her childhood.

She'd phoned his secretary, using her deepest and most professional voice, and made an appointment to discuss "new business on a potentially very lucrative account" (vocabulary she stole from the article) at the swankiest restaurant she could think of.

He was at first baffled when a teenager sat down at the table, then irritated, then amused when she laid out her list of demands: that he resume seeing Rachel because she was miserable without him, start paying child support, and admit in print to the same magazine that he'd fathered a daughter out of wedlock. She informed him that, regardless of said admission, she would not be changing her name because she'd gotten used to Mazrachi and it suited her. He bought her lunch and explained that he'd met Rachel when she was already five years old. But he liked her style and if there was anything she ever needed... She'd retorted with a stinging one-liner, something Mae West-y about fish and bicycles, and left with the upper hand and pride intact, or so she thought.

"Who do you think helped pay your medical bills?"

"For fuck's sake."

"Why are you taking this so personally?"

"Because he *used* you, Mom. For nearly ten years."

"Grown-up relationships are complicated. We got what we needed from each other. Passion."

"Oh God, I don't want to hear it."

"A safety net. Some kind of solace. It's lonely out there. But it ran its course. It was lovely while it lasted. But everything is finite. Life. Love. All this." She waves her hand vaguely at the assorted boxes. "Sadness too. Although that's harder to let go of than happiness."

"Oh, Mom." Kirby puts her head in her mother's lap. It's the weed. She would never do this normally.

"It's okay," Rachel says. She seems surprised. But not unpleasantly. She strokes Kirby's hair. "These crazy curls. I never knew what to do with them. You didn't get them from me."

"Who was he?"

"Oh, I don't know. There were a couple of options. I was at a kibbutz in the Hula Valley. They farmed fish in ponds. But it could have been afterwards in Tel Aviv. Or on the road in Greece. I'm a bit foggy on the dates."

"Oh, Mom."

"I'm being honest. You'd be better off doing that, you know."

"What?"

"Trying to hunt down your father instead of the man who...hurt you."

"You never gave me the option."

"I could give you names. Five at most. Four. Five. Some of them are first names only. But the kibbutzim would probably have a register, if it was one of them. You could do a pilgrimage. Go to Israel and Greece and Iran."

"You went to Iran?"

"No, but it would be fascinating. I've got photographs in here somewhere. Would you like to see?"

"Yes, actually."

"Somewhere..." Rachel nudges Kirby off her lap and paws through the boxes until she finds a photo album, the red plastic printed to look like fake leather. She flips it open to a picture of a young woman with her hair whipping round her, in a white bathing suit, laughing and scowling into the sun that slices a sharp diagonal of contrast across her body and the concrete pier she's scrambling up. The sky is a washed-out azure. "This was at the harbor in Corfu."

"You look annoyed."

"I didn't want Amzi to take a photograph of me. He'd been doing it all day and it was driving me crazy. So of course that was the one he let me keep."

"Is he one of them?"

Rachel thinks about it. "No, I was feeling nauseous by then. I thought it was all the ouzo."

"Great, Mom."

"I didn't know. You must have been there already. A secret to me."

She flips ahead—the photographs aren't in any kind of chronological order, because she goes past Kirby's crushingly embarrassing punk prom photos to a picture of her as a naked toddler, standing in an inflatable paddling pool, holding a garden hose and looking impishly into the camera. Rachel is sitting in a stripy canvas deck chair beside the pool, her hair cut boyishly short, smoking a cigarette behind oversized tortoiseshell sunglasses. The glamorous malaise of the suburbs. "Look how cute you were," she says. "You were always a sweet kid, but naughty too. You can see it radiating out your face. I didn't really know what to do with you."

"I can tell."

"Don't be cruel," Rachel says, but without heat.

Kirby takes the album out of her hands and starts going through it. The problem with snapshots is that they replace actual memories. You lock down the moment and it becomes all there is of it.

"Oh God, look at my hair."

"I didn't tell you to shave it off. They nearly suspended you from school."

"What's this?" It comes out sharper than she intended. But the shock of it is terrible. Dread like a swamp.

"Hmmm?" Rachel takes the photograph from her. It's mounted in a yellowed card with a looping friendly font: "Greetings From Great America! 1976." "That theme park. You were crying because you were scared to go on the rollercoaster. I hated that we couldn't go on roadtrips without you getting motion sick."

"No, what's *that* in my hand?"

Rachel peers at the picture of the wailing girl in a theme park. "I don't know, honey. A plastic horse?"

"Where did you get it?"

"Honestly, I can't remember the genesis of all your toys."

"Please *think*, Rachel."

"You found it somewhere. Carried it around for ages until you fell in love with something else. You were always fickle like that. Some doll with turnaround hair, blonde and brunette. Melody? Tiffany? Something like that. She had the most gorgeous outfits."

"Where is it now?"

"If it's not in one of these boxes, then it must have got thrown out. I don't keep *every*thing. What are you doing?"

Kirby tears through the boxes, dumping the contents on to the overgrown grass.

"Now you're just being selfish," Rachel points out calmly. "It's going to be much less fun cleaning that up later."

There are cardboard poster tubes, a hideous tea set with brown and orange flowers from Kirby's grandmother in Denver, who she tried to live with when she was fourteen, a tall copper hookah with the tip of the mouthpiece broken off, crumbled incense smelling of decayed empires, a battered silver harmonica, old paintbrushes and dried-out pens, miniature dancing cats that Rachel painted on tile blocks, which actually sold well for a while in the local craft shop. Indonesian bird cages, an engraved bit of elephant tusk or possibly warthog (real ivory regardless), a jade Buddha, a printer's tray, Letraset, and a ton, probably, of heavy art and design books bookmarked with torn-off bits of paper, tangles of costume jewelry, a weaver bird's nest and several dream-catchers that they'd spent a summer making when Kirby was ten. Some kids have lemonade stands, Kirby tried to sell fake spiderwebs with dangly crystals. And she wonders why she turned out like she did.

"Where are my *toys*, Mom?"

"I was going to give them away."

"You wouldn't have got round to it," Kirby says, brushing the grass off her knees. She heads back into the house and down to the basement, clutching the photograph.

She finds the discolored plastic trunk, eventually, stuffed inside the broken freezer that Rachel uses for storage. It's under a garbage bag full of assorted hats that Kirby once played dress-up with, half-crushed by a wooden spinning wheel that must be worth *something* to an antiques collector.

Rachel sits on the top of the stairs, resting her chin on her knees, watching her. "You're still a secret to me."

"Shut up, Mom."

Kirby pries open the lid, like an oversize school lunchbox. Inside are all her toys. A baby doll that she never really wanted, but everyone else at school had them. Barbies and their cheap generic cousins, in all kinds of career variations. Businesswoman with a pink briefcase or mermaid. None of them have shoes. Half of them are missing a limb. The doll with the reversible hair, naked, now, a robot that turned into a UFO, a killer whale in a trailer truck stenciled with the logo for Sea World, a wooden doll with DIY knitted plaits of red wool, Princess Leia in her white snow-suit and Evil Lyn with her golden skin. There were never enough girls to play with.

And there, underneath a half-built Lego tower manned by die-cast lead Indian braves, also from her grandmother, is a plastic pony. Its orange hair is matted with something dried and sticky. Juice, maybe. But it has the same sad-looking eyes and the goofy melancholy smile and the butterflies on its butt.

"Jesus," Kirby breathes.

"That's it, all right." Rachel shifts impatiently on the steps. "And now?"

"*He* gave this to me."

"I shouldn't have let you smoke. You're not used to it."

"Listen to me," Kirby shouts. "He gave this to me. The fucker who tried to kill me."

"I don't know what you're saying!" Rachel shrieks back, con-fused and upset.

"How old was I in that photo?"

"Seven? Eight?"

Kirby checks the date on the card: 1976. She was nine. But younger when he gave it to her. "Your math is terrible, Mom." She can't believe she hasn't thought about it in all these years.

She turns the horse over. There are stamps under each of its hooves in all-caps. MADE IN. HONG KONG. PAT PENDING. HASBRO 1982.

Everything goes cold. The static from the weed cranks up the volume, buzzing in her head. She moves to sit on the stairs just below Rachel. She takes her mother's hand and presses it against her face. Her veins stand out like blue tributaries amongst the fine hatched lines and first liver spots. She's getting old, Kirby thinks, and this is somehow even more unbearable than the plastic pony.

"I'm scared, Mom."

"We all are," Rachel says. She hugs her head to her chest and rubs her back as Kirby's whole body racks and shudders. "Shhh. It's okay, honey. It's all right. That's the big secret, don't you know? Everyone is. All the time."

HARPER

28 March 1987

First Catherine, then Alice. He broke the rules. He should never have given Etta the bracelet. He feels his control slipping, like a truck's axle off a jack.

There is only one name left. He does not know what will happen after. But he has to do it properly. The way he is supposed to. He has to set things right, align the constellations. He has to trust in the House. No more resisting.

He doesn't try to force it when he opens the door. He lets it open on to where it is supposed to be: 1987. He finds his way to an elementary school where he mingles with the parents and teachers moving between the displays in the hall under a hand-lettered banner that reads "Welcome to our Science Fair!" He walks past a papier-mâché volcano, wires and crocodile clips on a wooden board that light up an electric bulb when you touch them together, posters illustrating how high a flea can jump and the aerodynamics of jet planes.

He is drawn up short by a map of stars, actual constellations. The little boy standing behind the table starts reading from a card in a shy monotone. "Stars are made of balls of fiery gas. They are very far away and sometimes by the time the light reaches us, the star is already dead and we don't even know it yet. I also have a telescope—"

"Shut up," he says. The boy looks like he might burst into tears. He stares, lip trembling, and then bolts into the crowd. Harper barely notices. He is tracing his fingertip over the lines drawn between the stars, transfixed. Big Dipper. Little Dipper. Ursa Major. Orion with his belt and sword. But they could just as easily be something else if you connected the dots differently. And who is to say that is a bear or a warrior at all? It damn well doesn't look that way to him. There are patterns because we try to find them. A desperate attempt at order because we can't face the terror that it might all be random. He feels undone by the revelation. He has the sensation of losing his footing, as if the whole damn world is stuttering.

A young teacher with a blonde ponytail takes him gently by the arm. "Are you all right?" she says kindly, in a voice meant for children.

"No—" Harper starts.

"Can't find your child's project?" The chubby boy is standing next to her, sniffing, his hand clutching her skirt. Harper holds on to the reality of that, the way he rubs his nose with the back of his sleeve, leaving a smear of snot across the dark fabric.

"Mysha Pathan," he says, as if coming up out of a dream.

"Are you her . . . ?"

"Uncle," he says falling back on the explanation that has always worked so well.

"Oh." The teacher is thrown. "I didn't know she had family in the States." She studies him for a moment, puzzled. "She's a very promising student. You'll find her project near the stage by the doors," she points helpfully.

"Thank you," Harper says, and manages to tear himself away from the star map that is only a useless fetish.

Mysha is a little girl with brown skin and metal in her mouth like a miniature railroad, not unlike the wiring that once held Harper's jaw together. She is bouncing slightly on her heels, although she seems unaware of it, standing in front of a desk lined with potted succulents and a poster behind her head with numbers and colors that mean nothing to him, even though he looks at it very carefully.

"Hi! Can I tell you about my project?" she says, full of sparking enthusiasm.

"I'm Harper," he says.

"Okay!" she says brightly. This is not part of her script and it throws her. "I'm Mysha and this is my project. Um. As you can see, I grew cacti in, um, different kinds of soil with varying acidity."

"This one is dead."

"Yes. I learned that some soil conditions are very bad for cacti. As you can see by the results that I marked up on this chart."

"I can see that."

"The vertical axis represents the amount of acidity in the soil and the horizontal—"

"Do me a favor, Mysha."

"Um."

"I'm going to come back. Right away. As soon as I can. But it won't feel like that for you. You have to do something for me though while I'm away. It's very important. Don't stop shining."

"Okay!" she says.

Back at the House, it seems that all the objects are on fire in his head. He can still trace the trajectories, but for the first time he can see that the map leads nowhere. It folds in on itself. A loop he can't escape. The only thing left to do is surrender to it.

HARPER

12 June 1993

━━━━━━

He steps into the early evening 12 June 1993, the date displayed in the post office window. It's only three days since he killed Catherine. He is pushing up against the edge of things. He already knows where to find Mysha Pathan. It's printed clearly on the last remaining totem. Milkwood Pharmaceuticals.

The company is on the other side of town, deep in the West Side. A long, squat, gray building. He sits inside the window of a Dominos in the strip mall across the way, picking at the stringy cheese, and watches and waits, observing how the parking lot is mostly empty on a Saturday night, how the security guard is bored and keeps stepping out to have a cigarette, carefully disposing of the butts in one of the yellow fliptop trash cans at the side of the building. How he uses the tag around his neck to swipe himself back into the building.

He could wait. Until she comes out. Take her at home or en route. He could break into her car. The compact blue one that is the only one left, parked right next to the entrance. Hide in the back seat. But he is feeling edgier than ever, the headache burrowing through his skull and down into his spine. It has to be done now.

At 11 p.m., when the pizza place closes, he walks round the building, a slow circuit, timed to coincide with the guard's smoke break.

"Do you have the time?" he says, walking up to him fast, already unfolding his knife one-handed, hidden behind the swish of his coat. The guard is alarmed by Harper's pace, but the question is so innocuous, so ordinary, that he automatically looks down at his wrist and Harper stabs the blade into his neck and yanks it across, shearing through the muscle and tendons and arteries, at the same time spinning the man around so that the gush of blood splatters over the cans and not on him. He kicks him behind his knees so that he topples forward between the trash cans, which Harper pulls forward to hide the body. He snags the security tag and wipes the blood off on the man's pants. The whole thing takes less than a minute. The guard is still gurgling slightly as Harper walks towards the glass doors to swipe the keycard.

He takes the stairs, up through the empty building to the fourth floor, letting the feeling lead him, like a memory, past rows of locked doors, until he comes to Lab Six, which is standing open, waiting for him. A single light is on inside, above her workbench. She has her back to him, singing loudly and badly, half-dancing to the tinny music leaking from the earphones half-tucked under her headscarf: "All That She Wants." She's pulverizing leaves and then delicately transferring bits of the mush with some kind of plastic syringe to conical tubes filled with a golden liquid.

It's the first time he has had no understanding of the context. "What are you doing?" he says, loud enough to be heard over the music. She jumps and fumbles the earphones off.

"Oh my God. I'm so embarrassed. How long have you been

watching me? Oh jeez. Wow. I thought I was the only one in the building. Um. Who are you?"

"The new security guard."

"Oh. You're not wearing a uniform."

"They didn't have my size."

"Right," she says, nodding tightly to herself. "So, um, I'm working on seeing if I can grow a drought-resistant strain of tobacco, based on a protein from a flower in Namibia that can resurrect itself. I spliced in the gene and I've been growing the tobacco for a month, and now I'm checking to see if the protein I'm looking for is in there." She carries the conical tubes over to a flat gray machine the size of a suitcase and opens the flap to insert them into the tray. "Pop it in the Spectrophotometer for analysis..." She taps at the controls and the machine starts whirring. "And if the protein has been expressed successfully, then the substrate will turn blue." She smiles at him, pleased. "Did I explain that well enough? Because we've got a group of tenth graders coming in next week and—oh." She's seen the knife. "You're *not* a security guard."

"No. And you're the last one. I have to finish it. Don't you see?"

She tries to move so that there is a bench between them, scanning for things she could throw at him, but he has already cut her off. He has become efficient. He does what he needs to. He punches her in the face to get her down. He ties her wrists with the cords of her earphones because he has left his binding wire behind at the House. He stuffs her headscarf in her mouth to muffle her screaming.

But there is no one to hear her and it takes her a long time to die. He tries to be more elaborate to make up for the lack of joy this brings him. He unspools her intestines in a spiral around her. He cuts out her organs and places them on the desk where she was working under the lamplight. He stuffs tobacco leaves in the gaping wounds, so it looks as if the plants are growing out of her body. He pins the Pigasus badge to her lab coat. He hopes it will be enough.

He washes off in the women's bathroom, soaking his coat and stuffing his blood-soaked shirt into the feminine hygiene products disposal bin. He pulls a lab coat over his bloodied jacket and walks out of the building, wearing her name-badge turned around so that the ID is obscured.

By the time he is done, it is four in the morning and there is a different security guard, standing behind the desk, looking baffled and talking into his radio. "I told you, I already checked the men's bathroom. I don't know where—"

"Well, good night," Harper says cheerfully, walking out straight past him.

"Good night, sir," the guard says, distracted, registering only the coat and the badge and raising his hand in automatic greeting. The uncertainty kicks in a second later, because it's really late and how come he didn't recognize the guy and where the hell is Jackson? That will shift to crushing guilt in five hours' time when he is sitting at the police station, reviewing the pharma lab's security-camera footage, after the young biologist's body has been discovered, and he realizes that he let her killer walk right out past him.

Upstairs in the lab, a bloom of blue is spreading through the gold in the conical tubes.

DAN

13 June 1993

Dan spots her crazy hair right off the bat. Hard to miss, even in the clamor of the arrivals hall. He seriously thinks about getting back on the plane, but by then it's too late, she's spotted him. She half-raises her hand. It's almost a question.

"Yeah, okay, I see you, I'm coming," he grumbles to himself, pointing at the conveyor belt and miming lifting a suitcase. She nods, vigorously, and starts navigating the hordes towards him; a woman in a chador, like her own personal palanquin with the curtains drawn, a harried family scrambling to keep themselves together, a depressing number of obese travelers. He's never understood the thinking that airports are glamorous. People who believe that have never had to route through Minneapolis–St. Paul. Taking a bus is less tedious. Better view too. The only miracle of flight is that more passengers don't strangle each other out of boredom and frustration.

Kirby materializes at his elbow. "Hey. I tried to call you."

"I was on the plane."

"Yeah, the hotel said you'd left already. Sorry. I had to talk to you. I couldn't wait."

"Patience never was your strong point."

"This is serious, Dan."

He sighs, heavily, and watches a dozen not-his-bags inching past on the conveyor. "Is this about the junkie artist girl from a couple of days ago? Because that was an ugly thing, but it's not your guy. The cops already nailed her dealer for it. Charming fellow called Huxtable, or something like that."

"Huxley Snyder. No history of violence."

Finally his suitcase emerges from the plastic curtain and thumps down the chute onto the belt. He scoops it up and shuttles Kirby towards the exit to the El.

"History has to start somewhere, right?"

"I spoke to the girl's dad. He said someone had been phoning the house asking for Catherine."

"Sure. I get people phoning my house asking for me all the time. Most of them are insurance salesmen." He starts digging in his wallet for CTA tokens, but Kirby has dropped enough for both of them into the slot.

"He said there was something sinister about him."

"There's something sinister about insurance salesmen," Dan retorts. He's not going to encourage her.

There's a train waiting, already packed. He lets her take the seat and leans up against the pole as the doors-closing bell goes. Hates touching the thing. More germs on hand rails than toilet seats.

"And she was stabbed, Dan. Not in the gut, but—"

"Have you enrolled for the new semester?"

"What?"

"Because I know you're not talking to me about this shit again. You're practically under a restraining order."

"For fuck's sake. I didn't come here to talk to you about Catherine Galloway-Peck, although there are similarities and . . ."

"I don't want to hear it."

"Fine," she says coldly. "The reason I came to meet you at the airport was because of this." She swings her backpack round onto her lap. Battered, black, anonymous. She unzips it and pulls out his jacket.

"Hey, I've been looking for that."

"That's not what I want to show you."

She unfolds the jacket like it's some sacred bloody shroud. He's expecting proof of the second coming at least. Jesus's face imprinted in a sweat stain. But what emerges is a kids' toy. A plastic horse, the worse for wear.

"And this now?"

"*He* gave it to me when I was a little girl. I was six years old. How was I supposed to recognize him? I didn't even remember the pony until I saw a photograph." She hesitates, uncertain. "Shit. I don't know how to say this."

"Can't be worse than anything else you've said to me. All the crazy theories, I mean." Not the moment when she turned on him in the *Sun-Times* boardroom, raw with the betrayal that ripped right through him, leaving a residual ache every time he thinks about her. Which is *all* the time.

"This theory's the worst one of all. But you have to hear me out."

"Can't wait," he says.

She lays it out for him. Her impossible pony, which ties in to the impossible baseball card on that World War Two woman, which somehow ties in to the lighter and a cassette tape Julia wouldn't have listened to. He struggles to hide his mounting dismay.

"It's very interesting," he says, carefully.

"Don't do that."

"What am I doing?"

"*Pitying* me."

"There's a reasonable explanation for all of this."

"Fuck reasonable."

"Look. Here's the plan. I've had six and a half hours in airports and on planes. I'm tired. I stink. But for you—and really, you're the only person in the world I would do this for—I am going to forgo heading home to have the simple and very necessary joy of a shower. We're going to go straight to the office and I'm going to phone the toy company and clear this up."

"You think I didn't do that already?"

"Yeah, but you weren't asking the right questions," he says, patiently. "Like, for example, was there a prototype? Was there a salesman who might have had access to them in 1974? Is it possible that the numbers '1982' refer to a limited edition or a manufacturing number rather than a date?"

She's quiet for a long time, staring at her feet. She's wearing big clunky boots today. Half the laces are undone. "It is crazy, huh? Jesus."

"Totally understandable. That's a weird set of coincidences right there. Of course you want to try to make sense of them. And you're probably onto something big with this pony. If it turns out there was a salesman with a prototype, that could lead us straight to him. Okay? You done good. Don't sweat it."

"You're the one who's sweating," she says with a small tight smile that doesn't make it to her eyes.

"We'll sort it out," he says. And until they get to the *Sun-Times,* he actually believes it.

HARPER

13 June 1993

———

Harper sits at the back of the Greek diner, under the mural of the white church and the blue lake, with a short stack of pancakes and crispy bacon, watching passers-by through the window and waiting for the stoop-shouldered black man to finish with the newspaper. He takes cautious sips of his coffee, which is still too hot to drink, and wonders if this is why the House would only allow him as far as this day. Because he never goes back to the goddamn place. He feels remarkably calm. He's walked away from everything in his life before, too many times to count. He could be a drifter just as easily in this age, even with its crush and fury and noise. He wishes he'd brought more money with him, but there are ways and means to come by cash, especially with a knife in your pocket.

The old man finally gets up to go and Harper fetches another little packet of sugar and snags the newspaper. It is too soon for them to be reporting on Mysha, but perhaps there will be something on Catherine, and it's this bite of curiosity that lets him know that he is not done. He could stay here, but eventually he would find other constellations. Or make up his own.

It's only because the *Sun-Times* is folded over to the sports pages that he happens to see her name. Not even a real article, but a list of the Chicagoland High School Athlete of the Year awards.

He reads it carefully, twice, mouthing the names like they might help him unlock the glaring obscenity at the top: *"By Kirby Mazrachi."*

He checks the date. It is today's paper. He stands up slowly from the table. His hands are shaking.

"You done with that, buddy?" A guy with a beard to hide the fat around his neck asks.

"No," Harper snarls.

"Okay. Relax, man. Just wanted to check the headlines. When you're done."

He walks carefully across the diner to the payphone by the toilets. The directory hangs from a grubby chain. There is only one Mazrachi in the phonebook. R. Oak Park. The mother, he thinks. The fucking cunt who lied to him that Kirby was dead. He tears the page out of the book.

As he walks towards the door, he sees that the fat man has taken the newspaper anyway. He is overtaken by fury. He strides over, grabs the man by the beard and smashes his forehead into the table. His head ricochets back up, into his hands, his nose gushing blood. He starts whining in disbelief, a strangely high-pitched sound for such a burly man. The whole diner goes quiet and turns to stare as Harper shoves through the revolving door.

The chef with the mustache (gray, receding hair) is moving out from behind the counter, yelling, "Get out! You! Get out!"

But Harper is already on his way to the address on the listing crumpled in his hand.

RACHEL

13 June 1993

═══════

Shards of glass from the smashed window pane lie dull on the woven carpet just inside the front door. The canvases, mounted, not framed, along one side of the hallway have been slashed with casual hostility; someone dragging a knife along the wall as he walked.

In the kitchen, the replica Degas ballerinas and Gauguin island girls painted in strange juxtaposition on the cupboard doors look down with dainty indifference at the boxes that have been knocked over, their contents spilled across the floor.

The splayed-open photo album is on the counter. Pictures have been removed, torn up and discarded on the tiles; so much confetti. A woman in a white bathing suit squinting into the sun, her face sheared through.

In the living-room, the sleek round '70s table lies on its back with its legs in the air like an overturned turtle. The tchotchkes and art books and magazines that were on it are tumbled across the floor. A bronze lady with a bell hidden under her skirt lies on her side beside a china bird with its head snapped off, leaving a jagged wound of white ceramic. The bird's head stares blankly at a fashion editorial of angular young women in ugly clothes.

The couch has been cut up, long violent slashes that expose the soft synthetic innards and the bone of the frame.

Upstairs, the door to the bedroom is ajar. On the drawing table, spilled black ink is soaking into the paper, obliterating the illustration of a grimly curious duckling interrogating the skeleton of a dead raccoon in a bear's tummy. Some of the hand-lettered words are still visible.

It's too bad. I'm so sad.
But I'm glad for what I had.

A colored glass ornament sways slowly in the sun dappling through the window, casting crazy circles of light across the devastated room.

The neighbors did not come to investigate the noise.

KIRBY

13 June 1993

O h hey," Chet says, looking up from *Black Orchid,* which has a purple girl on the front cover. "I found something really, really cool in line with your mystery baseball card. Have a look." He puts aside the comic book and produces a printout from a microfiche dated 1951.

"This caused quite the scandal. A transsexual jumped off the roof of the Congress Hotel and no one knew she was a he until the post-mortem. But the best bit is what she's holding." He points at the photograph of a limp woman's hand, extending out from under a coat someone has thrown over her. There is a blurry plastic dial lying nearby. "Doesn't that look exactly like a contraceptive pill packet from today?"

"Or maybe a cute compact mirror with a beaded pattern," Dan dismisses it. The last thing he needs is Anwar encouraging Kirby's madness. "Now, do something useful and find me any information you can on Hasbro and when they introduced their pony range and toy patenting in general."

"Well, somebody woke up on the wrong side of the futon."

"Wrong side of the timezone," Dan grumbles.

"Please, Chet," Kirby intervenes. "From 1974 onwards. It's really important."

"All right, all right. I'll start with their advertising and take it from there. And oh, by the way, Kirby, you *just* missed a Grade-A crank who was in here looking for you."

"For me?"

"Real intense. Didn't bring cookies, though. Next time, can you ask him to bring cookies? I don't like to put up with that level of insane unless there's some kind of high-calorie compensation."

"What did he look like?" Dan's head comes up.

"I don't know. Generic crazy man. Well-dressed enough. Dark sports coat. Jeans. On the skinny side of built. Intense blue eyes. He wanted to know about the high-school best athlete stuff. He had a limp."

"Shit," Dan says, even though he is still processing this. Kirby is faster on the draw. After all, she's been expecting him for the last four years.

"When did he leave?" She's gone pale, her freckles standing out in sharp relief.

"What's with you two?"

"When did he *fucking* leave, Chet?"

"Five minutes ago."

"Kirby, wait," Dan grabs for her arm and misses. She's already out the door and running. "Fuck!"

"Whoa. Drama city. What's going on?" Chet says.

"Call the cops, Anwar. Ask for Andy Diggs or, shit, whatsis-name, Amato. The guy covering the Korean murder."

"And tell them *what?*"

"Anything that will get them here!"

Kirby flies down the stairs and out the doors. She has to pick a direction, so she runs up North Wabash and stops in the middle of the bridge, scanning the crowds for *him*.

The river is a Mediterranean teal today, the exact same color as the roof of the sharp-prowed tourist boat passing below. A tinny voice through a megaphone points out the twin corncobs of Marina City.

There are more tourists wandering along the river walk, identifiable by their floppy sun hats and shorts as much by the cameras slung around their necks. An office worker with the sleeves of his suit pushed up is sitting on the red girder by the railing, eating a sandwich, waving his foot warningly at the scavenger seagull edging closer. People cross the street in tight-packed clusters to the tune of the pipping walk signal and lose cohesion as soon as they're off the crosswalk. It makes it difficult to spot just one in the herd. She skips over them, micro-sorting by race and gender and build. Black guy. Woman. Woman. Fat guy. Man with headphones. Guy with long hair. Guy in suit. Guy in maroon T-shirt. Another suit. It must be getting to lunch-time. Brown leather jacket. Black button-up shirt. Blue jumpsuit. Green stripes. Black T-shirt. Black T-shirt. Wheelchair. Suit. None of them are him. He's gone.

"Fuuuuuuuck!" she screams at the sky, startling the guy with the sandwich. The seagull lifts into the air, screeching admonishment.

The 124 bus drives across in front of her, obscuring her view. It's like a reset on her brain. A second later, she spots him. The uneven motion of a baseball cap bobbing slightly as if the man had a limp. She's off running again. She doesn't hear Dan calling.

A tan-and-white taxi swerves to avoid her as she darts across Wacker without looking. The driver stops dead in the middle of the intersection, his hand still on the horn and rolls down his window to swear at her. Anxious hooting starts up on either side.

"You crazy? You was nearly toast," a woman in shiny pants scolds her, grabbing her arm and pulling her out of the road.

"Let go!" Kirby shoves her away. She pushes through the lunchtime shopping crowd, trying to keep him in sight, breaking past a couple with a baby stroller into the shadow of the elevated tracks. The oppressive daytime darkness throws her. Her eyes don't adjust immediately and in that split second, she loses him.

She looks around, desperate, mentally cataloging and dismissing people as she glances over them. And then the boldness of the red McDonald's sign catches her eye, dragging her attention upwards, to the suspended stairs leading to the El on the other side. She can only see his jeans disappearing from sight, but his limp is more pronounced on the stairs.

"Hey!" she shouts, but her voice is lost in the noise of the traffic. A train is coming in above her. She sprints across and up the stairs, digging in her pocket for tokens. In the end she jumps the turnstiles, hurtles up another set of stairs to the platform and shoves between the closing doors of the train without even seeing which line it is.

She's breathing hard. She stares at her boots, too scared to look up in case he's right there. Come on, she thinks angrily to herself. Come fucking on. She raises her head defiantly and sweeps her gaze over the compartment. The other passengers are applying themselves to ignoring her, even the ones who were staring when she forced her way in through the doors. A little boy in a blue camouflage track top glares at her with a kid's pure self-righteousness. GI Boy Blue, she thinks, nearly laughing in relief or shock.

He's not here. Maybe she was mistaken. Or he's on the other train, heading in the other direction. Her heart free-falls away.

She edges through the rattling car, making for the interconnecting doors, catching herself as the train swings hard through the corners. The perspex is scratched, not even graffiti, but hatchmarks scoured into the surface, accomplished over hundreds of rides by different people taking up the call with pen knives or X-Acto blades.

She peeks cautiously through into the next car and immediately ducks back. He's standing by the door, holding on to the handrail, his cap pulled down low. But she recognizes his build, the slope-shoulders, the angle of his jaw and his uneven profile, turned away from her, looking out over the rooftops swishing past.

She ducks back, her mind rocketing. She digs in her bag and shrugs into Dan's jacket to obscure her profile. She ties the scarf from her throat over her hair, babushka-style. Not much of a disguise, but it's all she's got. She keeps her head turned, enough to see him in her peripheral vision, to watch when he gets off.

DAN

13 June 1993

‗‗‗‗‗‗

Dan loses sight of her somewhere on Randolph. His mind a knot of panic, he made it through the traffic, setting off another round of enraged hooting, but he just couldn't keep up. He leans on one of the green trash cans, from the Chicago of yesteryear, like the streetlights with their gaslamp bulbs that look like inflated condoms. He's panting. He has a stitch clawing into his ribs and it feels like Dolph fucking Lundgren has delivered a round-house kick to his chest. A train goes rattling overhead, the vibration practically shaking his fillings loose.

If Kirby was here, she isn't now.

He takes a wild guess and walks over to Michigan, holding his side, breathing between his teeth. Pathetic. He is sick with panic and rage. He thinks about her lying dead in an alleyway somewhere behind a pile of trash. Probably passed right by her. They'll never catch the guy. What this city needs is cameras on every corner like a gas station.

Please God, he'll get in shape. He'll eat vegetables. He'll go to Mass and confession and visit his mother's grave. No more cigarettes on the sly. Just let Kirby be okay. Is that so much to ask, really, in the scheme of things?

Back at the *Sun-Times,* the cops have still not arrived. Chetty is in a fit of pique, trying to explain what's going on to Harrison. Richie comes in, pale and freaked out, to tell them that a girl was murdered this morning. Stabbed in a pharmaceutical lab on the West Side. Looks like the same MO. Worse. The details are even more gruesome. And a woman from the dead junkie girl's support meetings has come forward to identify a man with a limp who was asking about her.

No one quite knows how to take it, Dan realizes. That maybe she was fucking right about the guy all along. He can't believe that *pendejo*'s balls, walking in here and asking for her.

He goes to the electronics shop down the road and buys a beeper pager. Pink, because it's the window-display model and it's ready to go. He heads back to Chet and gives him the number and strict instructions to page him on it if they hear anything. Particularly from Kirby. He clamps down on the worry. As long as he keeps doing things, he won't feel it.

He goes to fetch his car and get something from his house. Then he drives to Wicker Park and breaks into her flat.

It's even messier than it was before. Her entire wardrobe seems to have migrated into the living-room, draped across the furniture. He averts his eyes from a pair of red briefs, inside out on the back of a chair.

She's been playing at being a proper detective, he sees. The contents of the evidence boxes are scattered all over the place. There's a map of the city blu-tacked to the broom closet. Every stabbing femicide for the last twenty years is marked on it with a red dot.

There are a lot of dots.

He flips open the file on the jerry-rigged trestle table. It's full of typed transcripts, neatly numbered and dated and clipped to the original news articles. Murder victims' families, he realizes. Scores of people she's tracked down and interviewed. *I've been doing this all year,* she'd said. No kidding.

He sinks heavily onto the painted stool, flipping through the testimonies.

I didn't "lose" her. I lose my housekeys. She was taken.

I go through every day thinking about how I will react when he gets caught. It changes, you know? Sometimes I think I'd like to torture him to death. Other times I think I'd forgive him. Because that would be worse.

They stole my investment in the future. Does that sound strange to you?

They make it sexy in the movies.

It's the most terrible thing to hear, but in a way, it was also a relief. Because if you only have one child, you know you will never get that phone call again.

HARPER

13 June 1993

―――――

A black rage swills through Harper's head. He should have killed the brown boy at the newspaper. Dragged him to a window and hurled him down onto the street. He played coy with him. He *humored* him. As if he was some empty-eyed idiot from Manteno State Hospital with his chin covered in his own saliva and shit in his pants.

It had taken every whit of his self-control to ask reasonable questions. Not how the fuck is she still alive and where is the cunt? But, is she in the office, he'd like to talk to her about *the awards*. He's very interested in the awards. Could he talk to her, please? Is she here?

He pushed it too far. He saw the boy switch from bored contempt to wary alertness. "I'll just call security to fetch her for you," he'd said, which Harper understood perfectly.

"No need. Tell her I was here for her, all right? I'll come back." It's immediately apparent how bad a mistake it was to say it. Enough that he buys a White Sox baseball cap on the street and pulls the brim down low over his face, because he half suspects the goddamn boy will call the police. He goes straight to the train. He needs to get back to the House to figure this out.

She'll be harder to find if she's spooked, but he can't keep the bile back. He wants her to know. *Let* her run. *Let* her hide. He'll dig her out like he used to do with rabbits, dragging her out of her hole by the scruff of her neck while she flails and screams, before he cuts her throat.

Watching the city slide past the windows of the train, he touches himself with the back of his hand through his pants. But his consternation is too overwhelming. It defeats him. Everything is slipping. It's *her*. He should have taken her when she didn't have the dog. There were other opportunities.

He feels terribly alone. He feels like plunging his knife into someone's face to relieve the pressure building up behind his eyes. He has to get back to the House. He has to fix this. He will go back to find her to try and unravel where he has gone wrong. The stars must realign.

He doesn't see Kirby. Not even when he gets off the train.

KIRBY

13 June 1993

She should walk away and call the police. She knows this deep in the base of her skull. She's found him. She knows where he is. But what *if,* the thought nags at her. What if it's a ruse? The house, by all appearances, is an abandoned wreck. One of several on this block. He could have gone into it because he was aware of her following him. She's not exactly subtle in this neighborhood. Which means that he might be lying in wait.

Her hands are numb. Just call the cops, you idiot. Make it their problem. You passed two payphones on the way here. Sure, she thinks. And both of them were trashed. The glass smashed and the receivers pulled off. She tucks her hands into her armpits, miserable and shaky. Standing under a tree, which Englewood, unlike the West Side, still has plenty of. She's pretty sure he can't see her, because she can't see the broken windows on the second floor. But she can't tell if he is peering through a crack in the plywood boarding up the windows downstairs, or hell, if he is sitting on the front steps waiting for her.

The plain, terrible truth is that, if she leaves, she will lose him.

Shit-shit-shit-shit.

"You going in?" says someone at her shoulder.

"Jesus!" she jumps. The homeless guy's eyes bulge slightly, making him look innocent or intensely interested. Half the teeth in his smile are gone and he's wearing a faded Kris Kross T-shirt and a red beanie despite the heat.

"I wouldn't go in, I was you. I wasn't even sure which one it was. But I kept watchin' him. He comes out at strange times, dressed funny. I been in. You wouldn't be able to tell from outside, but it's done up all nice. You want to go in? You need a ticket to get in." He holds up a crumpled piece of paper. It takes her long seconds to recognize it as money. "I'll sell you one for a hundred bucks. Otherwise it won't work. You won't see it."

She feels a jab of relief that he's clearly crazy. "I'll give you twenty if you show me where to go."

He changes his mind. "Nah. Nah, wait. I been in. It wasn't good. Place is cursed. Haunted. Devil's own. You don't want to go in. You give me twenty for the good advice and you don't go in, you hear?"

"I have to." God help her.

Everything she has in her wallet amounts to seventeen dollars and change. The homeless guy is not very impressed, but he takes her round and helps boost her onto the wooden staircase zig-zagging up the back of the house, regardless.

"You won't see shit, anyway. Not without a ticket. Guess that means you safe. Don't say I didn't warn you."

"Please be quiet."

She uses Dan's jacket to climb over the barbed wire that has been looped round the base of the outside stairs precisely to stop people getting in. Sorry, Dan, she thinks as the wire rips into the sleeve. You need new clothes anyway.

The paint is flaking on the boards. The stairs are rotten. They complain under her every step as she gingerly picks her way to the ground-floor window that gapes open like a hole in a head. There is broken glass all over the ledge. The shards are dirty and rain-spattered.

"Did you break the window?" she whispers down to the crazy man.

"You shouldn't ask me nothing," he sulks. "Your business, you want to go in."

Shit. The house is dark inside, but she can see through the open window that it's trashed. Junkies went to town in there. The floorboards have been ripped up, along with the piping, walls busted up and stripped to the bone. Through a door on the other side, she can make out the naked porcelain of a broken toilet. The seat has been wrenched off, the sink kicked to the ground and cracked open. It's absurd that he would be hiding in there. Waiting for her. She falters on the edge. "Can you call the police?" she whispers.

"No, ma'am."

"In case he kills me." This comes out more matter-of-fact than she would have liked.

"Dead people in there already," Mal hisses back.

"Please. Give them the address."

"All right, all right!" He whacks at the air. Swatting at promises. "But I ain't sticking around."

"Sure." Kirby mutters under her breath. She doesn't look back. She lays Dan's jacket down on the windowsill over the broken glass. There's a lump in the pocket. Her pony, she realizes. She hauls herself into the house.

KIRBY AND HARPER

22 November 1931

Time heals all wounds. Wounds clot, eventually. The seams knit together.

As soon as she crosses the window frame, she is somewhere else. She thinks she must be going mad.

Maybe she's been dying this whole time and everything has been an extended hero-trip, her brain's last huzzah as she bleeds out in the bird sanctuary with her dog tied to a tree with wire around his throat.

She has to push through the heavy folds of curtains that weren't there before, into a parlor, old-fashioned, but new. A fire crackles in the hearth. A decanter of whiskey sits on the side table beside a velvet chair facing it.

The man she followed into the house has already left. Harper has gone to 9 September 1980 to watch girl-Kirby from the parking lot of a gas station, sipping on a Coke because he has to hold on to something to stop him from crossing the street and grabbing the child by the throat with enough force to slam her off her feet and stabbing her again and again and again right there in front of the donut shop.

In the house, Kirby finds her way upstairs to a bedroom decorated with artifacts taken from dead girls, who are not dead yet, who are perpetually dying or marked to die. They shimmer in and out of focus. There are three that belong to her. A plastic pony. A black-and-silver lighter. A tennis ball that makes her scars ache and her head reel.

Downstairs, a key turns in the lock. She panics. There is nowhere to go. She yanks at the window, but it won't budge. Terrified, she climbs into the wardrobe and crouches there, trying not to think. Trying not to scream.

"Co za wkurwiaj‚ace gówno!"

A Polish engineer, drunk on his winnings and actual alcohol besides, fumbles around in the kitchen. He has the key in the pocket of his coat, but not for long. The door opens behind him and Harper limps in on his crutch from 23 March 1989, with a chewed tennis ball in his pocket and Kirby's blood still wet on his jeans.

It takes him a long time to beat Bartek to death, while Kirby hides in the wardrobe in the room and clutches her mouth. When the squealing starts, she can't help it, she moans against her palm.

He comes clomping up the stairs with his crutch, dragging his leg, one step at a time. *Tok-tok.* It doesn't matter that this has happened before in his past, because it is folded over into her present, like origami.

He comes to the threshold of the room and she bites her tongue so hard it bleeds. The inside of her mouth is dry and copper. But he passes right by.

She sits forward, straining to listen. There is a mad bear in here with her. Her breathing, she realizes. She's hyperventilating. She has to be quiet. She has to get herself under control.

There is the unmistakable porcelain clink of a toilet seat being lifted. The splash of piss. A faucet running as he washes his hands.

He curses softly. A rustling. The sharp tine of a belt buckle hitting the tiles. He turns on the shower. The curtain rings rattle as he yanks it across.

This is it. Your only chance, she thinks. She should walk into the bathroom, take up the crutch, and smack him in the skull with it. Knock him out cold. Tie him up. Get the cops. But she knows—if he doesn't wrest it away from her—she won't be able to stop until he doesn't get up ever again. The connections be-tween her brain and her body have petrified. Her hand will not move to open the wardrobe door. Move, she thinks.

The water sputters. She's lost her moment. He's going to emerge from the bathroom and cross over to the wardrobe to get clean clothes. Maybe if she rushes him. Shoves him and runs. The tiles will be wet. She might have a fighting chance.

The hiss of the shower resumes. The pipes playing up. Or he's fucking with her. *Now. She has to go. Now.* She shoves open the wardrobe door with her foot and scrambles out, across the floor.

She needs to take something. Some kind of evidence. She snatches the lighter from the shelf. Exactly the same one. She doesn't know how that's possible.

She steals into the corridor. The door of the bathroom is open. She can hear him whistling underneath the rush of the water. Something sweet and cheerful. She would be half-sobbing if she could breathe.

She edges past, her back pressed against the wallpaper. She is clutching the lighter so hard that her hand is aching. She doesn't notice. She forces herself to take one more step. Another. Not so different to the time before. And another. She forces her mind to blank out the man with his brains smeared across the floor at the bottom of the stairs.

The water turns off when she is halfway down. She bolts for the front door. She tries to step over the body of the Pole, but she's going too quickly to be careful and she stands on his arm. The give is horrible, too soft under the roll of her boots. Dontthinkdonthinkdontthink.

She reaches for the latch.

It opens.

DAN

13 June 1993

In here," says the owner of the Finmark Deli, showing Dan to the back office. "She was in a state when I found her."

Through the window of the door, Dan can see Kirby is sitting in a highback faux leather roller chair at a plywood desk under a calendar of fine art prints, currently showing a Monet. Or a Manet. Dan never figured out the difference. It's an impression of high-brow taste that is undone by the poster of the girl with her tits squashed between her fingers sitting on a Ducati on the opposite wall. Kirby looks pale and hunched up, like she's trying to shrink in on herself. Her fist is clenched in her lap. She's talking softly into the phone.

"I'm glad you're okay, Mom. No, please don't come down. Seriously."

"You think it's gonna be on the evening news?" Mr. Deli Guy says.

"What?"

"Because I should probably shave if it is. If they want to interview me."

"Do you mind?" Dan is going to deck him if he doesn't shut up.

"Not at all. Civic duty."

"He means, can you leave us alone, please?" Kirby says, hanging up the receiver.

"Oh, right. Well, it is my office," he bristles.

"And we're so grateful you're letting us use it to get some privacy," Dan says, half-shoving him out.

"You know I had to beg him to use the phone?" This time her voice cracks.

"Jesus, I was worried." He kisses her on the head, grinning in relief.

"Me too." She smiles, but it's not really a smile.

"The cops are there now."

"I know," she nods tightly. "I just spoke to my mom. The fucker broke into her house."

"Jesus."

"Tore it apart."

"Looking for something?"

"Me. But I was with you. And Rachel was visiting an old boyfriend. She didn't even know about it until she got home and found the place trashed. She wants to rush over here. She wants to know if they've caught him yet."

"Don't we all. She loves you."

"I can't deal with that right now."

"You know you're going to have to identify him. Down at the station. Will you be able to handle it?"

She nods again. Her curls are limp and dark with sweat.

"Good look for you," he teases, brushing her hair away from the nape of her neck. "You should chase down murderers more often. Most manageable I've seen it."

"That won't be the end of it. Still the trial."

"Sure, you'll have to be here for that. But we can avoid the media circus. Make an official statement and then we can book out of town. Ever been to California?"

"Yeah."

"Right. I forgot."

"Worth forgetting."

"Jesus. I was worried."

"You said." This time the smile is real. Tired, but real. He can't help it. He can't resist it. He kisses her then. Everything in her draws him in. Her lips are unbearably soft and warm and responsive.

She kisses him back.

"Uh," the deli owner says.

Kirby touches the back of her hand to her mouth and looks away.

"*¡Por Dios!!* Don't you knock?" Dan yells.

"The uh, the detective, wants a word." He looks anxiously from one to the other, trying to figure out how to turn this into a TV-friendly soundbite. "I'll be, er, I'll be outside."

Kirby pinches at the skin between her collarbones, absently rubbing the edge of her thumb against the scar. "Dan." The way she says his name unhinges him.

"Don't say it. You don't have to. Please don't."

"I can't right now. You know?"

"Yeah, I know. I'm sorry. I was just... Fuck." He can't even get a proper sentence together. Of all the stupid moments.

"Sounds about right," she says, not looking at him. "Hey. I'm glad you're here." She punches his arm. It's a brush-off. And something inside him breaks at the lightness and finality of it.

There's a sharp knock at the door a millisecond before Detective Amato pushes it open.

"Ms. Mazrachi. Mr. . . ."

"Velasquez." Dan leans against the wall, arms folded, making it clear he's not going anywhere.

"Did you get him? Where is he?" Kirby looks fearfully at the black-and-white screen connected to the shop's surveillance camera.

Detective Amato takes up a perch on the edge of the desk. Too familiar, Dan thinks, like he's still not taking her seriously. He clears his throat. "Hell of a thing. The guy coming to your office like that."

"And the house?"

He looks uncomfortable.

"Listen. It's been very stressful. It was very brave and stupid to follow him like that."

"What are you saying?"

"Easy to get turned around. You don't know the neighborhood."

"You didn't find it?" Kirby stands up, pale with fury. "I gave you the address. You want me to gift wrap him and put him under the fucking Christmas tree for you, too?"

"Now calm down, miss."

"I am perfectly calm," Kirby shouts.

"All right, everyone," Dan says. "Same team, remember?"

"We couldn't find the junkie you spoke to. I've still got guys asking around in the neighborhood."

"What about the house?"

"What can I tell you? It's abandoned. It's a wreck. Pipes have been pulled out, copper wiring stripped, floorboards yanked up. Anything of value has been stolen and the rest has been trashed for kicks. There's definitely nobody in there. But kids might have been smoking in there or having sex. We found a mattress upstairs."

"You actually went inside." Kirby says this with flat challenge.

"Of course we did. What are you trying to say?"

"And it was just a wreck?"

"Lady, come on. I know you're taking this hard. It's not your fault if you got mixed up. It's been very traumatic. Most people are terrible witnesses on a good day, let alone after they see the guy who tried to kill them."

"Coming back to finish it."

"So what happens now?" Dan asks.

"We're going door-to-door. We've got the description. Hopefully we turn up your junkie and he can direct us to the place."

"The *right* place," she says, bitterly. "And then?"

"We've got an APB on him. All stations. We find him, we bring him in. You have to let us do our jobs."

"Because you've done so well this far."

"Can you help me out here?" Amato says to Dan.

"Kirby—"

"I get it." She shrugs him off angrily.

"Have you got somewhere you can stay tonight? I can assign you an officer."

"She can stay at mine." Dan flushes as Amato's eyebrows twitch upwards. "I've got a sleeper couch. I'll sleep on that. Obviously."

"Have you caught him yet? Where is he?" Rachel demands, sweeping into the tiny room in a storm of nerves and patchouli.

"Mom! I told you not to come down."

"I'm going to claw his eyes out. Do we still have the death penalty in Chicago? I'll flip the fucking switch myself." She is full of fierce bravado, but Dan can see that she is at breaking point. Her eyes are wild. Her hands are shaking. And just her being here is winding Kirby up tighter too.

"Have a seat, Ms. Mazrachi," he says, nudging her towards a chair.

"I see the vultures are out already," she flings at him. "Come on, Kirby, I'm taking you home."

"Rachel!"

The detective's mouth narrows to a slit at having to deal with another crazy woman. "Ma'am, going home is not advisable. We don't know that he won't return to your house. You should book into a hotel for the night. And get some counseling. It's been traumatic for both of you. Cook County has someone attached to the emergency room. All hours. Or here. Call this number. It's a friend. Works with a lot of crime victims."

"What about the fucker who did this?" Kirby is furious.

"You let us worry about that. You look after your mom. Stop trying to carry this on your own." He frowns, not unsympathetically. "Now, I'm going to send an artist in to do an identikit with you and go through some photos, and then you are going to see the counselor and check into a hotel and take some sleeping pills. And you are going to *not* think about this anymore tonight. Got it?"

"Yes, sir," Kirby says, not meaning a word.

"Good girl," Amato says, wearily, not meaning it either.

"Sanctimonious prick!" Rachel says, throwing herself into the vacated chair. "Who the fuck does he think he is? He can't even do his job."

"Mom, you can't be here. You're upsetting me."

"I'm upset too!"

"But you don't have to try to be coherent for the police. This is really important. I have to get this right. I'm begging you. I'll call you when I'm done."

"I'll look after her, Ms. Mazrachi," Dan says.

Rachel snorts. "You!"

"Mom. Please."

"The Day's Inn is decent," Dan intervenes. "I stayed there when I was getting divorced. It's clean. It's reasonably priced. I'm sure one of the officers would be willing to drive you downtown."

She deflates. "All right, fine. But you'll come straight there afterwards?"

"Sure, Rachel," Kirby says, ushering her out. "Please don't worry. I'll see you later."

The atmosphere in the room changes the moment Rachel is out of the room. He can practically feel the temperature drop. There's a different kind of intensity—a terrible focus. Dan knows what's coming.

"No," he says.

"You're gonna stop me?" Kirby says, cold as he's ever seen her.

"Be sensible. It's getting dark. You don't have a flashlight. Or a gun."

"Yeah?"

"And I have both in my car."

Kirby laughs in relief and unclenches her fist for the first time since she left the house. She's holding a black-and-silver lighter. A Ronson De-Light Princess with an art deco design.

"Replica?"

She shakes her head.

"Not from the evidence room."

She shakes her head again. "It's the same one. I don't know how to explain it."

"And you haven't shown this to the cops."

"Would there be a point? *I* don't believe me. It's so fucked up, Dan. It's not wrecked inside. It's something else. I'm so scared we'll get there and you won't see it."

Dan folds his hand over hers around the lighter. "I believe you, kiddo."

KIRBY AND DAN

13 June 1993

She is tense in the car. She keeps playing with the lighter. Flick. Flick-flick-flick. He doesn't blame her. The pressure is un-bearable. Flick. Catapulting towards something that can be averted. A car crash in slow motion. Not just an ordinary fender-bender either. This is like your ten-car pile-up halfway across the freeway with helicopters and firetrucks and people weeping in shock on the side of the road. Flick. Flick. Flick.

"Can you stop that? Or at least stick a cigarette in the hot end? I could use one." He tries not to feel guilty about Rachel. About driving her daughter into danger.

"Do you have one?" she says eagerly.

"Check the glove compartment."

She pops the latch and the cubby dumps a bunch of crap in her lap. Assorted pens, condiments from Al's Beef, a squashed soda cup. She crumples the empty packet of Marlboro Lights.

"Nope. Sorry."

"Shit."

"You know there's still as much cancer-causing stuff in the light versions?"

"Never figured cancer would be the thing to kill me."

"Where's your gun?"

"Under the seat."

"How do you know you're not going to hit a bump and blow your ankle off?"

"I don't normally carry it around."

"I guess these are special circumstances."

"You freaked out?"

"Out of my mind. I'm so scared, Dan. But this is it. My whole life. There's no choice."

"We getting into free will now?"

"I have to go back is all there is to it. If the police won't."

"I think you'll find that's 'we,' pal-face. You're dragging me with you."

"Dragging is a strong word."

"So is 'vigilantism.'"

"You gonna be my Robin? You'd look good in yellow tights."

"Hold on there. I am definitely Batman. Which makes *you* Robin."

"I always liked the Joker more."

"It's because you relate. You both have bad hair."

"Dan?" she says, looking out the window at dusk creeping in over the empty lots and boarded-up houses and the rat-traps falling apart. Her face is reflected in the car window with the flame as she clicks the lighter again.

"Yeah, kiddo?" he says tenderly.

"You're Robin."

Kirby directs him down an alleyway, desolate even by this neighborhood's standards, and Dan suddenly has a lot of sympathy for Detective Amato.

"Stop here," she says. He switches off the ignition and lets the car roll to a stop behind an old wooden fence that leans out like a drunk.

"That one?" Dan says, peering at the abandoned rowhouses with the windows boarded up and weeds that have sprung up jungle-thick and blooming with flowers of trash. Clearly no one has been in here for a very long time, let alone set up a hidden den of yesteryear opulence. He tries not to let the doubt show.

"Come on." Kirby unlocks the door and climbs out the car.

"Hang on a sec." He bends down next to the open door of the driver's side, pretending to tie his shoelace while digging under the seat to retrieve his revolver. A Dan Wesson. The name amused him at the time. Beatriz hated it. And the thought they might actually need it.

As he straightens, he's blinded by the flare of light catching in the rear window from the sun, which is definitely on the way out. "We couldn't have done this eleven a.m. on a sunny day?"

"Come *on*." Kirby picks her way through the weeds to the rickety Z of wooden steps running up the back of the house. He holds the gun at his hip, out of sight of the casual observer. He'd settle for any observer. He's unnerved by how quiet it is.

She shrugs out of his jacket and drops it onto the barbed wire blocking off the stairway.

"Let me," he says. He shoves the heel of his shoe on the jacket, pushing down the razor-sharp coils, and extends his hand to help her over. He scrambles after her and, as soon as the pressure's off, the wire recoils like it's spring-loaded, tearing into the fabric.

"Never mind. I got it on sale. Bought the first one that fit me." He realizes he's shooting his mouth off. Never figured himself for a talker. Never figured he'd be breaking into abandoned houses.

They're standing on the back porch. The view through the window is as foreboding as fuck; dim light that casts everything in shades of green and detritus everywhere. It looks like the walls have been peeled and spread like confetti all over the floor.

He shrugs the jacket back on as Kirby sets one foot on the windowsill. "Don't be freaked out." Then she hauls herself through and disappears. Literally. One second she's there, framed in the window, next she's gone.

"Kirby!" He lunges for the window, putting his hand down straight onto a jagged slice of glass that's still miraculously intact. "Jesusfuckingshit!" She reappears and grabs hold of his arm. He half tumbles inside after her. Everything changes.

He stands there, stunned, in the dining-room. Disbelief like a concussion. She knows the feeling. "Come on," she whispers.

"You keep saying that," he says, but his voice is thick and far away. He blinks hard. Blood runs from his palm and patters on the floor in thick drops. He doesn't notice. The fireplace casts an unsteady orange glow over the floorboards in the dark corridor. There is no sign of the dead man she said she'd had to step over in the hallway when she made her escape before.

"Snap out of it, Dan. I need you."

"What *is* this?" he says, low.

"I don't know. I know it's real." That's not true. She's been doubting herself the whole way here. Thinking maybe everyone is right and she's the delusional freak and what she really needs is anti-psychotic meds and a hospital bed with a view of the gardens through the bars. It's such a terrible relief that he sees it too. "And I know you're bleeding. You should give me the gun."

"No way, you're unstable." He says it teasingly, but he's not looking at her. He's running his hand over the patterned wallpaper. Testing to see if it's real. "You said he's upstairs?"

"He was. Three hours ago. Wait. Dan."

"What?" He turns at the foot of the stairs.

She falters. "I can't go up there again."

"Okay," he says. More decisively: "Okay." He goes into the parlor and her ribs squeeze tight. Oh God, if *he's* in there, sitting in the chair, waiting. But Dan emerges, holding a heavy black poker from the fireplace. He holds the gun out to her. "Stay here. If he comes through the door, shoot him."

"Let's just go," she says, as if that's an option anymore. He jabs the revolver at her. It's heavier than she would have thought. Her hands are shaking badly.

"Cover all the entrances. Use both hands. There's no safety. You point and shoot. Just don't shoot me, okay?"

"Deal," she says, her voice shaky.

He starts up the stairs, the poker raised like a baseball bat. She presses her shoulder blades up against the wall. It's like playing pool. You have to breathe out as you take aim and release. No problem, she thinks with a flash of hate.

The key scratches in the lock.

She jerks on the trigger the moment the door swings open.

The fucker ducks as the shot nicks the edge of the doorframe, splintering the wood. (It cuts through 1980 and bores through the window of the house across the road, embedding itself in the wall next to a picture of the Virgin Mary.)

He is unfazed at being shot at. "Sweetheart," he says. "I was looking for you." He reaches for his knife. "And here you are."

She glances down at the revolver, a millisecond is all, to see if she needs to reload or click the chamber. Six rounds. Five left. Dan is already halfway across the room when she looks up. Right in her line of fire.

"Get out of the way!"

Dan brings the poker swinging down with force, but Harper, who is more experienced with violence, intercepts it with his forearm. It still cracks bone. He howls in pain and punches the knife into Dan's chest. There is a bright spray of red. The momentum carries both men up against the door. It's only on the catch. Not locked. They fall together, smashing through the boards nailed across the door, into another time. The door swings shuts behind them.

"Dan!" It's only a few yards, but it feels like forever. It might as well be. When she opens the door, it's on to the summer's evening she came from. There is no sign of them.

DAN

3 December 1929

———

They hold on to each other like lovers, tumbling down the steps of the front porch and into the cold and dark of early morning. The snow is a shock. Dan hits the ground hard enough to knock the breath out of him. He gets his knee up to shove the psycho off and scrambles like a dog on all fours into the street, trying to get distance.

Everything's fucked up. Somewhere else again. Where there was an empty lot before, a brick warehouse has sprung up. He thinks about banging on the door for help, but it's padlocked with a heavy chain. The windows of the houses are boarded over. But the paint is newer. None of it makes any sense; rolling around in the snow, bleeding on things, when it was June half an hour ago.

Dan's shirt is wet. The cold cuts through it. Blood runs down his arm and drips between his fingers, blooming in the snow in pink crystalline fractals. He can't even tell what it's from any-more, his ribs or the cut in his hand. It's all gone numb and burny anyway. The killer pulls himself to his feet using the railing, still holding the knife. Dan is already sick of that fucking knife.

"Give it up, friend," the man says, limping across the snow towards him. The guy has his knife and Dan has shit. He's crouching, his fingers digging in the snow.

"You want to make it harder?" The guy's diction is slightly off. Old-fashioned, almost.

"You're not going to get a chance to hurt her again," Dan says. Closer, he can see that the bastard smashed open his lip in the fall. His teeth are red with blood as he smiles.

"It's a circle that has to be closed."

"I don't know what the fuck you're talking about, man," Dan says, hauling himself up. "But you're making me angry." He shifts his weight onto his right foot, ignoring the pain in his side, winding up. The compacted lump of snow is gripped between his thumb and two fingers splayed wide like a four-seam fastball. He raises his knee and breaks his arms round in a pinwheel, pivoting his hips, and coming down on his front leg, letting the snowball glide, not snap, off his wrist at the sweet spot of the arc. *"Vete pa'l carajo, hijo'e puta!"*

It sings across the street, this improvised ball, the perfect pitch to rival Mad Dog Maddux himself, and smashes into the psychopath's face.

The killer staggers back in shock, shaking his head and brushing away the snow. It's enough time. Dan runs across the street, closing the gap between them. He's on him. He winds up again, smashing his fist into the man's nose. He's aiming low, hoping to drive the septum straight into the bastard's brain. But if it were that easy, it would happen all the time. The guy twists his jaw as the punch connects and Dan feels the cheekbone crunch under his knuckles. *Puñeta,* that hurts.

He shoves himself backwards, ducking the knife weaving through the air, falling onto his back like a crab. He rolls himself over, lashing out with his shoe, connecting with something solid.

Not the guy's kneecap or his balls, which would have been useful. His thigh, maybe.

The lunatic is still grinning through the blood running down his face from his nose. The blade in his hand is slick. The thought makes Dan feel sick and very, very tired. Or that could be the blood loss. It's hard to tell how bad it is. Pretty ugly, he reckons, by the red in the snow. Dan gets to his feet, reluctantly. He can't understand why Kirby doesn't come out of the house and just shoot the bastard.

He watches the hand with the knife. Maybe he can kick it away. Like some kung-fu master. Who is he kidding? He makes a decision. He lunges forward, grabbing hold of the guy's injured arm, squeezing and wrenching it, trying to pull him round, unbalance him as he drives his other fist into the bastard's chest.

The killer gives a surprised whuff as the air goes out of him, falling back a step, dragging Dan with him, but he is stronger and more experienced. He still manages to jab upwards with the knife, ripping into Dan's stomach, pulling towards his ribcage with a shearing meaty-paper sound.

Dan collapses onto his knees, clutching his stomach. And then falls down onto his side. The ground is freezing against his face. There is a shocking amount of blood spilling into the snow.

"She'll die worse," the man says, smiling horribly. He nudges Dan in the ribs with the toe of his shoe. Dan groans and rolls away, onto his back, exposing his stomach. He tries to cover himself with his hands, a useless gesture. There's something digging into his back, in the pocket of his coat. The goddamn pony.

Headlights sweep across the street as a boxy old-fashioned car turns the corner. Motes of falling snow swirl in the beams of the headlights. It slows as it catches them in the spot, Dan lying there bleeding to death and the man with the knife hobbling back towards the house as fast as he can, with dawn on the horizon.

"Help me!" Dan yells at the car. He can't see the driver's face past the sulfur glare of the round headlights, like spectacles. All he can make out is a man's silhouette with a hat. "Stop him!"

The car idles in front of him, the heat of the exhaust forming sputtering cumulus clouds of carbon dioxide in the cold. Suddenly the engine roars, the tires spin, kicking up bits of ice and gravel, and it swerves around him. Barely.

"Fuck you!" Dan tries to scream after it. "You fucking fuck!" But it comes out more of a jagged gasp. He cranes his head back to try and see the killer. He's on the porch stairs already, reaching for the door. It's hard to make him out, and not just through the flurries of snow.

Dan's vision is going furry-dark around the edges like a cataract. Like falling down a well and the iris of light getting further and further away.

HARPER AND KIRBY

13 June 1993

———

He kicks the door open, covered in blood and grinning insanely with anticipation, holding the knife and the key. But the grin dies when he sees what she is doing. Kirby is standing in the middle of the room, jerking the Ronson Princess De-Light to spray lighter fluid over a mound of stuff she's gathered in the middle of the room.

She's torn down the curtains from the window, soaked through with wet patches, piled up on top of the mattress from the spare bedroom upstairs. There are empty bottles carelessly tossed at the base. The kerosene from the kitchen. The whiskey. She's upturned the chair and torn it open so the stuffing leaks out in white clumps. The gramophone is smashed to pieces. Glossy splinters of wood and hundred-dollar bills and betting slips rammed into the dented brass horn. She's brought down everything from the room. The butterfly wings and the baseball card and the pony and the cassette with a snarl of unspooled black ribbon tangled up in a charm bracelet, the lab ID badge and a protest button, a bunny clip, a contraceptive pill, a printer's letter Z. A chewed-on tennis ball.

"Where's Dan?" Kirby says. The light from the fireplace behind her shines in her hair like a prophecy.

"Dead," Harper says. The snowstorm of December 1929 whirls behind him through the open door. "What are you doing?"

"What do you think?" she mocks. "You didn't give me anything to do but wait for you to come back."

"Don't you dare!" Harper says as Kirby flicks the flint. A steady golden flame flares up. She drops it into the pile. It catches a second later, oily black smoke twisting up from the paper, leaping orange flames.

He yells in anguish, lunging for her, the knife out, but something brings him up short.

He smashes violently into the floor, dropping the key, as Dan half-tackles him, on his knees, his arms clutched around Harper's legs. Still alive, even though blood is pooling under him, black and thick. He is pulling at Harper's pants to drag him back and keep him from getting at her. Harper kicks at him, frantically. His heel sends the key skittering across the floor, skidding through the blood, and coming to rest on the doorjamb at the very threshold of the House.

He manages to get in a lucky blow, catching Dan under his jaw with his shoe. Dan groans and his fingers release their hold on his jeans.

Freed, Harper scrambles to his feet, still holding the knife, triumphant. He will kill her and put out the fire and then carve up her friend slowly for the trouble he has caused him.

But then he meets Kirby's gaze as she levels the gun at him. The flames are hot at her back. She opens her mouth to say something and thinks better of it. She exhales slowly and squeezes the trigger.

HARPER

13 June 1993

The flash is blinding. The force spins him into the wall.

Harper touches the hole in his shirt where a dark stain is congealing. First it feels blank. Then the pain comes, every nerve along the trajectory of the hole the bullet bored through him lighting up at the same time. He tries to laugh, but his breathing is wet and wheezing as his lung starts filling with blood. "You can't," he says.

"Really?" She looks beautiful, Harper thinks, lips pulled back to show her teeth, eyes bright, her hair like a halo around her head. Shining.

She pulls the trigger again, blinking involuntarily at the crack. And again and again. And again. Until the chamber clicks. The detonations in his body register only dimly, as if he is already peeling away.

Then she throws the gun at him in frustration and falls onto her knees and buries her face in her hands.

Should have finished me, you stupid cunt, he thinks. He tries to move towards her, but his body won't respond.

His perspective is skewed, distorted at an obtuse angle. The whole scene is laid out beneath him, as if he is falling up and away from it.

The girl with her shoulders shaking, as the flames lick up from the tangle of chair and curtains and totems, spewing a black, chemical smoke.

The big man lying on the floorboards, swallowing hard, his eyes closed, holding his stomach and his chest, blood running between his fingers.

Harper can see himself standing against the wall. How can he see outside of himself? He is looking down on everything, as if he is wedged high against the ceiling, but still tethered to the lump of flesh with his face below.

Harper sees Harper's legs go slack. His body starts sliding down the surface of the wall. The back of his head smears dark globs of blood and brain over the cream wallpaper.

He feels the connection slip. And then it snaps.

He howls in disbelief, clawing to get back down. But he has no hands to grasp. He is a dead thing. So much meat on the floor.

He stretches out, reaching for anything.

And finds the House.

Floorboards instead of bones. Walls instead of flesh.

He can pull it back. Start again. Undo this. The heat of the flames and the choking smoke and the howling fury.

It's not so much a possession as an infection.

The House was always his.

Always him.

KIRBY

13 June 1993

=====

The room is getting hot. The smoke gets in through the sobs, catches in her lungs. She could just die here. Keep her eyes closed. Not get up ever again. It would be easy. Asphyxiation would kill her before the flames reached her. She could just breathe deep. Let it go. It's done.

Something is pawing at her hand, insistently. Like a dog.

She doesn't want to, but she opens her eyes to see Dan, squeezing her hand. He's on his knees, hunched over. His fingers are slick with blood.

"Little help?" he rasps.

"Oh God." She's still shaking, crying and coughing. She throws her arms around him and he winces.

"Ow."

"Hang on. I need your jacket." She helps him out of it and ties it around his waist as tightly as she can against the wound. It starts soaking through even before she's finished. She can't think about that. She crawls under his arm, braces against the floor and hefts up. He's too heavy, she can't lift him. Her boot skids in his blood.

"Careful, fuck." He's gone horribly pale.

"Okay." She says. "Like this," she rounds her shoulders so she takes on most of his weight, holding him up and shuffling forward. The fire crackles at their backs, jumping up the walls hungrily. The paper blackens and warps, wisps of smoke curling upwards.

And God help her, she can still feel *him* here.

They half-crawl, half-fall towards the doorway. She balances precariously and sweeps her foot out to kick the door closed on the ice and snow outside.

"What are you doing?"

"Trying to get home." She helps him onto all fours. "Hold on for another second. One more second."

"I liked kissing you," Dan says, his voice cracking.

"Don't talk."

"I don't know if I'm as strong as you."

"If you want to kiss me again, then shut the fuck up and stop bleeding to death," she snaps.

"Okay," Dan gasps, smiling weakly, and then more steadily, "Okay."

Kirby takes a breath and opens the door onto a summer's night full of police sirens and flashing lights.

POSTSCRIPT

BARTEK

3 December 1929

The Polish engineer pulls the car over two blocks away and sits with the engine running, thinking about what he's seen. A bad scene, that much he knows. He couldn't make out exactly what was happening. The man lying in the middle of the street bleeding in the snow. That shocked him. He nearly ran him over. He wasn't really concentrating on the road. Steering the car through the streets by rote equation that equals home, all the way from Cicero.

He's a little drunk, Bartek admits to himself. A lot drunk. When he starts losing, the gin comes easier to hand. And Louis kept the drinks flowing all night and into the small hours of the morning, long after he'd spent the last of his coin. And gave him credit on top of it. Enough to sink himself utterly. Now he owes Cowen $2,000.

The ugly truth is that he was lucky to be able to drive away in his car at all. They'll be coming for it Sunday morning right before church if he doesn't find a way to raise the money by the weekend. Better than coming for him, but that's next. Diamond Lou Cowen does not fuck around.

Gambling with known gangsters. Chumming around with personal friends of Mr. Capone. What was he thinking? He has enough problems on his plate without getting in the middle of a bloody altercation at five o'clock in the morning.

But he's intrigued. At the glow spilling out onto the street from the ruined house and the improbable sumptuousness he spied through the open door. He should go back and help, he tells himself. Or just go and have a look-see. He can always call the police if it's serious.

He turns the car around, circling back to the house.

The key is waiting for him on the front porch, barely on the threshold of the closed door, spattered with snow and blood-stained.

ACKNOWLEDGMENTS

Thanks to everyone who helped make this book what it is.

I had a crack team of researchers digging up information, out-of-print books, videos, photographs and personal histories on everything from illegal abortion groups to real-life radium dancing girls, the evolution of forensics, '30s restaurant reviews and the history of '80s toys. My dedicated researcher Zara Trafford, as well as Adam Maxwell and Christoher Holtorf of research and game design company SkywardStar, all found me strange and amazing things, elaborated on by Liam Kruger and Louisa Betteridge, and also Matthew Brown, who was always on call by dint of being married to me. Thank you.

In Chicago, Katherine and Kendaa Fitzpatrick were the best possible hosts, although it was a little weird taking Katherine's two-year-old daughter along on a murder scene playdate to Montrose Beach. Kate's husband Dr. Geoff Lowrey provided medical advice and fact-checking, as did ENT surgeon Simon Gane. Any gruesome errors are mine.

Twitter friend Alan Nazerian (aka @gammacounter) drove me round, accompanied me to Wrigley Field and introduced me to helpful people, including Ava George Stewart, who gave me invaluable insight into criminal law over the best Chinese food in the city at Lao Hunan, and Claudia Mendelson, who walked me through Architecture 101 over coffee at Intelligentsia. Claudia put me on to Ward Miller who talked about the city's most amazing buildings over dinner at Buona Terra. (Chicago is a foodie kind of town.)

Ghost tour guide, historian and YA fiction novelist Adam Selzer took me to the creepiest places in the city, including the back corridors of the Congress Hotel, and filled me in on intriguing Chicago history and the '20s and '30s in particular, much of which I couldn't fit into the book, and treated me to that Chicago institution: Al's Beef.

Longtime Chicago PD detective Commander Joe O'Sullivan (aka @joethecop, now retired) ran me through the inner workings of police procedure at the Niles police station, where he took me through some startling boxes of old evidence with haunting photographs. (Also: bacon and bourbon cocktails at divey bars.)

Jim deRogatis gave me the inside scoop on working at the *Chicago Sun-Times*, the paper's librarians, ink in the air, the editors and cranks and stories from the frontlines. I have taken liberties. He also provided in-depth intel on the '90s music scene, and sent me a copy of his brilliant, hilarious book, *Milk It: Collected Musings on the Alternative Music Explosion of the 90s*.

I'm grateful to sports reporter Keith Jackson and *The Tribune*'s Jimmy Greenfield who talked about the ins and outs of sports journalism with me, as well as philosophies of baseball.

Ed Swanson, a volunteer at the Chicago History Museum, offered to read the novel for me, fact-checking the history, Americana and El (or L as it was previously known) routes with an eagle-eye. Any mistakes are mine and some minor ones, like the actual release date of *The Maxx* or the presence of *any* African-

American workers at the Chicago Bridge And Iron Company in Seneca, are intentional nudges in service to the story.

The newspaper article on the murder of Jeanette Klara owes much to a real piece of journalism about a real-life radium dancer, "In New York She Is Dancing To Her Death" by Paul Harrison, published in the July 25, 1935, edition of the *Milwaukee Journal*. Thanks to the *Milwaukee Sentinel Journal* for permission to quote some of the great lines from the original.

Pablo Defendini, Margaret Armstrong and TJ Tallie were very helpful with excellent Puerto Rican swear words while Tomek Suwalksi and Ania Rokita translated and double-checked the Polish dialogue, also obscenity-laden.

Mutant-protein-wrangling scientist Dr. Kerry Gordon at the University of Cape Town advised me on Mysha Pathan's research.

Nell Taylor at the Read/Write Library gave me a deep history of Chicago zines, while Daniel X. O'Neil talked me through the '90s punk and alt theatre scenes as well as Club Dreamerz and sent me off with original flyers. Thanks also to Harper Reed and Adrian Holovaty for hanging out at the Green Mill listening to '30s-inspired gypsy jazz band Swing Gitan.

Helen Westcott loaned me all her criminology textbooks and serial killer reading matter, and Dale Halvorsen kept me supplied with great true crime podcasts he found. My studio mates Adam Hill, Emma Cook, Jordan Metcalf, Jade Klara and Daniel Ting Chong kept me grounded with funny YouTube videos and daily merciless teasing. And thanks to all at animation company Sea Monster, for letting me hide out there to work when our building was being renovated.

Thanks to my friends and family and strangers on Twitter who leaped to help with useful suggestions or translations or medical advice or Chicago recommendations, and anyone I have neglected to mention.

I'm not going to list the full bibliography of my research, but some of the most useful and entertaining reference works included: *Chicago Confidential* by Jack Lait and Lee Mortimer, an amazing, sexy, fun guide to the seedier places and people of the city published in 1950; the wonderfully accessible *Chicago: A Biography* by Dominic A. Pacyga; *Slumming: Sexual and Racial Encounters in American Nightlife 1885–1940* by Chad Heap; *Girl Show: Into the Canvas World of Bump and Grind* by A.W. Stencell; *Red Scare: Memories of the American Inquisition* by Griffin Fariello; the Chicago Women's Liberation Union's Herstory resources on Jane at The University of Illinois Chicago's website, including transcriptions of personal histories; *Doomsday Men* by P.D. Smith, about the history of the atom bomb (and extracts Peter emailed me from his new book, *City: A Guidebook for the Urban Age*); *Perfect Victims* by Bill James; *Whoever Fights Monsters* by Robert K. Ressler and Tom Schachtman; *Gang Leader for a Day* by Sudhir Venkatesh; Jack Clark's *Nobody's Angel*; *The Wagon and Other Stories from the City* by Martin Preib; Wilson Miner's talk on how cars shaped the world in a tectonic way at Webstock 2012; *Chicago Neighbourhoods and Suburbs* by Ann Durkin Keating; as well as *The Lovely Bones* by Alice Sebold; *I Have Life: Alison's Journey* as told to Marianne Thamm; and Antony Altbeker's *Fruit of a Poisoned Tree*, which all gave me devastating insight into what real victims of violence and their families endure. Studs Terkel's oral histories were invaluable for conveying real people's stories in their own voices.

First readers Sarah Lotz, Helen Moffett, Anne Perry, Jared Shurin, Alan Nazerian, Laurent Philibert-Caillat, Ed Swanson, Oliver Munson and time-travel plot advisor genius Sam Wilson all made great suggestions on making the novel better and more interesting.

The book wouldn't have made it into the world without super-agent Oli Munson. Thanks also to everyone at Blake Friedmann and their international co-agents. I'm especially grateful to the editors and publishers who believed in it right off the bat, especially John Schoenfelder, Josh Kendall, Julia Wisdom, Kate Elton, Shona Martyn, Anna Valdinger, Frederik de Jager, Fourie Botha, Michael Pietsch, Miriam Parker, Wes Miller and Emad Akhtar.

I wouldn't have been able to write it without the love and support of my husband, Matthew, who played single dad for weeks at a time to our daughter, while I was away on research trips or in lockdown behind my desk writing and editing and is always first among first readers. Thank you. I love you.

The
Shining
Girls

Lauren Beukes

AN INTERVIEW WITH
LAUREN BEUKES

Tell us about yourself. Who the hell are you?

Jeez, that cues all kinds of metaphysical philosophical quandaries. Can I be a mismatch of atoms and carbon and mind thoughts in the restless dreaming of a post-dimensional crocodile god?

Okay, seriously, I'm a South African writer who is incredibly lucky to get paid to make up stories all day. It wasn't always like this. Over the last fifteen years, I've been a journalist, a TV scriptwriter, a documentary maker, and a mom to a small and amazing daughter—and had to find time to write novels in between.

I guess I'm best known for winning the Arthur C. Clarke Award and the Red Tentacle in 2011 for *Zoo City,* a black-magic detective story set in Johannesburg about refugees, redemption, criminals with magical animals, and the evils of autotune.

Give us your 140-character story pitch.

Harper, a time-traveling serial killer, is untraceable, unstoppable, until one of his victims, Kirby, survives and turns the hunt around.

Where does the story come from?

This is a little embarrassing. I was messing around on Twitter instead of writing (as you do) and threw out the idea in the middle of a random conversation. I immediately deleted the tweet because I was like, YES! That must be my next book! Quickly! Before someone else thinks of it!

But I think that's often the way of interesting ideas—they come around when you're least expecting them, in those moments when you've let your subconscious off the leash to romp in the grass.

How is this a story that only you could have written?

There are a lot of social issues that leak through my novels. It comes from having grown up under a terrible repressive racist regime (aka apartheid) and ten years as a journalist, getting backstage in the world.

I could have done a *Bill and Ted's Excellent Killing Spree* from the dinosaurs to the Middle Ages to killing Hitler, or a *Jack the Ripper Doctor Who,* but I wanted to mess with the conventions of both genres.

I wanted to use time travel as a way of exploring how much has changed (or depressingly stayed the same) over the course of the twentieth century, especially for women, and subvert the serial-killer genre by keeping the focus much more on the victims and examining what real violence is and what it does to us. The killer has a type, but it's not a physical thing—he goes for women with fire in their guts, who kick back against the conventions of their time.

What was the hardest thing about writing The Shining Girls?

Keeping precise track of the multiple timelines was tricky, but really the hardest thing was the killing. I wrote deep portraits of interesting women, from an African American World War Two single-mom welder to a troublesome broad architect accused of pinko sympathies in the fifties to a gentle abortionist and a burlesque dancer with a terrible secret . . . and then I had to kill them.

The attacks usually happen from their perspective, so you're not riding along with the killer, complicit in the murder, getting off on it. You're with the women, feeling their fear and their outrage and grief and trauma, and that was pretty hard to write, to make it more than a gratuitous murder, to get at the shock and emotion of it, because violence should be shocking. It should punch us in the face, that this is what it means when a murder is reported on the news or a woman turns up dead in a story. It was about creating characters rather than pretty corpses.

What did you learn from writing The Shining Girls?

That history is amazing! Okay, I knew that already. But the resonances of stuff that happened then with stuff that is happening now was a little scary.

There are a lot of echoes, some of them obvious, like the Great Depression and our current recession, or the Red Scare's tactics coming up again in the War on Terror, sneakily eroding our privacy and stirring up fear for political control, or the fact that women's rights to control their bodies are apparently still up for debate, somehow? Which just makes me sad and mad.

But there were others that creeped me out, like the Motion Picture Association of America's role in McCarthyism and politics, which explains so much about their political clout now in trying to get people cut off from the Internet for illegally downloading a movie. Seriously. Losing access to the Internet, which the UN has determined is a basic human right and is pretty fundamental to the way we live now, because an entertainment company is pissy that you pirated *The Hangover 3*? Not okay.

(Which is not to say I'm endorsing piracy—pay creators, kids, but that's a lot of political power for a movie organization.)

And a lot of amazing detail I just couldn't fit in, except in passing, from the first labor case, by the women who painted undark dials on watches during World War One with radium paint and died horribly of radiation poisoning, or how abortion got legalized in New York or the first nuclear fission in a lab under the University of Chicago's football field. So. Much. Good. Stuff.

What do you love about The Shining Girls?

The women. All of them, how they're sharp and bright and curious and ready to set the world alight in some small way, and if they're scared, they find a way to push through that. Especially Kirby. And I love her relationship with Dan. The love unfolding, if only she'd let it, if only she hadn't let her whole life be derailed by her obsessive quest to find the man who did this to her.

What would you do differently next time?

I really want to write Nella's story. She's the daughter of the African American welder who is killed in 1943 and starts trying to put the puzzle together before Kirby does, because Harper left an impossible clue on her mother's body—a 1993 Jackie Robinson baseball card—but real life gets in her way and there are too many missing pieces, literally, as she develops Alzheimer's and can't keep track of the threads anymore. I may still do it as a short story.

The original version of this interview appeared on the website Terrible Minds, www.terribleminds.com.

ALL THE PRETTY CORPSES . . .

Pop culture has a nasty habit of producing them. You know the type: the girl in the trunk with her long bare legs dangling over the bumper; the torture victim in the basement in a dirty vest and panties, matted hair over her face; the broken ingénue with glazed eyes and her dress fetchingly rucked up and one high heel kicked off and blood pooling under her.

The murder victim becomes a bloody puzzle that has to be solved. She is the sum of her injuries, rather than her life.

We focus on the gory details—the exit wound of the bullet, the angle of the knife, the pattern of the blood spatter, the DNA under her nails, the defensive cuts on her hands. We learn it from TV. This is what is important: what was done to her. Passive voice. Because there's no subject anymore. Only object: the dead girl, the body. And a body doesn't mean anything. It's an empty snail shell. It's okay to look. There's no one in there now.

But there was once.

Which is why I wrote *The Shining Girls* to be a book that is as much about the victims' stories as the killer's.

Serial-killer folklore maintains that they often have a type. Ted Bundy was into young women with middle partings and brown hair, for example. But what if my killer was not into physical characteristics but some inner quality that shone out of them? Bright young women full of spark and curiosity, engaged with the world, kicking back against convention and pushing past their doubts and fears. What if the story was more about their lives than their deaths? What if the pretty corpses had voices and that's part of why they were cut down?

I was interested in writing women who were exceptional in ordinary ways, who didn't quite fit in, who took a stand and would have made some kind of contribution in their fields if they hadn't been robbed of their potential, from a microbiologist to an artist, an architect, an activist, a single-mom welder, a transsexual dancer, an economist.

If the violence in the book is shocking, it's because it is supposed to be. Because real violence is. All those pretty corpses and raging gun battles and torture porn onscreen have made us virtually immune to violence and the ripples it sends out. But it should be gut-wrenching and upsetting, it should be emotional. It should be about the victim.

Of course, in the real world, real violence is usually not perpetrated by a serial killer. Usually it's someone the woman knows. A partner or husband or friend or neighbor. But the truth about violence is that it is all domestic. As in everyday, playing out with tedious regularity in any number of configurations. Ask any cop, any social worker, any paramedic or crime reporter. Bodies lose their flavor. Often they don't even make the news. Especially if they're not a pretty corpse or a celebrity, if there's no whiff of scandal. Especially if they're poor.

Writing this book was very personal.

In 2009, Thomokazi, a twenty-three-year-old friend of my family, was attacked by her abusive boyfriend. He stabbed her, poured boiling water over her head, locked her in his shack in one of Cape Town's desperately poor shantytowns, and just walked away, like she was nothing.

Five days later the neighbors called the cops to break down the door because of the moaning. There were flies thick on her skin, the smell was terrible, but she was alive. We didn't know it was already too late. With burns, the infection sets in deep, the same way violence sets into society. She died four months later. The public hospital put it down as "natural causes," because maybe that kind of thing is.

I tried to help the family. We tried to get justice. Three months after Thomokazi was buried in her traditional home up-country, I accompanied her sister to court. But before the case was called up, the prosecutor summoned us into his rooms and told us—furiously—that he couldn't try the case. The police docket was one pathetic page. The cops hadn't bothered to investigate, hadn't bothered to interview anyone. The only witness was Thomokazi. It was her word against his and she was dead and the dead cannot speak for themselves.

But I thought I could. I got the case into the papers, because I'm middle-class and I have a voice and I know how to use it and I believe in justice. With the support of the prosecutor, I got the investigation reopened. I gathered hospital records, the names of other witnesses who could testify that he'd punched her before, pulled out her hair, and found out which neighbors had called the cops.

Then her family phoned me. They couldn't bear to go through all of it again. They couldn't face having to exhume her body for a police autopsy. They couldn't talk about it anymore. All the words had been used up. They asked me to let it go.

I still haven't been able to. I'm still angry. About the violence that happens every day, about all the girls and women, like Thomokazi, whose deaths go unmentioned, who will never have a voice, whose obituaries come down to their autopsies. As Kirby says, "How am I supposed to let this shit go?" How are any of us?

At least in fiction, unlike real life, you can get justice.

Lauren Beukes

QUESTIONS AND TOPICS FOR DISCUSSION

1. Harper tells his second victim, Zora, "You shine. I need you." What does shining mean to Harper and what makes each of these very different women a shining girl?

2. Kirby Mazrachi is the only person to survive Harper's attack. Is she already a shining girl, or does her survival make her one?

3. *The Shining Girls* takes place in Chicago. What role does the city play in the story? How would another setting have changed *The Shining Girls*?

4. When Harper enters the House—before committing any of his future murders—he finds the names of his victims scratched into the wall, in his own handwriting. What is the House and why does it have a hold on him?

5. What is the significance of the objects Harper takes from his victims? Why does he feel the need to connect them?

6. Harper is obsessed with signs and portents and feels like he is fulfilling a destiny. What role do free will and fatalism play in *The Shining Girls*?

7. Could Kirby have used the House to go back and fix the past and stop Harper before he killed all the women?

8. What is Kirby and Dan's relationship? How does it develop and change them?

9. What is the role of Bartek and how does he fit into the loops of the House?

10. How does *The Shining Girls* illustrate the ways that women's roles and social issues have changed (or not) throughout the twentieth century?

MULHOLLAND BOOKS

You won't be able to put down these Mulholland books.

Visit mulhollandbooks.com for
your daily suspense fiction fix.

Download the FREE Mulholland Books app.